THE GIRL WHO
INHERITS THE DEAD

ALESSA WINTERS

To the maybe four people who will get the joke.

1

Her entire life, Delina Frisse has always felt she's missing something.

Something big.

Something defining. That once she figured it out, once she unlocked whatever it is inside, she would fundamentally change as a person. She would fundamentally know herself, and all of this hand shaking, dust covered nothing inside of her will disappear.

Sure, everyone thinks her life is pretty grand. She has a semi-cushy job messing with spreadsheets for people who can't, she lives in a condo in Prescott paid for in full because her bio-mother was some strange rich science person, and she has a doting boyfriend. Her dad lives in Sedona, just close enough that she can visit him and get home cooked food but just far enough away that it's not suffocating.

She gets to dress well, more polished than the cowboy fashion in Prescott, drives to a bigger city to get her hair done, keeps her manicures up to date and her nails sharp, and everyone thinks she is the one that has her shit together. That nobody that composed could have something missing.

She used to think it was because she never knew her bio-mother. That it was some deep psychological need for her to know the person who gave birth to her, but that just took one college psychology class to dismiss. By all accounts, her bio-mother was some odd scientist up the coast of Vancouver who didn't really want a kid, and definitely didn't want a husband. Her dad spoke of her with a detached fondness, but even he shrugged when the notification came that she had passed.

Maison, Delina's boyfriend, had just sat and listened when Delina told him of the weird feelings over her bio-mother's death, his handsome face completely unmoving, before he took her out to the brewery that night and got them both absolutely trashed.

He's good like that.

But there's still something, some nebulous something out there, that should be different. It creeps along the edges of Delina's vision when she isn't paying attention, itches at the back of her mind. Like a lost tooth or a phantom limb or another sense that she just doesn't have access to. Like sometimes, if she touched things, she could expect something else to happen.

It never does. She's completely normal, completely generic, run of the mill person. She's just another person, even with the nagging sense that she's not.

And, of course, it all gets blown to hell by something as simple as a phone call on her day off.

～

THE DAY STARTS OFF NORMAL, in her normal day-off routine in her normal, boring life. Maison wakes before she does, for the long commute to his work from home office, where he sits in a chair that's bad for his back and fiddles with photoshop for some graphic design company or another, leaving Delina alone in bed for a good hour and a half.

She stares up at the ceiling, blank and white in the late October sun of Northern Arizona, until she can work up the energy to do something about it. Work up the energy for another day where she should be completely content and completely happy.

That never comes.

With a sigh, she forces herself to get up, to get dressed in the cute matching gym clothes that should spark joy but don't and to throw her blonde hair into as fashionable of a ponytail as she could muster.

Maison stirs from his desk as she strides by the office, sticking his head out the door. His soft brown hair sticks up a bit in the back, a tell-tale sign that he didn't bother brushing it before starting in on his art, but the glance he gives her is as alert as it ever is.

"Morning, Delly-girl," he murmurs, catching her by the wrist and kissing the palm of her hand like he's some knight in a story book. "Sleep okay?"

"I guess," she says, and he gives her one of his smiles, crooked with a dimple.

He's one of those people who seem generically good looking, generically handsome, until she gets his attention focused on her. Then all ideas of anything in her mind, any unhappiness or discontent or worry, all gets blown away.

It's a smile that says she's safe. A smile that says she's the most important thing in the world. A smile that says there is nothing else that matters to him but looking at her, nothing else that matters but their small bits of connection.

She had called it charisma, when she first met him. Her friends called it a crush.

He's everything anyone would ever want in a long-term boyfriend. He's handsome, he's kind, he makes her food and makes her laugh, so the moment he had worked up the guts to ask her out she practically jumped him, and hasn't looked back.

"I might get to paint today," Maison says with an almost dreamy smile of his own, jerking his thumb back towards his computer setup. "That is, unless they decide to give me an entire second project."

He's always in a better mood when he paints. Always emerges like he's discovered a new world, discovered something groundbreaking and can't wait to share it with her. She has a hundred small paintings he's done, tucked into her wallet and used as bookmarks and everything in between. He paints on small scraps of newsprint, on the back of receipts, on whatever good paper he can collect in the world.

It's a little magical how he can conjure something out of nothing, where the most creative she gets is a particularly satisfying pivot table.

His grey eyes flicker up to hers, quickly perceptive in the way that leaves her marveling. "You okay?"

"Having one of those days," she says, and he nods, pulling her towards him until he can wrap his arms around her.

They've talked, at length, about her 'days'. About the times she feels hollow, the time she feels something is missing.

So she leans against him, against the familiar strength in

his shoulders.

"I'll be fine," she says, because he almost needs the reassurance more than she does. "Just woke up like this."

He pulls away, smoothing his hand over the back of her workout tank top, fiddling with the hem. "Anything you need, I'm right here," he vows, and he's said it a million times, but it's always a balm. "Don't beat yourself up, do something fun instead of just the norm."

"Do you need coffee?" she asks, shaking her hand loose so she can grab her purse, her original plans be damned.

Another smile, and it's almost like she doesn't need to worry about feeling unsatisfied.

It doesn't last, of course. She's not even to the coffee shop before her phone rings and ruins everything.

Delina sighs, of course, because who the heck actually makes phone calls this day and age, before letting her car answer the phone. "Hello?"

She hopes her voice is as annoyed as she feels.

There's a delay, then a click on the line, and she clutches her white leather steering wheel out of annoyance, before tapping her nails on it.

"Yes, is this Miss..." the voice on the other line trails off, as if reading from a prompter, "Delina Joyanne Frisse?"

Delina raises a blonde eyebrow out at the rock dells outside her car. Most people don't say the middle name. "Who's calling?"

"This is the Prescott post office at city square. Your PO Box is full, and we called to check since nobody has been in to clean it this year."

Delina coasts her car into the coffee shop parking lot,

then brakes, unwilling to step outside of the air conditioning for this call. It's just now starting to tilt into the coolness of fall, but in the full sun it's still far past what she would consider reasonable. "You must be mistaken. I don't have a PO Box."

Nobody has a PO Box anymore.

"Your billing address is on Willow Court Way, right?" She wasn't going to confirm that, of course. "Birthday October Eighth?"

"That's..." She trails off, squinting out of the car.

"We have on our records that it was set up by a Dr. Joyanna Frisse fifteen years ago, and it is cleaned out at least once every six months," the impersonal voice rattles off. "With strict instructions to call this number if it ever gets too full."

She sits up straight at her bio-mother's name, then straighter when she does the mental math.

Delina and her father had moved into Prescott fifteen years ago, back when she was a struggling preteen and he wanted a bit smaller of a town to deal with her in.

"Well, shit," Delina says, still sitting in her car. "I guess this is for me."

Something a little bit like wonder peeks into her mind, replaced quickly by a thin sheen of anticipation.

She knows her bio-mother was strange, but creating a mystery PO Box for her daughter is some mystery movie shit.

"If you can stop by the post office this week, we can deliver the items to you."

"I don't have a key," Delina informs her, which feels like an important part of this conversation, unless the media has lied to her about how PO Boxes work. "I didn't even know about it, that's my mother." She winces at that, unintentionally blurting out personal details.

"Oh, that's no problem, miss, our instructions say your ID is sufficient."

Delina glances at her car clock. "What are your hours?"

IN THE END, the post office was the least of her worries.

"Oh, wow, you look just like her," the petite Post Office clerk says, the moment Delina flashes her ID. "I mean, her hair was gray and all, but..." she gestures at her face. "It's like you're a clone."

"That's not weird, not at all," Delina says, syrupy sweet, but her heart is pounding. "Did she come by often?"

"Every six months, like clockwork. Nice lady."

Her own mother, setting this up and then returning twice a year, but never bothering to stop by and introduce herself. Just mysterious behavior suited for a spy story. "Sure."

The clerk grabs an old-fashioned ring of keys, then gestures for Delina to follow her deeper into the post office, past brass and mahogany boxes. "We thought it weird when she didn't come by last summer."

"Oh, she totally died," Delina says, still syrupy sweet. "If I had known about this, I would have stopped by sooner."

The clerk eyes her. "My condolences?"

"I didn't know her," Delina continues. "So this is a bit weird, you know?"

"Guess so," the Clerk says, voice now wary. "Here."

It's a normal looking PO Box; one in a long row of other boxes, with nothing but a number to indicate any difference, and now Delina's stomach flip flops all over the place as the clerk deftly unlocks it, pulling out packet after packet of papers.

"Here, this should be it," the clerk says, and Delina's actually holding something from her bio-mother in her hands, something that's not just a check printed by a bank, before the Clerk puts another letter on top of it. "She said to have you open this one first."

It's a clean envelope, brilliantly white and expensive looking, with her name printed neatly on the front. Just her name, not her father's, not the bank's, just her.

"Okay," Delina responds, unsteady. "Anything else?"

It feels like there should be more, if this was as important for her bio-mother to set up and maintain.

"The box is pre-paid for the next ten years. Do you want to keep it open?" the Clerk asks, and Delina just shrugs, then turns on the heel of her expensive gym shoes and strides out of the post office.

The sun slaps her in the face, it always does, but she doesn't stop until she's in her car and can dump all the paperwork in the passenger's seat, her arms shaking.

One package is a neatly compact will, with more properties and bank accounts listed than she can read, her eyes blurring together. One package is a textbook—maybe—in a language she can't read, beautifully bound in embossed leather with gold lettering.

And then...the envelope with her name on it.

Instead of opening it right away, she cradles it in her hands. There's little indentations from the force of the pen, like her mother wrote with some fierceness. Like she pressed against the envelope with all of her might, so that even if the ink faded, the shape of her name would still be there.

Living with Maison for the last five years made it

unavoidable to not notice the paper, so she runs her fingers over it. It's high quality, the sort of paper that would give Maison a fit that it was used for something so mundane as an envelope.

Careful to not rip it, she slides her nail under the wax seal, popping it open and setting it aside. Maison'll be able to paint over it, make some sort of art with it. It's an old habit at this point, to collect fine bits of paper so he can use them.

Inside is a key, simple and normal with a red ribbon tied on it, and a single, folded up piece of paper, of much lesser quality. Printer paper, if she had to guess, the flimsy sort, and the words on it are scribbled with much less care, the blue ink skipping over the lines.

She can't make herself read it, not immediately.

She tucks the key into her purse, a bit unnerved.

At the top, there's a messy sort of symbol, scrawled in cheap blue pen, like someone tried to write all the letters of one word on top of each other, and she peers at it, bringing the paper up to her face, but nothing makes sense.

"Weird," she mumbles, before she brushes her thumb over the symbol, as if that could get her to understand it.

With a snap, a static shock arcs from the paper and into her thumb, sending pins and needles through her hand, and she jerks back, the letter falling harmlessly onto her lap.

And before her very eyes, the scribbled-on symbol fades, until all that is left is the indentations from the pen.

"What the fuck?" Delina says aloud, staring down at the paper, shaking out her hand before examining her thumb. It's fine, her hand is fine, her manicure still untouched, but her thumb feels like it's been coated with a thick dust.

Careful, she sets the letter down in the passenger seat and starts the car. She's gonna need coffee for this.

∾

AFTER GETTING her espresso milkshake and Maison's overly fancy caramel monstrosity of a coffee, she idles her car back in the parking lot, staring at the letter, still half unfolded in the seat next to her.

It's tilted enough towards her that she can read the first line.

DEAREST DELINA, my daughter,

"OKAY," Delina says, nervy, then picks it back up. No static shock, nothing. Just a normal piece of paper, she's just going a bit nuts from the anticipation.

I'M SO sorry I never got to meet you. If this letter is in your possession, then I am either dead or in prison, and if they put me into a prison, I doubt I'm getting out.

DELINA TAKES the moment to glance out at the white sands and stone beyond the coffee shop parking lot.

Her mother's dead, she knows her mother is dead, but even reading those words feels odd.

SORRY ABOUT THE rune at the top, it's all I could manage without setting off alarms. I'd unlock everything inside of you, but they'd catch on. If you touch anything magical with the hand that touched the rune, you'll be able to tell.

You don't know about the world, about the actual world, so I'll rip off the band aid fast. Magic is real and there's magic in you. The world is far more vast than you think it is, and there are ghosts and demons and monsters around every corner.

DELINA RESTS the letter on her lap and takes a huge drink from the espresso milkshake.

Not only is her mother dead, but she's also insane.

WHEN I WAS pregnant with you, I was starting on experiments, and a ruling counsel—the College—deemed it immoral for me to be around you, and locked away your magic. Everything about your life is a lie, and you have been watched and controlled for your entire life.

SO HER MOTHER is really insane. A nice fancy insane nut job. Delina breathes out hard through her nose.

YOU CAN'T TRUST ANYONE. Your father knows, he's complicit in keeping you locked away. Your boyfriend, Maison, isn't real. He's a spy from the College, vastly powerful, and has been in charge of keeping you in control for at least five years. Don't trust him, he's not who you think he is.

SHE TAKES another long sip from the espresso milkshake, disappointment flooding through her. Her own mother knew her boyfriend's name, but didn't know her, and was apparently convinced of a grand conspiracy.

. . .

They track your cell phone, they track your car, they track your email. Go to Northern Washington, near the Ferry service, there's a cabin that will help unlock your full potential. Leave your phone behind, buy a plane ticket with cash, there's some in the textbook. The address to the cabin is in the will, page 24, line 9.

Delina leans over to flip through the will, and sure enough there's a property listed.

I love you, and you will one day be magnificent.
  Joyanna Jhyoti Frisse

And that's it. Just some insane ramblings from someone she never met. Claiming magic was real, that there were ghosts and shit.

After a beat, Delina tosses the letter aside, then picks up the textbook again, this time leafing through the pages.

Symbols, like the one that zapped her thumb, adorn every page, but she doesn't touch them, instead turning them.

At the start of the second chapter, a crisp hundred-dollar bill.

"Okay, Mom, that's nice," Delina says, then continues flipping.

Third chapter, another. Fourth, another.

There are twenty-eight chapters in the book, and all of the bills are perfectly clean and unused and, because Delina's the person to check for these things, all unmarked and non-sequential.

When they had first found out about her mother's death, Delina had gotten a nice sum of money deposited into her bank account, but this seems somehow even weirder.

Her mother was insane, dead, and left her a key and a bunch of cash in a book. Just what every little girl dreams of.

2

Delina allows herself about five minutes of wallowing and drinking her espresso milkshake, staring blankly out at the austere desert around her, before her phone dings.

MAISON <3 (9:21 AM): You okay? Something wrong with the coffee shop?

Delina stares at it, at the little thumbnail of his face, and really doesn't want to explain to him all the emotions and completely derail his day.

DELINA (9:22 AM): Yeah, sorry. OMW back now.

MAISON <3 (9:23 AM): Didja make an extra stop? :)

She shivers, then shakes her head. Of course he would ask that, she was gone for a full hour longer than she should have, but she hesitates before answering.

DELINA (9:24 AM): Ran into work buddy, chatted for a while.

And even telling that lie sends her stomach into a pit of guilt.

"Oh fuck this," she mumbles, then folds up the now

alarming wad of cash and shoves it into her purse, putting the car into reverse and pealing out of the parking lot.

She's not supposed to be the one who reacts to things like this. She's supposed to have her shit together.

Mashing the buttons on her car until it calls her dad, she drives towards her condo, a knot in her throat, while the phone rings through.

"Hello?" her dad's voice says, distorted through the speaker.

"Hi, yes, can I come over today?" Delina asks, and her voice is smaller than she would like. "Do lunch or something? It's my day off."

"Sure," he says, easily. "Always."

"Cool, cool," Delina rambles. "I'll be there in a few hours."

Her father would know what's up. Would tell her she's being irrational. Would tell her everything's okay and that her mother was merely weird.

The thought propels her until she's back at the condo, balancing the coffees with her purse, and her hands shake while unlocking the door. Her thumb is still numb, of course, making it much more difficult than it should be.

She's too old for fairy tales and madness.

"There you are," Maison says, and he's standing in the kitchen, washing paint from his hands. His eyes crinkle up into a fond look when she walks through the door. "I was getting worried."

"Sorry, sorry," she says, the knot in her chest growing. "I didn't mean to."

He swoops over to her, plucking the coffees from her hands and setting them aside before pulling her into a kiss, tilting her head back and making her eyes swim, then breaking it just as fast as it started. "All good," he says, his voice deep. "I painted another note card for your dad, got inspired. I think he'll like it."

"I'm going over to him for lunch," Delina blurts out, and Maison nods, idle. Like he already knew.

"Anything interesting happen?" Maison asks, turning and grabbing his coffee. "You met with..." And he trails off, raising an eyebrow at her.

"Juliette," Delina fibs, making up a coworker then and there. "You haven't met her."

He shrugs, then gives her one of the smiles. One of the smiles that shows his dimple and makes her knees shake and makes her stomach drop with the lies she's telling him. "Love you."

"Love you too," she replies, automatically, though her heart is beating fast, way faster than it should, as he turns back towards his home office, pulling out his phone as he walks away. "Want me to take the drawing to my dad's?" she calls after him out of habit, wandering into their bedroom, staring uselessly at it.

Maison's blue button up from yesterday hangs haphazardly over their hamper, and his slippers are neatly tucked into their place on his side of the bed. Her books are strewn all over her side table, and his phone charger is fraying at the cord end, like his always do after a few months of use.

His sketchbook lays propped open, from where he obviously started to sketch something the night before, and the random collection of too fancy pens that are always around clutter up the top of his dresser.

She's known him since undergrad. She's lived with him for five years. She knows what laundry detergent he prefers and his favorite brand of string cheese. She's slept next to him and heard his soft snoring and cuddled against him on the rare snowy night in northern Arizona, and dozed next to him on top of the sheets when the air conditioning broke two summers ago. He likes pretzels and dislikes peanut butter and wanted to work in animation before he got pulled into corporate graphic design.

And now she's lying to him based on an obviously insane letter from her biological mother that she's never met.

"Sure," he says, voice slightly muffled by the door between them. "Tell me if he likes it."

Impulsive, she shoves an extra pair of underwear in her purse, then coils up her own, non-frayed phone charger, her heart pounding, then she drifts back into his home office.

She shouldn't be this affected.

The light streams through the window blinds, and he has two computer screens with photoshop open and three messy watercolors drying on the desk next to his keyboard as he pokes on his phone, a frown across his face.

Heart still pounding, she kisses the top of his head, and he leans against her for a brief, familiar second, before pulling away.

"And nothing weird happened while you were out?" he asks, brow furrowing at his phone. "No weird phone calls or anything?"

That's not a question he would have asked.

That's not a question anyone would ask, and she blanches, before he glances up at her, eyebrows drawn together, confusion in his lovely grey eyes.

"Oh, just the...post office?" Delina says, trailing off, tapping her nails against his desk, next to the paintings. "Wrong number."

His eyes clear with something resembling relief, and she gets a hint of the dimple again before he gestures to one of the note cards on the desk, the one with the vague impression of green rolling hills and trees just beginning to turn. "Here, for his wall with all the landscapes."

"Yeah," Delina says, past the lump in her throat. "He'll love it."

THE RED ROCK drive to Sedona does nothing to calm her nerves, so by the time she pulls up to her father's completely beige suburban home, she's practically vibrating out of her skin and her hands hurt from clutching the steering wheel.

The will, the letter, and the textbook are still in her passenger seat, growing in awareness until it's all her mind can think about.

Her dad kneels in the garden, leather gloves on his hands, as he pulls up some weeds that somehow sneak up through the reddish gravel surrounding his cacti. He gives her a quick smile, before laboriously climbing to his feet.

"What's got you all tied up, Delly?" he asks, patting her on the shoulder. Her father gives everyone the impression of useless joviality, of maximum harmless-dad, and the suburban garden get up does nothing to combat it. "Your face is all twisted."

She looks at him, catching his eyes and keeping them, drawing herself up as much as she can muster. "Dad, I want to talk about my mother."

He doesn't react for a moment, then raises his eyebrows. "Okay...?"

"I got a letter from her, and it...says some things."

This time, her father blinks twice, then slumps, like she's never before seen him do. Like someone lets the air out of him, taking away all the fun and the joy and leaving a haggard, worn-out man instead.

It lasts for only a second, before he straightens again. "I'm gonna go get some lemonade, go in the backyard, there's no cameras pointed there," he says, voice quieter than normal. "Pretend to be normal."

HER FATHER TAKES TWICE AS LONG to come out to the backyard as usual, and his dog has thoroughly slobbered all over Delina's gym shoes by the time he comes out with two glistening glasses of lemonade and, for some reason, an old-fashioned pager.

"Dad, what's going on, why are there cameras?" Delina blurts out, and he just hands her the cup instead, placing the pager on the glass outdoor table between them. "Why would you think that, what are you going on about?"

"Did the letter, ah, tell you what she did for a living?" her dad asks instead, sitting heavily on the camp chair he keeps there year-round.

"She said magic's real and that I have it like some really bad kids' book," Delina says, clutching the cool glass. "And that you knew and Maison knew and everyone knew."

"Maison knows?" her dad asks, sharp.

"I don't know, I didn't ask him, the letter said he did, Dad..." Delina gapes at him, "Are you insane?"

"Probably," he says with just a trace of his usual jocularity. "But yes, your mom was somehow a magician, I wasn't allowed to tell you or the child support would stop, half your elementary school teachers were plants, and Mrs. Reed from down the street growing up was definitely one of them." His dog loses interest in Delina's shoes and plops down in front of him instead. "Didn't know about Maison. I liked him."

Delina carefully sets the glass on the table and, as primly as she could, turns to him and brings as much imperiousness as she possibly can to her next words, "Dad, what the fuck?"

"Fair enough," he sighs, then nudges the pager towards Delina. "Was there a symbol on the letter?"

Delina stares down at the outdated piece of electronics, at the faded black plastic. "Yes."

"Did it feel like static electricity?"

She hadn't told him about that, hadn't shown him the letter.

"Yes."

"Touch the pager," her dad instructs her, and she looks at him, sharp.

Her father had raised her as a single dad, all through her horrid teen years and through her extremes. Through her tantrums and her tears and everything in between.

And he had never done anything that could bring her harm.

"Why?" she asks, and despite all her control, her voice breaks.

"Before she left, she told me to keep this in case you broke free, for some proof," her dad says, and she hardly recognizes the look on his face. "Said that you would need proof, if you were anything like her."

"Proof would be nice," Delina replies, staring down at the pager, like just glaring at it could reveal its secrets. "Are you sure I'm not insane?"

"All the therapy you got as a teen suggested you're fine," he says. "Some depression, but fine."

"Thanks, Dad," she snipes back, then, like it'd bite her, she pokes the pager with her thumb.

At first, there's nothing, and she glances up at her dad, before the plastic snaps in two, shattering apart.

She jumps back in the camp chair, clutching her hand to her chest. Her dad's dog scrambles up, sprinting to the other side of the backyard with a whine.

The pager smolders, black smoke curling up from it, and a spare wire sparks uselessly.

Her father sits back, with a sigh, and he looks old, far older than she's ever seen him.

"Did she leave you someplace to go? She always said she would."

"A cabin in Washington," Delina says, horror creeping in. Her dad is supposed to be the sensible one, the one that tells her to research mortgage rates and check her tires before long drives.

"Cash to get there?" he asks, and then nods back at her. "Leave your phone in my car, I know that's tracked."

After a brief explanation that makes no fucking sense, her father ends up taking her to her least favorite Target store in the state to buy enough toiletries and changes of clothes for a few days, plus a bright pink rolling suitcase, and Delina can't quite stop shaking. There's a flight to Seattle at six PM with a ton of open seats, and despite everything, despite all the earth-shattering insanity that has been told to her that day, Delina still can't quite grasp that she's actually going on a plane.

She can't quite grasp that she broke a pager.

"Act a bit more natural," her dad mutters to her, as they go through a drive through for fast food burgers, of all things. Delina hasn't eaten a burger in three years, but this seems to call for it.

"I'm..." Her phone chimes, and they both fall silent.

MAISON <3 (3:21 PM): I'm making tacos, can you pick up some cilantro on your way back?

"He knew I had a phone call from someone strange," she says, and her dad holds out his hand for her phone, as they inch along the drive through. "He knew that without me telling him."

"So we'll keep your phone in my car, and if they have the location tracked they can come to my house," her dad reminds kindly. "I'll feign ignorance. I'll park your car some-where else, and if it's nothing, you can come back and tell him your friend had a crisis and you left your phone."

It's so far outside of her normal behavior, that she knows, she just knows, that there's no way Maison would buy it.

"Did you ever see Mom..." she trails off, still unsure what she could actually say, "do magic?"

"Four times," her father says. "Saw her light something on fire with her fingertips. Saw her draw something in midair and cause an explosion. Saw her write something in a Sharpie and it glowed. Saw her..." he hesitates long enough to order for the two of them. "Saw her aim some-thing at her stomach while pregnant with you, and she had a seizure and you both almost died before you could be born."

"Was she..." Delina trails off, blinking down at her hands in the Arizona sun, "trying to get rid of me?"

"Oh, god no, honey," her dad says, reaching over the parking break and grabbing her hand reassuringly. "Nothing like that, she wanted..." and here he sighs, weary once more. "More than anything, she wanted to give birth to someone powerful. I think that's why."

Delina just watches the cars pass them on the main street, drumming her nails on the passenger's side door, just like she used to do when she was a teen and upset about small things.

The textbook and the will are safely tucked in her new pink suitcase, and the letter in her purse.

"Do you really think Maison is a spy?" she asks, leaning her forehead against the warm glass of the window, her throat tight.

He had made her a smoothie yesterday before work, put chocolate milk in it and everything.

By then, her father had gone over the letter with her, had read that crucial, heartbreaking detail, and had given her a hug over it.

"Your mother seems to think so," he says, still gentle. "She knew that world, not me."

"Why would he be with me for so long if it was just some...ruse?" Delina says, blinking too fast. She had put on mascara before the gym, like she always does, and she doesn't want to ruin it before a flight. "But he...I thought he was going to propose."

Her father reaches across the car and grabs her hand again. "I don't know, Delly. I thought he was good for you."

She doesn't have a response to that.

"He seemed decent, maybe she was wrong about this thing," he says. "She wasn't right about everything, she had her flaws."

She rubs her face, carefully avoiding the already precarious mascara. "Should I just talk to him?" she asks, and it's like she's back as a high schooler, woefully asking her dad for advice. "Maybe there's some explanation?"

He pauses long enough to accept the food from the take-out window, and remains silent until his window is rolled up enough to drive away.

"Delina," her father starts, and he so rarely calls her by her full first name, "go to this cabin first. Take a few days to get your head on straight, see what your mother left you. If you still want to talk to him, talk to him then. You have bigger things to worry about."

He's right, of course, her dad is usually right, but everything presses down hard against the back of her eyes.

"Right, like magic, because that's apparently a thing," she snips back, accepting the hamburger.

"There was a reason your mom hated the College, though I never knew it," he says, digging into the bag for his fries. "And there was a reason they wanted to keep you in the dark."

~

IT STILL DOESN'T MAKE sense, even if she accounts for the idea that magic is real and even after three midday airport margaritas.

Somewhere in waiting for her now woefully delayed flight, she pulled out her trusty planner and tried to sketch out some lists, make some sense, anything, and nothing added up.

"I need more information," she mumbles, looking wistfully in the pocket of her purse where her phone usually resided. "This is bullshit without information." The balding bartender throws her a look, and she waves him away. "Just talking to myself."

Even if magic is real, and broken pager notwithstanding she's not sure it is, there's not any reason to keep it hidden from her except in revenge for her bio-mother, and Delina just doesn't have enough information on her to figure that out.

There's always the option her bio-mother was insane even by magical standards, but that's not exactly better, and she tugs at the collar of her gym clothes, suddenly and viciously wishing she had thought to change into something else before driving to her dad. Something more comfortable, something less spandex-y. Something soft, something that she could snuggle into and forget everything that's going on.

Her dad had left her instructions on how to pick up an untraceable cell phone in Seattle, because that's a skill he apparently has now, and had given her even more cash, to the point where Delina's basically a walking target for an enterprising pickpocket.

Maison would always insist on her depositing too much cash, that it was dangerous for her. Insist that she needed to be safe, needed to not take any risks. Would fret at her doing anything remotely risky, worry that she's going to get harmed by some nebulous...something.

If that nebulous something was something magical, she's gonna be pissed.

Across the bar, just far enough away that it's almost ignorable, her eyes catch on a woman staring hard at her. Her graying hair is in a haphazard bun and she's on the dumpy side of fashionable, but her eyes are way more skeptical than most people who look at Delina.

So, of course, Delina lifts her chin and stares right back. Pours all the self-confidence she's not feeling and all the frustration into the look, until the woman's gaze drops.

Drops directly to her hand. To her thumb.

Delina shivers, tucking her hand away, and the woman smirks, throws down a twenty on the bar, and striding away.

By the time her flight takes off, however, the drink has led to a creeping doubt and a deep-down horror that everything Delina's doing is a mistake.

If Maison is a spy, he'll be able to find her. If he's not...

she's doing the worst thing she has ever done, and she's not quite sure how there would be a way to come back from it. From hurting him, if that is what will happen.

But her thumb still tingles, and she swipes it on the window of the airplane, and there's no reaction. None of the spark or static that she felt with the pager, nothing.

Except...

All at once, the tiny hairs on the back of her neck raise, and she shudders, glancing up from her seat.

The entire airplane is cool, filled with tired people who obviously would prefer to be somewhere else than on a plane in the middle of the afternoon. Three rows over an elderly gentleman sleeps, his head leaning against the back of his chair, his wispy white hair fluffed up. Two rows back, a young mother bribes her tear-streaked child with a toy, and the kid shakes his head angrily.

But near the front of the plane, almost still, someone stares back. He's propped up, standing from his seat despite the seatbelt light still on, and despite looking like the most boring middle-aged businessman ever in a slightly wrinkled suit, his eyes lock onto Delina with something approaching malice.

If the seatbelt light wasn't on, Delina would march up to him and ask him what his problem is.

But instead, she glares back at him, lifting an eyebrow. People don't stare at her like that, with that intensity. Either they're staring at her boobs or they're ignoring her, their eyes sliding off of her as yet another blonde girl of Arizona, blending into the background.

This man stares at her like he knows what she did wrong. Like she is wrong.

The stewardess leans over to him, and he cocks an ear to

her, before continuing to glare at Delina, his lips curling up into a sneer.

"Fuck you," Delina mouths to him, and he flinches back, before finally lowering himself back down into his seat.

She settles back down, grinning to herself just a bit, for a second, just a little bit alive.

THE MOMENT she lands in Seattle, before the familiar haggling for a rental car (trickier when she's paying with cash) and the wrangling of suitcases, a strange fog enters her.

She's still aware, of course, but everything matches the weather outside. Like something inside of her was transformed by the three-hour flight, changing her from someone terrified and afraid to someone...separate. More akin to viewing her life from outside a window, watching herself move through the motions, but not connected to them.

Like she's a different person.

Her thumb still tingles, her hip aches like it always does after a flight, and she fumbles with opening the car door more than she should.

The mist of the parking lot chills against her cheeks and tugs at her hair, chilling her to the bone as she stops and buys a cell phone from the first sketchy store she can find, a gas station/convenience store charmingly named Buggies. The outside is less than inspiring, with broken glass all over the asphalt and paint peeling off of a sign that claims the grand reopening was less than a month ago.

Her dad told her to find some place that looked less than

ideal, and if he hadn't she would have never pulled over to such a spot.

"Buggies, huh?" she says, the moment she shrugs off the mist and steps inside.

The inside smells a bit too much like damp, the sort of humidity that never happens in Arizona, but the disinterested clerk in a polo shirt doesn't question her at all. Despite the disrepair outside, however, the floor is pristine, mopped clean and scrubbed within an inch of its life. All new shelving adorns the walls, and none of the packaging is even dusty.

She gives the clerk her widest grin as she places the phone on the counter, the sort of grin she uses to get free drinks at bars, but he barely glances at her. He's missing more teeth than not, and wears weathered overalls over the bright red polo shirt.

The counter has a smear of glitter on it, even though everything else is clean. A small sign hung off the end of the counter, says the counter is 'part of the original build.'

"You re-opened?" Delina asks, after the clerk is still completely silent, counting her dollars.

He nods, giving her a slightly suspicious look.

"What happened?" she asks, something digging inside of her to have the conversation, to have some little bit of normalcy.

"Explosion," he replies, gruff. "Took a year to rebuild."

Out of all the answers, that wasn't one she anticipated, so she cocks her head at him, her ponytail exaggerating the movement.

"Are you on your way to Canada?" he asks, finally, opening the brand-new cash register with the same suspicion he gave her.

"No, to...above Bellingham. Up the mountain." she says,

trailing off, thinking back to the will in her pink suitcase. "I'm...in the area, visiting friends."

That sounds plausible.

"That's a two-hour drive." Slower, he re-counts the money, like he's not used to seeing such crisp bills. "There's food in Bellingham, not much more until you go to Woolley, and even then it's not great." He raises an eyebrow at her, at her pristine gym clothes. "No cell signal there, this will be useless."

Of course her insane mother had to give her a property with no cell signal. "I'll make do."

Finally, he pushes the cell phone across the counter, and she grabs it as fast as she can, her hand grazing the counter.

An audible snap cracks out the moment her thumb touches the glitter, and she jerks back, almost dropping the phone.

He gives her a blank look.

"Sorry, must be static," she says brightly, her heart pounding. "Not used to the weather, you know?"

The clerk scowls at her, hands her the receipt, then busies himself reorganizing the candies, an obvious dismissal.

"Wow," Delina says aloud, then strides out, gripping the phone, and stands by the rental car long enough to punch in her dad's number.

DELINA (10:23 PM): Made it safe.

DAD (10:23 PM): Good!

She shivers in the mist, and her hair is going to frizz into something unmanageable, before she glances back at the Buggies.

So. Her hand responded to another thing. This time something closer to her mother's house.

DAD (10:26 PM): Maison has called four times. I played

dumb. He definitely noticed you weren't where you were supposed to be before he should have, hours before.

Delina stops herself from biting her cheek at that.

DELINA (10:27 PM): Tell me if he suggests to you that he knows?

DAD (10:28 PM): The moment he does, I will. Be safe and have a good drive! It's pretty up there!

Delina glances up, and she's not sure she can see the tips of the trees for all the mist.

DELINA (10:29 PM): Gas station clerk says I might not get cell signal, so don't worry.

DAD (10:30 PM): I will!

With one last shiver, she shoves the phone in her pocket, then climbs back in the car. It's a ratty sedan, far lesser than her sleek car at home, but it chugs out of the parking lot without a problem.

Bringing her closer to her mother's cabin.

BY THE TIME she drives by the little town of Woolley, nestled charmingly in the mountains among the spruce and the dying fall grass, she's over it. She's over the cutesy storefronts and the Americana coffee shops and the rain pelting onto the windshield and the moss on every tree and the advertisements for a winter snow festival in just a month.

Sure, Prescott occasionally gets snow in the winter, but it never lasts, and she gets a creeping dread that the snow might be a bit more intense up here.

So if she stays—her mind blanks out for a few seconds, and she coasts the car to the side of the two lane winding highway—she'll need better coats.

If she stays.

If, for some reason, there's something here for her. If there's magic and her full potential and whatever bullshit that's supposed to be.

If she has to stay in hiding, away from Maison, away from whatever nemesis her mother has. If she has to abandon all her possessions, never to get them back.

She takes a big, gulping breath, the only sound the absolute drumbeat of rain against the roof of her car, drowning out every other noise.

If she can't go back, if she can't resume her job, if she has to live off the inheritance and whatever houses and other things in the will and...

She shuts her eyes, thudding her head against the lumpy seat cushion.

"I just have to go to the cabin," she whispers to herself, though it's lost in the thrum of the rain. "Everything else can wait until I've gotten to the cabin."

It's only a ten-minute drive from where she's parked, and the only light is her headlamps. With the clouds drumming so heavily, there's no moonlight, no stars, and certainly no streetlamps.

She lets herself despair for five seconds, then throws the blinker on out of habit, coasting back onto the highway.

DELINA (12:46 AM): Losing cell signal.

Her phone blinkers out before she can get a response, so she drives on, exhaling hard out of her nose.

The highway turns into a winding road, bumpy and half overgrown with dead blackberry vines, before, finally, to a gravel driveway, leading her through a narrow pathway of tall, overarching trees that disappear into the clouds, until she finally turns around a bend, to a cabin.

It's a cute cabin, the sort you see in rustic postcards and

advertisements for the Pacific Northwest. Rough-hewn logs, floral curtains, stained glass window on the door with light peeking out.

Light.

Her breath catches.

The lights are on, shining bright into the forest around them, and a plume of smoke curls from the chimney.

There's another car in the driveway, a beat-up looking jeep with rust adorning the tire well and chains wrapped around the back.

Someone else is here.

4

Delina idles the car, a knot in her throat.

Throughout the day, she never even entertained the idea that the property might be inhabited. That she might be rolling up, well after 1 AM, with a key to the place and the deed in the will, and be kicking someone out.

She had driven by a ton of cutesy bed and breakfasts not ten minutes back, she could probably just stay the night at one of those.

A figure walks by the window, followed by another, silhouetted against the cutesy floral curtains.

So they're also awake at this ungodly hour. Whoever they are.

Carefully, she turns off the headlights, the rain clattering on the roof of the car until the only light is beaming from the cabin.

The cabin that belonged to her mother. The cabin that her mother sent her to, with the express reason to help her, whatever that may look like.

Maison would have a fit laughing at her right now,

chewing on her lip like she's a person who gets shy. He would tease her about it, probably throw his arm around her shoulders, guide her to the door to knock. Say something pithy like, 'you're not one to let other people stop you,' or, 'if it's yours it's yours.'

For some reason, contemplating the actions of her maybe-fake boyfriend doesn't help.

"Fuck this," she mutters, palming the key with the red ribbon in her hand and kicking the door to the sedan open into the sheets of rain. The downfall immediately plasters her hair to her face and her ponytail unpleasantly to her neck, but she yanks out the rolling pink suitcase and stomps through the gravel to the front door.

On the concrete slab, instead of a welcome mat is a complex circle with symbols scrawled all over it, neatly spray painted in a shiny, chromatic gold.

The key in her hand grows warm as she approaches.

Not hot, not painful, but she presses her thumb against it for a small reassuring thrum, then strides across the circle and all but shoves the key into the door.

The lock clicks, and she throws her shoulder into the door to open it, before it creaks and relents, stumbling inside.

And all at once, three things are obvious.

One. Those stupid symbols are scrawled everywhere. One on the roof, a few embroidered onto pillows on the floral couch, some etched in the dark wood over the fireplace and on the granite counter tops, all the same glistening gold.

Two. Two people stare at her like they've been caught doing something they really, really shouldn't.

Three. One of them has a gun.

Delina yanks in her pink suitcase from the rain, and

pulls herself as tall as she can, fixing her best glare on the man with the gun. "Who are you and what are you doing in my cabin?"

The man opens his mouth, then closes it with a click. He's blond with floppy hair, and holds the gun like he thinks it'll bite him. He's maybe the same age as her and looks like he's never done a hard day's work in his entire life. He's even wearing a pressed suit.

The woman shoots him a look, then focuses back on Delina. Large, thick rimmed glasses dominate her small face, and short cut black hair gives her the overall impression of a mad scientist going through a rebellion.

Delina just pulls any self-confidence she can into herself, crossing her arms.

"Uh," the woman says, and her voice is surprisingly high pitched. "Who are you?"

"I asked the question first," Delina snaps back.

"How'd you find this place?" The man breathes, still holding the gun limply. "Nobody should be able to find this place."

"My mother left it to me in her will, apparently," Delina says, wishing there was something she could throw at him. She grew up in Arizona, she could hold a gun better than whoever this guy is. "So legally you're the ones who aren't supposed to be here."

The man and woman glance at each other, eyes wide, and the guy slowly lowers the gun, and the only sound is the crackling of the fire.

In the middle of one of the embroidered pillows on the couch, a tabby cat sleeps, curled up.

"Oh my god," says the woman, her brown eyes light up. "Oh my god, you're her." She covers her mouth with one hand, and her fingertips are stained with gold spray paint.

The guy sets the gun onto the side table—just the side table, no security whatsoever—and crosses his arms over his chest. "Aren't you supposed to be ignorant somewhere in the south-west?"

"Excuse me?" Delina says.

"Oh my god, Gurlien, stop," the woman says, then she stands, shaking herself visibly. "I'm Chloe, we didn't know you'd ever find out about this place, I'm so sorry."

"Delina Frisse," Delina responds, narrowing her eyes at her. "Why are you here?"

The man—Gurlien, apparently—scowls, a somewhat hopeless scowl, like he's just as lost as she is. "But seriously, we thought you were under lock and key in New Mexico or something," he says. "Not able to stride across an active trap circle like it's nothing."

"Trap circle?" Delina asks skeptically. "You think a little bit of spray paint is gonna stop me?"

Chloe glances at Gurlien again, and they have a brief, wordless argument, the sort of non-verbal communication that immediately highlights how much of an outsider Delina is, before Gurlien sighs.

"When did you find out that magic is real?" he asks, disgruntled. "The official line from the College—" he throws the word out with some real disdain, "—is that you weren't ever supposed to find out."

"About fourteen hours ago," Delina replies, finally allowing herself to squeeze out her drenched ponytail. Her fingers are already like ice, after just that brief walk outside. "Been a bit of a weird day."

"Oh no," Chloe mumbles, rubbing her face. "Oh no, and you have to find out from us." She paces across the room, like this is somehow her problem and her crisis as well.

Gurlien pays her no attention, just squinting at Delina, a

shockingly fake bored expression over his face. "And you booked a plane and drove out?"

"Pretty much," Delina says, losing patience and stomping over to the open-air kitchen and grabbing a floral towel. "You two still haven't explained what you're doing in my cabin."

"Oh that's easy," Chloe pipes up from her pacing. "We needed a place to hide that the College wouldn't get us, and Gurlien did like all of Dr. Frisse's estate paperwork so he pulled this as a good place to run."

"You knew my mom?" Delina asks, as fast as she can.

"Unfortunately," Gurlien snips back. "Where's your jailer boyfriend?"

Delina flinches.

"We know you have one, he was supposed to stop you from figuring this out, where is he?"

"God, Gurlien, don't be a nightmare," Chloe says. "Think, we need to think. If she's here," Chloe jerks a thumb at Delina, "then we really need to figure out some more defenses."

"Why?" Delina asks, finally drying off, the floral towel much softer than she would have expected.

The two of them freeze again, staring at each other, like she's thrown a wrench into all their plans.

Before Gurlien sighs, put upon once more. "I'm going to make some coffee," he announces, pointing to the couches. "Might as well get comfortable, this is going to be significantly not fun."

Turns out her mother also had an affinity for over complicated coffee machines and it takes him forever, so Delina gets an opportunity to grab a throw blanket and kick off her shoes so she can properly curl up on the couch and approach comfort for the first time since she read the letter.

The cat blinks up at her with tranquil green eyes, but ultimately decides to not move.

Gurlien carries three mugs—all chipped and worn—and sets them on the coffee table next to the gun. Chloe doesn't stop staring at Delina like she's going to grow an extra head.

"You do have a boyfriend, though, right?" Chloe asks, after they all take a few sips of the coffee in silence. "We know they assigned someone to you."

"Don't know who, though," Gurlien says, tucking his legs underneath him on the giant armchair. He's still wearing pressed slacks, completely out of place in the rustic cabin.

Chloe, at least, is wearing functional overalls, and the pockets clink with tools.

"Yes," Delina forces herself to say. "Found out about that fourteen hours ago, too."

"That's rough," Chloe replies immediately, and it's just enough sympathy that the hard shell of Delina's composure starts to crack. "How'd he react?"

"Oh, I didn't tell him," Delina says, clutching the warm mug against her icy fingers. "I just...left."

It still feels weird to say.

"What's his name?" Gurlien asks, clinical even over coffee. "What, we need to know who we're up against."

"You think he's going to follow me?" Delina asks, blinking at him.

"If his whole job was preventing you from finding out about your mother, he's going to try to collect you," Gurlien says. "Drag you off to the College and wash his hands of you."

"Oh my god, Gurlien," Chloe mumbles.

"So us knowing who we have to defend this place against would be helpful," Gurlien continues. "Chloe's good with traps, she can ward this place all to hell."

"Ward?" Delina asks, and they both sigh.

"Just...what's his name?" Chloe asks, way more gentle than Gurlien. "We both used to be in the College, we probably knew him, so we can plan."

So these strangers probably knew Maison as well.

Knew him better than she ever did.

"Maison Shutze," Delina says, and it feels like a confession.

The two people in front of her give her identical blank looks.

"So a code name." Gurlien recovers first. "What does he look like?"

The entire conversation tugs at the sadness in her chest, but she wills her composure back into place. "Brown hair, grey eyes, about six feet tall? Has a dimple on the right side of his chin and freckles on his chest?"

Still nothing.

"He's an artist." she continues, her voice tilting up. "Works in graphic design?"

"Devin, Freddy, or Lutes, what do you think?" Chloe remarks, picking up a pen from the coffee table and drumming it against her leg.

"Devin would be the easiest option. If it's Frederick, we're fucked," Gurlien says, and Delina's known him for all of an hour and swear words still seem out of place in his mouth. "Lutes would give up, though, so maybe that's better."

"Devin is the best looking, though," Chloe says, still drumming the pen, the muffled thumping noise horrible. "If

I was to send a boyfriend to a mark for a long term, I'd pick the handsome one."

"He is good with snares," Gurlien remarks, and it's like they're discussing the weather. "He could have trapped her in a seduction spell, then got close to her."

"Ew," Chloe says.

Delina carefully sets the coffee on the side table away from the gun, then rubs her face. "I have pictures on my Facebook," she says.

"Yes, because the internet works here," Gurlien says. "Please tell me you left your phone elsewhere?"

To that, at least, Delina can nod.

"We'll drive into town tomorrow," Gurlien declares, "get the picture, then make a plan."

"Wait, isn't Shutze Freddy's mom's maiden name?" Chloe asks, tilting her head. "Or was it Schmidt?"

"Schmidt," Gurlien quickly replies, "but if it's Frederick, we're fucked, unless..." He snaps his attention onto Delina. "Did you sleep with your boyfriend?"

Delina and Chloe lock eyes.

"I've lived with him for five years," Delina says.

"That's immaterial," Gurlien says.

"Gurlien, she's saying yes," Chloe murmurs. "Subtext."

He shrugs that off, scowling. "I hope it's Devin," he says instead. "You can easily overpower Devin."

"Can one of you two tell me about who these people are?" Delina asks, pitching her voice up. "So I'm not just here guessing about what wild person I apparently slept with for the last five years?"

"Devin is a moderately skilled spell weaver who's excellent at snares and bespelling people, and he's a dream to look at," Chloe ticks off a finger. "Freddy is a Half Demon who I thought was on assignment in France or something, and Lutes is an alchemist specializing in art forgery."

She says all these things like she's expecting Delina to understand. Spell Weaver. Demon. Alchemist. Traps.

"Demons exist?" Delina says skeptically. "Do angels?"

"Not as far as we know," Gurlien says, just as skeptically, like she's the one being somewhat ridiculous, then ducks his head. "You should know about demons, regardless."

Delina crosses her arms.

"Your mom was obsessed with doing experiments around them," Chloe chimes in. "Near as we can tell, pissed off a lot of them."

"She wanted their power," Gurlien says clinically. "Wanted it controllable in a human form, ended up creating a monster."

"Monster, right," drawls Delina. "That sounds possible."

"Demons can only possess dead bodies. She put one in a live one, then lost control," Gurlien lists off, and Delina's skin crawls. "The entire College has been working for decades to carefully gain access to demon skills, and she just blew up all the research and knowledge with one super careless act."

Delina stares down at her hands, the shiver winding up her back again. "So they might've sent a half-demon to watch me."

Makes a certain kind of twisted sense.

"Oh, Frederick's more human than the College would have liked, they call him a failed vector of the experiment," Gurlien says, which isn't better. "Still powerful, not what they wanted, can't even teleport. That's like...basic demon shit."

"Wait, Lutes," Chloe says, brightening up and snapping

her fingers. "He did all that research in Necromancy against Frisse, six years ago. Stopped her from getting that grant."

"Fat lot of good that did," Gurlien says, then, as an aside, "your mother found a necromancer. It was a disaster. There were two, maybe three, demons that got drawn in, half of America got their magic destabilized, and there's now at least three formerly dead people up and walking around."

"Is...one of them my mom?" Delina asks, moderately horrified.

"Absolutely not," Gurlien replies, and Delina isn't sure if she should feel relief or not. "In fact, the necromancer used the power from your mom dying to kill one of the demons, we think, though the theory is real shaky."

Delina stares at him. "They told me she died in a car accident?"

"No, it was a demon battle, anyways," Gurlien starts, "that does put Lutes back in play. He would stick around to make sure everything was done, he hated Frisse."

The idea that Maison, her Maison who listened to all of her rants about not knowing her own mother, would have strong opinions, sits so very poorly with Delina. Like an open maw of hurt, widening inside her gut.

"Okay, I'm done," Delina announces, pushing the cup of coffee away and jolting to her feet. "It's two AM, you two can give me a list of definitions in the morning. Is there a room in here that isn't already inhabited by you two?"

"Master bedroom, there's a bio-trap in there," Chloe says nonchalantly, then sits up straight. "The bio-trap, do you think it's for her?"

"What, and I mean this politely, the fuck is a bio-trap?"

"It's a spell circle meant to do a specific thing for a specific person when they walk in it," Gurlien recites, like it's practiced. "Everyone else it's useless, but for one person it'll do...something."

And the letter sent her here to unlock some nebulous power.

Right now, she just wants to unlock some sleep.

"Can I get in the beds without tripping the trap?" Delina asks, and they both nod, so she yanks her pink rolling suitcase down the hall and slams the door.

5

Delina wakes up in an unfamiliar bed, cold and alone, and immediately wants to tear everything down. Wants to grip the stupid floral curtains and rip them in two, to smash the antique dresser and the overly ornate mirror on top of it; wants to rend the squeaky door to the closet away from its hinges, until everything is destroyed and everything feels better.

So she blinks hard up at the wooden ceiling, spreading her arms and legs out on the bed wide, as if taking up more space would do it.

All things considered, the room is...fine. A bit dusty, but fine.

There's a gigantic bed smushed against one wall, and a circle of spray paint in the opposite corner, staining the perfectly baby blue carpet. There's a bathroom attached, with an overindulgent cast iron tub and a separate shower, and two twin vanities and sinks that each have their own mirror.

She splashes water on her face, but it does little to wash away the circles under her eyes, or her truly destroyed makeup that she had applied all the way before leaving for coffee.

Her stupid cheap phone with no signal tells her it's around 10 AM, but when she creeps into the kitchen, there's no lights on and no sound but the rain against the roof.

Which, fair. She kept them up until two AM, and who knows what sleep schedule these two oddballs keep.

She dejectedly pokes at the espresso machine until it refuses to chug to life, but even that action seems unreal.

"Wait," she whispers to herself, then swipes her thumb over the top of it, one quick action.

Immediately it whirs, grinding coffee in a smooth motion, like it had just been waiting for her to do that.

If that's what her mother meant by magic, she's going to be simultaneously excited and really, really disappointed.

"You're telling me Dr. Frisse put a bio-lock on her coffee machine?" Chloe pipes up, startling Delina. Chloe's hair sticks up on the sides, and she's wearing an oversized T-shirt and some basketball shorts as pajamas. "Jeez, she was insane."

The machine pours a beautiful shot of espresso without her needing to do anything, and they both sort of numbly watch.

"Just so you know, Gurlien's gonna watch you do that like a hundred times while we figure out what kind of magic you have," Chloe says, after Delina's poured the shot into a glass of milk and started the next shot of espresso. "Indulge him a bit, it'll be easier to work with him that way."

"So there are different types of magic," Delina says, taking a fistful of ice and then some chocolate syrup she found for her coffee.

"Oh, you know nothing," Chloe says, opening the cupboard and pulling out a box of PopTarts. "Jeez."

Delina holds out her hand, and Chloe thoughtlessly hands her one of the PopTarts. She hasn't had one of them in years, but she had a burger, might as well kick the rest of the clean eating streak away.

The cat from the night before wanders into the kitchen, stares at them, before idling back out, butting its head on Chloe's leg once.

"There's about as many types of magic as there are people, though the College likes to pretend there's only three or four," Chloe says over a mouthful of PopTarts, popping herself up so she sits on the counter. "Dr. Frisse was an experimental Spell Weaver, she specialized in finding new ways of combining and twisting magic to her purposes. She was obsessed with new magics, like necromancy and demon shit, all super dangerous and rare." Chloe gestures at herself with the PopTart. "Me, alchemy. I make things into other things. The older the thing the easier it is."

Delina crosses her arms. It's still before breakfast.

"Gurlien was also a spell weaver, he mostly did diagnostic shit, but his magic got exploded in a big accident, that's why the College kicked him out," Chloe continues. "I left because they were dicks."

"Exploded?" Delina asks. Too many people used that term to her in the last twenty-four hours.

"It's gone," Chloe replies helpfully. "Caput. Non-existent. He's now the second person in the world it's happened to and the College thought it could be contagious so..." she jerks her thumb over her shoulder, "he's out." She swings her legs off the counter, and Delina can't quite grasp if she's much younger than her or not. "Don't ask him about it, he'll pout the rest of the day."

"And me?" Delina asks, finally taking a bite of the PopTart. "What am I?"

"We won't know until the bio trap, and I don't pout," Gurlien breezes in, already wearing a neatly ironed shirt. "I have appropriate emotional reactions to stimuli."

Chloe and Delina just glance at each other.

"And Dr. Frisse had libraries full of research on how to make someone powerful," Gurlien continues. "I read the report on you, they locked your magic up because nobody had any clue what she did to you."

Her dad had said she had a seizure.

"They think something weird," he continues, like it's not emotional. "Like she deliberately tried to make you... dangerous. They didn't want to deal with that, with all the training and guidance and making sure you weren't a psychopath, so...locked away."

Delina stares down at her thumb and the silence stretches on.

"Her magic responded to the coffee machine," Chloe says, instead of anything else.

Gurlien's eyes light up.

DELINA ENDS up making five cups of coffee while the two of them make a bunch of remarks that might as well be Latin to her, before she shuts herself back in the room without either of them.

The spray-painted circle is still there, tucked neatly in the corner, with no chance of her accidentally stumbling into it.

And she's here, in a cabin owned by her actual mother, without so much as a basic internet connection, with nobody but two practical strangers for company.

And some sort of nebulous magic she may or may not have.

Her mother wanted her dangerous.

She flops onto the overly soft bed.

So dangerous that an organization she's never heard of locked it away and sent her minders and boyfriends to keep her happy. So dangerous that her mother did some weirdness with a P.O. Box instead of picking up the phone and calling her.

So dangerous that her boyfriend of so long had been faking it the entire time to just make sure she didn't figure anything out.

"Oh, he was never gonna propose," Delina says aloud to the room, to the exposed wooden beams and the furniture that looks like it was bought to be cutesy. "It was just going to be us living and lying for forever and him never telling me."

Saying it doesn't make it feel better.

From outside the room, she hears the cat make a warbled meow, and the soft sound of someone replying to it.

Delina spreads her fingers over the quilt, but her thumb doesn't react to that, so she sits up, pulling the textbook and the will out of her suitcase and laying it on the bed, before someone raps on the door.

"No," she calls out.

"I'm just saying we're gonna drive into town once the weather breaks to get cell connection," Chloe says, muffled through the wood. "Are you going into the bio-trap right now?"

Delina glances to it. "Not right now."

"Okay cool." Footsteps thump away from the door.

The letter gives her nothing else, no new revelations, and the will is even worse, a clinical description of bank accounts and properties and everything else. No hint of the danger, no hint of anything.

She stares back at the completely useless cell phone.

The first number she had put in was her dad's. The second, Maison.

It says something about her, she decides, laying there on the quilt, that she's way more torn up about Maison than the possibility of magic. Even after all the bullshit with the coffee machine, even with the pager, it still seems...not real.

———

6

The day passes in a haze of information while they wait for the weather to break. Of hearing more about her possible boyfriends, about hearing more and more descriptions of magic. Of learning about all those mythical creatures her mother mentioned in her letter.

Of hearing the massive amounts of crimes her mother committed in the pretense of becoming powerful. It's almost dizzying.

Gurlien takes the letter and the will, examining it with a magnifying glass, and Chloe leafs through the book (and finds two hundred dollar bills that Delina missed) idly, like it's something she's familiar with.

"So this," Gurlien says, pointing at the faded place where the symbol that zapped Delina's thumb was, "is really just a buffer rune."

"You say that like I know what it is," Delina says, petting the cat when the cat deigns to curl up next to her.

The cat's name is Chance, apparently. Chloe claims it

because it was chance that brought it to them, Gurlien says because the cabin had been a new chance for him.

Delina's not sure which one to believe, but Chance the cat still wanders everywhere like he owned the place, and considering how Chance was here first, she's not about to evict him.

Chloe says it lived in the cabin and hunted outside, but its glossy fur definitely suggests someone actually taking care of him.

"It's designed to slide between existing protections, nullifying them, providing a way in," Chloe replies, as if it's memorized. "I use them for breaking into things."

"Tombs, she means," Gurlien says, as if that makes it any better. "Chloe breaks into tombs."

"Archeology is fun," Chloe says when Delina raises a manicured eyebrow at her. "So many things we don't know about how people used to do magic, so many dead runes that have juuuust enough spark in them to be bitey."

This time, it's Gurlien and Delina exchanging a glance at how weird the third is.

"So it's just to get in between all the protections on me?" Delina ventures a guess, and they both nod in unison. "Cool."

"It's smart," Gurlien says, begrudging. "For someone who ruined so many lives, your mother was smart."

"Gurlien, she was a genius, no need to dance around it," Chloe says, turning another page in the book. "Just because she was immoral doesn't mean she wasn't the mind of a generation."

Delina, having heard enough stories of her mother's loose definition of morality by this point in the afternoon, weighs stopping being offended.

"She didn't care so much she had a daughter, she wanted

a powerful minion," Gurlien says, and it hurts, of course, even though Delina had always heard her mother was disinterested in her. "I'm just surprised she didn't try again after you."

"I definitely touched Maison with this hand, so it's not perfect," Delina says, hoping to save the conversation.

"If he was paying attention he would have noticed," Chloe says, and Gurlien nods along. "Means he was complacent."

The complacency doesn't quite feel right, but Delina just stares up at the wooden beams of the ceiling and pets the cat, who purrs at her touch.

"What are the chances he was actually in love with me?" she asks, and for a few seconds the only sound is the drum of rain against the roof.

"It's possible," Chloe says gingerly.

"I'd say eight percent," Gurlien answers. "None of the three men, if it is one of them, are the type to be frivolous with work assignments."

That still hurts, so she narrows her eyes at the roof and the cat gives a small mrrr sound.

"Then why stay with me after my mom died?" Delina asks, finally, after letting the moment stretch on. "If the danger passed after she died, that makes no sense."

"It makes plenty sense, if you consider you as an actual danger and not just an extension of your mother's will," Gurlien says, and Chloe looks up from the book long enough to roll her eyes at him. "Seriously, whatever you do could be world ending."

"That's not likely," Chloe says, "what's more likely is you're just really strong with flexible morality, which is almost worse."

The idea that she could be powerful still makes Delina smile, even just a bit, though she squashes it down.

"But we won't know until the bio-trap," Gurlien points out, and Delina avoids looking back at the room. "I don't know why you're avoiding it."

"I'm not avoiding, I'm collecting information," Delina says, and Chloe coughs out a laugh into the book. "Wouldn't you want to when faced with life changing information?"

Gurlien gives her a flat look over his glasses. "I wasn't given the option."

By now, Delina's heard all about how he lost his magic, about how much vitriol he has about being kicked out, all that fun stuff. And Chloe feeling stifled, until she couldn't do anything she actually liked, deemed too dangerous or too protected.

"But it could be exciting," Chloe says, almost dreamily. "Finding out what's been missing your entire life."

And Delina has to swallow down that one, letting her head lean back towards the room, fear and hope warring in her heart.

What she's been missing.

"Give us some additional firepower when your boyfriend shows up to collect you," Gurlien says, almost clinically. "If you don't want to be just imprisoned by the College, having some power could be useful."

Right. Imprisonment.

"You don't think they'd train her?" Chloe asks, propping herself up. "I don't think they'd go directly to imprisonment."

"I do," Gurlien says, darkly. "They wanted to for me."

He and Chloe exchange a significant glance, one that leaves Delina wondering how much more she's missing.

"Yours was just an injury," Delina says, halfway to help out and halfway to make sure she's understanding the problem. "Why imprison you if it's just an injury and nothing you did wrong?"

Chloe finally looks up from the book, closing it with a click. "Because that's what the College does," she says, solemn. "Too many people are imprisoned for shit they didn't do, just dangers they present."

Gurlien scowls, then ducks his head. "And I was completely okay with it until it was aimed at me."

There's a lot of self-hate in that statement; self-hate that Delina doesn't have the inclination nor the knowledge to deconstruct, but Chloe reaches out and pats him on the shoulder.

"So avoid going to this College, right, got that," Delina says, breaking the moment. "The whole never letting my bio-mom meet me thing kinda convinced that."

"If I wasn't like this, I could do all sorts of diagnostics," Gurlien says, still full of frustration. "Figure out exactly what things they put on you, probably be able to trace who your boyfriend was by just the magical signature. But no. I'm useless."

"You're still knowledgeable," Chloe points out, "you're still knowledgeable and you're still useful."

Gurlien frowns, but it's obviously not aimed at Chloe. "Do you think Alette over at Frisse's compound would help?"

Delina eyes him. "She had a compound?"

"She had several," Gurlien says, which isn't better. "But Alette was trained by her, she might."

"But she hates you," Chloe reminds, and he rolls his eyes. "You did kinda almost destroy her world."

Gurlien shrugs, but doesn't dispute that. "I still talk to Axel, he could convince her."

"You don't talk to Axel, you two call each other and yell

on the top of your lungs for twenty minutes, then you go get drunk," Chloe says, and it's an amusing image. "They're not gonna help."

THE RAIN DOESN'T SO MUCH LET up as much as the wind abruptly stops blowing, and both Chloe and Gurlien raise their heads at the same time.

"How long have you two been here?" Delina asks, unnerved.

"A few months," Chloe says, cagey. "Long enough to get the idea when the weather's good enough to go out."

She scrambles up, disappearing into one of the smaller bedrooms in the back of the cabin, and emerges holding two rain jackets.

"Here, yours is not good enough for the rain," Chloe says, and the jacket at least appears to be two sizes too small for Delina. "Here."

With a flick of her wrist, Chloe shakes it, and it grows in size.

Resisting the urge to back away, Delina cocks her head. "Did you just..."

"Yes, clothing is the most basic of alchemy tricks, she's just showing off," Gurlien shrugs on his own neon orange jacket, out of place over his otherwise nice clothing. "If you're an alchemist, she'll teach you how."

That, at least, seems to be the first practical example of magic since this whole thing happened. "Neat."

"It's really not," Gurlien says, before he holds the door open for them.

Outside, rain splashes into every available surface, in the puddles of the driveway and the eaves of the cabin. Leaves and pine needles litter the floor, and bright yellow birch leaves are plastered all over the roof of Delina's sad little sedan. The entire outside glistens with water, a sharp, fresh smell, sending a chill down her back.

She'll have to figure out how to get it back somehow. She only got a ten-day rental.

And here they were, about to go into town to solve one of the main mysteries in her life.

THEY GET ALL the way to almost the highway before a felled tree stops them in their path.

"Really?" Gurlien says, as he coasts the car to a stop.

Chloe kicks open the door, her hair immediately plastering to her head in the downpour, but she pays it no mind.

"Can you move it?" Gurlien calls after her, definitely not getting out in the rain.

Delina can't blame him. The rain is still coming down in sheets and the temperature is what she would charitably declare as horrid.

"It's a whole ass tree, she can't move it," Delina tells him as they both watch Chloe poke around at the tree branches.

"She might," he responds, distracted. "Depends how long it's been down."

Delina eyes him, then shifts in the car so she can get a better view of Chloe.

The tree is gigantic, branches splayed down everywhere, feathering the road.

"She needs to do the matter shift," Gurlien continues, craning his neck to watch Chloe. "She's been practicing, if she tries, she could do it, but she's too insecure."

"Is this a magic thing?" Delina asks, and he nods, still

distracted. "You're telling me that magic could make that tiny person move this tree?"

That gets him to glance at her. "Yes." He sighs, though, and rolls his eyes. "She gets weird with organic material. If it was stone, she could do it, but because it has a different cell structure, she has issues."

She stares at him, flat.

"Some alchemists have no problem with wood or plant matter, it's all in her head," Gurlien continues, like that's the part she's bumping up against. "She has problems with wooden doors sometimes, it's embarrassing."

Outside the car, getting completely soaked, Chloe kneels down on the asphalt, making a complex motion with her hand that's only partially visible in the sheets of rain.

Nothing happens.

Gurlien sighs again, then cranks down the window just enough. "Try shifting it towards petrification, that worked with the cacti," he yells, and Chloe stands long enough to cheerfully flip him off. "It's just a tree."

"I'm going to assume I can't do anything, right?" Delina asks as he rolls up the window, and he glances at her again. "Not without the spray paint in my room?"

"Do you want a lecture on sealed magics right now?" Gurlien asks, face completely serious. "Because to answer that, you'll need the lecture."

"I'll pass," Delina replies.

Outside the warm dryness, Chloe straightens, shifts her weight, and...

The entire air seems to snap around her, blurring and obscuring her, until the branch nearest to her crunches, then shatters into a million stone-like shards.

Delina flinches.

"Okay, good," Gurlien says, sarcastically. "Now she just

has to do that for a whole tree. Just managed one branch."

In between one moment and the next, before she can tell herself that this is a bad idea, Delina throws her shoulder into the car door and strides out into the unpleasantness.

Rain immediately soaks through her shoes, squishing in her socks, but she stomps over to the stone branch.

Even despite the chill, Chloe's breathing hard, twin splotches of red on her cheeks.

"You just did that?" Delina asks, stooping down and picking up a chunk of stone.

It even has the same pattern of tree bark as all the spruce up here.

"It shouldn't be this hard," Chloe grumps, which is again, not the point. "I should be able to just transform it and sweep it out of the way."

Delina turns it over in her hand, brushing her thumb against it, and it snaps at her, staticky.

Chloe straightens, blinking through the rain sheeting down on them, her eyes wide. "That's just from the one rune?" she yells, and it's almost difficult to hear her through the weather.

"Yeah," Delina says, staring at the stone. The stone that, completely and inarguably, used to be relatively alive wood.

Chloe sighs, staring at the tree, then back at Delina. "There's no way I can do this entire thing," she says, like it's a moral failing and not incredibly fucking intense that she turned tree into stone right in front of them. "We can try to walk out there, but it's a twenty-minute walk from here to signal."

"Yeah, no," Delina says, peering at the stone.

Dimly, she's aware of Chloe stomping over and repeating the same to Gurlien, but this...this is even stranger. Despite the coffee machine, despite the pager, she's holding something in her hands that used to be something completely fucking different.

And Maison is some flavor of this fucked up too and never told her.

She kicks at one of stones near her foot, sending it skittering along the pavement.

The tree trunk towers above her, even on its side, branches splaying out every which way. It's a pine type tree, the type not common in Arizona but seemingly everywhere here, and even in the pouring rain it's fragrant.

The needles are still vividly green.

She stares at it, at yet another barrier in figuring things out. Yet another thing in the way of her actively figuring out who Maison actually is, what they need to do to prepare, everything.

"Fuck this," she says in the pouring rain, then walks back to the car.

SHE STREAMS past the rune circle painted on the front porch, unlocking the door with the same key with the red ribbon, throwing her shoulder into the door until it tumbles open.

"How..." Gurlien mutters, before both he and Chloe sidestep it to get in the house.

Delina pays him no attention, instead dumping her uselessly soaked rain jacket on the bench next to the door, shucking off her shoes, before she whirls and faces them.

"I'm going to ask just one question, and I want you two to answer plainly," she says, and they both give her a wide-eyed look. "Am I in any danger if I step in that stupid circle of paint?"

"Bio-traps aren't stupid, they require an insane amount of knowledge and precision," Gurlien starts.

"Maybe," Chloe interrupts. "We don't know what it does, just that it's locked to one person or bloodline. What," she directs that to Gurlien, "that's what she asked."

"Could Lutes, or Fred, or whatever his name actually is lift that tree?" Delina asks, pointing back in the vague direction of that road.

"Devin probably couldn't," Gurlien answers. "It'd be child's play for Frederick, and Lutes could get around it."

"Devin could," Chloe argues. "He had no problems with barriers in school."

"Right," Delina says, ire seeping into her. "You two went to school with all these people."

She glowers at them as Gurlien uses an honest-to-god satellite phone to radio in for road clearing, and Delina's practically vibrating from the frustration of all of it.

Chloe throws herself on the couch, disrupting the cat who skitters under the armchair. She had been silent the entire drive back, her face as stormy as the weather outside.

Instead, Delina sits on the armchair, ignoring the meow of protest from underneath it when she does. "So what's the plan now?" she demands once Gurlien hangs up the clunky satellite phone. "I don't know what prep work you guys can even do, I don't know how to help, I barely know anything."

Gurlien has the gall to look at her as if she's the illogical one. "So we wait. Either the state troopers will clear the road and we can get out, or we wait for the weather to be nice enough to walk into town."

Neither of these sound particularly great at the moment, so Delina squeezes her eyes shut, desperately wishing she could actually affect something for once. Actually do something.

"If I step in that bio-trap," she starts, and both of them in front of her perk up, "what are the chances that I'll be able to do something to that tree?"

"Maybe!" Chloe says enthusiastically.

"About four percent," Gurlien replies, a bit more clinically, but he too is staring at her over his glasses. "Especially without training, it would require natural power of a specific type to do that right off the bat."

Delina glances at the closed door to the bedroom. "And...would Maison be able to tell I did that?"

"Depends on how in depth he was in your wards," Chloe says, only halfway muffled by the couch. "Freddy or Lutes, it would tell them immediately. Devin would get a call from someone else."

"I can't believe his name might be Lutes," Delina says, because her filter seems to have gone the way of her patience. "Lutes is an objectively stupid name."

"If it's Lutes, stepping into it would be a giant road flare," Gurlien continues, "he'd know where you were and how to get to you."

"Freddy, too," Chloe says, and Freddy might be a worse name. "Though that would be from the sleeping with him part, not the bio-trap."

"Frederick might just collect her in a few minutes," Gurlien responds.

With as much power as she can muster, she turns towards the room, and behind her Gurlien hisses out a breath.

"I don't want to just wait for someone to come and collect me," Delina says, and even she doesn't know the reason for her hesitation. Doesn't know the reason she's holding back. "I don't want to face someone who can lift a fucking tree with fucking magic."

"Chloe, get the first aid kit," Gurlien says behind her, his voice far away. "In case this goes bad."

That doesn't help the hesitation, and she can see the paint circle from where she stands, just the corner of it from the door.

"Do you think my mother would hurt me?" she murmurs, but even she doesn't know the answer to that. "She sent me here for a reason."

"Yes, and —"

Outside, a giant thud reverberates through the cabin, and they all flinch.

"What?" Delina asks, turning back towards the door. "How..."

The door shudders, then, with a crash, splinters.

7

F our things happen in fast succession.

One, the beautiful door with the stained-glass shatters apart, wood splintering all over the bucolic sitting room. Shards of glass spike into the wall, slashing open the wallpaper and imbedding into a pillow. Delina jerks herself back, pressing herself against the bedroom door as if that could help her.

Two, Gurlien grabs the gun and snaps off a shot, striking the doorjamb and splintering even more wood away. The bang blasts through Delina's mind, plugging her ears and ringing her brain.

Three, the cat hisses, spitting and arching its back, yowling before dashing away.

Four, in the doorway, his eyes flashing red, half crouched, the paint circle ablaze in fire, is Maison.

There's a quick, vicious moment of silence, before Gurlien aims the gun again and snaps off another shot.

Maison just shifts, still in the circle, the bullet passing harmlessly by.

"Where is she?" Maison growls, his voice distorted by

the circle around him. The very air wavers, and his eyes glint, unreal. "Where did you take her?"

Delina presses herself against the door, and the flicker of motion draws his gaze to her.

He blanches, paling, drawing himself up out of the crouch. "Delly," he starts, stepping towards her and getting jerked back into the circle. "Delly, are you okay?"

Delina opens her mouth to speak, then closes it, words gone like the wind whistling through the shattered door.

His eyes are still red, flashing, unnatural.

He tries to take another step, but gets yanked back once more from the circle on the doorstep.

"Delly, did they hurt you?" he asks, like she's the only person in the room and like he didn't just fucking obliterate the door to the cabin.

Slowly, she shakes her head.

"She came to us, Freddy," Chloe says, suddenly, and both of them flinch. "Glad to know her mother left a functioning demon trap."

"Didn't know a demon trap would work on a half one," Gurlien says, staring down at the vivid fire surrounding Maison's feet.

Maison shoots them a quick glance, then back to Delina. "Whatever you're thinking, it's not real," he says, dipping his voice down, as if he could deny anything with his eyes glowing red and the circle ablaze at his feet. "Whatever they told you, whatever you think is going on, it's not it."

"Delina," Gurlien says, his voice clinical, "I would advise going into the other room for this."

"Or what, Gurlien, you're going to try to shoot me?" Maison snipes back. "I can block that in my sleep and we both know it."

So he does know them. It's not just a bad prank, it's not just a misguided letter.

It's worse.

With composure she sure as hell doesn't feel, Delina pulls herself to her full height, staring Maison down.

He winces again at her expression, and she can't even see the gray of his eyes behind the red.

"Can you move?" she asks, finally, after letting him stand in silence in the doorway. "Over...whatever the hell that thing is?"

"Oh we are not letting him in," Gurlien says, as Maison shakes his head no. "There is no way he's coming in here, not when —"

"You knew about my mom," Delina interrupts him, and the panicked expression bleeds into Maison's eyes again. "You knew about my mom and never told me."

"Delly," Maison starts, then trails off.

"Don't call me that," Delina snaps, and he flinches. "You knew."

And Maison's handsome face closes off, and he leans back, away from the doorway, still trapped in the circle. "You wouldn't understand."

"Oh fuck that," Delina says, and there's something unreal about fighting with him in front of other people. All their arguments, all their fights, had always been in private before. "Make me understand."

Out of the corner of her eye, Chloe grabs Gurlien, pulling him back, whispering something frantic to him, but honestly, she can't make herself give a fuck about whatever it is.

Maison obviously does, his gaze flickering between them and her as his jaw works. It's his thinking face, when he's grabbing at straws for something to say.

"And what, your name's 'Freddy' now?" Delina asks, and a dim part of her realizes that this is probably not the best place to have the argument. "You have a different name, you are apparently magical—"

"—Half Demon," Gurlien calls out, even though Chloe's tugged him into the kitchen.

"And you're...you're just here because you were paid." At that, her voice cracks, embarrassingly so, and Maison's expression softens. "And you knew my entire life was a lie."

He remains silent, but he often does when she shows emotions like that, letting her piece together what she wants to say, not interrupting, before he sighs, leaning so he can see more of the cabin.

"How long have you known?" he asks, voice dipping down. "Where did I go wrong?"

"Literally yesterday," Delina answers. "My mother set up a PO Box, they called me when it got too full because she didn't clear it out."

He grimaces, like this is a mistake made in loading the dishwasher, before his eyes dips to her hand. "You're still warded."

It's not a question, but she's known him long enough to hear it in his tone.

"Chloe, you're good at undoing traps, mind letting me in?" he asks, and his voice is back to the casual Maison she knows, the one who chats about paint and hugs her when she's feeling down. "Clearly, I need to explain some things."

A big part of her wants to let him.

Instead, she just presses herself deeper into the doorway of the bedroom, throwing a glance over at the bio-trap.

Maison's eyes follow her gaze, and he draws himself straight. "Don't go in there," he says, and she's known him long enough to hear the distress in his voice.

It was the same distress that came out when they got in the car accident two years ago.

"Why not, Maison," she says, and he obviously struggles with his words. "Worried you'll get fired for not doing a good job?"

He flounders, visibly so, and she's so used to helping when he does that it itches along her awareness. "We can still go back," he says. "We can still go back to how it was before, as long as you don't step in there."

That settles it, firm in Delina's chest, and she turns and strides into the room.

Behind her, Maison makes a wordless noise of agitation, and she can dimly hear Chloe and Gurlien exclaiming or arguing, but her eyes are just locked on the single spray paint of gold.

It's harmless, more like a bad movie decoration on something too low budget for an art department. Like something Maison would call out as sloppy worldbuilding when they watched movies.

And somehow, it holds whatever her mother thinks is the key to her 'potential.' The potential that Maison thinks she shouldn't have.

She tosses a look to him over her shoulder, then steps over the gold paint.

He flinches, like she struck him.

Immediately, sparks crackle up around her, snapping and vivid, spiraling up her ankles and her legs, sending pinpricks of sensation along her skin.

It's not painful, necessarily, but it's near to it.

She turns, so she's facing out towards the door of the bedroom, but the world blurs outside the barrier of the circle, and all other noise falls away.

And she waits.

The sparks flicker over her skin, nestling into her arms and itching at her face, but she breathes out hard, shuddering, and the air catches in her throat.

She tries to form words, but no sound comes out, her throat as dry as the deserts in Arizona.

A shiver of dread drips down her spine, and the world jerks once, twice, then spins, tugging her legs out from underneath her.

A dim part of her fights whatever it is, fights falling to the ground, fights the onslaught of sensation and sparks and terror, before...

Darkness slams into her.

8

Nothing makes sense.

No, nothing feels like it makes sense.

Her arms ache, her legs ache, her head thuds with the pounding of her heart, and her eyes struggle against her to stay shut.

Above her, someone speaks and it's not someone she knows.

Wait, yes. It's Chloe, they just met, answered by Gurlien, just as close.

Their voices are muffled, like they're speaking through several thick panes of glass.

Delina scrunches her face, and her head is on someone's lap, and someone's hand in her hair.

"She's coming back," Maison says, his voice clear, so clear it's almost startling. "Delina? Delly girl?"

She told him not to call her that.

She told him not to call her that, and he had lied for five years.

She opens her mouth to say something back, but nothing comes out.

Chloe speaks again, and it's just outside of her aware-ness, and the cat meows in response.

The cat's perfectly audible, at least.

"You're okay, we got you, you're fine," Maison says, and she can feel the rumble of his words, so she pries her eyes open.

The world blooms in gold.

There's gold on the edges of the doorway, gold streaks along the ceiling of the cabin, and the outline of Maison's jaw as he leans over her.

She tilts her head over, and Chloe is outlined in a similar sheen of gold, though Gurlien is dark, without a trace.

The cat sits on its haunches, close to her, and at least it's fucking normal.

Chloe says something, Delina can see her mouth moving, but the words still don't reach her.

"Delly, can you hear me?" Maison says, and she tilts her head back. Of course she's leaning against him.

She tries to speak, tries to say something, but nothing comes out, so she swallows and nods.

"She needs some water, go get some water," Maison instructs, and the completely dark form of Gurlien dashes to the kitchen. "It's okay, everything's okay, you passed out."

She passed out?

For a few moments she marvels at it, at the idea of being unconscious, before the memories cram into her brain. Of the door flying in, Maison trapped outside. Of the gunshots. Of Chloe and Gurlien yelling.

Of herself striding into the circle left by her bio-mother.

She jolts upright, scrabbling up, before all her blood rushes to her head and she lists to the side, thumping against Maison's chest instead of falling to the ground.

They're splayed out on the floor of the bedroom, with the baby blue carpet and the floral curtains.

There's not a trace of paint where the circle used to be.

"Here," Maison says, and he holds a glass of water out to her. Gold lingers on the glass where his fingertips touch, and it distracts her enough to actually take a drink from it. "You'll be okay, your body just dumped the last few decades of magic into your system at once."

She twitches herself away from him, and though her head swims and she wobbles, she doesn't fall back over. "Don't touch me."

Right. Magic.

And he lied to her.

"Why are you..." she trails off, getting a glimpse of her hands.

They shine gold, bright.

"Here," Gurlien says, and she can barely hear him, though he crouches down in front of her, holding a pen light in one hand. "Look...me."

She blinks owlishly at him, and he shines the light into her eyes.

There's something off about him, too, besides just the darkness around him. His hands are hurting him, somehow she can tell, and there's something fucked up with the tendon in his left wrist.

She looks to Maison, wordless, and his brows are drawn together. His feet ache, his legs are almost trembling, and there's a sharp spike of pain in his forehead, even though she can see no injury.

She reaches a hand up and touches the spot on his forehead, but there's nothing there to suggest anything.

But it still hurts him.

She can feel it in her bones. Some newfound certainty,

like a color she's never seen before, but is suddenly, vividly, there.

Chloe crouches next to Gurlien, and her boots pinch at her toes, annoying but ultimately ignorable.

"Why does your head hurt?" she mumbles, the words mealy in her mouth. "Your head hurts."

Maison and Gurlien exchange a glance. Maison had been trapped outside, she's sure of it. She's sure of it, there was a circle, and—

She leans away, looking past the door to the bedroom. Not a trace of the magic still exists, nothing's burning on the ground where he had been trapped.

Rain still blows in from the gaping hole, but it's normal. Completely normal.

The scribbled rune over the top of the doorway's gone, too.

The golden thread in one of the pillows lays shredded on the floor, like someone had taken a seam ripper to it.

"Okay," she mumbles, and Maison holds the glass for her to drink again but she pushes him away. "I don't want to sit on the ground right now."

THEY GET her to the couch, Maison holding her up like he did when she sprained her ankle, and her skin crawls the entire time. The moment she's able to support herself on the couch, she jerks out of his grasp, sitting as far away from him as the couch and her swimming head would allow.

The cutesy living room with the cute couch is absolutely coated with gold. Gold dusts the creases in the fabric, the lining of the pillows, and the cracks in the hardwood floor.

Rain blows through the doorway with every gust of

wind, and Gurlien and Chloe busy themselves with hanging a heavy blanket over it as Delina sips water and tries to make sense of the world.

Every little bit of protection her mother had written into this place is gone. Every scrawled rune, every carefully placed ward, all of it.

Even without looking, she knows the one sketched on the bathroom wallpaper is gone.

All the little details threaten to overwhelm her, and she shakily sips from the glass, hyper aware of Maison staring at her, sitting next to her on the couch.

"How'd you get inside?" she attempts to say, though the words come out half garbled.

He catches her hand holding the glass, setting it on the table for her, and there's even rings of gold around the surface of the table, like they too had been collected with condensation on warmer days.

"Don't worry about it," Maison says in his attempt to be soothing, and she shoots him a glare. "We'll talk later, it's okay."

"No," she says, and her voice is loud even to her plugged ears. "I'm not okay, I want to know now."

From hanging up the blanket, both Gurlien and Chloe look back at her.

There's dust streaked along Chloe's face and Gurlien's hair is firmly out of place.

"How long was I out?" she asks, the attention overwhelming in the silence. Chance the cat jumps on the arm of the couch, sitting upright and staring at her as well.

"About...minutes," Chloe says, and Delina blinks at her, still missing words.

"Twenty," Maison murmurs to her, like he can tell she

can't hear that well. "The wards fell, you convulsed, we stabilized you, then you woke up."

She doesn't miss the word 'we.'

"They let you in?" she asks, and both Chloe and Gurlien wince as Chloe hammers a nail in place, then quickly tucks away a step stool.

"...couldn't...came in...sorry," Chloe says, drawing close and sitting on the far edge of the couch, as far away from Maison as she can.

Her toes still hurt in the boots.

"Without the wards, they couldn't stop me," Maison supplies at her blank face. "She's not hearing you guys well."

"Don't talk for me," Delina snaps, though even her own words feel muddy.

Gurlien steps close, the pen light still in his hand, and she leans away from that. "I've seen this before," he says, speaking slowly, and this, at least, she can hear. "The sound processing...in a few hours."

"You'll be fine in a few hours," Maison murmurs, despite her glare.

Delina rubs at her face, and even her skin feels rubbery, her eyes crunchy.

When she thought about getting magic from her mother, she didn't think it'd be like this.

"Why is everything gold?" she asks, plaintive, and all three give her identical uncomprehending looks. "Everything shines with gold."

Maison and Gurlien glance at each other, and despite the fact that Gurlien had shot at him and Maison had destroyed a door, there's still some sense of them knowing each other. Some sense of shared history that she wasn't a part of.

"That'll probably go away," Maison says, though his voice isn't as declarative as before. "Your body had a shock."

"Don't baby me," Delina says, before shakily reaching for the glass again and missing it completely.

Maison grabs it for her, holding it out, and she considers ignoring it before taking it anyways.

"Why can I hear you?"

"Half-demon," Gurlien says, slowly and deliberately, and that, at least, she appreciates. "Magic doesn't ...by normal rules."

"Thanks," Maison snipes back.

"What does half-demon mean?" Delina asks, before screwing her eyes shut to block out some of the glaring gold.

"I will explain it later," Maison says, and she peeks an eye open, only to see more of the gold along the edges of his cheekbones and in his soft brown hair. "Tell us your symptoms."

Both Chloe and Gurlien nod, and Gurlien pulls out a notebook and an honest-to-god fountain pen from the coffee table.

"Chloe is good at figuring things out, and this asshole has a ton of diagnostic knowledge," Maison continues, gesturing at Gurlien. "If there's something we can do, they will know."

She stares at all of them, at the gold everywhere, at her boyfriend who was actually fake and these people she just met, and seriously considers just leaving. Just getting into the tiny sedan and getting out.

"Did you clear the tree?" she asks, instead.

"Not fully," Maison says, and there's still the sharp pain in his forehead, itching at her awareness.

"He wouldn't...to," Gurlien says, and nothing makes sense still, and she shuts her eyes again.

"Everything's covered in gold. I'm dizzy, my ears are plugged up, and I can tell your head hurts, your boots are bothering you, and your left wrist is messed up," Delina says, pointing to each of them, but keeping her eyes closed.

She doesn't want to see their expressions, so she squeezes her face as small as she can scrunch it, trying to think.

Everything is still too much. Too many things she's aware of, too many sensations.

"The scribbles in the bathroom are gone—"

"The runes," Maison murmurs.

"—and everything is too much. There's too many details, there's too much to think about, I'm getting a headache."

She ventures her eyes open.

Gurlien's brows are drawn together, a thoughtful expression on his face, his pen still on the paper. Chloe drums her fingers on her legs, her head cocked, frowning.

Maison's leaning back, his face unreadable.

"There's some sort of animal outside, I think it's dead under a tree and some leaves. There's ants on the outside of that wall, and I still want to know why he's allowed in here and why you two didn't do anything."

Gurlien glances at Chloe, then holds up his left hand. "Translate...sense."

"He's asking what you sense when he does something," Maison says, his voice distant, like his mind is racing and he's on autopilot.

In front of her, Gurlien taps each finger to his thumb, and there's a trace of pain when his ring finger comes in contact.

"There," Delina says, and after everything, with how shitty she feels, with how much her head pounds, a smidgen of curiosity worms its way inside of her. "That one hurt."

Gurlien nods, then says something rapid fire to Chloe, too fast for her to have a prayer of understanding. His eyes dark, he stands, striding into the other room.

"He's going to walk into town to make a call," Maison says, his grey eyes staring hard at her. At least they're not red anymore. "You're not going with him."

There's no way she could make that walk right now, but she levels her best approximation of a glare at him. "Are you going to arrest me?"

"What?" Maison says, then shakes his head—which doesn't help the sharp pain. "No, Delly, I'm not going to arrest you."

"Don't call me that," she says, crossing her arms.

Chloe says something outside her hearing and she doesn't feel like concentrating to understand it, but the sarcastic tone is obvious enough.

"No, I'm not going to do anything until she feels better," Maison argues, "then we'll plan and we'll figure something out; until then, the College doesn't need to know."

"I thought you worked for them or something," Delina says. "Great big reason why you were with me."

Maison exhales, looking away, and in the motion she could swear she sees a glint of red in his eyes before he blinks and it's gone.

Chloe clears her throat, the sound soft against Delina's awareness. "Delina," she says, slowly, deliberately, leaning forward and peering over her thick rimmed glasses. "We may have bigger fish to fry right now."

She didn't even miss any words that time.

Delina shuts her eyes again, thumping her head against the couch. "So what am I, Chloe? You're the one who knows the types of power."

There's silence, not the normal muffled speaking, which doesn't help.

"Still figuring that out," Maison says finally. "Might take a bit."

There's the sudden, overwhelming emotion of exhaustion. Of experiencing too much in too little time.

"Is it safe for me to sleep?" Delina asks instead. "Or is this a concussion sort of situation?"

SHE ENDS up curled on the couch with a blanket thrown over her, the dim sounds of Maison and Chloe discussing something in undertones in the kitchen.

It's not better, and the nap that she knows in her soul would make her feel better evades her.

Chance stretches himself out next to her, at least, purring like nothing's wrong in the world. The cat's back right paw is a bit sore, like he stepped on something prickly, but she would have never known by the sound of the purr.

It's worse than her horrid hangover in undergrad, but she focuses all of her will to doze off, like that could fix everything.

At one point, Chloe steps outside, comes back drenched, holding a piece of plastic siding. Without even bothering to explain or anything, she holds it against the open-door jamb.

It's far too small to cover it, but Delina watches her through lidded eyes as the air blurs, bursts gold, and a door forms in its place.

A fully functioning door, if a bit warped. Still made of plastic, down to the doorknob, but Chloe yanks down the blanket and opens and shuts it several times.

The rain stops leaking in, and the wind echoes outside instead of through the living room, but Delina can't find it in herself to be appreciative of it, not quite yet. Let them think she's actually asleep.

Maison putters in the kitchen, with the familiar sounds he makes, with mixing bowls and measuring cups. He's always been the one out of the two of them to bake when stressed.

How much of that is fake?

Delina stills her hand on the cat, and the cat meows at her in response.

There's so many small things that could be real, could be fake, and she would've never known without her mother's letter.

So instead, she listens to the familiar clinking of pans of the oven door opening and closing, all slightly muffled, the anger slowly replacing itself with something closer to sadness.

9

She manages to actually doze off, so by the time Gurlien makes it back it's dusk outside and the smell of cookies permeates the air of the cabin.

And everything is louder.

"Axel didn't pick up his phone, and Alette cussed me out before hanging up, and I still don't have the other's number," Gurlien mutters to Chloe, along with the tell-tale sounds of someone stripping off a wet rain jacket. "I tried Luis the scholar, he didn't take my call, and I couldn't risk anything to Kirk."

Delina blinks her eyes open, not moving from underneath the blanket, but they're all in the kitchen.

"I found the dead bird," Chloe says, and Delina instinctively thinks towards the spot she could tell it was.

Somehow, it's colder, like the leaves covering it were a burial blanket.

"That's bad," Gurlien snips. "I don't think either of you two know how bad this is."

"I have a little inkling," Maison says, his voice a rumble, and Delina sits up at that.

Immediately, they all look to her. Gurlien's hair is literally dripping from the rain.

"Can you hear now?" Chloe asks, the first to break the awkward silence.

"Yeah," Delina says muzzily. "Thanks for the door."

"Oh that's...that's no problem," Chloe responds, almost puzzled. "Just had to find a material that would work."

Maison scowls at the room, his arms crossed, though his head is certainly better.

"Why is it bad?" Delina asks, when none of them speak again. "You said it was bad, why is it bad?"

They all look at each other, like gauging what lie they can tell.

"Frederick should take this one," Gurlien says, "since he knows how bad it could be."

"Don't call me that," Maison replies, plaintive, and that, at least, is something. "Nobody calls me that anymore."

"Is it actually your name?" Delina asks, reaching towards the water on the table.

"Legally," Maison says, disgruntled. "My mom calls me Maison."

Delina raises an eyebrow at him. He never talks about his mother, changing the subject sourly whenever she brought her up, to the point where she thought they had a horrible relationship or something.

But no, his mom calls him Maison.

Her hand shakes a little with the glass, but not nearly as much as before, so she pushes herself up to standing and wobbles.

"Take it easy." Chloe says, her voice lilting up. "You're probably still dealing with a fair amount of shock."

Delina shoots her a glare, and gets a surprised grin from Maison, before she strides in to join them in the kitchen, shamelessly grabbing a cookie from the pile. "Talk," she orders.

Again, she's met with silence.

"I mean it," Delina says, leaning against the counter, the same counter she brewed coffee just that very morning. "I can hear now, I'm upright, I deserve to know. Go."

"Good lord, she is just like her," Gurlien mutters in sotto voice, and she levels the stare at him. "It's not a good thing to be like your mother."

"We can't confirm anything," Chloe finally says, as Maison crosses his arms again. "So we don't want to panic you, but in whatever magic your mom did...it might be bad."

"Understatement," Gurlien says.

Maison just frowns deeper.

"Bad like drag me off to this College bad? Or bad end the world bad?"

"You're not going to end the world," Maison says, finally. "At most you might be on the run for your entire life."

"That's not better," Delina informs him, and his jaw twitches.

"We want to run some more tests," Chloe says, and Gurlien nods. "But you need time and energy for those."

"Do I have time for that?" Delina asks, tossing her ponytail behind her and immediately regretting it. "Or is my ex-boyfriend here going to take me to this College that my mom wanted me to avoid?"

There's a flash of something across Maison's face, gone before she can even pinpoint it down, but he shifts, squaring his shoulders.

It's his 'ready to fight' stance.

"They don't know I'm here yet," he says, and Gurlien's eyebrows flash up. "And I'm not going to tell them until we have more answers. If they track my GPS, I'll say we went on a surprise vacation."

"Charitable," Gurlien shoots at him.

"And," Maison says with a glare to Gurlien, "like you pointed out, there may be bigger issues."

"Which you aren't telling me," Delina snaps, stealing another cookie.

"We're trying to not be alarmist," Chloe says solemnly, "and if we act like the bad option is true before we know it is, then we could do things that aren't necessarily a good idea."

It's something, at least, but it sits poorly with Delina.

"And," Chloe says, raising her voice just a bit more, "we can go into town to test it tomorrow. Weather is supposed to clear up and the forest service will take care of the tree."

"And there's something to be said in not telling you, as to not influence the results," Maison says, which is, again, reasonable, but Delina seethes with it.

Gurlien's staring hard at Maison, like he's trying to will him into explaining himself, and Delina could have told him that rarely works. "Chloe," Gurlien says, "I need to run something by you."

Chloe glances at him, startled, her brows drawn together. "Now?"

Gurlien nods, a quick jerk of his head, still staring at Maison, before the two of them abruptly walk away, down the hallway on the other wing of the cabin that Delina still hasn't explored.

Leaving just her and Maison.

She grabs another cookie, needing the idle motion, and he scowls.

Once, two years into their relationship, they had fought over her taking a job he thought was underneath her, and she thought he'd leave her out of frustration. He had insisted she was better than it, she had insisted that it would be easier, and they didn't speak to each other for almost a week.

This scowl reminds her of that.

"Ex-boyfriend?" he starts, like that's the upsetting part of all of this. "Just like that?"

She stares at him, and he doesn't look away.

"You were never planning on telling me," Delina says finally, and the yellowing kitchen lights do nothing for his complexion.

"I couldn't," Maison says, leaning back against the fridge.

"Bullshit," Delina informs him, and he bares his teeth at her in an almost smile. "You could've and we could've figured something out."

"Yes, that would go well," he says, and if he's using that sarcastic tone he must be really upset. "'Hey, Delina, your mother was an evil magician and I have dubious parentage and you might be magical, but we don't know, wanna get frozen yogurt after work?' That'd go over just peachy."

"I dunno, these two nerds managed to show me some proof pretty quickly," Delina shoots back. "Your eyes were fucking glowing, that might've convinced me."

He crosses his arms again.

"You listened to me talk about my mom so many times, and you never even said 'oh hey I know her,'" Delina continues, a bile taste in her mouth. "Instead, I had to find out from a letter."

There's a long stretch of silence, where the only sound is the continued hum of rain on the roof and the faint purr of the cat on the couch.

There's a brush of gold where she had touched the espresso machine that morning, weakly glittering.

"You would've left," Maison says, his voice awful, "you would've left and then the College would've sent someone worse your way, or just...arrest you."

She stares at him, and he has the gall to look like he thinks he's in the right. Gold still glints around him, through his soft brown hair and around his jaw.

"You should probably rest more," he murmurs, after shifting under her examination for a good minute. "You're new to this, don't do anything rash or make any fast decisions for a bit."

"You're just trying to get out of this discussion," she says, because he totally is. "You're uncomfortable because you lied to me for five years and you're trying to convince yourself that it was the right thing to do."

That makes him look away, and she wants to thrill in the little victory of it, but the sour taste doesn't go away.

It never does, whenever they've fought.

"I can't believe you would do that," she whispers, and her voice breaks, no matter how hard she tries to keep it under control. "Five years, and it was fake the entire time."

Her head pounds, and she squeezes her eyes shut again.

"Do you think they went in the other room just so we could fight?" Maison asks, his voice low.

"You're the one that's known them for longer than you've known me," Delina says, and it's just as bitter.

"Then probably," Maison says, shifting uncomfortably. "Gurlien hates emotional situations, even before...whatever happened, happened, and Chloe follows the lead of those around her."

"Right," Delina says, then shrugs. "Yes, ex-boyfriend. Just like that."

There's still the well of hurt inside of her, bubbling forward and mixing with bile, at her saying the words. At her actually speaking them aloud, as if she had kept silent the last two days wouldn't have happened.

So instead of seeing that terrible expression over him, she turns on her heels to leave, her throat aching with something else unsaid.

Before she can take a step away, Maison catches her by the hand, like this is a normal day and he's pulling her in like he always does.

But the moment his fingers grasp her, a loud snap echoes through the tiny kitchen, and a single spark of gold arcs from her hand and nestles into his skin.

Delina flinches, hard, and Maison jerks, his hand tightening around hers.

"What was that?" Delina breathes, then chances a look up at Maison's face.

His eyes reflect the light back at her, unreal and unmoving, and the expression over his face is an unholy amalgamation between horror and hunger.

She freezes, like a mouse caught in a cat's gaze.

"Delina," Maison says, his voice deep, a tremor hiding beneath it. "Did you do that on purpose?"

Slowly, she shakes her head, and his expression doesn't shift, though his fingers shake against the palm of her hand.

Even without explanation, she somehow knows it's bad by the stillness in his body, and by the horror growing in his eyes.

Like she's the frightening one here.

"Delina," he says again, his voice softer, "if that happens with anyone else, you need to tell me. Tell Gurlien and Chloe. And nobody else."

"That's not good, is it?" Delina asks, small, like the one spark of energy shrunk her down in size.

He hesitates, for a bit too long, then shakes his head and releases her hand.

Her palm is cold without his grasp.

They stare at each other for a few more seconds, his eyes never returning to normal, before she clutches her hand to her chest and flees to the bedroom, slamming the door behind her.

AFTER A FEW HOURS of curling up on the bed, halfway between horror and fear warring inside of her, she ventures out of the bedroom.

It's just Chloe in the kitchen, thankfully, busying herself by sautéing something fragrant in a cast iron pan, though her face pinches together when Delina comes into view.

"Feeling better?" Chloe asks, forcefully cheery. It's awful.

The answer is no, but Delina shrugs.

"Well, Gurlien and Freddy are outside arguing in the dark if you want to join them," Chloe says, bright and sunshiny and fake. "They haven't seen each other in six or so years, they probably have a lot to yell about."

Maison hardly ever yells.

"Freddy already got a chance to stress bake, so it's my turn." Chloe says, pointing down at the pan. "Do you like frittatas?"

"I think I scared them," Delina blurts out, like she's a child who has no control over what she says. "I don't know how, though."

"I'd say you did," Chloe replies, as delicate as a hammer. "Don't worry, we'll get it all figured out."

Chloe certainly is worrying, that's for sure, as she pours

in an egg mixture over the top of the veggies, then shoving it in the oven.

"But are you feeling better?" Chloe asks once the idle motions are done. "Physically. Does your head hurt and are you seeing gold still?"

"No on the head, yes on the gold," Delina replies, thankful for the direct question for once.

"And can you tell if I'm uncomfortable?" Somewhere in the conversation, Chloe's face had turned clinical.

So Delina breathes out, and thinks.

Her mind immediately snaps over to the dead bird outside, cold and horrid, but she wrangles it in to the person in the room with her.

Chloe's changed her shoes, now padding around in a pair of comfortable slippers, though the tips of her fingers hurt, like she had grasped something from the freezer for a bit too long.

"Did you touch something really cold?" Delina asks. "Like, ice cold?"

"Nice," Chloe says, and the encouragement is a welcome surprise. "Yep, you got it."

The plastic door slams open, bouncing against the door-frame, and Maison strides in, hair damp and wild, with Gurlien scrambling after him to keep up.

"What did you just do?" Maison demands, and whatever horror or upset he felt earlier is gone from the lines in his shoulder.

"Calm down, I asked her to scan me," Chloe says mildly.

Maison doesn't look very calm.

"She succeeded, too," Chloe says, crossing her arms.

"That didn't feel like a scan," Maison says, and he has no leg to stand on, so Delina levels a glare at him.

"It shouldn't matter to you," Delina says, arching an eyebrow at him. "Ex, remember?"

Gurlien edges his way past Maison, who's blocking most of the doorway to peer at Delina.

"Delina," Gurlien starts, slowly, "do you feel up to a walk around the property?"

AFTER A BRIEF PROTEST FROM MAISON, Delina shakily puts on the magicked rain jacket and this time takes the stupid looking hat, before they all exit out of the plastic door into the night.

It still boggles her mind.

Maison's quiet, his chin tucked in and his eyes narrowed, and whatever argument is brewing there isn't going to be good, but she can't bring herself to care.

Not after he lied to her for five years.

They tromp around the edge of the cabin, and it's far larger than she thought it would be, reaching back into the forest, a simple gravel pathway around it. Rain beats down overhead, shaking the birch leaves and sending pine needles to the forest floor in the darkness.

There's still gold out here, but less. It's on the walls of the cabin, like someone trailed their hand across it while walking, and old footsteps in the gravel, but the rest of the world is thankfully normal.

"Okay," Gurlien says, once they're around, facing the vast black open forest behind the cabin. "Tell me what you feel."

"Irritated," Delina says, and Chloe giggles behind her.

"I mean through magic," Gurlien responds, clearly exasperated, like he's not the one who blacked out that day.

"Close your eyes, concentrate, meditate, whatever feels more natural."

"Just don't fall over," Chloe says helpfully. "First time I tried, I fell over."

Delina eyes her, but Maison shifts, his arms still crossed until he's right behind her, so she shuts her eyes instead, trying to think past the sensation of rain beating down on the hat.

The wind's mostly died down, thankfully, and though the leaves shake, they don't seem distressed. Like the tree is built for this weather.

Cold drips down her cheeks, derailing her thoughts, but she exhales past that, past the wrong sensation that she's trying to think of something that's not there. Like reaching towards a missing tooth.

There's a whisper of something, soft, almost outside of her reach. Like hearing words through a wall, or seeing what might be headlights far away while driving all alone at night.

Her breath puffs up around her, almost palpable in the chill.

"Okay," Gurlien says, and his wrist is still hurting him. "Without opening your eyes, point where you could tell the dead bird was."

That's easy.

Even without her eyes open, there's something tugging at her behind her belly button, towards the left and deeper in the forest, so she points.

There's the trademark sound of Maison walking through the underbrush, and though his legs are tired they no longer shake.

She could tell his footsteps anywhere, even without the weird bio-feedback she's getting from him. He's brilliant against her awareness, almost outlined, even with her eyes closed.

She breathes out again, reaching out towards the missing thing again, and Chloe's there as well, a dimmer sort of presence, always moving or twitching, but not nearly as bright as Maison, who almost dominates the environment. Even in the rain and the chill and the dead thing that pulls at her.

"I can tell when you're doing that!" Maison calls out, closer to the dead bird but facing the wrong way.

"Okay, so she can scan *that* easily, that's useful," Gurlien mutters.

"Can I open my eyes now?

"How far away is he from it?" Gurlien asks instead of answering her question.

"He's facing the wrong direction, I think," Delina says, right as a big drop of water lands on her shoulder and splashes up to her face. She flinches, and all of the awareness of everyone immediately drops away.

She jerks back, her eyes opening, scrubbing the water from her face.

"So your concentration needs work," Gurlien says, crossing his arms against the cold but still holding the flashlight. "But some senses are there."

"Of course her concentration needs work, she's never had to use it for that before," Maison says, stomping back in the underbrush, shifting leaves around, getting closer to the dead bird.

"Now," Gurlien says, his voice low, and Delina doesn't think Maison would be able to hear him. "What do you want to do with the dead bird?"

Chloe whirls around and smacks him in the arm. "That's too much," Chloe says.

"It's cold?" Delina says, unsteady. "I'd probably bury it so it wasn't so cold."

Both Gurlien's and Chloe's eyebrows do a funny thing, like they're trying to not show their expression and fail miserably.

"We definitely need to take you into town," Gurlien says, with a confidence that settles something inside of Delina. She's always liked a steady plan.

10

Delina awakens the next morning to more lingering chill in the bed and a growing awareness of the dead bird outside.

She flops over onto her back and stares up at the open beam ceiling, letting her mind wander.

A bug crawls over the exposed bone in the bird, sending pinpricks of sensation towards Delina, and she hates it. Hates hates hates it.

The world no longer shines in gold, thankfully for her eyes, and despite the late-night walk through the woods, she's back to her normal time waking up early, as if she still has an office job and a gym routine.

The main room of the cabin is empty, cold, though the plastic door still stands against the wind and Chance the cat sleeps on one of the pillows, barely opening his eyes to glance at her before falling back asleep.

The espresso machine still summons a perfect shot of espresso at her touch, and Delina watches it, detached.

In all of this magic, in all of the stress of the day before, and her mother had still somehow coded the machine to her. It's almost obscenely silly in her mind, to bother doing something so small when the rest of the magic was so...big.

Scrounging up a slice of leftover frittata, she throws it in the microwave right as Maison wanders into the room.

He freezes at the sight of her. Delina doesn't know where he slept, but by the look of the circles under his eyes, it wasn't well.

"I don't want to talk to you," Delina heads off, clutching the chipped coffee mug to her chest, as the microwave takes the longest time possible.

"I gathered," Maison replies, guarded, moving into the kitchen.

Delina skirts around the counter to avoid being in the same place as him, her heart pounding.

He attempts a try at the espresso machine, and it does absolutely nothing for him, and a thrill of victory goes through Delina at his frustrated scowl.

"My bio-mom coded it to me," Delina says, after the third attempt at checking to make sure the cord is seated properly.

"Of course she did," Maison grumbles, then sighs. "I don't know what they've told you, your mother is dangerous."

"I should've been the one to decide that," Delina says, then, before she can stop herself. "Why are you still here?"

This seems to short out his brain. "What?"

"You got through the tree, you can get out." The microwave beeps, but he's standing right by it, and she's not about to skirt by him to get her food. "Why are you still here?"

He rubs his eyes. "Can I answer that after coffee?"

"No," Delina responds and, for some reason, he smiles just a bit, which makes her blood boil even more. "I own this cabin, apparently, and I want to know why you bothered to stick around."

He weighs his words, obvious even behind his bleary eyes, for far too long.

"I don't want a pretty answer, I want the honest answer," she says, after he doesn't say anything. "Stop trying to put it into palatable words."

"Safety, then," he responds, trying and failing again with the coffee machine. "You're in danger, I don't like that, and I'm gonna stick around until you're not."

She rolls her eyes, finally skirting around him to get to the still beeping microwave. "I don't believe you," she shoots, before taking her frittata and amazing coffee and slamming the door to her bedroom.

SHE DOESN'T EMERGE until she can one hundred percent hear Chloe and Gurlien in the kitchen, and she intentionally makes quite a few shots of espresso for them.

The air of the cabin is charged, but with what she could never tell. Something between eagerness and nerves, between fear and excitement, and all Delina can think about is the dead bird still outside.

Chance the cat is in rare form, batting at everyone's ankles as they walk by, then meowing pitifully when he inevitably got his claws stuck in Gurlien's pant leg until he carefully untangled him.

"Okay!" Gurlien says, after the strained conversation comes to a lull and the dishes are put away in the surprisingly modern dishwasher. "Going into town, let's do it."

Maison's gaze is once again on Delina, but she ignores

him. "I should bring my phone to check in. Tell them everything is fine, nothing to worry about."

"No," Gurlien snaps, as Chloe audibly scoffs. "I don't know the codes anymore, I don't trust that."

Maison crosses his arms. "I'm coming, I'm not letting you two assholes be the only protection for this."

Chloe bristles, but Gurlien waves his hand at that.

"Yes, yes, you're powerful, we know, that's not news," Gurlien replies.

"I've worked too hard to separate from them, I'm not letting you blow that up," Chloe says, and it sounds a bit like a vow. "If I think you're going to rat us out I will put you in a trap circle."

Maison spreads his arms, like that's an insult.

"And I don't want them to know this place exists," Gurlien finishes. "The moment they do, then all the research in the basement will belong to them and they'll bury it."

"This place has a basement?" Delina interrupts.

"It's super creepy," Chloe responds, as an aside.

"I think it's better that I give them an 'all clear, this is fine' than them suddenly wondering why I dropped all communication," Maison says, and it's so close to reasonable that Delina squints at him. "The first—and last—time I missed a check in was...not good."

"When was that?" Delina asks, and he avoids her glance. "No, it was my life, I deserve to know."

"And what happened to make it 'not good'," Gurlien follows up. "Define not good."

Maison scowls at him. "Delina had a personal emergency," he reports, "we were out of contact for two days because the mountain had no signal."

Delina blinks at him for a few seconds. "Do you mean when my dad broke his ankle up at the Horse camp?"

He nods, though Gurlien scoffs.

"They didn't let me see my mother for three months," Maison continues, quieter. "They didn't let her outside of the compound and see the sky for the entire time."

Chloe and Gurlien recoil back, and Delina stares at him, hard. Maison just scowls, crossing his arms and not looking at any of them.

No wonder he never spoke about his mother.

Gurlien recovers first. "So that's how they've been keeping you in line, I always wondered," he says. "It didn't make sense why you didn't go freelance."

"Gurlien..." Chloe trails off, rubbing her face. "Okay, Freddy, that makes complete sense, sorry."

There's a lump in Delina's throat, another crawling horror.

Maison's jaw twitches, like he wants to flee the conversation but is forcing himself to continue it.

"So yes, I would very much like to do a check in that everything is fine and say Delina surprised me with a trip," Maison says. "Combined with nobody knows who or what is going to come out of the woodwork because she—" he jerks his thumb at Delina, still not looking at her, "—is a beacon right now to who knows what out there." He then pushes himself up, striding off into the wing of the cabin Delina hasn't explored yet, his shoulders a long line of tension.

Chloe blinks over at Delina, twisting her hands together. "You didn't know?"

"Of course she didn't know, she didn't know anything," Gurlien says, though his brows are drawn together. "Explains why he took a long-term contract and stuck with it."

Long-term contract, that must be Delina, and it still doesn't taste any better.

Explains why he was so patient with her and why even at their worst, he didn't want to break up.

"Chloe, bring your laptop to town, let's see if we can find records of his mother," Gurlien commands. "Use the cached version we have of the surface records, don't try to hack, not right now."

"Do we know if his mother was the demon or his father?" Chloe asks, standing up with something resembling purpose. "That'll narrow it down."

"Mother was the human," Gurlien calls after her, as she walks briskly into the other side of the cabin, then he glances sideways at Delina. "I want to make sure he's telling the truth before we let him."

She had thought she knew all of Maison's tells when he was lying, but apparently not. "I've never met any of his family."

"And you were with him for five years and you didn't find that odd?" Instead of being skeptical, Gurlien leans forward, like he's honestly curious and bewildered by that. "I thought that would be odd for most people."

Delina leans back, desperately not wanting her personal space to be filled by anyone at this moment. "I take it you haven't had many relationships where one party has things they don't discuss."

Gurlien just shakes his head, as Maison strides back in, carrying the navy not-quite rain jacket he practically lives in when it's blustery outside.

"You and Chloe wouldn't know subtlety if it hit you over the head," Maison says. "I'll give you my mother's exact name and cell number if you need verification on your records."

Oh, he's angry. And still avoiding looking at Delina.

"That'd be nice," Gurlien replies without a trace of irony.

"Here," Maison says, then tosses Delina his phone, without even looking. "Have her hold it until you determine I won't rat you out."

The phone is off, cold, but the case is the one she bought him a year ago when he got a promotion.

If that promotion was even real.

"I know your dad has your new number, I'd leave that behind because they could use him to trace it back to you," Maison tells her, jaw tight. "That's where you'd have to worry about the tracking, I at least knew to turn off my phone when going to an unknown location."

"There wasn't any signal," Delina protests, and he looks at her, really looks at her. Like she's transparent, like he can see every thought and instinct and hurt that she's having right now, and none of it is good enough. "And, to be fair, I'm new to this conspiracy stuff."

"Well, you seemed to get a good grasp of it quickly," Maison shoots back. "Quick enough to run away."

Chloe tromps back in, a normal school backpack over her shoulder making her look even younger, then stills in the doorway, caught in the uncomfortable moment, until Delina gestures her in.

"I'm bringing my kit this time," Chloe says, and by their nods, both Gurlien and Maison know what that means. "If we get caught off guard, we'll have some materials for me to work with."

"Good," Gurlien says, then honest-to-god puts the gun in his coat pocket, completely unsecured. "Let's do this."

11

The town is a mere twenty-minute drive from the cabin, now that the tree is neatly chopped to pieces and branches cleared off to the side.

Delina stares out at them as they drive by, the frustration and awfulness of even the day before almost foreign to her, but they're past it in a blink of an eye, the break in the foliage small.

"Okay," Gurlien says, as soon as they're into the small town, with its Americana stores and tiny cafes. "Chloe, you need the library or Charlies?"

"Charlies," Chloe says confidently, hoisting her backpack over her shoulder once Gurlien parks on the sparsely populated street. "Internet's better and we can get coffees."

Without the biting wind, the rain drifts like an afterthought once Delina steps out of the car, but she pulls the jacket tighter around her chest as Chloe and Gurlien step into one of the indistinguishable cafes.

Mason catches her by the elbow before she can follow them in, just touching her jacket and not her. "Delina, one sec."

In the chill air, his cheeks are pink, and the rain settles into his brown hair like a mist.

She jerks her elbow out of his grasp. "Yeah?" she says, and they're actually in public, there's some people across the street, she doesn't know what could be said when out and about like that. There's still so much she doesn't know, an aching chasm of unknowing.

Maison hesitates, then leans forward, as if they were still a normal couple and they were discussing something idle. "If you don't want to do the test they're going to put you through, tell me, and I'll get you out of there." His grey eyes flicker up into the cafe, tracking Gurlien ordering something and Chloe opening the laptop and plugging it in. "There's a chance it won't be nice and friendly."

The sarcastic, biting comment is on the tip of her tongue, but the tension still across his shoulders stops her from speaking it.

So she exhales, consciously, attempting to loosen up the knot of hurt. "It would help if I could make an informed decision on what it might be," she says, trying to keep her tone just as soft as his but failing miserably. "I don't like going into things blind."

"I know," Maison says, "I want them to be wrong. I don't...I don't think they're wrong."

Delina can't think of anything to say.

"But if they're not wrong, then we have more important things to deal with than a missed call into the College," he continues, though his face twists. "I can do a lot, but I can't defend against everything."

The half answers itch at her mind, but she nods. "My mother was really that bad?"

"I read her research, she was insane," Maison says, and it's so close to his normal grumbling of people that it tugs at

Delina. "Utterly batshit, made enemies right and left, couldn't be trusted with anything. She tried to..." he trails off, conspicuously so, then sighs. "She's lucky she didn't kill you before you were born, there's no way anything that she did was ethical. It's a miracle you're not...it's a miracle you're at all normal."

"Can I read it?" Delina asks, and he raises an eyebrow at her, the hint of the dimple coming back for the briefest of seconds. "The research. So I know?"

He narrows his eyes at her, and it's his expression like he thinks she's making a foolish choice, but he's not sure he wants to dispute her on it.

How many of those decisions on disputing things like this were because they threatened his own mother if Delina left him?

"I don't think you'd like it," he says instead, then steps ahead, opening the door to the coffee shop for her. "Ask Chloe to download it."

The inside of the coffee shop is far warmer, so Delina sheds the rain jacket as she sits next to Chloe, who studiously ignores her, tapping away at the computer

"Anything I can help with?" Delina asks, sinking into the overly comfortable chair. No coffee shop chairs should be this comfortable.

"No, it's not that complicated," Chloe says, tapping away. "I'm only doing this because Gurlien's afraid he'll get caught."

Maison drifts over and joins Gurlien next to the register, the frown still on his face.

"Did...did your College do this a lot?"

"You're gonna have to be way more specific," Chloe says, still tapping away.

"Keep people prisoners?"

"Oh you have no idea," Chloe responds. "Anyone they might consider dangerous, they either lock up or they leverage things against them." She throws a nod towards Maison. "My bet is he's too useful, so they went with the leverage. Or his mom is also something strange, but I feel like that would've been mentioned by now." She glances up at Delina, brief, before her brown eyes return to the screen. "Like I said, they're dicks. They're just the dicks in charge."

Delina glances back over at Maison, where he and Gurlien are obviously arguing in whispers while waiting for the coffees to come out. "I take it they didn't get along well in school?"

"Gurlien got along well with absolutely nobody, and Freddy always avoided all his classmates when he could," Chloe answers, and it's so much information on Maison, so much she doesn't know. "Sure, he was nice when he had to interact, but you know, it was obvious he'd rather be anywhere else."

When they had first started dating, Maison had been so obviously twitchy at parties, though that'd calmed down completely after just one year of being with her.

She had just thought he was sheltered before undergrad. Her dad had told her she helped him come out of his shell.

"And then nobody's seen him for years, we all thought he was doing fancy things in France with research scientists," Chloe continues. "Which made sense, he's way more powerful than the average student and he didn't like us anyways."

"Nope, just in Arizona," Delina says. "Working on graphic design in a small town."

Though who knows how much of the graphic design job was real and how much was just a smokescreen to prevent her from figuring things out.

"And...got it." Chloe taps a few more beats, then gestures for Delina to glance in. "Carolina Schmidt, kept in cell 82C on the fifth basement of the Atlanta branch."

The screen is grim, just a diagram of an architect's drawing, with numbers over way too small of rooms.

"He always had business trips to Atlanta," Delina says before she can stop herself. "One a month."

All this time, he was just visiting his mom.

"Here." Chloe double taps on the diagram, bringing up a too-short paragraph. There's a small picture of an unsmiling woman, hair gone white, and if Delina squints then she can see the hint of Maison's nose and eyebrows in her facial features. Her eyes are gray, just close enough Maison's that it suddenly sends some homesickness through her.

"Carolina Schmidt, age 58, gave birth to half-demon at age 23. Monthly visitation, library use allowed, no research facilities. Must remain warded at all times."

And then there's a long string of numbers, completely incomprehensible.

"Those would be the wards placed around her, I think half of those are demon related, don't know the other ones," Chloe says, poking at the computer screen, her lips pressed together. "So that part checks out."

"That's it, they keep her locked up because she gave birth to him?" Delina asks, sitting back, as Gurlien and Maison walk over, both carrying multiple coffees.

Chloe immediately spins the computer to Gurlien, and Maison only glances at it, before blinking away, his face pinched. He passes a cup to Delina, and though their fingers graze, there's no snap of whatever magic had happened before.

Gurlien disinterestedly clicks on the computer a few times, though his eyes are sharp. "All this tells us is there's someone with that name who had a Half Demon," he says. "Not that it's you, not that your sob story is correct."

"I have pictures of me and her on my phone," Maison replies, his voice tightly controlled. "I don't even have to touch the phone, I'll talk her through the check in."

"They don't even make you do voice check ins?" Gurlien asks, then glances to Chloe, and they have one of their brief nonverbal arguments.

And the woman had his eyes.

"Alright," Delina drawls, pulling out the phone and pressing the on button. "Let's see this."

"Hey," Gurlien blurts out, but Maison just sits back, something satisfied glittering in his eyes.

The phone clicks back to life, and his lockscreen is still the picture of them on their third anniversary, when they had driven to the Texas coast and spent the entire weekend getting horrendously sunburned.

"Code is one-zero-zero-eight," Maison says, and it fits the pattern she always saw him swipe. "Pictures are in the google drive, under the folder titled floral references." He shrugs, though he watches her like a hawk. "Figured nobody would snoop there."

Sure enough, picture after picture of Maison and the white-haired lady, one for each month of the year going back ten years. Of him before she knew him, of him when they first started dating. Of him that one time he got his haircut way too short and he looked like a stranger for a month.

"Is that proof enough?" Maison asks, the same shimmering anger underneath his words.

Chloe's already nodding along, though Gurlien scowls.

"Go in the messages, there's a contact named Human Resource Director."

Delina does. Text after text from Maison, all with the date, time, and the words "check-in all good."

Gurlien hovers over her shoulder, and it feels like an invasion of privacy.

"If you scroll up, you can find one of the last times we traveled and the reason why," Maison continues. "But type in the 'day, time, check-in all good,' then put 'flew with target to Seattle for surprise.'"

"Target?" Delina asks, and he shrugs.

Gurlien scrolls up, leaning well into Delina's personal space, until a similar text is in view, then he sits back as well.

Before she can second guess if it's smart, before she can second guess if he's telling the truth this time, she types it out and presses send.

And, just minutely, Maison's shoulders relax. Just enough that she could only tell because she watches.

"You should have verified more," Gurlien says, but he sighs, grabbing at his coffee instead. "We're still going to turn your phone off before we get to the cabin."

"Sure," Maison replies.

∼

AFTER A BRIEF TIME TO drink the rest of their coffees, Gurlien drives them to a derelict corner on the outskirts of the small town.

"Oh," Maison says, as they once more step out into the chill. "I see why you picked this place for the test." He bounces on his toes, eyes alight.

Delina eyes it. There's a run down, boarded up church on one corner, a burnt-out husk of a restaurant, and what looks like a house nobody has lived in for years, blackberry brambles growing up the sides of the brick.

The rain has settled into a fine mist, squashing all sound, as if they are the only people within miles. The pavement is cracked, and dead leaves blow across the street.

Chloe conspicuously heaves the backpack off of her shoulders, unzipping it and settling it at her feet.

"Okay," Gurlien says clinically, "this is going to have three parts. One," he holds up a finger, "we're going to see what you naturally sense without any augmentation. Two, we're going to put a small amplification circle, and then you're going to try again. The third..." he trails off, glancing at Maison, who's giving him absolutely nothing to go off of. "The third will depend on the first two."

"But there will be three parts," Chloe chimes in. "Standard beginning test when you find someone in adulthood."

"Not quite standard," Maison grumbles.

All three of them watch Delina, all of the sudden, and if she could be swallowed up by the pavement she would. "Okay...?"

"Close your eyes and tell us what you feel," Gurlien says, and Chloe's nodding. "Yes, this is vague. That's important."

With one last glance to Maison—he looks distinctly unhappy—Delina lets her eyes shut, and focuses on her breathing. Focuses on reaching for that strange bit in her mind that feels like a loose tooth, like she has to worry at it until she figures it out.

Immediately, there's a gut punch of awareness, right past the church, blossoming and growing until all she can perceive is...there. Something on the other side of the church, many somethings, old somethings, laying cold in the ground, the dirt crawling over with damp and bugs and mold and moss and—

"Stop," Maison's clear voice commands, and she pops her eyes open, and wobbles. "This is unnecessary."

"Do you want a surprised magician only using instinct? Because unless we learn specifics, it's going to be instincts only and that is not going to be a good thing the first time she gets in danger," Gurlien shoots back. "Delina, what did you tell?"

She opens her mouth to speak, but everything's dry, like she fell asleep in the Arizona sun for too long.

Maison's eyes reflect red at her, inhuman and bright, but he crosses his arms and huffs, his breath puffing out in the chill air.

"There's something in the ground behind the church," she says, shakily. "I don't..."

Maison glares over at Gurlien. "We don't have to do more, Delina, you can sit down."

Well now she's not going to, so she shifts until her feet are stronger underneath her, until she doesn't wobble, then strides off towards the church.

A rickety wooden fence, half broken, surrounds the back property, back where the crawling sense of horror pulled at her. She ducks underneath one shattered beam, the throat clawing tightness just getting worse.

"Delly," Maison catches her by the elbow again, and this time, another crackling spark hits him, but he barely flinches. "Delly, don't..."

She rips her arm out of his grip. "Don't touch me."

Inside...is a graveyard. Cracked tombstones, overcome with moss and blackberry brambles, the dirt rich and black.

And underneath them...

Delina's legs shake, and she sits down, hard.

12

It's not so much that she blacks out as that she comes back and time has moved a bit faster than it should.

She's sitting on the mossy damp ground, her head balanced on her knees, her vision swimming and shivers going up her arms, even under the rain jacket.

Chloe's spray painting something on the cracked church foundation, the gold paint sparkling in the mist as she draws something Delina vaguely recognizes as one of the symbols that had been at the cabin before she tore them all down.

It's elaborate already, so it must've taken some time.

Gurlien crouches in front of her, staring too intensely at her, and Maison's hand rubs Delina's shoulders.

"Did you pass out or did you get overwhelmed?" Gurlien asks, clinical. "That just looked like overwhelmed to me."

She blinks at him, then sits upright, twisting to look at Maison.

His face is pinched, his eyes red, but he doesn't say anything.

"I'm okay," Delina says, and even without concentrating,

there's the same pull from whatever is in the graves. Like by sensing it at all, she can't go back to not knowing.

A bug crawls over one of the things, moisture trickling in from above.

"Breathe, it's okay," Maison says from behind her, and she takes a big, gulping breath. "Do we need to do the amplification circle?"

"Yes!" Chloe calls over, still spray painting.

"It's standard procedure," Gurlien responds, though he too looks conflicted.

"This is two instances of her immediately sensing the dead," Maison replies, his voice deep. "I don't want to risk calling something down on us for the sake of scientific propriety."

Dead.

Delina pushes her damp hair out of her face. One of the gravestones is smaller than the other, and the years carved into the moss-pocketed granite says the person only lived for two years.

Two years, a hundred years ago.

Again, the punch of awareness, an itch along her fingers to reach out, dig into the ground, shove the dirt aside, and grasp.

"Right, because you have such vested interest avoiding another one of you," Gurlien shoots back.

"Yes!" Maison replies, immediately. "If she tries to bring something back then yes, the chances of a full demon finding her are incredibly high and I don't want that."

"Bring it back?" Delina asks, and they both fall silent. "You mean I could..."

"No." Maison interrupts. "No, you absolutely cannot."

She shoots him a glance, and his jaw is set.

"You don't want me to do any of this," she tells him, and he narrows his eyes at her, flashing red.

"We don't know if you can bring anything back," Gurlien says instead. "But trying on century old bones would be a bit of a bad place to start."

Delina stands, even though she sways, and Maison steadies her immediately.

The bug crawling along one of the bones stills, deep beneath the earth.

"So, what, my mom gave me some sort of zombie powers?" Delina asks, and from her spray-painting Chloe covers a laugh with a cough. "That's what you guys have been all vague about?"

Both Gurlien and Maison remain silent.

"A warning would have been nice, because this is gross."

Gurlien opens his mouth, as if to answer, but Maison beats him to it.

"She doesn't know anything, don't be an ass about it," he shoots to Gurlien. "Delly —"

"Don't call me that," Delina interrupts.

"Delina," Maison corrects deliberately, "I need you to understand, each time you're going to try to use any of your magic, you're going to be in danger."

"That's an exaggeration," Chloe calls out, calmly stepping out of the mess of symbols she has spray painted on the foundation.

"Maybe," Gurlien interjects.

"There's that other Necromancer, she's still alive, and she's been active for a while now, it's clearly possible." Chloe tosses the spray paint in her bag like she's used to keeping it with her. "Besides, an amplification circle doesn't mean she raises the dead, just that she can see more. It's passive, not active, and Necromancers only send up flares when they actively do things."

Necromancer.

She's only known about all of this for a few days, but even her cursory knowledge of fantasy books tells her what that means.

But the word clearly, clearly has more meaning to them.

Gurlien rubs his face, like speaking it aloud makes it worse, and Maison sighs—a deep, weary sigh. The sort that usually only happens when he can't sleep for days.

"Did you know?" Gurlien asks, directed towards Maison. "Did you have any inkling for however long you slept next to her, that she's someone your father would kill in an instant?"

"What?" Delina asks, as Maison shakes his head. "What do you mean?"

"That's why necromancers are rare, Demons kill them." Gurlien crosses his arms to the cold. "This subsect of magical beings that can teleport across the globe and wreak havoc on local power structures...kill necromancers on sight."

The words hang in the mist, with Maison refusing to look at any of them and the dead bodies lying cold in the ground, and Delina scrapes at her mind for something to say.

"So this circle, it'll do what?" Delina asks, instead of the fear and the horror and everything else. "Any chance of summoning vampires or any other mythical creature I need to be aware of?"

"No," Chloe says sunnily. "Don't touch anything dead though."

"Cool." Delina shakes out her hands, approaching the

cracked pavement. "At least you'll talk to me normally. What do I do, what do I look for?"

Chloe seems just as hell bent on not discussing dire things as she is. "Step inside, same prompt as before. The world will be a lot busier, a lot more intense, and whatever you're getting from the bones will feel a lot more real."

That doesn't sound terribly pleasant, but Delina cocks her head at it anyways. "Can you teach me all of these symbols?"

"Gurlien would be better at teaching it," Chloe says, and Delina's not going to look back at the two men bent on being dire. "But sure."

"So all I need to do is avoid raising things from the dead and I'm cool?" Delina asks, and to this, Chloe looks back over to Maison. "Cause I'm pretty okay with not touching dead things."

And before she can convince herself otherwise, for the second time in only a few days, she steps into a spray-painted circle.

There's a pause, when nothing happens, before the world blooms once more with gold. Gold dripping from Chloe's fingertips, gold highlighting in Maison's hair, gold illuminating Delina's skin.

"It's just the everything has gold on it again," Delina calls out, though she can still see and hear everyone just fine. The world doesn't shift, the sound of the wind still echoes around her, and the mist still drifts around her hair.

The bones in the ground grow larger in her mind, until it's almost a physical itch under her skin. Until all she wants to do is dig, claw her fingernails into the dirt, and pull something up.

Even more, beyond the century old bones, there's a dead mouse in the church, an assortment of dead bugs under the canes of blackberries, and something that might've once been a cat but just gives her echoes of terror and cold.

So instead, she just looks towards Maison, and he tucks his chin in, staring at her. His eyes glint red, of course, but every other line in his face and motion in his body is immediately familiar.

"That's not a bad sign," Gurlien says, though he too looks pale. "Look out to the street."

It takes her a moment to break eye contact with Maison, but she glances out towards the broken pavement and empty buildings.

Flickering in the road, like a drip of a current, is a single line of gold, fluttering merrily along, completely unencumbered by the wind or any physical barriers.

"So there's a rope?" Delina asks. "Right in the middle of the street."

"That was easy," Maison murmurs.

"I didn't expect Dr. Frisse to do anything by half measures, much less any experiments on her flesh and blood," Gurlien says, dusting off his hands, though his face is still pinched. "Of course it was easy for her."

"Congrats, even without the Necromancy you'd be considered powerful, that's neat," Chloe says, completely sincerely. "Normally we'd try for a demonstration but…"

"No," Maison immediately interrupts.

"Yeah," Chloe finishes lamely. "Not the best idea."

"There's a dead mouse—maybe squirrel—in the church," Delina says, and even though the bones are closer, the mouse reads fresher. More possible.

Like it would take less.

"No," Maison repeats.

"And bugs in the brush, those seem small," Delina

finishes, raising an eyebrow at Maison. "A lot easier on the mind than all the bones."

"Oh my god," Chloe mutters. "Oh my god she's going to be like this."

"Though," Gurlien starts, "why your mother would attempt to give you powers that are close to a death sentence is a bit of a mystery."

"And if she unlocked the powers but never got trained, she'd absolutely bring down a demon on her within the month," Chloe continues, which isn't helpful.

So instead, Delina just focuses on the world around her.

Without the pounding headache, the gold isn't that bad. Almost pretty, definitely surreal.

Maison's head isn't hurting him anymore, though his legs shift restlessly and his shoulders are tight, though she could've told him that just by looking at him. Gurlien's wrist aches—worse in the cold—and the skin on his cheeks is a bit chapped. Chloe herself is a bit headachy, in the sort of lack of caffeine way (despite the espresso and the coffees), maybe dehydration.

"That's still weird," Maison says, voice a grumble, the same tone when she made salads for dinner. "Do all necromancers do that?"

"How would I know?" Gurlien asks.

"You're the one who's dealt with one before," Maison responds, though beyond the red glinting in his eyes, he's thoughtful.

"They hid her from me, I never actually met her, just one of the people she raised," Gurlien says, and he shakes out his wrist, an unconscious action that momentarily relieves some of the discomfort. "They didn't like me, remember?"

"Does anyone actually like you?" Maison shoots back, but he narrows his eyes at Delina.

She narrows her eyes right back.

"Tell me," he says, stalking closer to the circle, which draws Delina's back up straight. "What do you see when I do this?"

He waves his hand, some elaborate motion, the sort that he'd make fun of on their movie nights, and the ribbon of gold from the street jerks itself over, snapping around his fist.

A shiver races down Delina's spine.

"Shit," Chloe mumbles, then grabs a gawking Gurlien by his collar, pulling him a few steps away.

Clearly, it's meant to impress her, so Delina crosses her arms. "The thing in the street is now in your hand," she says, pouring every bit of authority she doesn't feel into the sentence.

Maison hates when she turns that tone to him, and his jaw twitches from it, before a hint of the dimple appears.

Like somehow, she answered correctly.

"And this?" Somehow, he digs his fingertips into the ribbon itself, and it shreds apart and...

Detonates.

The pavement underneath him cracks, dust and pebbles floating upwards, his hair lifting in the air. A root beneath the foundation snaps, sudden and green.

A warping, blinding sphere of gold surrounds him, his clothes fluttering around him, and somehow...

Everything in it, everything but him, is dead.

Every bug beneath the surface, every small microorganism she hadn't even known existed, dead. The root, dead. The fly buzzing around his head hits the cracked pavement, brilliant against her mind.

"Are you okay?" Delina blurts out, completely against

her wishes, as Chloe drags Gurlien further away, against the hollowed-out shell of the church.

Maison blinks at her. "Yes?"

"Okay, cause you killed a lot of bugs with that," Delina says, then, before he can stop her, steps forward and reaches out, tangling her fingers in the warping sphere of gold.

Maison flinches forward, but stops himself.

"That was foolish," he says, still within the sphere. "Never touch anything magical without knowing what it can do."

"What, should this hurt me?" Delina shoots back, and the gold threads are warm and pliant against her hand. "Feels like yarn."

"Oh my god," Gurlien mutters, barely on the edge of her hearing.

Maison cocks his head at her, eyes narrowed, as she twists a strand of the gold in between her hands. "We need to have a long conversation about basic magical safety," he says, but there's something close to wonder in his voice, as she weaves the gold in between her fingers. "But that should not be that easy for you."

It's not a rebuke, this time, at least.

"Then why'd you do this?" Delina asks, and even though she's outside of the amplification circle, the bubble still glows bright.

"Because if you see anyone else but me do this, you need to get out of there," Maison replies, voice dipping down low. "This is the basis of what demon magic looks like, and if you see this, you're in danger."

There's something serious on his face, something that gives her pause, so she bites back the sarcastic comment, bites back what she wants to say out of hurt.

"Why'd all the bugs die?" she says again, staring down at the dead fly at Maison's feet.

"Because any living thing—"

"Besides Necromancers! We proved that with the last one!" Gurlien yells over.

"—that's in here when I do that, dies." Maison's eyes glint red, sudden, and her heart jumps. Like she's looking at a predator. "This isn't something you mess around with, this isn't something kind and friendly, this isn't just a new curiosity for you to chase after. Demons wreak havoc on people around them, they take lives without any respect for it, and any time you use that power, you become a beacon to them."

She stares down at the ground, at the cracked pavement and the pebbles still stirring in an invisible wind around his feet.

"And to you?" she asks, finding no other words that aren't hurtful. "Do I look like a beacon to you?"

Surprise filters over his face, before he grins, sudden, foreign and strange. "You do when you do that."

13

Despite his attempts to scare her, Delina's back to feeling hollow by the time Maison takes down the bubble, one thread at a time, and she sits against the wall of the shell of the church, watching him.

After a few minutes of inspecting, then spraying over the circle to invalidate it, Chloe sits next to her, watching as well. Gurlien is inspecting Maison's work as close as he dares, and the pinched off expression is back on Maison's face.

She hates that expression. Always has.

"Can you see all the gold?" Delina asks, after a few minutes of silence, shifting against the damp concrete.

"Not easily," Chloe responds, muted. "That bubble? Yeah. They train us pretty early to see those."

They watch for a few moments, as more and more of the threads disappear back to the ribbon on the street, and the gut punch of death lessens.

"So Necromancer?" Delina asks, and Chloe nods. "Is he telling the truth about the danger or is he trying to control me?"

"Oh, he is absolutely not exaggerating the danger,"

Chloe says, stretching out her legs. Her feet are back in the boots, pinching at her toes. "I have no clue how we're going to teach you control without bringing down an actual demon." She glances, sidelong, to Delina, her brown eyes serious behind her glasses. "At least with Freddy here, he can absolutely do some defense, but I don't know if he could stand up to an actual demon."

"I still feel like I'm missing a massive piece of this puzzle," Delina admits, even though ignorant is the worst thing she could be. "You three were raised in it."

"Eh, Freddy and Gurlien were raised in it, they found me when I was like twelve," Chloe says, chewing on her lip. "Turns out, when you transform a Bunsen burner into a padlock in the middle of your eighth-grade science class, it gets back to people real quick." She shrugs, digging in the backpack. "Still feel the dead?"

"Ugh," Delina responds, but the answer is yes. The bugs and the bones and the small creatures, all neon in the back of her mind, though the wrongness of the bubble is fading into the mist. "So not only did my mom get me the worst power imaginable, I can't ever use it."

Chloe tilts her head, her eyes narrowing. "We are still going to have to teach you control," she says, her voice suddenly calculating, like she took too many lessons from Gurlien, but there's a flicker of mischief in her face. "I have some ideas. Want to break into the church basement?"

"Why?" Delina asks. Her head still hurts and the bones still itch in her mind.

"She's just offering because she's bored," Gurlien calls over. "There's nothing in there."

"You don't know that!" Chloe calls back, then gives Delina an encouraging smile. "He's a little correct."

"No, I'm okay," Delina replies. "I don't really want to go digging into anything I can't tell won't include dead things."

MAISON INSISTS on her getting a proper lunch and Gurlien retreats to try to call the magicians who know of the other Necromancer, and Chloe takes one look at the two of them and immediately scampers into one of the stores instead.

Delina can't blame her. If she could get out of the awkward situation, she would.

But instead, she finds herself getting corralled into a cozy booth with shiny maroon leather benches and a table that's been colored on too many times, and her ex-boyfriend immediately sitting across from her.

"Rule one of magic, of any sort of magic, is you're going to need way more food than you think you will," Maison says, as soon as the waitress swings two waters over to them, and if he's going to act like this is completely normal than she most definitely is not. "If you think there's a big chance, you'll have to do something in a day, bring extra food."

"Does that explain all your extra granola bars in your car?" Delina asks, prickly, pretending to study the menu extensively. "And in every one of your coat pockets?"

She had thought it a cute quirk.

He nods, relenting at that. "You got attacked far too often for me to not."

She glares at him over the plasticky menu. "Excuse me?"

"That was the other part of this—" he gestures between the two of them, like it's a business partnership that she had a say in, "—they wanted me to keep you alive, too, and the moment any of your mother's enemies found out you existed, they all tried something. All of them."

"And what, you were the one who had to protect me?" Delina asks, then glares down at the menu. "Sure. Right."

Even over the menu, she can see Maison pinch the bridge of his nose. "Yes, exactly."

"I don't believe you," Delina informs him, aiming for cold, but her voice breaks anyways. "For all I know you're just lying again."

In her pocket, his phone beeps, and the two of them lock eyes.

Because for all the hurt, there's still all those pictures of his mother on his phone.

"Okay," Delina says, pulling the phone out again, punching in the code. "Your Human Resource Officer wants to know when you're returning to, and I quote, 'the Prescott base.'"

"Jesus Christ," Maison mutters, then leans over the booth to peer at the message with her. "Type in 'unknown, target organized trip as a surprise.'"

"Can I text my dad?" she asks, waving his phone at him, and his face twists. "Just let him know all is good, so he doesn't worry."

"They absolutely track my texts, I wouldn't," Maison says, sighing. "If we had thought ahead, we could've established a code, but..."

"Wait, they track your texts?" At his nod, she wrinkles her nose. "Even when you were on your business trips?"

He nods, blankly, then winces.

"When I sent you those..."

"Probably," he says gingerly.

"Ew!" Delina says. "I don't want some gross guy from Atlanta to see my nudes!"

He rubs his face. "I don't think they read every text, just

when...when things went wrong? I think?" It's weak, and he knows it.

"Gross," Delina informs him, and his lip twitches up into the barest hint of a smile before he gets it under control.

The waitress swings over to take their order, and throughout the entire time, three dots appear on the phone, then disappear, as if the person on the other edge is typing, then decides not to press send.

"We're going to have to figure that out," Maison says, leaning forward on his elbows over the table. "What we are going to do with you without...putting my mom in danger."

Which is another horrible aspect of this.

"Would you have worked for them if your mom wasn't held?" she asks, and he's already shaking his head before she finishes.

"Never in a million years," he says, voice low, like it's a confession. "The moment they would have let me out of their sight as a teen, I would have run away and never looked back."

"Never would've dated me, never would have moved in with me?" Delina continues, and his jaw twitches. "Probably never even looked at me twice."

"Delly," he sighs, then stares out at the tiny cafe, at the single waitress and the only other table with one other person. "One sec."

With his fingertip, he traces something, some symbol, into the wood of the table, and it glows briefly, before all sound around them slips away.

The waitress still taps her heels against the tile, the other person still folds the daily paper, but no sound reaches Delina's ears.

"Neat," Delina says, before she can stop herself. "Will I be able to do that?"

"Probably not," Maison says dryly. "Maybe if you worked for ages at it, but it's highly unlikely. Necromancers are, supposedly, one purpose only."

"Ew," Delina says, and he cracks a smile, briefly, before it falls. "Just saying, that would've been useful in the apartment above the bar."

"And if I hadn't been forbidden from doing exactly that, I would have," Maison replies, and it's so close to their normal banter that it hurts.

The waitress swoops by with the food, with Maison's pastrami melt and Delina's club sandwich.

"Sorry about your mom," Delina continues, after a few moments of him watching her and her attempting to find the food palatable. "If I had known it would put her in danger or anything I would've talked to you first."

Finally, he nods, his face solemn. "I wish you could meet her," he says, wistful and a bit sad. "I think you two would get along."

There's nothing to be said at that. It's a nice, pretty statement, the sort of statement she wants to believe but finds it out of her grasp.

The sort of statement she would have treasured before.

They eat in the awful, artificial quiet, until all that's left is the fries she would usually steal off his plate and the lettuce she picked off.

"Did you ever meet your dad?" Delina asks, finally. "The...demon one?"

"Yes," Maison says, eager, like the silence broke at him too. "Three times. They weren't...exactly pleased about my existence."

She raises an eyebrow at him.

"The College apparently did a hell of a lot of magic on my mom to make it even possible, and apparently not

knowing about that ahead of time is annoying for demons."
This, at least, is something he can talk about, and the line in
his shoulders relaxes some. "They visited once when I was a
teen, trying to figure out if they could do something with
me." Maison briefly cracks a smile, his dimple perfect.
"They couldn't figure anything out, and I tracked them
down a few other times with questions before I met you."

"How?" Delina asks, and it's a relief to just talk as well.
They always talked, about the little and the big things, and
the lack of it...hurts.

"Eh, I can do just enough demon junk to figure out the
communication lines," he replies, with a wave of his hand,
like that explains everything. "It was the weirdest fucking
thing of my life."

Considering that his life apparently involved keeping
her alive from mysterious assassination attempts, that in
itself is interesting.

"So demons...possess other bodies to communicate,
right? The dead bodies?" Maison says, as if that's just
common knowledge. "First time I met my father, the other
person of the genetic mishmash, they were in a female body.
Blew my little teenage mind." It's so close to how he would
tell stories of his workday, back in the condo in Arizona.
"Next time, male body. Incredibly confusing. Turns out most
demons are like that, not really caring about that aspect of
the body they're in, and the fact that I couldn't just switch
when I got tired of this one absolutely annoyed the shit out
of them."

"So now you just have a gender-neutral parent that's just
out there somewhere?" Delina asks, and if she hadn't spent
the entire morning incredibly aware of dead bones it would
be a lot weirder. "Who has no idea how to deal with you?"

"Exactly," Maison says, and at least he's treating it like it's an amusing story, his dimple on his chin. "Any magical person meets me, they always want to know how much I know about my father, like they think I just have them on speed dial."

"Could...your other parent help with...all this?" Delina asks, gesturing at herself. "Get your mom out so we don't worry about it, make other demons back off so I'm not in danger?"

"No," he says, almost before she finished talking. "Because they wouldn't help, they would kill you, and me asking them not to wouldn't mean a thing." The brief, fragile peace of them just chatting shatters, and his face pinches. "I don't ever want them to find out about you."

"Okay, scratch that," Delina says, unnerved, "how about breaking your mom out?"

"She's warded, demons can't get in there," he says. "I asked a while ago, they asked me very politely why I think someone would risk getting trapped for someone they slept with a few decades ago and didn't bother bonding with."

"Grim," Delina says, because it is, and he nods. "So we figure something else out."

"I have been trying to figure something out for my entire adult life," Maison informs her, and this, at least, she believes him. "Unless there's some aspect of Necromancy I'm just not aware of, I don't know."

The lack of options is annoying, but to be fair, Delina's only really known about the problem for a few hours.

"So we can ward against demons, for me," Delina says, and he wavers his hand. "At least so I can learn a little?"

"I mean, that might work, but I don't like it," Maison replies. "Professionally speaking, there's nothing to stop the demon from just waiting until you step out of the wards."

He would know more about the limitations than her, and even that irks her.

"I have been...wanting to talk to you about this for ages," he says, almost in a rush. "Find out your perspective, get your ideas, rant about all of this."

"I'm sure keeping a secret and dating someone because it was a job was so hard on you." Her throat sticks at saying that.

"Okay, that's fair," Maison says, begrudging, and it should feel like she won something, but it doesn't. "Would you believe me—"

"—No," Delina interrupts.

Once again, he cracks a smile like he didn't expect that of her, before he shakes his head. "Okay," he says, a little bit slower. "I don't exactly know what to do or say to convince you to trust me of...well, anything...but can I try?"

It's not what she expected him to say, so she folds her arms as the waitress soundlessly swings by to refill their waters.

He had clearly expected her to say something, so he stares at her, obviously scraping for words.

"Why?" Delina asks, after a horrifically long moment, picking at the remnants of her fries. "I know now, we just have to figure out a way to not get your mom hurt and then you don't have to deal with me anymore. Why do you care if I believe you?"

"Because five years," he blurts out, immediately, then he blanches. "Because I don't..."

She raises an eyebrow at him over the remains of her sandwich, picking out the less than ideal looking lettuce.

"Look, Maison, or Frederick, or—"

"Yeah, don't call me that," he interrupts.

"Or whoever you actually are," Delina pushes on, and

there's still the knot of hurt in her chest, pounding. "I'm not delusional enough to think I'm easy to get along with, even before finding out that my bio-mother is apparently a psychopath. But you don't have to try now, I don't have to believe you, you don't have to pretend to like me."

He hesitates, watching her from underneath his unfairly long lashes.

"It does explain why you were so willing to stick around when I was awful," Delina says, poking at the remnants of her sandwich again. If she's supposed to be hungry after the morning, it hasn't kicked in yet. "I bet the paycheck helped with that."

The silence, with that briefly glowing rune, now itches underneath her skin. Something, anything, besides his lack of words would be welcome.

Suddenly, Gurlien sits at the booth right next to Maison, startling them both, and Chloe slides in on Delina's side.

"The problem with silencing spells is you need to be aware of your environment so you don't miss something," Gurlien says, and Maison flinches, like the sudden noise is too much. "We were calling your names from across the shop, you asshole."

Chloe pokes at the rune, and it glows briefly at her touch. "Why'd you go with this one?"

Outside the table, the world is still silent, still muffled, and Delina has to crane her neck to look out, just to make sure.

"Because people get disgruntled when you start to throw around the word demon all over the place," Maison says, before something pokes at Delina's brain.

Something wrong, like something at the base of her neck, brushing against her awareness.

She turns and looks at Chloe, who's inspecting the rune still, like it says more to her than it does to Delina.

And in her backpack, in a small plastic, airless container like a coffin, wedged between an extra jacket and a thin metal clipboard, is something dead.

Delina breathes out, and it's the small fly that Maison killed in his bubble, now perfectly preserved in the plastic container. It's still, entirely motionless, and one of the wings must've bent on its fall to the ground.

Chloe finally glances up at her, raising a sharp eyebrow, then shakes her head at her.

Message clear. Don't talk about it.

14

~

The fly sticks in the back of her mind the entire drive back, warping and pulling at her thoughts, until she thinks she's going to vibrate out of her skin with the knowledge of it.

Chloe chats like it's nothing big, and whatever she's doing must not be giving off any of the trackable Necromancy vibes because Maison remains calm, though his face is more thoughtful than it usually is.

Normally this is when he'd lock himself in a different room and not emerge until something inconvenient got painted.

The death in the car tugs at her attention, despite all attempts to stop herself from thinking about it, to redirect her mind from obsessing.

It's gross, it's disgusting, and by the time they pass the downed tree and come into view of the tiny cabin, her head pounds and her hands tremble.

Gurlien and Chloe had kept up a steady stream of

discussion, of magical terminology and history, but she's retained none of it, and she pushes herself out of the car as fast as she can, barely before the car is off.

Even once past the plasticky door, she can still sense the fly outside, deep in Chloe's backpack. And what's worse, now the dead bird is vivid, brilliant and shimmering with potential.

Delina flops over on the couch, and Chance mrrrs at her, blinking his green eyes at her.

The wing on the dead bird is crumpled beneath it, the feathers bent and its spine broken, and even if she touches it, it would never fly again.

Even if she touches it.

She stares down at the cat, who matches the eye contact.

"I don't want to touch it," she whispers at Chance, who yawns at her, showing all his fangs. "This is the worst."

"What is?" Gurlien asks, striding back into the cabin and shedding his rain gear, and Chloe and Maison file in after him. "I think it's a nice cabin, lack of internet notwithstanding." He gives her a brief, critical glance, then an obvious one to Chloe's backpack as she disappears down the hall with it.

So he knows, too.

"Everything," Delina says, and just by the feel of the dead fly, she knows Chloe turns the corner down the hall, then descends some stairs.

So, the creepy basement.

"I'm also probably fired from my job," Delina says, and Maison snorts out a familiar laugh as he strides into the other room. "That's not fun to think about."

"I've seen your mom's accounts, you never have to work again," Gurlien says, dismissing her concerns with a wave of his hand. "You can spend the rest of your life in far off exotic locales and doing whatever research your heart desires with a fake passport, easy."

"Thanks," Delina says, hopefully as sarcastic as Gurlien's comment, before she pushes herself up, the dead fly almost pulling her to movement. "Because fake passports are definitely not a difficult thing to get."

"Chloe's an alchemist," Maison replies, returning with his small travel paint set tucked underneath his arm. "Give her enough paper to work with and she can get it without any issue."

"How is that not outlawed?" Delina asks, as Maison sits at the cutesy carved kitchen table, rolling out the kit, setting the watercolors to one side in practiced motions.

She's seen him do so a hundred times, on trips out to coffee shops and their yearly vacations.

"What are you doing?" Gurlien asks, finally turning to stare down at Maison. "Those would be shitty for runes, and that paper wouldn't do a thing for any spell keeping." He pokes at Maison's watercolor book, like it'd bite him.

"I want to think some," Maison says, with the infinite patience he only gets when he really wants to yell at someone but is keeping it in. "So I brought this along."

"Is this just...normal paint?" Gurlien says, his face wrinkling. "That's useless."

Maison's gray eyes flicker to Delina, before he goes about ignoring Gurlien.

So they don't know he paints.

They don't know this crucial detail of Maison, part of what makes him him. They don't know that this is the first thing he does when stressed, the first thing he does when happy, the first thing he does when sleep deprived. They grew up next to him, at whatever childhood the College let them have, and Gurlien never knew he painted.

"It's not useless if it helps me think," Maison replies, filling up one of the chipped mugs with water. "Some of us went about developing hobbies outside of magic instead of making it our entire personalities."

The cat watches Maison paint with avid eyes, slowly raising a paw like he's going to bat at the paint brushes before Gurlien scoops down and picks up the cat away from the temptation.

Gurlien rolls his eyes at him. "Some of us had to work for our abilities instead of being granted with unlimited potential just because of how we were born," he rebuts, before glancing up at Delina, then obviously towards the hallway Chloe went down.

Message received. Whatever it is that they want her to do with the dead bug, they don't want Maison to know immediately.

"Well, I'm going to explore this strange cabin my mother left me," Delina says, rolling her eyes performatively at Gurlien. "Have fun arguing."

"Don't touch anything you don't understand, it could be dangerous," Maison calls after her, because of course he does. "Your mother was a lunatic."

The cat pads along behind her, far enough away that she can't pet him, as Delina steps down the dark hallway.

A few steps past three obvious bedrooms, Delina's ears pop and the air abruptly cools.

The wallpaper transforms from the floral everywhere else in the cabin to a gray, clinical shade, something akin to a dentist's office. The baby blue carpet stops, giving way to bare, enameled concrete.

All vestiges of a personality, however cutesy, vanish. All small decorations, all kitsch and Americana, stop.

"Alright," Delina whispers, finding the staircase half by sight and half by the sense of the dead fly. "Grim."

She flips the light on over the stairs, and it's bright and florescent, out of place with the warm lamps of the front rooms and master bedroom.

Clearly her mother wanted to give at least the appearance that this was someplace normal at first.

At the bottom of the stairs, Chloe pokes her head around the corner. "Okay good, it's just you. Gurlien annoying Freddy?"

Delina nods, trailing her hand against the wall, her fingertips tingling.

"Welcome to the real benefit of this place," Chloe says, and she's sitting in a rolling chair, the tile clean. "Underground basement that isn't on the will or the deed to the place."

"All basements are underground," Delina murmurs.

The single room is cavernous, giving vibes halfway between a school library and science room gone wrong. Shelving packed with books and scrolls and papers line every wall, with cardboard boxes holding more scrolls stacked haphazard in every corner.

The middle of the room has a drain in the center, and is completely empty, but for a stack of spray paint off to one side. Stains and smudges of paint mar the enameled concrete, all worn down or washed away or completely harmless.

Along the edges are cold metal tables, like a mortuary, with an array of readings and tech equipment and everything in between.

"So when you said mad scientist, you meant it," Delina says, cautiously sitting in one of the rolling lab chairs next to a table. "What are the chances someone's died in here?"

"Well..." Chloe thinks for a few moments. "Probably

higher than we're comfortable with."

The dead fly, still in a tiny plastic container, sits on one of the tables. The small coffin she sensed, the thing keeping all the air out, is nothing but a normal travel pill container.

"So you sensed this within moments of me sitting next to you," Chloe starts, gesturing at it. "Gurlien and I thought it would take you longer."

"It's incredibly obvious," Delina replies on autopilot.

"Good to know," Chloe says. "Rule one of magic, the earlier it is in the process for you to reverse something or the closer it is to the original state, the easier it is. This goes for undoing a spell, for identifying what went wrong, for changing something into something else, and, most likely, bringing something back from the dead."

Bile creeps up Delina's throat, but she nods.

"So while it might be possible for you to raise century old bones, it wouldn't be a good place to start, and you'd probably have significant trouble with it," Chloe continues. "Just like it's far easier for me to transform a sheet of plastic into a door, rather than a tiny slip of plastic wrap. It's closer to what I want it to be."

That almost makes sense.

"We know that the Necromancer currently active was able to raise someone from the dead who had been dead for fourteen hours, and a cat that had been dead for four days. We don't...really want to test you on a person, for obvious reasons."

"So a dead bug."

"A dead bug. Courteously killed instantly, so you don't have to worry about correcting any injuries."

"No, its wings are bent from when it fell," Delina says, and Chloe blinks owlishly at her. "It's...I can tell."

"Alrighty," Chloe says, a little bit more unsteady. "So this is going to be pretty different from all my other experiments, isn't it?"

Delina can't think of anything to say, so she nods.

"I don't want you to raise it, not yet," Chloe says, and Delina's skin crawls. "But we want to record what you can sense from it, so we get a baseline." She sets a quick, simple recorder on the table, the sort you find reporters using on the field. "Can you repeat that?"

Delina does, and Chloe just nods, swinging in the chair.

"Based just by what you're feeling, could you tell me how long it's been dead? Forgetting that you already know."

Delina squints down at the travel pill container.

Time doesn't seem to have passed for the bug, still frozen in the worst moment. There's no blood to cool and nothing for her to gauge.

"Maybe a general sense of hours, but nothing concrete," she says, finally, after the lights overhead buzz. "The bird outside is a few days, at least, if not a week."

Her mind flashes over to it, and there's decay over some of the exposed skin.

"I'm gonna need to learn timelines for things like rigor mortis, aren't I?" Delina quips, though the very idea is awful.

"Can you tell what killed the bug? As clinical as you can, not what you know killed it, but what in its body killed it?" At her owlish look, Chloe sighs. "If it had been squished, the answer would be the organs were compacted. If it had been attacked, it would be because pieces were missing. That sort of thing."

Delina doesn't know enough about fly biology, but she huffs anyway and tries to think.

"Can the answer be the nervous system stopped?" Delina asks, then lets her mind wander back outside. The bird's organs are more clearly defined, easy to read, and there's an echo of another set of talons piercing through the skin, through the ribs and shattering one, and into the lungs. "The bird was attacked by another bird."

"Good," Chloe says, enthusiastic. "That's exactly the sort of thing we're trying to figure out if you can figure out."

It doesn't feel very good, but Delina nods, trying to match the enthusiasm. "This seems useful for murder investigations."

"Oh, true, though it wouldn't hold up in court," Chloe says, off handed, then pauses, deliberate. "We want to see about giving you a space to practice without Freddy knowing immediately."

As if she hadn't figured that out by the secrecy and the attempts to distract him.

"I and Gurlien are firm believers that you cannot control something you don't practice, and without control you'd be a sitting duck. I know you and Freddy..." Chloe visibly flounders. "Well, you have history, but we don't know exactly what his motivations are to keeping you ignorant."

So they think he's still lying about something.

Which makes sense, though it settles inside of her just as wrong as everything else.

"I'm glad he seems to want to keep you alive," Chloe says, which is an understatement, "but without knowing how he intends on reporting this, I don't think we can trust him with anything else but that."

"Yeah," Delina says, and it's a bitter taste.

"And we don't know how much of your necromancy he picks up from you," Chloe continues. "Demons feed off of necromancer power or life source, it's unclear, but that's why they die. As a Half Demon, he might...want some. And that's not even bringing in the sleeping with him part, he could've done something there to make you easier to track."

Delina rubs her face.

"If I were him, I would be working really hard on convincing you that I feel bad and that I still want to be with you," Chloe continues, as if that's not exactly what he had been doing on their lunch. "Try to re-establish a rapport, show that he is this person you knew and loved. Be charming and give you every piece of information. Work real hard at –"

"Got it," Delina interrupts. "Can't trust the ex-boyfriend."

"Yeah." Still, Chloe looks uncomfortable. "We have to keep him here so we can at least monitor his communications."

"So don't piss him off so much he decides to just leave, got it." Still doesn't feel great. "Haven't had this much drama in my life since my sorority days."

"When he's not actively annoying Freddy, Gurlien's going to look up cloaking runes that I can put out, so you can practice safely without him noticing when he's still in the building." Chloe glances up at the ceiling, where the two men are. "Because if this does go south, it'd be good to have him here as some defense."

Her head hurts all over again.

"Okay," Chloe says, obviously still off kilter. "Can you tell me how old the fly is?"

AFTER A GOOD FEW hours of thinking real hard about a dead bug, Delina's headache has escalated to a respectable migraine.

She begs out of more tests, and leaves Chloe to her notes

in the cold basement, and the cat climbs the stairs with her to the much warmer main cabin.

Three paintings dry on the kitchen table, spread out and glistening, and Gurlien has his feet up on the couch as Maison bends over a fourth.

"I assume you found the library?" Gurlien says with a raised eyebrow, glancing up over the edge of the book.

Belatedly, she realizes it's the one her mother left her in the PO box.

"If you can call it that," Delina replies, and the sound of her voice lifts Maison's head.

His hand is well and goodly cramped, and his eyes hurt from squinting.

"Your ex-boyfriend is boring," Gurlien drawls, and it's so obviously to get a rise out of Maison that it's almost funny. "And you put up with him for five years?"

"It's not like I'm a barrel of laughs," Delina replies.

Maison refuses to rise to the bait, instead setting down the paintbrush and shaking out his hand, giving Delina an even glance. "Get enough of your scanning done in this library?"

The paintings on the table are, of course, beautiful. Long aching swipes of watercolor with the impressionistic suggestion of the doorway of the cabin surround the greenery outside, all on a small piece of paper about half the size of a normal letter sheet.

He had done it three times, changing the perspective ever so slightly each time, changing how the piece reads. The emotions, the view, everything.

"Does your hand always hurt when you paint for that long?" Delina asks instead.

He flexes his fingers, rotating his wrist. "It doesn't really hurt."

"Liar," she says, and even though he doesn't smile, his dimple briefly appears. "It's cramped and everything."

"I really need to get ahold of Axel and Alette," Gurlien says from the couch. "See if the pain thing is part of Necromancy or something else."

"Feels like necromancy," Maison replies, almost as an aside. "Same color and everything."

And Chloe's words still echo in her mind about trusting him. About all his knowledge, about what he's telling them, everything.

"So these two know of another Necromancer," Delina says, and Gurlien nods along. "How is your College not breathing down their necks?"

Gurlien raises his hand in almost a jaunty wave. "I happened. They don't want it to happen again."

Maison's eyes sharpen, and she gets the sudden sensation that he's filing that information away. That in the time he's been here, he hadn't learned what happened yet and hadn't asked. "The Necromancer did that?"

"Not at all," Gurlien replies. "I didn't even get to meet her."

Disappointment briefly flashes over Maison's face, barely identifiable, before he masks it. Delina raises an eyebrow at him, and he catches her expression.

Instead of saying anything, he holds out his hand to her, like he always does after painting, and the tips of his fingers are wrinkled from the watercolors. "Seriously though, scanning went okay?"

"Dead things are gross," Delina informs him, definitely not taking his hand, not after the talk with Chloe. "I'd much rather have the making things into other things ability."

"So does every beginning magician," Gurlien interrupts, and Maison slowly withdraws his hand, the hurt quickly

15

The next day passes in a haze of information, of Gurlien bringing up runes and Maison contradicting him, of Chloe suggesting things and Gurlien shooting them down, all in languages that sound more like Latin than English to Delina's ears, before a knock raps against the fake plastic door.

Everyone stiffens, and Maison stands from the table, his eyes immediately reflecting back the light.

"Delina, go downstairs," he orders, and Gurlien nods, pulling the gun out from the living room table drawer. "Don't..."

Even though it's locked, the door swings open, bouncing off the hinges. "Don't try to hide her."

An older woman, meek and short, strides in. Gray laces through her hair, wiry and uncontrollable, and she's a good foot and a half shorter than anyone else in the room.

"Who's there?" Gurlien asks, his voice declarative, blinking wildly around the room.

Maison steps around the table in one smooth motion, pulling Delina behind him, like he can protect her with that.

The old woman just leans to glance around him, locking

eyes with Delina. "You're the new one."

"Who are you?" Maison demands, and Gurlien stiffens, looking around, and Chloe's the same way.

They can't see whoever this person is.

The old woman smiles, but it doesn't reach her eyes. "You're the one looking at the dead?" At Maison's tension, she sighs. "I'm not going to threaten her, I'm just evaluating our risks."

"Frederick," Gurlien says slowly, deliberately. "What are you seeing?"

The woman sighs once more, put upon, and then the very air around her shivers, and Chloe recoils back.

Gurlien, however, just narrows his eyes at her.

"Are you a local wight?" Gurlien asks, voice strident. "Can you communicate with Zoel and Alette?"

The woman shoots him a glare, but Gurlien doesn't react to it. "I only communicate with whom I want."

The air shimmers around her again, and both Gurlien and Chloe startle again.

Back to them not seeing her, apparently.

"And you are..." the woman says, fixated on Delina. "You haven't been around here before."

"She's new," Maison says, still keeping Delina behind his broad shoulders. "She doesn't know about any regional politics."

The woman lifts her unreal eyes to Maison. "And you do, demon child?"

Though her voice is mild, the hair on the back of Delina's neck raises.

"No," Maison admits freely. "I'm here to make sure nobody else comes for her."

"Good," the woman says, sharp. "We don't want any more of you. Half of one is already enough."

For a few seconds, she thinks Maison is going to bristle, before he obviously relaxes his shoulders. "I'll notify you if anyone comes for her," he says, and the woman nods, like this is expected. "If you can tell me if any new Demons or unknown magicians enter your territory."

The woman shrugs one shoulder, casts another critical eye to Delina, then disappears.

This time, Maison flinches, then shakes out his hands, turning back towards the others. "The local flavor knows we're here," he says, grim.

"No shit," Chloe mumbles.

Delina weighs saying something about so clearly being talked over, and someone clearly coming in to be a show of force, before she sighs, sitting down at the table instead. "Another magical creature?"

"Wights are more guardians of the lands, they're generally benign as long as you don't disrupt their flow of magic," Gurlien says, reciting again. "Sounded like she was just letting us know she knows about her." He jerks his thumb at Delina. "Don't disrupt the magic here and she'll leave you alone."

"I don't know how to disrupt magic, remember?" Delina says wearily. "I don't know anything."

"Why can Necromancers see them naturally but we cannot?" Chloe asks Gurlien, curiosity in her voice.

"Same reason why Necromancers can see demons but we can't," Gurlien answers, almost offhand.

"Great," Delina says. "Another perk."

"Good idea about other magicians," Chloe says, "Give us a heads up if the College comes after her."

"If anyone from the College comes after you —" Maison starts.

"How would I know they came after me?" Delina interrupts, which she feels like is a perfectly good point. "The amount of people I know in the College are you three."

"If anyone suspicious comes after you," Maison corrects, "stand behind me. They won't try to kill me."

Delina stares at him. "Why would they try to kill me?" Her voice tilts up into hysterics, and even she knows it. "I have literally done nothing!"

Maison glances to Gurlien and Chloe for help, and they give him absolutely nothing.

"You're the one still pulling a paycheck from them," Gurlien points out.

"Because they're scared of anything they don't know, and you'd be one giant question mark," Maison finally pulls together. "Combined with the absolute batshit of your mother, it's probably smart to be cautious until I can let them know you're not a threat. Somehow."

"You're telling them nothing," Delina challenges, having heard enough, and he holds his hands up in surrender. "I don't care, it's my life, I want to be in control over something at least."

Maison crosses his arms, still staring hard at the door. "I want to ward this place better. She shouldn't have been able to just waltz right in."

"You mean like you did?" Delina asks, rubbing her forehead.

"You mean after your bio-trap took down all the protections? Yes." Maison snips back, then sighs. "Gurlien, do you want to help pick out the runes?"

Gurlien visibly brightens, before he narrows his eyes in suspicion. "Why?"

"Because if I don't include one of you, you'll think I sabotaged it," Maison replies, still standing like the door will attack him. "And you're better at defensive runes, no offense, Chloe."

"None taken!" she replies, giving him a thumbs up. "I can try to break them after if you want."

Maison blinks at her, and it's his very-close-to-being overwhelmed expression, the one Delina rarely sees, before he strides out the door.

The moment he's out of sight, Chloe's cheerfulness drops. "That's not good," she says, sitting at the table next to Delina, running her finger over the carved wood.

"So my entire life I could've been seeing non-human people and just never known?" Delina says, and the cat paces up to her and butts its head against her leg, so she idly dangles a hand down to scratch its head. "This just gets better and better."

"No, him asking Gurlien for help," Chloe replies, then she stares back down the hallway. "If I were him, I'd be trying with you instead. You don't know enough and then it'd be time with you."

Having heard more of the trust issues Chloe has, Delina has no patience for it, so she pushes herself up as well.

"I'm going to see if my mom has anything actually interesting to read, or if it's just textbooks," she says, desperately hoping Chloe doesn't just follow her back down.

⁓

16

T he next day, after using up the last of her meager travel hair conditioner and thoroughly breaking her travel comb, Delina informs everyone else that she's absolutely going to drive to the nearest big box store and get supplies.

Of course, this gets met with scoffing on Gurlien's part, some truly dire suggestions from Chloe on what she can use instead, and flat-out denial from Maison, but Delina does what she does best and ignores all of that and grabs her car keys instead.

"Wait," Chloe blurts out, dashing back into her room and coming back with a notebook and a pen, of all things. "If you're actually going—"

"Not alone," Maison grumbles.

"—then actually make a supply run."

Delina holds out her hand for the book, and Chloe hands it to her, and the list is full to the brim of obscure ingredients and herbs and components.

"You actually think Target is going to have one of these?"

"If you go to the Target past Birmingham, there's the tractor supply store and the gardening store," Gurlien replies idly, because the two of them have actually been here a while and, apparently, have all the local town stores memorized.

Chance the cat is curled up next to him on the couch, the tip of his tail flicking, eying them all.

Maison grabs the list out of Delina's hands. "You are not sending her on a run to get ingredients for a tomb break," he says, deeply skeptical. "Are there even any tombs here for you to break into?"

"Surprisingly, yes, lots of bunkers, that sort of thing," Gurlien drawls, then he sits up straight. "You're not going with her to a major city alone."

"Ugh," Delina says, because now this seems like it's become a thing. "Sort yourselves out, I'm gonna get the car started."

Outside, sun streams down muted through the tree branches, and her breath puffs up around her face, ethereal. Birds chirp in the forest, like they've been waiting this entire time for the sun to come out from behind the clouds, and an idle breeze dances through Delina's disastrous attempts at a hair style.

Spruce needles litter the floor of the dirt driveway, fragrant and damp, and even though it's almost winter, green underbrush still shines around the trees and twists among the deadened blackberry canes. A squirrel dashes between trees, almost too fast for her eye to track.

And the dead bird still overshadows all of it.

More bugs crawl over its bones, and the sharp chill of the air seeps deeper into it, until all that is there is the cold.

"Maybe we should burn it." Maison steps outside the

plastic door, his jacket tossed over his shoulder. "If it bothers you so much, giving it a proper sendoff might work."

"And then we can see how far along into that process you can sense it," Gurlien says, following after him, and Chloe's carrying her backpack. "Good data."

"And does that normally affect Necromancers?" Delina asks, to which all three shrug. "Ugh."

Burning it doesn't sound better, except maybe to ward off the pervasive chill. Something to stop the eternal cold that is imbedded in the bones.

"You're gonna need to be careful around hospitals," Chloe says, shooing the cat back away from the door and then locking the door behind them. "And any graveyards bigger than the one the other day."

～

THE ENTIRE TRIP down to the nearest target takes an hour of driving through the mountains, and Delina wants to claw her own face off at the constant squabbling between Gurlien and Chloe.

It's not that they're not getting along, but that everything they do and everything they say immediately gets a comment from the other, spiraling down into tangents and counter arguments and examples half explained from their background until Delina's...exhausted.

There's a reason why she's usually insular. Usually an introvert.

Chloe splits the moment they park back behind the store, heading straight for the garden store.

"Remember to actually make sure the seeds are accredited this time!" Gurlien calls after her, and Chloe waves back without even looking at them.

Maison's still scowling, standing close to Delina, like he's half afraid something's going to jump out at him and that by being close enough, he could somehow ward off everything bad.

It's something he used to do when they traveled, though she had thought he got over it.

But the best she can do is ignore it, and she strides quickly into the familiar store.

Given enough time and inclination, she could absolutely spend hours wandering the store, smelling all the candles and browsing the clothes, but she instead heads immediately towards the hair care supplies with both men trailing after her.

It crawls underneath her skin, at the constant monitoring, but there's the ever-pervasive sensation that if she tried to get rid of them, she couldn't.

"So every time I made you come with me to the store, were you always just there to make sure I didn't get shot or something?" Delina asks Maison, raising an eyebrow at him.

They hadn't talked much the last day, not directly at least, and it doesn't help.

"Not every time," Maison replies, almost plaintively. "Just when there were known threats."

"I'd hate to see those security briefs," Gurlien says, and thankfully he got a basket too and seems to be filling it with actually normal things. "What, 'mother of target pissed off Shaman group, keep an eye out for people with staffs chanting ominously?'"

"Not funny," Maison sighs.

It's a little funny.

"Or 'Frisse attempted to destroy the world again, keep an eye out for FBI agents,' was it that sort of thing?" If Delina hadn't spent the last few days with him, she would swear that Gurlien is actively trying to bait Maison, but no, he just talks like that. "Frisse bought property in France and we don't know why, don't let any Frenchmen near the target?"

Delina snorts.

"The France thing wasn't a problem," Maison reassures her, and she quick flashes over to evaluate her life in the fact that he didn't reassure her over the other ones and she has to find out in the hair care aisle. "You were never in any danger with that one."

"You're kidding me," Delina says, grabbing her favorite shampoo and conditioner in their actual sizes. "You two are absolutely just messing with me now, you joined forces with the sole purpose of getting me to believe the most ridiculous things about my mother with no actual reason."

Maison smiles, suddenly, with a brightness she hasn't seen since the letter, and her knees almost go weak at the shock of it. "If you want ridiculous stories, I have ridiculous stories."

"He's just trying to charm you, don't fall for it," Gurlien says, and the smile is gone from Maison's face in a flash. "If you truly wanted ridiculous stories, you can find them in the basement."

Delina hesitates at the lost smile and at the reveal of information. "When we get back, both of you decide on the funniest, most ridiculous story, and let me know."

Both the men still, wide eyed.

"Why?" Gurlien says, recovering first.

"Because she's probably only heard bad things about her mother so far, I'm going to guess," Maison says, and it's absolutely correct. "It's not like this entire thing has been fun for you."

Which is even more true, but she doesn't want to give

him that, so she moves on to adding actual skin care products to her cart before pushing it towards the clothing.

"Her mother was awful, though," Gurlien continues, honestly confused. "I don't see why we should sugar coat anything."

"Which you've made clear," Delina says, grabbing a few shirts blindly and thinking fondly of her closet back in Arizona. "But if I was under threat by mysterious Frenchmen—"

"—You weren't," Maison interrupts.

"—then I at least want to know the funny things."

They follow her in silence, as they get the items they need, and Delina refuses to think of this place as permanent, despite all the things she's purchasing to make it so, and Maison adds a few familiar items of his own. His favorite brand of pretzels, his preferred deodorant, a razor that won't mark up his skin. All things she has memorized in the file in her mind for him, all things she would buy if she had the need to get something for him.

It hurts, just a bit. To do something so normal as shop through a Target with him, and have everything about their relationship be so completely ruined.

In her purse, his phone beeps, and all three of them still in the junk food aisle. Beyond the daily trips into the town for the check-in, there had been no response to his work phone.

Gurlien straightens, staring Maison down, like he could fight him in the same place they were discussing cheez-its.

"Okay," Delina says, half placating and half annoyed. "I'll just..."

HUMAN RESOURCE DIRECTOR (3:21 PM): trg spt grp 1 rpt.

"Oh that's interesting," Maison says, though his voice is anything but happy.

"Are they really saying there's an active threat right now?" Gurlien asks, crowding around them because of course he can read that jumble of text.

"Group 1 is around the Prescott condo," Maison informs him. "All the condos on the block and the bar at the corner."

"Someone's threatening Lyzzards?" Delina asks, glancing back at the words that still make no sense.

"No, someone they have marked as a danger to you showed up in that block," Maison says, squinting down. "If we were there, it'd be important, but we're...not."

"What are the chances it's an automated report?" Gurlien asks, deeply skeptical.

"Slim," Maison says. "Type out 'still in Washington with target.'"

She still bristles at being called target, but does anyways, and his hand comes up to the middle of her back, the same motion he used to do to soothe her.

She throws him a glance, flat, and his hand falls away, his face pinched.

"How often did you get these?" Gurlien asks, shattering the moment to pieces. "Are they really that common?"

"At least once every six months," Maison replies, which isn't a number she wanted. "When her mother was dealing with the Terese project it was once a week."

Terese was apparently the demon in the live body, Delina knows that by now, but that doesn't make it better.

"Did you ever see her?" Gurlien asks.

"Terese? Twice." Maison's lips tug down into a frown, a clear indicator he doesn't want to talk about it. "Not from close, and she wasn't coherent."

"Surprised she didn't try to off Delina, you wouldn't have

been able to do much to stop that," Gurlien says. "No offense."

"Thanks," Delina responds, the want for shopping waning drastically. "I'm gonna have to learn how to protect myself, the way this is going."

Maison's lips tighten at that, like she's honestly supposed to believe that he's just going to stick around forever just to protect her, before he looks away.

"We should get back to the cabin," he says, instead of anything else. "If they think there's a threat to Delina, then we should be somewhere defensible."

Delina's not going to leave without paying, but Maison's scowling the entire time, bouncing on the balls of his feet, like he does when they've stayed too long at a party.

Or, apparently, when he's on the lookout for threats. Which was all the time, if she had to judge it, and the fact that so many moments of the two of them had him distracted because of nebulous dangers leaves a bitter taste in her mouth.

It'd be easier if he isn't here, and the thought pops into her mind unbidden as she watches the clerk bag their items. That if he had just washed his hands of her, then all these complicated and awful emotions would be further away.

But now he's just an arm's length away, waiting at the end of the checkout line, his arms crossed and his eyes sharp, an ever-present reminder that he only dated her and lived with her for the job.

"Whatever you're thinking, don't," Maison says, suddenly. "What, that's your thinking face, you're thinking of something frustrating."

"That just looks like her normal face," Gurlien chimes in, which doesn't help.

"Thanks," Delina throws back, picking up as many bags

as she can before Maison takes them all from her, like in addition to defending herself she's incapable of carrying a bevy of Target bags.

Gurlien just shrugs. "Congrats, this is the nearest place of civilization to your cabin."

For a dingy target next to a tractor store and a garden shop, it's not exactly inspiring hope, though the air is crisp and fresh as they step back outside to begin the annoying trek back to the car.

"Chloe loves it, but she grew up rural," Gurlien continues. "One gas station and one fast food sort of town in the middle of cornfields, so this is downright cosmopolitan."

It's not that she lived in a big city or anything, but at least it has more than this. More variety.

"Prescott wasn't bad," Maison says, in a way of conversation. "Anything we couldn't get local, there was always Sedona or Flagstaff or Phoenix. It had its charm."

Gurlien squints at him. "The smallest city you've lived in was Atlanta."

"And now Prescott," Maison insists, and it's such a nonsensical argument. "We had a brewery and a meadery and all the weird whisky bars you could ever want."

"There's a brewery half an hour away, if you want to go sometime," Gurlien says, and it's just a breath away from normal. "They do a good Irish Red and a decent Cream Stout."

Maison actually looks interested, before he shrugs. "Maybe in a few days, after this threat."

"There's also the dive bar in Sequim, it's awful but it is cheap." Gurlien ticks it off his fingers. "And there's the family diner that has a surprisingly respectable variety of wines, when Chloe and I have people visit—which does happen, by the way—we usually go there. Chloe takes dates there, that sort of thing."

It's true, Delina hasn't really thought hard about their social life outside of the tiny little cabin, but it's logical they have one.

"I like a decent wine," Delina says, once again approaching the sensation of normalcy, of not being entirely ripped away from everything she knows. "I like this idea."

Maison shoots her a glance, his dimple on his chin.

Right before everything goes to shit.

They swing around the building to the view of the car, and Chloe's standing there, her backpack clutched to her chest, with a strange man right next to her, a hand gripping the back of her neck, holding her there.

Immediately, Maison drops the bags, swinging Delina behind him, her shoes skidding on the still-damp pavement. The bags burst open, products rolling and clattering around.

The stranger is tall, clearly in his mid-fifties, with grey-blond hair and annoyingly blue eyes, and Delina abruptly shudders when his gaze glances off of her.

Something about him is wrong.

Very wrong.

On the ground beneath him is a neatly drawn circle, similar to the one spray painted in the graveyard.

After a split second, Gurlien strides forward, his shoulders back.

"Korhonen, hello," he calls, and Maison tenses, his hand tight on her arm. "Thought you'd never stop by."

The man doesn't look at Gurlien, not even a glance, instead focusing on Maison, unnaturally still.

"It's been what, a year?" Gurlien continues, and by the

whites of his eyes, he's bluffing. "How's your family, how's the job?"

Maison takes a step back, still holding Delina behind him, forcing her back as well.

"It's been interesting up here, you know," Gurlien says, still chatting, "Never thought the College would take an interest in us up here."

Ah. The College.

"Delina, you might need to run," Maison whispers, barely audible over Gurlien's chatter, his back straight. "If I tell you to run, you need to run."

The man—Korhonen, apparently—tilts his head at Delina, and her skin crawls again, before he idly waves his free hand at Gurlien.

As if hit by an invisible brick, Gurlien reels back, and even from this far away she can feel pain blossoming across the side of his head. He staggers, keeping his feet under him, before another wave of the hand crashes against his stomach and Gurlien doubles over.

All in complete silence, all still keeping a hand on Chloe.

"So, you failed," this man speaks, and his voice is slightly accented, some Northern European country that Delina can't place. Norway or Finland or something. "And instead of calling in, you just followed her up here, to this...town. Frederick."

Chloe makes a small sound, barely over a squeak, but again, the man pays her no attention.

Maison takes another step back, and his shoulders ache from the tension.

"And you found...what, she has some talent?" Korhonen says. "Found some dusty research papers of her mother's with two delinquents?" He gestures again, a welcoming gesture, and Maison backs up another step, the hand tightening on her arm.

And all at once, the gold blooms in her vision again, and Delina gasps, before Maison taps his fingers against her arm. A signal.

The stranger in front of them has his hands tightly tied in with two strips of magic, tight and angry, one of them pressing into the back of Chloe's neck.

"Is it worth it?" he asks. "Throwing away a promising career and the contact with your mother just for some...girl?"

Maison inhales, but doesn't move.

"So what are you?" he directs at Delina, and the magic coils around his fingers, sparks shivering down the length. "What did your mother do to you?"

"We don't know," Delina lies baldly, and Chloe's eyes are wide. "We haven't figured it out yet, not really."

The man thinks for a few moments, obviously evaluating. "Pity."

"Let her go," Delina says, and Maison backs her up another step, practiced. "I can chat with you, you don't need to hurt anyone."

"Frederick?" he asks. "What is she?"

Maison opens his mouth, then closes it. "We don't know."

"No ideas?" the man asks, and Maison shakes his head. "No educated guesses on the bomb her mother left in the world?"

And Delina's mind races.

Gurlien's still huddled on the blacktop, pain across his face and his stomach, and Chloe practically vibrates with the need to be anywhere else. His grip on her hurts, viscerally, in a way Delina can't quite get her mind to touch.

The man himself...is blank. Not a black hole like Gurlien is, not vivid and bright like Maison, but something more akin to an oil slick, all light slithering off of him until she can perceive nothing.

"Delina, stop," Maison breathes, and she does, shuttling her mind to the surroundings, to the vivid gold elsewhere. "She's not a bomb, she's completely safe."

Completely safe sounds like a misnomer, but she's not going to chime in now.

"That's not for you to judge," Korhonen says, then gestures Delina forward, his hands still full of magic. "That was an interesting scan. Come over here, let me see."

There's no way Delina's going to do that, not with his grip on Chloe or Gurlien still doubled over, and Maison's hand on her is downright terrified, but he doesn't need to know that.

"Can you let Chloe go?" she asks, and her voice doesn't quiver. "Let her step away?"

The man releases Chloe, who scrabbles over to Gurlien, the pain vivid on the back of her neck, burning, as her knees hit the damp pavement next to Gurlien, but still clutching her bag.

Her bag with all her supplies.

Delina forces herself to not look, to not give it away. "I want reassurances that you're not going to hurt them," she says, and Maison breathes deep, like he recognizes her tone of voice. Like he recognizes her bluffing. "And don't do anything to Maison's mom."

"His name's not Maison, that's a lie," he says, before inclining his head. "That can be arranged."

Out of the corner of her eye, Chloe slowly, deliberately slowly, unzips the backpack, every motion slight to not draw attention.

The magic coils tighter in his fists, and the man pays it no attention, like he doesn't know she can tell.

The creepily blue eyes bore into her, barely visible from over Maison's shoulder, and all at once it's like she's drenched in water, cold climbing over her skin, shuddering through her body.

"Don't scan her like that," Maison blurts out, skirting her further back behind him. "She doesn't know—"

His hands tightening over the magic is the only warning, before it snaps out towards Delina, the air cracking in its wake.

Maison jerks his hand forward, and the magic crackles to the ground, useless, sparks shimmering through the air.

"You found one," the man snarls, all pretenses of civility gone, abrupt, "you can't let her live free, you can't."

"Delina," Maison starts, before the man twists the magic again, crackling it against whatever barrier Maison puts in place. "You need to run."

Delina backs up, half turning before the strip of magic snaps at her, shattering through whatever barrier.

Maison grabs her, a spark cracking between them, yanking her back, and the spike of magic just grazes by her shoulder, ripping into the rain jacket and sending a long line of fire down her arm.

She stumbles, her own pain blocking out everyone else's for one brief second, and she gets one crystal clear moment of seeing everything.

One crystal clear moment, where Korhonen twists his hands around more magic, a bored expression on his face. Where Chloe draws her hand out of the backpack, a dagger in her fist, balanced for a throw. Where blood wells up against her cut, immediate and vivid red, redder than she would have ever thought. Where the pavement is damp and the sun is shining and there's nobody else around and birds trill in the background and Maison's in front of her and the line of his shoulders is long and —

Korhonen snaps the magic over to her, lancing towards her, too fast, too fast for her to move, too fast for anyone, too fast for her to breathe, too fast for her to evade.

Maison grips her arm, and jerks himself in front of her.

The magic lances through his chest, bright, crackling blinding against her awareness, and blood splashes against her.

He doesn't make a sound, doesn't say a thing, just slumps back towards her, heavy, and she scrambles to keep him upright, her hands catching on his jacket, fumbling.

Chloe screams, high pitched and loud, and Delina catches a glimpse of a dagger in flight, striking Korhonen deep near the hip, before he twists away and disappears, the dagger clattering to the ground.

And all at once, all the sound slams back into Delina, and she staggers, her hands slick with blood already, and—

"Here, get him down," Gurlien is saying, and his hands help her lower Maison onto the damp pavement, and Maison's face is pale, too pale, his eyes wide open and panicked.

"Here, put pressure," Chloe says, pressing a sweatshirt into the wound on Maison's chest.

Maison gasps at the contact, like he can't quite take a breath, can't get enough air. There's pain, somewhere in all of it, almost drowned out by the fear and horror and terror.

Delina scrabbles for the sweatshirt, holding it against the blood, against the actual wound in Maison, but there's blood bubbling up in Maison's mouth, so acrid Delina can almost taste it.

He's scared. She can feel it in the throb of her shoulder

and the wheeze coming from his breath and brilliant fire of pain in his chest.

"Gurlien, help here," Chloe instructs, and Gurlien does, leveraging his weight onto the sweatshirt.

There's too much blood, and a distant part of Delina refuses to latch onto that, and her hands shake. He can't be this injured, he can't, he was just joking about her mother and Frenchmen and grabbing the bags from her.

Maison's grey eyes lock on hers, his hand curling up around her wrist, a small sound wrenching from his throat.

There's blood on his hand, too, slick against her skin.

He gasps, again, and not enough oxygen is getting to his brain, electrical signals going haywire, sparking against her awareness like static.

"It's okay, I got you," Delina babbles, as Chloe unrolls bandages from her bag, moving fast. "It'll be okay, you'll be okay, it's okay—"

And then, with his hand holding onto her, he dies.

It punches through Delina, wave after wave of contradictory sensations, knocking the breath out of her.

But his brain stills, his nerves cooling and settling to stillness, and his eyes are still open.

He's vivid against her awareness, unmoving, his blood not pumping, his heart quiet, all crystal clear and bright and...and...and...

Dead.

"Shit," Chloe says, scrabbling at her bag. "Shit shit shit."

Dead.

"Fuck, no pulse," Gurlien is saying, his fingers against Maison's pale skin, and there's blood smeared there, too. "Call an ambulance, make a defibrillator, something."

Dead.

Some deep part of her knows that a defibrillator

wouldn't do a thing. That it might shock his heart, a few beats might happen, but it would stop again, and it would happen all over again.

The wound is too big, stretching through his lungs, grazing past an artery in his heart, tearing a ragged hole in it, the blood still leaking.

She can't see it, she can't see anything but the crimson and black blood splashed all over his front and the terror in his still open eyes and his paling skin, but still, she knows. The injury is too big, would need too much repair, too much effort.

It pulls at the back of her stomach, at the wrongness, at the brightness and the itch in her hands and whispers that she could change this.

That she could fix this.

Not seeing, she scrambles until she can press her hand against his cheek, and...and lets whatever that is in her snap into place.

Her ears pop, and again, no sound reaches her, like she's back at the cabin in the bio-trap, but gripping his cheek she pushes the blood back into place, snapping the artery closed and smooth again, purging the liquid starting to pool in his lungs.

His body jerks like it's fighting her, but she just leans in more. Like putting her body weight against him could make this work, like she could actually do something.

"No, stop." It's Gurlien, but his voice is far away. "Shit, stop."

There's a chip of bone off of one of his ribs, she sockets that back into place. Smoothes over the skin, though blood still smears over it, soaking into his clothes.

Then, with one last bit of something inside of her, she

clenches her hand and sends a spark of electricity into his heart.

And for a beat, nothing happens.

Her stomach drops, and she stares down at his still open eyes, her head swimming.

Then all at once, he sits bolt upright, gasping, coughing, hacking up blood, and her hand falls away from him.

"Fuck," Gurlien says, scrambling away from them.

Maison clutches at his throat, then at his chest, then looks up in horror to Delina.

"Hi," Delina says, and her own voice wavers, her head light for a few giddy moments, before she blacks out.

17

It's not like she wakes up, not quite, but more like something gradually pulls her upward, tugging her back to awareness, one torturous moment to the next.

She's laying on something cold, something chilled and hard, and though she fights to keep her eyes shut, there's a bright, sterile light above her. The cut on her shoulder stings, distant.

And the creeping sensation of the dead fly, still in the plastic pill case on the table.

She pops her eyes open. The dead fly.

The fluorescent lights above her shine, painfully, too much, and she flops her arm over to cover her eyes.

"Delly?"

It's Maison's voice, quiet and subdued, and for a few moments her mind rejects it. He had been bleeding, she felt him die, she felt his brain stop and his heart still and everything go wrong.

"Delly, you need to sit up."

She tilts her head over in the direction of his voice. She's laying on the bare concrete of the basement, a spray-painted circle of gold wide, encompassing almost the entire room. The tables are pushed to the side, the bookcases pressed against the walls, as far away as possible.

Maison's sitting cross legged, a few good paces away, and his eyes glow red at her.

She glances to the circle, it's exactly like the one that had been in front of the door when she first got here.

There's blood still on Maison's cheek, like he had missed a spot while washing, though he's pulled on a new shirt and a hoodie somewhere along the line. His lungs ache, bone deep, and the skin across his chest itches and tugs at Delina's awareness.

"You died," she says, dumbly, then makes a face at the taste in her mouth, pushing herself up to sitting.

Her head swims, and she blinks through the dizziness.

"Is this a demon thingy?" she asks, pointing to the spray paint. "The trap?"

Maison nods, his expression something awful.

He's sitting in there with her, which means he can't leave.

"You've been out for about three hours, we got you back here. Gurlien and Chloe are now putting every anti-demon ward on the house they can possibly think of, carving it into the very forest floor." His voice is still soft, like he's expecting volume to hurt her. "You are very, very lucky."

There's a pallet of water bottles, helpfully put in the circle with them, and Delina makes an aborted motion towards them, before Maison scrambles over, pulling one out and opening it in one smooth action.

"You were dead, though," Delina says, after a long glug of water. Her own head aches, her fingertips tremble, weak.

His face twists. "Yeah."

"The...other guy, he did something, he killed you." The

more she says, the further away it feels. "I saw it go through you, you died."

Maison rubs his face, and there's still blood underneath his fingernails. "And you're a necromancer, and you panicked."

She stares at him for one long moment. "You're welcome?"

He huffs out an approximation of a laugh, but it hurts the skin on his chest. "You could have died so easily right then, it's just luck that you're not dead."

She crosses her arms, and his fingerprints where he had gripped her and pulled himself in front of her are still there, almost bruises.

They had obviously tried to clean the blood off of her, wiping off her hand, though her shirt still sticks uncomfortably to her skin.

For a long moment, the only sound is the buzzing of the lights overhead.

"You should eat, too," Maison says, gently. "You put so much power into me your body shut down."

Food sounds like the opposite of what she wants to do, but he tosses her a pop tart and she rips open the cheap wrapping, her hands shaking.

"Is everyone else in danger?" she asks, her voice smaller than she wants. "Are they okay, too?"

"I don't think Gurlien's gonna sleep tonight, his face is one mess of bruising," Maison reports, "and Chloe is way more twitchy and spooked than she wants to say. But they're only in danger of being collateral damage, and each ward they put down decreases that possibility."

Doesn't explain why he's down here, where he can't escape.

"Does everyone always feel like ass when they do their

magic?" Delina asks, and gets the barest hint of a dimple in return. "Cause this sucks."

"I think anyone who, completely untrained, put as much of themselves into doing some as you did, would feel just as shitty." He stretches out his legs in front of him, and there's a scrape on his shin that she didn't notice when her hand was on him. "You didn't just bring me back, you apparently tried to fix the entirety of the injury itself."

"Well yeah," Delina says, finishing the water bottle and immediately grabbing the other one. "It felt like you would just...die again if I didn't."

He raises an eyebrow at her, then shakes his head, and there's an echo of pain as he did that. "That's terrifying, and I don't think you realize this."

His skin is still paler than it should be, and there are circles under his eyes.

"Is there anything else to eat besides a pop tart?" Delina asks, glancing around the makeshift circle. A duffel bag sits to one side, but she very much does not want to touch something she's not supposed to.

"Five-hour energy drinks, power bars, a bag of chocolate chips, and some beef jerky," Maison says. "What, they left their emergency food bag, they didn't want to spend time cooking something."

"No, that's fine, it's just..." She attempts to push herself up to standing, but her knees wobble and she sits down hard on the concrete floor. "Weird options."

"When they're done, Chloe mentioned something about cooking an actual meal, but nobody's coming into this circle until they've finished the wider one." Maison digs into the duffle bag, tossing her a five-hour energy shot and the bag of chocolate chips.

"There is no way I'm drinking this," Delina informs him.

"I guarantee you'll feel better if you do," he snips back.

"Gross," Delina says, then opens it anyways. "Aren't these outlawed in a few states?"

"I mean, they should be," Maison says, taking one himself and shooting it in one go before coughing at the taste.

Which, of course, tugs at the skin and the ache in his lungs.

"Sorry," she blurts out, and he raises a single eyebrow at her. "Your lungs hurt."

Deliberately, he sets the shot to the side, then leans forward. "Delina, and I mean this completely seriously, don't fucking worry about it."

She blinks at his word choice.

"The College sent one of their best battle mages to kill you, you literally brought me back from the dead, you almost got yourself killed, I could not give two shits that I'm a bit sore."

It still bugs at her awareness.

"I'm alive, you're alive, I could be full of broken bones and I would not care."

"That's fair, I guess," she replies, and stretches, her entire body angry that she was apparently asleep on concrete for a few hours. "Glad we didn't bring a demon down on us."

"That's because we threw you in the car and broke way too many speeding laws getting out of range of the flare you put up," he says, then, slowly, reaches a hand out to her. "I know you're still mad that I lied, I know you can't trust me, but can I please see that you're alright?" His voice lilts up, suddenly vulnerable, and he swallows that down, his throat moving.

Even in their fights, even in their bad moments and their close calls, she's never seen him like this.

"Okay," she says, nervy, and he scoots over to sit next to her, cross-legged. "I feel like shit but I'm okay."

He rests his hand on his knee, palm facing up, and he's so close it's overwhelming.

"Why are you down here, anyways?" Delina asks, before gingerly placing her hand in his.

He inhales, then clears his throat. "In case they couldn't get the demon traps upstairs set up in time." He curls his thumb around her palm. "I'm going to do a basic scan on you, it won't feel like the one Korhonen did on you, it'll be gentler."

"Right, because he could tell what I was."

"What he did is considered very unethical, so you know." He briefly squeezes her hand, and a warmth spreads through her entire arm. "This is much milder, and if I was actually a demon, I would be able to do this just by glancing at you."

She shivers, even though it's warm.

"You need to eat way more," he says, his eyes half closed, staring off into nothing. "You will have a blood sugar crash soon if you don't."

"Alright," she says, then opens the bag of chocolate chips with one hand and pops some into her mouth. "That's doable."

"You're so low energy," he says, distant, "if anyone tried to scan you right now, they'd think you were completely normal."

"That's good, right?" Delina says, resisting the urge to pull back her hand so she can hug her knees into herself.

"No, it's very much not good, it means you're defense-less," Maison says, snapping back to full attention, but keeping the grip on her hand. "Just..."

He sighs, and with the paleness of his face and the

circles under his eyes, it's like the last few hours have aged him.

"You stepped in front of me," Delina says, softly, after a few moments of silence pass under the harsh fluorescent lights.

He nods, circling his thumb on the back of her hand.

"That would've been a convenient way to get out of your problems," Delina continues. "Nobody would blame you if you didn't protect me now."

He looks up at her, really looks at her, like he can see all the way through her, and a thrill half akin to fear spirals up her spine. "I would blame me."

It's so close, so close to some sort of confession, something she so desperately wants to hear that she has to blink back tears in her eyes. She always cries at inopportune times, and this would be among them.

"Aww, no, Delly," he says, and his voice breaks. "Don't..." He tugs her into a hug, one of his wonderful hugs, wrapping his arms around her on the cold concrete floor, surrounded by gold spray paint and her dead mother's old research. "Don't cry."

"I'm not," she declares, before burying her face into his chest, right where she can hear his heartbeat.

It beats strong, perfectly in rhythm, and new tears well up in her eyes.

He strokes back her hair, gentle, as she shakes apart, real tears spilling over her cheeks, as everything in the last few days catches up to her, all at once. At the letter, the betrayal, the stares, the strangers in the house, the bio-trap, and Maison actually fucking dying, everything.

"You're okay, I'm okay, it's okay," Maison whispers, and she clings to him, to the clean hoodie and the still soreness in his lungs. "You'll get through this, you're going to live and figure this out."

It's not quite what she needs to hear, but she can't bring herself to say anything, just cries.

~

SOME TIME LATER, when her tears have subsided but she can't pull herself away, someone clatters down the stairs and Maison abruptly stiffens. All the warm comfort, all the soft touches and gentle arms around her, immediately transforming into something foreign.

"All clear," Chloe's voice says, and Delina tugs herself away, sitting upright. "Oh good, you're awake."

Her tone suggests it's anything but good.

"And the forest floor?" Maison asks, deeply skeptical.

"Let's just say, any plant biologist would absolutely lose their shit if they ever did any research, and someone will have to let you in and out every time you want to leave for a bit." Chloe looks past him at Delina's ruined makeup. "Are you feeling okay?"

The answer is no, but she shrugs.

"Of course she doesn't, she hit burnout on her first time using her powers in any substantial way, nobody would feel okay after that." Gurlien steps down the stairs after Chloe, and a startlingly purple bruise mars his cheekbone and his eye is half swollen shut, but he crosses his arms at them. "Have you told her she was stupid yet?"

"I told her she was lucky," Maison responds, standing up, and his eyes still flash red.

"That's a nice way to put it," Gurlien says, then nods at Chloe. "Go ahead and let him out of this one."

Delina watches as Chloe sketches something midair, and the curve of the circle closest to her blurs.

"Is it safe for me to leave?" Delina asks dully, her head now good and truly pounding like it always does after she cries.

"Should be," Gurlien says, voice deeply skeptical. "That was insanely stupid of you."

Maison offers her a hand, pulling her up, and she sways.

"Now they know you're you, they know our general area, that Chloe and I are up here, they know that Maison double crossed them, and they know how to get back at him."

"They probably think I'm still dead," Maison says, with a glance back at Delina. "Hopefully, no getting back at me."

"And they know she's a Necromancer, nobody in their right mind is going to think you're still dead," Gurlien says, and by the tightness in his lips, he's frightened, too. "My former boss smacked me away like I was a fly, they're not going to assume anything and they're going to come down hard."

Maison scowls at him.

"I'm reheating some soup from our freezer, and Gurlien's already has bread in the oven," Chloe says, and soup and bread sound just about perfect. "Think you can manage the stairs?"

The answer to that is also no, but Delina nods anyways, and they all tromp upstairs, Maison's hand steadying on the small of her back the entire way.

Chance meows at her the moment she's back on the couch, before butting his head against her arm and crawling into her lap.

"Aww, the cat likes me," Delina says, holding as still as she possibly can, feeling wrung out.

"The cat does that to anyone who's feeling bad, don't take it personally," Gurlien says.

"Gurlien, stop," Chloe mutters, and he does, sitting at the table and accepting an ice pack for his face.

"What's the likelihood of them tracking us directly here?" Delina asks, as Chloe offers her a glass of water.

"Relatively unlikely but not impossible," Gurlien says, waving the hand not pressing the ice pack to his eye around. "Depends on how in-depth their knowledge of Frisse's properties is. This building is pretty well hidden, if they don't have directions to it."

Delina glances over at Maison, and he's staring blankly out at the door, like now that they're upstairs and out of the demon circle, the entire day is catching up to him.

"Oh, he found you because you slept with him, so unless you've slept with other members who just so happen to have innate tracking powers and bonds, you don't need to worry about it," Gurlien says, and Delina's gathered something of the ilk, but it's still...weird.

"What he's saying is we should be safe for now," Chloe says from the stove. "We just don't know how long that will last."

18

L   ater that night, long after the sun sets and the wind
      starts whistling through the chimney and
      everyone else has gone to sleep, Delina lays awake
on the giant bed, alone.

There are a hundred reasons for her to still be awake,
she knows this, but the most annoying by far is the dead fly
still in the basement below.

She could make a map of the basement, merely by the
location of the fly.

Sure, the others are sorta in her awareness. Chloe fast
asleep, unmoving. Gurlien a black hole of no magic, tossing
and turning. The cat pacing up and down the hall like a
patrol, tail flicking right and left.

And Maison sitting up in his bed, down the hall from
Chloe, skin still pulling at his injuries.

Delina's breath catches in her throat at the sudden
knowledge that she's not the only person awake, and quickly
lets her mind flash back to the dead fly, to the bird still
outside.

There's a bug crawling over the bird, small, it's many feet

leaving tiny pinpricks of sensation over the one exposed bone, sending echoes of shivers down Delina's back.

"Yeah, I can tell when you do that," Maison speaks from the door to the bedroom.

Delina briefly contemplates pretending to be asleep, before she sighs, tossing off the blankets and sitting up.

He's silhouetted against the doorway, in a soft T-shirt and his sweatpants, his hair sticking up in the back.

"Well, you can go back to sleep, I'll work hard at not accidentally scanning you," Delina says, though her pulse flutters against the skin of her neck.

"Eh, I wasn't sleeping well," Maison says with a half-shrug. "Bit hard to in a strange bed, completely forgetting the fact that I, you know, died."

And her heart hurts all over again, at the casual conversation after midnight. Like it's just another sleepless night with the two of them chatting, like nothing has changed and she still trusted him.

Slow, she clicks on the aged lamp on the bedside table, casting a warm glow across the baby blue carpet and the floral quilt.

There are circles under Maison's eyes, a vivid reminder that they're not in undergrad anymore and all-nighters can be a bit rough.

"Dead bug too distracting to you?" Maison asks, leaning against the door frame. "I know other late bloomers, when they become aware, get driven nuts by their powers until they get used to it."

"That would've been good for my mom to include in her letter," Delina says and Maison smiles. Actually smiles, like she's the only person in the world and nobody else matters.

It catches in her throat.

"Do you want hot chocolate?" Maison asks, going for the

jugular and offering her favorite late-night drink. "I can make a few mugs."

"Sure," Delina says, before she can stop herself, before she can think it's a bad idea.

SHE PULLS on a sweatshirt by the time he returns, and by then she's had enough time to steel up her spine and shore up her defenses.

One look from him, still sleep rumpled, threatens to tear them right down again.

"Here," he says, setting it on the bedside table, before he sits next to her on top of the quilt, smoothing his hand over the wrinkles They're not touching, but all it would take is a twitch of her hand to grasp his. "They didn't have the type with the marshmallows, but at least it wasn't the fat free stuff."

With all the turmoil of the day, with the ache still in his chest, she doesn't know how to respond to that.

"How's the lungs?" she asks, after a long stretch of just sipping hot chocolate in the warm light.

It's a wan attempt at conversation, she can tell they ache, less so than a few hours ago but still enough to tug at her awareness.

He offers her a crooked smile, before ducking his head. "I'll be okay."

By now, she doesn't think the wound is going to tear open again, that the artery will stay in place, but the anxiety of it still tugs at her mind.

"You realize if you lie to me about that, I can tell now," she says, aiming for arch and coming off a bit pathetic.

Her hair is still a mess, the bags full of hair supplies and snacks most likely still on the blacktop behind the Target, but she pushes it away from her face anyways.

"Well, it's not comfy," he replies, wry. "But most likely better than being dead, can't imagine anyone like me would have a great time in an afterlife."

She blinks at him, and the light from the lamp cast deep shadows in the room around them. "Is there an afterlife?"

"Nobody really knows," he says, with a wistfulness that's almost like homesickness.

"They told me that there were some other people who had been raised who were, you know, dead for longer than a minute, they might know?" Delina ventures, and he cracks a smile. "Pretty sure you wouldn't even have had the chance to figure that out, your eyes were still open and everything."

He flinches, and she wishes she could pull the words back.

But then, there's so many words she doesn't know how to even begin to say, the confusing mess of emotions sitting behind her breastbone leaving a knot behind her throat.

Because she had panicked, it's true. She had panicked and instead of letting him die, immediately did something that everyone had decried as foolish. Because just moments before, he had looked at her and smiled when she talked about wine.

"Oh, I've made a mess of things, haven't I?" Delina says, watching as the dust mites cast shadows over the baby blue carpet.

"Well," Maison says delicately, taking the time to sip from his own mug of hot chocolate in an obvious stalling movement. "I think Korhonen carries the bigger blame than you, personally. I've known him since I was eight," he turns to her, still sitting there on the quilt, "Since I was eight, and he had no problems with striking me."

It's entirely not what she means, but she nods.

"I've had drinks with him and his wife, and he just...was completely okay with killing me."

In all her angst, all of her exhaustion, Delina didn't factor in the betrayal side of it for him. That it's not just the injury, it's from someone he knows, someone he used to trust.

"And now, I did everything they asked for my entire life, and it's...they're still going to take it out on Mom." He looks down at his hands, and somewhere in the last few hours he had obviously taken the time to clean the blood from under his fingernails. "Even if they still think I'm dead. Which I still can't wrap my head around."

Before she can stop herself, Delina puts her hand on his arm, and he cuts off, inhaling suddenly.

"I'm sorry," she says, and means it.

He searches her face for something in the dim, warm light, and she doesn't know if he finds it.

"I probably shouldn't have come in here just to rant," he mumbles, wrapping his own hands around the mug, and his fingers tremble, just a bit. "You should absolutely be getting some sleep."

"I dunno, I had a pretty good nap in the middle of the day," Delina says, and gets a hint of the dimple. "You know. Sometimes I just don't sleep."

It's true, though less frequent than it used to be, and he nods. Because of course he knows, he would lay beside her on those long nights, a hair's breadth away from her, so she can see his chest rise and fall even when sleep evaded her.

"Maybe those other people have a support group?" Delina says, and he huffs out a weak laugh. "I dunno, Gurlien said one of them had been dead for like fifteen hours, that could be something."

She still has her hand on his arm, she realizes distantly, right on the edge of his sleep shirt, at the creases that came from packing, and the smart thing to do would be to lean away. To go back to drinking the hot chocolate and then pretend to fall asleep again, and let her ex-boyfriend go back to whatever it is he should be doing.

But in the warm light of the lamp, all those 'shoulds' seem awfully far away.

"I don't know how to navigate this," he says, voice softer than the quilt. "I don't know what to do right now, and so much of my life has had a clear purpose and set of rules to follow, and now..." for a long moment, he doesn't speak, before he sets down the mug of hot chocolate and rubs his face again. "Sorry."

The apology carries some weight, something unsaid, something bigger than the whole room, and it hangs in the air between them.

"So for once in your life, you're not beholden to just doing what they want you to do," Delina says, and he blinks, like it's not something he's considered. "You don't have to behave, you don't have to toe the line, the worst has happened."

He's still, barely breathing.

"You've betrayed them, you tried to stop them, nothing you do right now will convince them otherwise, right?" she continues, and he gives her the most minute of nods. "Then you can do what you want. Live your life how you want, do whatever reckless thing that crosses your mind. Move where you want, do whatever magic you want, fall in love with whomever you want." The moment is crystalline silent, not even a stir of air through the entire house except what is between the two of them. "You can do anything."

He looks down, away, his lashes casting shadows over his cheekbones.

"You don't even have to stay here if you don't want to," Delina says, and though she knows that would be the good option, that would be the healthy option for both of them, the words are bitter in her mouth. "You can go anywhere, forget that this chapter of your life ever happened."

"I don't want to," he says, finally, swallowing.

"Okay," Delina says, and he smiles at her, heartbreaking in its beauty.

Slowly, telegraphing his motions, he shifts, lifting his hand to tuck a wayward strand of her hair behind her ear, like he used to do when she needed some touch but couldn't ask for it.

"May I ask you some things?" His voice dips down, low, as if to not wake the other two people in the house, even though Delina can tell with merely a thought that they're still asleep.

She nods, swallowing, and he cradles her chin.

"Why'd you bring me back?"

Once more, the words hang between them, and Delina can't parse what's the right thing to say. Can't sift through her options and find what's correct, what's smart, and what's accurate, all thoughts mishmashing together in her mind.

"Because five years?" she says, her voice lilting up, and she knows, the moment she says them, that they're too honest. Too honest and too ill advised.

His face is unreadable, like stone.

"I mean, also I panicked," Delina says, hoping for a joke. "I don't know how your magic demon bullshit worked but it was pretty intense for me all of the sudden, and—"

He swipes his thumb against her cheek, cutting off her

words, and to her horror she realizes that she had let tears fall for the second time that day.

She jerks herself back, yanking a tissue from the box on the nightstand and wiping the tears away. "Sorry," she says, though if you held a gun to her head she couldn't tell you what she was apologizing for. "It's been...it's been a day."

He leans back as well, crossing his arms. "I've seen you cry already today, you don't have to apologize."

"Obviously," she snips back, then presses the heels of her hands into her eyes, flopping backwards on the bed. "I hate that everything I do now is complicated."

The bed dips down, the familiar weight of him laying next to her, not touching her. They're still on top of the quilt, they're still both fully dressed, but she feels fully naked. Naked and vulnerable.

"I'll try not to send you into any more moral quandaries," he says, and she smiles, briefly, still shutting her eyes against the world. "And I wouldn't say everything but... yeah bringing someone back from the dead is pretty complicated."

"Not to mention it's you." She exhales, finally blinking her eyes up to the exposed wooden beams of the ceiling. "First person I tried to bring back, first anything I tried to bring back—"

"Please don't try anything else," he interrupts, and she leans her head over to give him a glare, but they're so close, flopped on the bed, that the retort just evaporates from her mind.

It's no different from when they were first dating, in those first few months, before they really knew what to expect from each other. When everything was tentative and everything was unknown. When sometimes he seemed so skittish around her, she had no idea what to do.

It makes sense, in retrospect, the nerves from him. If he messed up, the looming threat to his mother was always behind him.

But here, with his lashes casting shadows on his cheeks and his hair messy and his lungs still aching against her mind, she finds herself without words.

He's content to let her blink up at him, watching her intently with his grey eyes so familiar.

"Why are your eyes only red some of the time?" she asks, instead of all the emotions clogging through her. All she would have to do to kiss him is shift forward, ever so slightly, and all he would have to do is drape an arm over her and so many things could happen.

"You shouldn't see that outside of circles," he replies, but there's a half smile lurking in his expression. "Maybe it's a Necromancer thing."

"Weird," she says, but doesn't move away.

His eyes flicker down to her lips, only a brief second, so short she might've imagined it.

"You really should sleep," he says, also staying exactly where he is. "We'll deal with all the complications and everything tomorrow."

"Sure, that sounds responsible," she says, and he laughs, quiet, before he sits up and clicks the lamp off, stealing the warm glow away, so the only illumination is the filtered moonlight through the floral curtains, before settling down next to her.

Not touching, not holding her, but she can hear the rise and fall of his breath and see the vague silhouette of his jawline in the shadows.

Tentative, she reaches out, tangling her hand in his, and he grips her back.

19

She wakes the next morning with him still fast asleep, his arm thrown over her midsection, tugging her until her back's pressed against his chest.

Where his lungs are much less painful, just a twinge on the crest of every deep inhale, and the skin no longer stretches annoyingly.

It's exactly how they would wake up on cold winter mornings in the condo in Prescott, on the rare occasions of snow.

For a few moments, she gives herself the luxury of cuddling, no matter how ill advised. Of closing her eyes to the warm comfort of being against him in a bed, as if nothing in the last few days had happened. As if she still didn't know, still thought of him as the perfect doting boyfriend, and she still worked the job doing spreadsheets for people who couldn't.

It's such a little thing, to be held like this in sleep, and she can't help but relax into it. To cherish it, as if it might not ever happen again.

She blinks out, the sunlight muffled through the floral curtains.

Because he's alive, he's well, but he's still...someone who dated her just because of a job.

No matter the familiarity, no matter how wonderful this feels, there's still the gaping maw of what he did. Of the confusion of which part of emotions from him are real and which emotions and habits are just from him sleeping next to her for so long.

"Ugh," she whispers to herself, too quiet to disturb his sleep. Because she knows that off hand.

She needs to figure this out, she decides. Figure out which parts of her are angry and which parts of his actions are habits.

Though stepping in front of her for a strike that was aimed to kill runs deeper than just habits.

It would be far easier if he resented her, but the twin chipped mugs of hot chocolate on the side table and the ache in his chest says otherwise.

She wiggles out from underneath his arm, and he mumbles something in his sleep at the movement, before squishing his face into the pillow.

His hair is even more messed up than it was the night before, but the circles under his eyes are lighter, and Delina stares down at him for probably too many moments to be excusable before she abruptly turns and heads into the kitchen.

Chance chirps a greeting at her, stretching his paws out on the couch, before jumping off it and meandering over and butting his head against her leg.

"Aww, good morning," Delina whispers, scratching under his chin, and he leans into the touch. "You are just a sweetheart."

The espresso machine brews just as good of a shot of espresso as the day before, and even though she can't find where the beans are reloaded into it, it's just as fresh and rivals most of the coffee shops she's ever been into.

She takes her time, crafting an elaborate breakfast and an exquisite drink, settling into her bones. The familiar actions bring something closer to peace, despite the busyness in her head.

Somewhere between chopping up veggies and grating a bit of cheese for a scramble, Gurlien steps into the great room, giving her a suspicious look.

"What?" Delina asks defensive, before he even says anything.

"Are you a morning person?" he replies, poking dejectedly at the coffee machine until she swipes it with her thumb. "I haven't been a morning person in a year."

Considering he lost his magic and his job all at once, that would disrupt anyone's sleep schedule.

"It's ten AM," Delina says, adding a few more veggies to the pan. "And not really, but it's been a few strange days."

His suspicious glance doesn't go away, though he curls up on the couch, tucking his legs underneath him. "Did you sleep with Frederick again?"

Delina considers throwing the spatula at him. "Only technically."

He squints.

"He brought me hot chocolate then we dozed off in the same bed," she clarifies, and he nods in understanding.

"I can't believe he defied them," Gurlien says, and it's too close to what she's been thinking that she doesn't bother to get him on a different track. "That's definitely not how I saw that going."

Delina can't think of anything to say to that, so she aggressively stirs the scramble instead.

"Good to know your Necromancy is strong enough to bring back a full person," he muses, and it's still disorienting to hear it spoken so blatantly. "Inconvenient in terms of security, nice in terms of, you know, still being alive."

"Thanks," she replies sarcastically.

"There aren't really any known and accepted methods of training Necromancers, but I would say that your gut instincts served you decently," he says, staring somewhat blankly down at the coffee. "And Frederick…"

Delina waits for him to continue, stirring the eggs.

"I don't know what to think." Finally, he glances up and there's a scowl on his face, as if the world hasn't prepared him well enough for this moment. "I just don't."

"You and me both," replies Delina, shoving her scramble on a plate. "And now we can't even leave without demon threats."

"It'll subside in a day or so without you using it, or it should, in theory."

"That's not comforting." Delina sits down at the table with her over indulgent scramble and her over indulgent coffee, as Gurlien grabs a power bar from the cabinet. "Are you and Chloe going to have to move?"

He hesitates. "Not yet," he replies, guarded. "They know we're in northern Washington, but Dr. Frisse has eighteen properties in the area, so it doesn't narrow it down. We'll have to avoid those three close stores, but there are options. I destroyed Frederick's phone, so they can't use that for tracking a confrontation anymore."

The phone with all the pictures of his mother.

"I created a local backup," Gurlien says, and it must've

been written on her face. "Too many good contacts to just erase forever. And besides, he gave it to me to do so."

That helps a little bit, and they descend into silence for a few minutes.

"I guess the possibility that he actually likes you is higher than eight percent," Gurlien all but mumbles, after a good solid five minutes of ignoring each other.

"Thanks," Delina responds.

"I'm not good at that sort of thing, but I doubt he'd take a kill shot for most people. He's a selfish asshole."

Delina briefly considers attempting to defend Maison, because selfish asshole has never been in the descriptors for him, but Gurlien knew him through whatever equivalent of high school and nobody is their best during that.

"So today we wait?" Delina asks, instead of any emotional statement, as possibly crying in front of Gurlien sounds like a nightmare. "Wait until whatever Necromancy power burns off?"

He's already nodding. "The circle is a five-minute walk in any direction, you can't miss it and you won't cross it without knowing."

AFTER BREAKFAST and taking care of her dishes, she escapes outside the moment Maison emerges from the bedroom, still sleep rumpled and handsome.

She's not running away per se, but things are definitely still too confusing to contemplate this early in the morning.

So she clutches her mug in her hand and paces outside the cabin.

There's a well-worn trail around it, filled in with gravel, though moss grows thick over some of it, and anything off that path is thick with blackberry bramble, dying in the chill of fall, and she's not sure her tennis shoes would survive a fight with the thorns.

The dead bird is still bright to her awareness, but she skirts to the opposite side of the house, as if that could lessen it, finding a more or less beaten trail leading deeper into the woods.

It's not nearly as quiet as she would think, with the wind in the branches and the live birds singing in the trees, but as she steps through the trail, the cabin disappears from view, almost as an optical illusion.

"Ah," she whispers, to the air around her. Of course her mother took pains to hide this place, and even in death it still works.

She tromps until she hits a burned strip, about as wide as a foot, curving around the property, and the hair on the back of her neck rises.

The demon trap, it must be.

Besides the visual signal, there's nothing else that would set it apart. The birds still chirp on the other side and the wind still blows through.

"It's clever," a voice says, and Delina jumps.

The woman with gray hair—the Wight? Spirit? — appears a few steps away, on the other side of the trap.

"I guess?" Delina says, her voice lilting up, and the woman bares her teeth in a smile. "I don't know enough about it yet to tell you."

"The magicless talked the alchemist through it, they're both very talented." The woman glances down at it, almost idle. "We can't cross it, and I'm not sure anything can."

"Good to know," Delina says, clutching her coffee mug as if it could give her strength. "Sorry if it hurt anyone or anything."

The woman shakes her head at that. "Merely an inconvenience. Have to walk around instead of going through. Worth it to keep the demons at bay."

A lump in her throat, Delina nods.

"Though I think one or two of them checked out your flare down south," she continued, conversationally. "So they definitely know there's another one active."

And the woman fixes her eyes on Delina, sharp, like she can see through her and find her wanting.

"The weak ones will be scared off by the Half Demon. The strong ones won't."

"Creepy," Delina says, and she gets an honest smile in return.

"I don't want a full demon in my forest again anytime soon," she continues, pacing in front of the burned line. "So do all your raising away from here."

Delina swallows. All her raising. As if there would be much more.

"The bodies can last a little while longer, the other one doesn't need it to be immediately after death."

"I panicked," Delina says, and the woman's mouth thins. "Sorry about...all the drama."

"It's good he's already bonded with you," she continues, and it's so close to an actual answer that Delina perks up.

"What does that mean?" Delina asks, raising an eyebrow. Her gut instinct is to lift her chin and demand an answer, but something inside of her tells her that wouldn't work in this case.

"You should ask him directly," the woman says, and Delina wants to tear her hair out at that. "See what he says... it's more demon magic than it is human." She watches as Delina obviously tries to keep her temper. "It's the one fallacy of demons. They form bonds with those they deign to care about. It's their weakness and often the only thing preventing them from full chaos and insanity."

"Okay," Delina responds, unnerved, then, "do you know how I can hide from demons? Besides this circle?"

This time, the woman's smile is full of teeth. "You will always send up blinding flares whenever you draw someone back from death. Every demon close can see it. Learn to spread it out, diffuse it, and they won't be able to find you."

Delina nods, though her heart pounds.

"We liked the Grand Magician," she says, and it takes Delina a few seconds to realize that she's probably talking about her bio-mother. "We were sad to hear of her passing."

"I think you're the first person to say that," Delina replies. "Thank you."

The woman nods, and the lines around her face make her look, ever so briefly, ancient. "Stay alive, it'll be good to have someone strong in our forest again."

Before she, of course, vanishes.

Delina exhales, staring out at the now empty woods.

20

It takes another day and a half of nerves, a day and a half of Maison jumping at each sound, and a day and a half of Delina desperately wanting to be anywhere but the cabin her mother gave her, before Gurlien declares that it's "probably" safe for them to let Delina out of the demon trap.

Delina's barely seen anyone in that day and a half, with Maison steadily avoiding her. She steps into the common room, he disappears down into the basement. She wanders down the stairs, he finds a reason to go back to his room. There have been no more midnight hot chocolates, no more kind but confusing conversations.

Instead, he just acts as if he's going to jump out of his skin whenever she gets close.

Gurlien's mostly kept to himself in the stacks of research, occasionally conferring with Maison, but mostly ignoring everyone else. Chloe's been running around, reinforcing runes and wards, as well as attempting to transform half of their items into things more usable.

It's the most awkward Delina's ever felt, and that's saying something.

"So I take it no going back to that Target," Delina says, bouncing on her feet as everyone shakes their head no.

Everyone's uneasy. Everyone's on edge.

"There's the grocery store one town down, it should have about half of what you need," Chloe says, and she's honest-to-god writing down some sort of math equation in a notebook. "It's about a twenty-five-minute drive if you take the overpass."

"It's next to the brewery," Gurlien says, direct at Maison who blinks owlishly.

It'd be interesting if he wasn't still avoiding her and every attempt she made to talk to him.

"What are the chances you would let me go alone?" Delina asks, and Maison blanches. "I need to be out of this cabin before I throttle one of you."

Chloe glances up at her, skittish, and the back of her neck is still raw. Korhonen had left some unholy amalgamation of a burn and a bruise when gripping her, and ironically, it's still the most painful out of all the collected injuries.

The math equations are all titled 'defense' on them, so Delina's not going to pry into that.

Gurlien and Maison glance at each other, and a silent battle of wills ensues, one completely foreign to Delina. An eyebrow raised, a twitch of a scowl, a crossing of arms, before Maison stands, definitive, and grabs his jacket from the other room.

"What was that?" Delina asks Gurlien, who fakes another bored expression. "No, that was something, what was that?"

"He's just trying to be an ass, don't worry about it," Chloe chimes in, already hunched back over the notebook.

"Which he?" Delina asks, as Maison strides back in the room, coat thrown over one arm. "If I'm just going to be a burden, you don't have to come."

Maison rubs his chin and he has the beginnings of stubble growing along his jaw, which is further than he's ever let a beard grow before. "That's not it, Chloe, disable the trap?"

DELINA DRIVES, this time, and she idles the crappy rental right on the other side of the burned-out line, as Chloe and Maison both inspect it, before the now familiar air shivers in front of the car tires.

Through the windshield, Chloe crosses her arms at Maison, bristling, both of them talking too quietly for Delina to hear in the car, before Chloe stomps back off in the direction of the cabin, the mist swirling behind her.

Maison watches her walk back, a scowl on his face, before he yanks open the car door and sits back down, his hair damp from even that brief time in the mist.

"You don't need to babysit me if it's that big of a deal," Delina says, driving over the remnants of the trap. The back of her neck prickles, like something's going to rain down on them, but nothing happens, just the slow movement of the blackberry canes along the deadened branches.

Maison leans his head over on the neck rest, watching her, like he used to do whenever they drove long distances, whenever they made road trips. "It's not that big of a deal."

"Everything else you're doing suggests otherwise."

Delina clutches the steering wheel, before drumming her nails on it. "Am I still glowing or whatever?"

"I'm not a good judge of that," Maison grumbles, and Delina chances a glance away from the gravel road to look at him. "You're fine."

"So what's crawled up your ass the last few days?" She's probably being a bit too rude to him, a bit too mean, but the day and a half of almost ignoring her after such a tender moment in the middle of the night, she can't make herself care.

They pass the broken tree, and the stone chips turned by Chloe are still there, scattered into almost pebbles.

"Would you believe me if I said that things feel incredibly weird for me?" Maison asks, after a long pause.

Things are incredibly weird for everyone right now, but as the car slides through the mist to the paved street, Delina still scowls, before a thought occurs to her.

"Weird like the whole death thing? Is your chest having issues? I should be able to tell, but..."

"Weird like I don't know how to talk to you," Maison interrupts, then sighs. "And yes, the death thing."

"Talk to me about the death thing," Delina demands, a horror itching under her skin. What if she did it wrong, what if it reverses itself, what if the repair work unravels and his artery rips open and his lungs fill up...

"I don't want to talk about the death thing," he says, surly.

"No, tell me, what if I did it wrong, what if something happens, what if—"

"You didn't do it wrong," he interrupts again, and Delina coasts the car to the side of the highway, throwing it into park and turning in her seat to face him. "Delly, I'm fine. Absolutely fine. Stop worrying about it."

They stare at each other, his eyes the same gray as the mists around them.

"If I scan you, would it draw demons?" Delina blurts out.

For a long moment she thinks he's going to refuse to answer, before he crosses his arms. "Don't try to fix anything."

It's enough permission for her, so she slaps her hand against his chest, right where the bolt pierced him, even though his skin stopped hurting a day and a half ago, and exhales.

The artery still holds, healthy and flowing into his heart, as if it had never broken. His lungs are clear, not even a hint of a hitch in their motions. The muscles in his back are together, reknit in her healing and just as strong.

She lets her eyes flutter shut, follows the motion of his blood. It surges up to the brain, back down, perfectly clear of any obstruction.

His shoulder is a bit unhappy, like he slept wrong, and his ankle is annoying him.

"Okay," she says, opening her eyes again, not removing her hand. "Alright, you're okay."

His own eyes glow red, and she flinches.

"Red eyes again," she tells him, nervy, and he blinks, before the color vanishes to the grey again.

"So you can tell when I'm tapping into something demon," he says, like it's a separate side of him, but at least he's talking to her. "I'll hold it back."

"You don't need to." If they were together, actually together, she would curl her fingers around the collar of his Henley, pull him closer, and plant a kiss on his cheek, but as they are she just keeps her palm against his beating heart.

There's something akin to exhaustion thudding against his mind, halfway to a headache.

"You're not sleeping well again," she says, instead of anything else. "Did I interfere with that?"

"You are always the reason I lay awake," Maison replies, and his face pinches off, like he didn't mean to reveal so much. "Gurlien has his theories, I think they're bullshit, he's pulling the rank of actually talking to someone who's been raised before, I think a sample size of two isn't nearly enough."

That sounds like him, at least.

"What does he think?"

Maison's lips thin. "That my mind is unsure how to deal with the fact that I died for a bit so it doesn't want to sleep."

"So like...trauma?" Delina hazards, and he scowls at her. "I dunno, dying is traumatic, it has to be."

"I'm not traumatized," Maison protests, which is absolutely something someone dealing with shit would say. "He thinks it's physiological, not psychology."

"That's still trauma," Delina says, then slowly removes her hand and glancing back at the misty road. "Tell me if things start to feel like they're falling apart."

He obviously bites back a reply to that, like she's said something wrong, before he nods. "I will."

She coasts the car back to driving, merging back onto the empty highway.

"You're doing well with the scanning," Maison says after a few minutes of driving through the mist. "It must be natural for Necromancers."

"Can you do it?" Delina asks, and it's an opportunity to talk, to not be so awkward.

"Not like that, what you're doing is far out of my skill set. I can, at most, tell how much energy you've used and if you're close to empty." Out of the corner of her eye, in the way she's not supposed to look while driving, she sees him shrug. "It's useful in battle."

There's a strange charm to him talking about things he does as battle. Completely out of her image of him as a mild-mannered artist, but somehow completely fitting into the seriousness he sometimes falls into.

Like this is the missing part of him, as well, and now she gets to see it.

And, of course, now that they are completely complicated and broken up but still acting like this.

"You had promised ridiculous stories," Delina says, after they pass the nearest other inhabited house, a small trailer nestled in the woods, a rusted-out car in front.

"Gurlien was right, I was just trying to charm you," Maison says, instead.

"Does that mean you don't have them?"

He's quiet for a few more minutes, until they pass an actual neighborhood of three houses, clustered around what looks like a Christmas tree farm. The paint peels off the sidings of the house and there's tires in the driveway, but the rows of trees are pristine and perfect.

"Do you remember our trip to Phoenix, the time when we got hit by the monsoons and the road back flooded out?" he starts, leaning his head against the window.

Of course she does, it was a pain in the ass, and she missed two days of work before they repaired highway 89.

"Your mother had just lost control of the Terese project, and we didn't know anything, so I was told to take you back to the base—back to home—in no uncertain terms. They could not grasp the idea that a flooded road would prevent it."

He had seemed stressed the entire time, beyond the

normal lack of home, and he had paced a line in the carpet of the crappy hotel they ended up stuck in.

"The Terese project pissed off...a lot of people, and whenever that happened, someone almost always sent someone to try to hurt you." It's not where she thought the story was going, so she perks up. "You desperately wanted to go out and have fun in Phoenix, but there was an actual sniper in town, so I had to balance trying to get home over flooded road, my bosses texting me every half hour with either demands to get you someplace else or updates on people your mom pissed off, and you wanting to go to the club. That was ridiculous."

In the end, they had gone to a dive bar after poking their heads into half a dozen lounges, before Maison found one he liked, and he ended up getting trashed on a much too strong margarita that neither of them anticipated, and she had loved it. They had gotten back the next day and it took him a day after that before his hangover was gone.

"Crazy that there was a sniper there," Delina muses, instead of the strange wistfulness of a happy memory of hers being so stressful to him. "That has to be why you picked the bar with no windows."

"Yup," he says, popping the p sound. "And I really didn't mean to get drunk, and you were so pretty in the neon lights and there was a fucking sniper in town searching for you."

He sounds...resigned. Delina hates it.

The pitted highway smoothes out, as they pass a school and an actual grocery store, before cruising into something that approaches a downtown. Flags hang in every storefront, and a few people scurry between stores.

"Considering how I was never sniped, I think you did a good job," Delina says, pulling into a parking space in front of one of the grocery stores.

He gives her a startled look as she climbs out of the car.

"And how I had no clue my life was in danger, that's also pretty impressive." She doesn't know why she's pushing herself to compliment him. Doesn't know why she desperately wants him to know that she appreciates it, appreciates the stress, appreciates the effort. "Glad I didn't get shot or anything."

He squints at her, his eyes briefly flashing red before that too vanishes. "You're welcome?"

She tosses her mess of a ponytail over one shoulder. "Let's get some supplies, see if they have your pretzels."

21

E verything goes smoothly, no hint of anything harming her or him. They pick up some of the rather gourmet cat food on the grocery list, and Delina holds it up to Maison.

"And they claim Chance just hunts in the wild," he grumbles.

"There's cat treats here, too," Delina says, definitely grabbing some extra of those. "I knew they must spoil him."

Maison tosses a cat toy into the basket as well, the sort that someone will absolutely trip and twist their ankle over.

The store had acceptable hair products and gorgeous apples and she ends up getting enough to actually make some comfort foods, before they pile it into a cooler with ice packs Gurlien had insisted they take.

It's so close to how shopping back in Prescott used to go.

"Gurlien told me to go to the brewery," Maison says, almost disgruntled, and there's some context that she's missing there, something, but if it keeps her out of the cabin a little longer, she's not going to protest. "Gave me a list."

"He doesn't strike me as a beer drinker," Delina says with a shrug, though her curiosity is buzzing.

"Me neither," Maison replies, "but he was oddly insistent about having me try some. I think he was trying to be social." There's a long pause after that. "Or trying to apologize."

"Not so good at that, is he?"

"Not at all."

THE BREWERY IS CLOSE, and Maison's just about to vibrate out of his skin with the same unnamed tension.

"Do you think someone's going to attack me here?" Delina asks dryly.

"No, they tracked me by my phone, don't have that anymore," Maison replies idly, which thankfully answers that question. "Unless they're just coating the entire seaboard, and in which case, there's not much we can do."

"Can Necromancy be an offensive power?" Delina asks, as they step inside the brewery.

It's barely after midday, so only a few disinterested bartenders linger at the front, and Maison tucks them in one corner, conveniently away from any window, and it's so familiar, it's so normal, that it makes her heart stick.

The bar is raw wood, the tables made from old fashioned stumps, and the light is on the dimmer side than most industrial style breweries. The floor is more raw concrete, and the tables have stools rather than proper chairs.

He orders for them, referring to an actual physical list written down by Gurlien, and comes back precariously balancing two flights.

"Did Gurlien want to apologize or to get you drunk?" Delina asks, raising an eyebrow at them.

"Good question." He places one in front of her, then cheers her with the first glass from his. "Yes, Necromancy can work on the offense, in theory. If you can provide something with magic, you can almost always take something away."

She shivers at that, then shivers at the sensation of helplessness she felt stuck behind Maison, with someone intent on killing her. "So can you teach me?"

He hesitates, taking a drink from his first beer to stall, then making an impressed face at it. "I don't know if I'm demon enough to do that."

She sips from hers, a surprisingly fizzy wheat beer, and watches him underneath her eyelashes as he obviously wrestles with his emotions and expectations.

"I can—possibly—teach you some basics," he says, after savoring the entirety of his first sample, a dark, rich looking amber. "In general, people are taught by the same genre of magic."

"Were you?" she asks, and he swallows, the long lines of his throat moving. "Are there a lot of Half Demons?"

"No," he admits, "though when I found my other parent, they gave me some...additional help."

The beer seems to loosen him, his shoulders relaxing just a touch, to more of the normal person she's used to, despite the oddness of the conversation.

"But a rule is, if you're to be trained in something, you should be willing to use it," he says, finally focusing an intense look on her, pinning her down.

"I'd be willing to kill someone who's attacking me, that's for sure," Delina says, surprising a smile out of him. "I don't want to cower whenever a threat comes by."

She picks up her second beer, and it's sharp and fruity, almost sour, and by instinct she offers him to taste.

Like nothing's ever changed.

"And if I can attack first, maybe they'll think twice before sending someone after me, maybe they'll let me live in peace," she continues, and he nods, tentative. "You know, set a few examples, disrupt their ways of thinking, that sort of thing."

There's a ghost of a smile across his face, something so close to how he used to look at her when she did something clever, when she had a smart turn of phrase while arguing.

She used to think he enjoyed her being smart and sharp.

"By all accounts, the other necromancer is peaceful." he says, and it's a bit amazing, getting another little hint of information. "I think that you going on the offense would be one of their worst fears."

"Good," Delina says, and can't help herself from being bitter. "They kept me from my mom, they tried to kill me, I should be their worst fear."

Another glimmer of a smile, before it fades.

"They shouldn't be able to hurt your mom, they shouldn't have been able to lock me away, they shouldn't have, you know, shot you. Killed you." The words flood from her as if she could ever stop them. "Maybe my mom should've still been blacklisted, she sounds awful, but...not me."

"I told them, once, about two years ago, that if you ever found out you'd be angry," he murmurs, almost too low for her to hear. "They dismissed me, said I was overreacting."

She sits up, towards him and he reacts in kind. "You were patient with me the entire time, you dated me when I was at my worst, and they thought you just overreacted?"

And he picks up another one of his beers, a dark beer so

almost black, and downs it in one go, before he leans close to her, intent. "Delina, you were not the difficult part of the job."

She lets her hand fall to the small glasses on the tray.

"The hard part was never you, it was the net of politics and things I had to do for my bosses, the awfulness of all the lies, and the ridiculousness of the people going after you. Never actually you."

Delina squashes down her first instinct to scoff, to deny it, and instead just stills herself. Makes herself listen.

"The times I could exist with just you, not have to deal with the fear over my mom, over the net of responsibilities and expectations, those were probably the only times I wasn't stressed out of my mind."

Delina cheers him with her next glass, out of a lack of anything else. "Glad I was the easiest part of the job."

He sighs, which she honestly anticipated at that. "You know what I meant."

She thinks she does, if she dares to hope instead of actually use her brain, but she just takes a drink instead.

"I couldn't ever just be a normal person," Maison says, sitting back. "My entire life I was always the kid Half Demon who couldn't do anything they wanted me to do. I was always the failed experiment, good for some things but not what they wanted at all. You were the first person who treated me like I could be interesting outside of that."

"Well, yeah," Delina says, and her heart pounds. "You were the hot guy in the apartment next door who painted pictures on the back of envelopes, of course that's interesting."

His eyes crinkle up at the edges. "They put me on assignment with you because I can do half decent shields and they said you didn't form friendships with the other people they tried. I applied for it because doing research on demons in France was boring, and maybe I would actually have free time to take some art classes."

Knowing that's the reason he applied for his specific job should be hurtful, should be painful, but instead, her lips tug up in a smile. "Of course you did."

When they had first started dating, back when she was finishing her degree, he had taken nightly classes in painting and sketching, and would bring them back to her to show.

"Of course, all I knew about the assignment was that you were getting threatened, I had—of course—known about your mother, heard they locked away any magic, and that's... it." He gives her a sheepish smile. "Nothing about your personality, what you wanted to do with your life, nothing. Nothing about your dad, nothing about anything you were trying to accomplish, nothing about how you were, you know, actually fun."

Dimly, she knows this should be slightly insulting, but still she just props up her chin on her hands, looking at him.

Maybe it's the week she's had, maybe it's the growing awareness that she can feel his heartbeat with merely a thought, maybe it's the fact that she brought him back from the actual dead, but the part of her that should be angry with him wanes.

But one bit wriggles under that shield.

"I talked to the Wight again," she starts, and Maison jolts upright, all traces of softness and fondness gone from his face. His eyes glint red for just a brief second, before returning to normal.

"When?" He asks, sharp. "When and what did she say?"

"Cool it, you're not on bodyguard duty right now," Delina says. "She couldn't get through the circle trap."

"I'm always on bodyguard duty," Maison replies automatically, then wrinkles his nose at her. "Of course not, Chloe does nothing subtly. What did she say?"

"One or two demons checked my flare in the parking lot. She said you would deter a weak one."

Maison absorbs that information like he would anything else, like she just informed him of dinner plans or a cancellation of a night out. "That's charitable of her."

"And," Delina pushes on, despite some instincts telling her she should cool it, she should back off, "said that because we were bonded, it would scare people away. What," she flicks her eyes to his, as if she could tell his honesty just by that, "did she mean by that?"

For a few long moments he remains still, before he pushes himself up. "Do you want another round?"

"You're avoiding the question," Delina says, crossing her arms. "Get me one of the first glass."

He nods, then whirls away, taking their empty flights back to the bar, leaning against it as the beer tender pours the glasses, before he turns towards her, still leaning against the bar but watching her.

His chin dips down, his gaze somewhere between terrified and emboldened, and she hasn't seen that expression in years, so she sits back, her heart pounding.

He looks like he'd consume her if she let him, and it scares him just as much as it should scare her.

It only lasts for a heartbeat or two, before the bartender passes him their beers, and he's back on his way as if nothing happened. As if the expression never occurred to him, as if they were a normal couple.

"First thing to know is I didn't know this would happen," he responds, handing her the glass, and she would bet anything that he spent the entire time mentally rehearsing.

"That's an auspicious start," Delina says, taking a sip. "I feel like my barrier for accepting information is far, far lower now. You could tell me any number of things and I don't know if I'd have a reaction besides 'sure.'"

She gets a flash of a dimple.

"Sometimes demons form bonds with people they have connections with," he says, which is about what she surmised. "Human research doesn't know if it's intentional or not. My...parent...told me it isn't." He takes a large drink from his beer and, besides herself, she notices that his hand is trembling. "I think I did that to you."

"You think?" Delina prods, and he gives her an honest-to-god dirty look, his fingers tight against his glass. "So what's the ramifications?"

There had to be ramifications. He wouldn't be this nervous without ramifications.

He runs a hand through his soft brown hair, sending it sticking in all directions. "To you, none."

"Again, auspicious," she says, and gets another almost smile. "Good to know, what are they?"

"You're not going to like this," he warns her.

"I'll be the judge of that," she says sharply. "In the last week or so I found out my mom was a magician, insane, and possibly a war criminal. I can raise people from the dead, someone tried to kill me, and my entire life was a lie. Spit it out."

"I can always find where you are," he starts, slower than she would like, but any answer is better than none. "It might take me a few days to pinpoint, but I can always tell what direction you're in."

"Good if I get kidnapped," Delina says.

"Yes, that's a plus, that's how I found the cabin, that's what I thought happened until I got there," Maison says, almost dismissive. "If I concentrate and I'm close, I can tell your general emotions. Happy, sad, pain, angry, that sort of thing. Like a minor feedback loop. Apparently, that's stronger in actual demons." Here he trails off, staring down at the raw concrete floor. "For actual demons, it's a...claim. Raising a flag in the sand. Warning of others to back off. So no other demon would get close."

Delina's heard enough about magic and about demons and about all the unfair rules of the world than to know better than to ask if it's breakable. Nothing in her world would be that simple, for him or for her.

The despair and embarrassment in his eyes tells that for her.

"Was this in your College's plan?" Delina asks, instead of poking at him, instead of any of the storm of emotion welling up inside of her. "Make you bond with me so you wouldn't complain about being stuck with me?"

He regards her, steady, and the light hits his hair just right, casting shadows across his face and highlighting his cheekbones. "If it was, they didn't tell me."

"Fair enough," Delina replies. "Is this something else I should apologize about?"

"No," he all but interrupts her. "Not at all."

"Just makes things a hell of a lot more complicated for you?" She ventures a guess, and he nods, something close to misery on his face. "Makes you feel shitty about me finding out and all? As if your mom wasn't enough of a motivation?"

He lifts one shoulder into a shrug, and there are a few other things buzzing in the back of her head, implications and struggles and commitments it entails.

"So when I called you my ex," Delina forges on, and he closes his eyes, like he's waiting for the ax to drop, "that's more complicated for you than it was for me."

He doesn't confirm it, but neither does he deny it, just taking a drink from his beer, and a smidgen of hurt worms into her.

So not only was the relationship fake, not only did he lie to her, not only was he set up to stay with her for forever, his drive to convince her to stay, the glimmers of affection she still saw in him, all of those were borne from some non-human instinct that she can't fully grasp.

And he was stuck with it.

"Wow, yeah, this is shitty," she says, drinking the fizzy beer perhaps a bit too fast than she should, and it almost burns down her throat. "You're right, I don't like this."

"Didn't think you would," he responds, surly. "That's why I didn't mention it."

"Okay no, stop that," Delina says, setting her glass down with a thunk. "Stop keeping things from me just because you think I won't like them, stop holding shit back. I don't care if you think I won't like it, I don't want to be left in the dark for the rest of my life about anything. I'm tired of that."

His lips thin, but he nods.

"Any other big bombshells? Any other bullshit that I should absolutely know about?" All fondness from the earlier conversation is erased, and she pulls herself as tall as she can while sitting on the cold metal stool. "So I can actually make informed decisions for once in my life?"

He just stares at her, a pillar of misery and frustration, his jaw tight, and drinks his beer.

ON THE DRIVE BACK, Maison flinches, then grabs Delina's hand resting on the shifter.

"What?" Delina asks, the knot sitting in her chest still prickly.

"Drive faster," he says, voice strangled, and when she risks a glance his eyes are red.

So she does, pressing down on the gas, speeding the ratty little sedan down the empty, misty highway.

Maison doesn't let go of her hand until they're over the demon trap, and Delina guides the car to a stop right on the other side of it, and he stares at her as she clumsily puts it back together, his eyes glittery.

"What was that?" Delina asks, after the circle clicks back into place with a finality she swears echoes in her bones.

Maison exhales, finally, and shakes out his hands, his jaw tight.

"That," he starts, and his voice cracks, just a bit, "was a blanket demon scan of the entire area."

Delina blinks at him. "Oh shit."

"Yeah," Maison replies, harshly. "Not good."

"Did they...did they find me?" Delina asks, and they're still standing in the mist, on the side of the road leading to the cabin.

"I don't..." he swallows, and she can see his throat bob. "I don't think so. I think I camouflaged you fast enough, I think."

Delina stares at him, and he's pallid in the mist, leaning against the ratty sedan.

"Okay," she says finally, now even more unsure of footing. "Thank you?"

He blanches.

"I mean, I'm alive, you're alive, job well done?"

"Please don't thank me for stuff like that," Maison replies, as if it pains him. "I really don't like that."

"Fine," Delina says, opening her car door again. "I take it

22

The next day, Chloe takes Delina out of the cabin, deeper into the woods until they come across the other side of the burned circle.

Maison didn't look at her after they returned from the brewery, and didn't crawl into her bed the next night, plunging Delina into even more confusion.

"Okay, masking a magical flare," Chloe says, tucking her hands into the pockets of her hoodie. "Every magic gives them in some way, different people can see them. A demon —or, you know, Freddy—could tell just with a glance based on the type of feedback they give off. Like a vibe."

Delina nods, and the sun is just starting to peek out from the morning mist. It's colder than the last few days, and each breath draws icy lines into her throat.

"So do you know anything about diffusers? For lights and cameras?"

"I thought flare was less literal than that," Delina says, trying real hard to keep the sarcasm from her voice.

"Yes, just like how magic isn't actually in threads, it just looks like it," Chloe replies, bouncing on her feet. "Be as literal or as figurative as works for you. I like literal, it helps me picture things."

Delina scuffs her toes right up to the mossy line, before everything is abruptly burned. "Maison's the one that pictures things, not me."

"And he's the one currently moping, so that's on him. If he wanted to come help, he'd be welcome."

That doesn't help, so Delina huffs out a breath, which puffs around her face. "Yeah, I'm halfway certain he's mad at me."

Chloe gives her a look, her brown eyes sharp. "Yes, of course, he's mad. That's what it is. Not scared out of his mind."

"I'm not scary," Delina says, and Chloe responds by rolling her eyes. "What? I'm not. I'm an accountant, I deal with spreadsheets."

"Necromancers are terrifying," Chloe shoots back. "Nobody understands them and you basically can hold someone's life in the palm of your hand. Countries would kill for that power to be under their control, rich men would hoard them, and demons are drawn to them. There's nothing that isn't scary."

"Cool," Delina says.

"It's one thing to think that the person you've been sleeping next to for years might be a spooky sort of magic, it's an entire other thing for her to put it to practice on your dead body." Chloe finally slings off her backpack from her shoulder. "If I were him, I'd be evaluating every little thing of my life after that."

In the cold air that hurts her nose, Delina can't bring herself to roll her eyes right back at that.

"He'll come around, or he'll get so annoyed by Gurlien pestering him for theory that he'd do anything to run away with you again," Chloe says. "Gurlien has my back, I have his, but good lord is he good at ignoring clues that the other person is bored out of their mind."

"Glad I'm not as bad as that," Delina says, then toes the border again. "So, diffuser."

"If drawing the magic to you is light, then think something blocking it, so they can't pinpoint it directly." Chloe switches courses easily, as if there's nothing else to it and she didn't just leave Delina with a sour taste in her mouth. Out of her backpack, she pulls out a thin sheet of plastic, then a tiny flashlight. "Flashlight by itself, thin beam, you know where it's coming from. Then this," she shakes the plastic sheet, and in the warble it turns from clear to almost opaque. "This happens."

She hides the flashlight behind the sheet and instead of a thin beam, the entire sheet of plastic lights up.

"There's still light," Delina points out, intrigued besides herself.

"Do a big enough diffuser, all they'd be able to figure is your general area. Think big enough to disguise mountain regions. It's possible, in theory."

"So what, right now you want me to raise something from the dead and then hide it?"

"God no, just imagining the plastic in your hands, that sort of thing." Chloe stores the now frosted plastic back in her backpack. "Think about the place your necromancy comes from, think about how it feels, just...don't touch a dead thing."

The dead bird is a good few minutes' walk away, which helps, so Delina settles her feet wider, then...thinks.

No place in the forest is truly devoid of something dead, not with the moss decaying under the thin layer of frost that glittered earlier that morning, not with bugs crawling and dying and leaves and fallen branches and browned grass.

There's new growth moldering over the dead bird, lessening the punch, but the knowledge that she could still bring it back sits beneath her spine.

The handprint on the back of Chloe's neck, hidden underneath the hoodie, still burns in the cold air.

"Should we get antibiotics on your neck? Did the skin break?" Delina asks. "It's inflamed, whatever it is."

Chloe just blinks at her. "No?"

"It hurts, still."

"Well, yeah, Korhonen is real good at damaging people, that's his shtick," Chloe replies, almost dismissive. "I'll scar but I'll be okay."

"Dude," Delina says.

Chloe shrugs. "They did worse to me in the Toronto base," she says, as if attempting to dismiss it. "That's where I broke out, and their defenses...let me tell you." As if Delina needs the proof, she hikes up her jacket and shirt in the chilled air, revealing a mess of scars across her ribcage. "I barely managed to stop the mechanism that did this before it shredded me, left all my research behind, a little burn of a hand isn't gonna take me down."

Delina resists the overwhelming want to poke at the scars, to test to see how deep they are, if they still hurt, but Chloe tucks her shirt back into place. "This is starting to sound more war criminal-y than I'm comfortable with."

Chloe gives her finger-guns. "You're not wrong! There's a reason I left, and people like him are a big part of it. Concentrate, diffuser."

Delina rolls her eyes again, then, feeling more than a little bit foolish, tries to imagine that sheet of plastic.

It does nothing, but the plastic front door to the cabin slams open, and Chloe gives Delina a wicked smile.

"See, told you he'd find you more interesting."

Sure enough, Maison's striding towards them, hunching in under his coat, a scowl across his face.

"I'm just practicing her concentration," Chloe says merrily, before he even has anything to say. "Just some visualization work, nothing risky."

Maison doesn't even spare Delina a glance. "I felt it."

"You're also only a few feet away, you're attuned to everything she does, and you're paranoid," Chloe says, then shoots Delina a merry smile. "Try it again, see what Freddy sees."

"Stop calling me that," he mumbles.

"Well, if you're going to be out here, you can be helpful." Chloe gestures for Delina to continue, as if the entire outside didn't get insanely more awkward. "Remember, plastic sheet."

Maison crosses his arms. "Visualization's not going to help her, she's not an alchemist."

"Then any ideas?" Delina asks, her voice sharper than she really wanted, and the flicker of hurt flashes over Maison's face, familiar, before it smoothes over into his confident mask.

It's the same mask he put on when he first met her dad, and she doesn't buy it one bit.

"Don't think about a plastic sheet, try to spot where the threads of magic flicker through the property," he says, gruff, and the tips of his ears are cold, turning red and derailing her train of thought for a few moments. "Like this."

Without her even thinking too hard, the strip of gold is in his hands once more, tugging from between the trees.

Chloe throws up her hands. "Or yes, do advanced demonology, that's practical advice, thank you, Freddy."

He ignores her, before gesturing for Delina's hand and

dumping the strip of magic on her palm.

Her heart jolts, almost unpleasant, like she grabbed a live wire, but nothing else happens.

"There's a reason demons want necromancers," Maison says, still barely looking at Delina, despite the strip of magic coiling in the palm of her hand, shockingly warm. "Using natural defensive tactics is much smarter than trying to force her concentration into a box."

"She's not always going to have you around to drop it in her hand," Chloe argues, which is a very good point. "Don't make her dependent on your protection."

"Delly, draw the magic between your fingers like it's an accordion and it can expand," Maison instructs, also choosing to ignore the valid points. "Like that paper art your dad uses to decorate for Christmas."

Unfortunately, Delina completely understands that reference, and she sighs. "That's just a different sort of visualization," she says, then pokes at the magic with a finger.

A spark snaps between her finger and the chord, but a quick glance at Maison doesn't show any additional worry, so she shrugs it off, picking it up gingerly, testing to see if it can spread apart.

It does, a crackling, warping net, and she shudders.

"I mean, that might work," Chloe replies, tilting her head sideways to look at it, her eyes crossing slightly. "Looks more like a basic shield than anything else."

When she lifts her gaze to him, Maison's eyes glow red. "On a bigger level, it would confuse the hell out of a demon if she does it properly."

"Okay, I'll practice," Delina grinds out, and despite the chill of the air, her hands grow hot, like she laid out in the direct sun.

He scowls at her, and she lets the magic go with a snap.

He flinches at the abrupt motion. "Don't do that," he says, then hesitates, obviously torn, before the confident expression filters over him again. "Maybe do that if there's a demon in your face about to kill you. It's disorienting."

"Oooh, really?" Chloe asks, eager, and Delina reaches for the strip of magic again, her hand falling harmlessly through it. "How disorienting?"

"You know those flash bangs Gurlien used to do to startle people before doing a diagnostic? Like that." Maison shakes out his hands, grabs the strip again for Delina. "Except not physical."

"Ew," Chloe replies helpfully.

"Flash bang the demon, got it," Delina says, pulling the magic into the same net shape as before, though her fingertips crackle with sparks.

"Might give you a chance to run," Maison says, and briefly, ever so briefly, he meets her eyes. "Snap it large enough so they can't see you through their magic and most demons don't pay that much attention to the physical appearance."

Delina swallows, at the harsh reminder of the fate that could possibly befall her with a face to face with an actual demon, before she spreads the magic a bit further, until her hands are wider than her body.

Sparks swirl around her hand, nestling into her skin, and Chloe's breath hitches.

"Is that okay?" Chloe asks, her voice hushed. "That doesn't seem good."

"That's only not good if she's a spell weaver, don't worry," Maison replies, his eyes glowing as he evaluates her, before he obviously widens his stance, bracing himself. "Okay, let it go."

Delina raises an eyebrow, then, discomfort fitting inside

her, snaps it.

There's a brief moment of surprise, of Maison's eyes widening and the golden power reflected in them, before he tumbles to the ground with a small 'oof.'

Chloe stands there, completely unaffected, a puzzled look on her face.

"You okay?" Delina asks, as he awkwardly climbs back up, damp moss all on his pant legs. He's not in any pain, not that she can tell with a brief scan.

"Yeah, definitely do that if you come face to face with a demon," Maison grumbles, brushing himself off. "Not sure if it affected me more because I'm less powerful, or if it affected me less because I'm only half."

It bothers her a little, when he calls himself half, but she tosses it behind her. "Should we go in the basement where we can set up that padding?"

"I don't need padding," Maison shoots back, "don't knock me into a tree and I'm good."

She narrows her eyes at him, and he lifts his chin.

If he's getting competitive with it, so can she.

She reaches for the strip of magic again, and this time there's a little bit of resistance before her hand falls through it once more.

"Freddy..." Chloe trails off, at something in his face, before she throws up her arms once more. "This doesn't do anything except still make it so she has to run."

"But she has time to run now," Maison says, but he doesn't take his eyes off of Delina, as she tries to grab the magic again. "Stop thinking of it as something you pick up, that won't work."

"Thanks," Delina responds. "That's helpful."

"Think of it as a current in a stream, and you're grabbing some pine needles that are riding along the current,"

Maison says, and his gaze feels like fire against her, deep in her stomach.

He looked at her like this when he wanted to fuck her.

She swallows again, and tangles her fingertips against the strip, and his eyes flicker down to her lips before coming back to her eyes.

That one-minute motion is a spotlight to his wants.

It's strange that he would still look at her like that, now. That he would put on that face when he doesn't have to, look at her like he still is very much attuned to her body.

Her mouth goes dry.

"Delina?" Chloe asks, startling her so much that she almost drops her tenuous touch on the magic. "Everything okay?"

"Yeah," she replies quickly, twisting the magic in her hand as fast as she can, then spreading it apart and snapping it together.

Maison reels back, stumbling but not falling, before he regains his footing. "That wasn't as powerful that time, do it again."

His words are back to clinical, like whatever moment never happened.

23

"Hey, just found a locked bunker about twenty miles away through some satellite pics, wanna come?" Chloe asks the next day, when everyone is otherwise peacefully sitting around.

Maison and Delina briefly lock eyes.

"What do you think you'd find?" Maison asks, crossing his arms. "We're in upstate Washington, you're not going to find riches and treasures in a bunker."

"Maybe guns, though," Chloe responds. "Usually, the abandoned bunkers up here have guns. Sometimes expired food."

"How do you know it's abandoned?" Delina asks, curiosity getting the better of her. "And isn't that...insanely illegal?"

Chloe shrugs at that. "Near as I can tell, nobody has gone in or out in around seven years, that counts as abandoned to me. One time, we found a bunch of hundred-dollar bills and a skeleton."

Outside of her control, Delina cocks her head.

"No," Maison replies, cutting her off, which just pushes her into motion.

"Want to make sure you're not going to run into any skeletons before you get to the front door?" Delina asks, and Chloe answers with a grin.

THEY DROVE AS FAR as they could in Chloe's car, and had to hike in the last mile, and Gurlien complains the entire time.

"I didn't move out to the middle of nowhere for hiking," he says, as they tromp through the underbrush. His face is still mottled and bruised, the color mostly faded between a sickly purple and yellowish tone, but it doesn't hurt him much according to Delina's brief scans.

Maison, at least, doesn't complain, just watches the forest around them with a sharp eye.

"How many of these have you found since coming here?" Delina asks. The air is cool against her cheeks and the remnants of frost glitter on the forest floor, but blue sky peeks between the branches of the spruce trees.

"Not nearly as many as I'd like," Chloe replies cheerfully. "Probably eight or so, this is the closest, though."

"It's a miracle you haven't been caught," Maison grumbles.

"That's why I pick the abandoned ones," Chloe says, turning and hiking backwards while talking to him. "More likely to be old, more likely to not be discovered as broken into. And I don't steal much."

"Much," Gurlien deadpans. "It's where we got our gun."

After a few moments of quiet, a phone beeps in Gurlien's pocket.

"Oh hey, signal," Chloe says brightly.

"It's just Luis the scholar," Gurlien says, screwing up his face. "Yep, the College is searching for us, reached out to 'known associates.'"

Maison breathes in, deep, as if trying to keep himself calm.

"Looking for me, Chloe, a 'tall blonde woman with uncontrollable powers,' and maybe Frederick," Gurlien continues. "Hey, you're uncontrollable."

"Thanks," Delina says, and a scowl settles over Maison's face. "So they're unsure if you're alive."

"Apparently," Maison replies skeptically.

"You should dye your hair," Chloe suggests, and Delina isn't sure if that's the worst thing she's heard or not. "That'll throw them off. I cut mine when I left, they all knew me with super long hair."

"Well, that'll restrict our ability to get help," Gurlien says, sticking his phone back in his pocket. "Luis says he's gonna go dark for a bit."

A bit away, probably a few meters deeper into the forest, a brief strike of terror grabs at Delina, then a death punches through her stomach, filling her lungs, striking her across the chest.

She reels back, shoulder thumping against Maison's chest before she regains her footing.

"What was that," he asks, abruptly, a hand gripping her elbow.

Delina blinks, then breathes out hard through her nose, resisting the urge to double over.

They're all looking at her.

"Uh," she says, at a loss for words, at loss for how to describe what just happened. "Um, something...died. Over there."

Even as she points, the picture firms up in her mind. A

small mammal, a chipmunk or something, struck by a bird of prey, rapidly moving through the air until the distance grows, lessening the punch.

Though her eyes still water.

"Jeez," Gurlien mutters. "Talk about passive perception."

"Were you actively scanning?" Chloe asks curious, as Delina shakes her head. "You could just...tell?"

"Apparently," Delina replies, and she can feel the beat of the wings of the bird flying away in her heart. "Small animal got grabbed by a hawk, I think. Died really quick."

"Could you tell," Gurlien asks Maison, "when she could? Any flares?"

"No flares," Maison responds, and his hand is tight on her elbow, comforting. "Was about as bright as a normal scan, just all of the sudden."

She twists to look at him, and his eyes glow red.

"You okay?" he asks, voice quiet, like it's just for her.

She nods, swallowing, making sure she's steady. "Just...startling."

His jaw clenches, but he nods back, releasing her elbow. "Tell me if you need anything."

It's a strange thing to offer after the last few days, but she just breathes out of her nose again, hard, as if that could get the stink of it out of her system.

THE REST of the walk is easy by comparison, but the lingering death sticks in the back of her mind like a loose tooth, and the hush hangs over the group as they approach the bunker.

It's nothing more than a door nestled into the side of a

hill, abrupt in the woods, no pathway leading towards it or away.

"Oh, it's a boring one," Gurlien says, even as Chloe bounces on her toes as she inspects it. "There's not even any booby traps."

"There doesn't have to be booby traps for it to be exciting," Chloe replies, barely paying him attention. "There's three locking mechanisms alone!"

Delina and Maison glance at each other, and he shrugs.

"You grew up with these people," she says.

"Don't put this on me, they were weird before I met them," Maison says, and they share a brief, ridiculous smile.

"Statistically, you are far weirder than either of us," Gurlien informs him, watching as Chloe wanders over to the door, tracing her finger along the seams. "There are probably hundreds of alchemists, maybe two thousand spell weavers, and what, nine Half Demons? Ten?"

"Depends if you count the hybrid attempts like Terese," Maison says, but genial, like they're actually friends. "Then there's much more."

"I definitely don't count them, only what, two or three of those survived? Including Terese?" Gurlien shrugs, too casual. "And now there's a grand total of two necromancers alive and in existence, so both of you are the weirdos."

Maison turns to look at him, his eyes narrowed in just the way they do when he's about to get very, very competitive, and Delina raises an eyebrow. Competitive Maison is rare, but usually fun. "Only two former magicians who have lost their magic."

"I guess," Gurlien replies, with a twist of his face. "That's unfair, I wasn't born like that, you were." Then he smiles, actually smiles, like this strange conversation is actually fun.

"You've actually died and come back. That's exceedingly weird."

Delina coughs out a laugh at the put-out expression on Maison's face.

"You're in league with two or three other undead people, plus a cat, apparently." Gurlien grins, bouncing on his feet. "How does it feel to be in the same category as a cat? A cat that I've heard is stupid?"

"Is this how you two talked all the time?" Delina asks, a bit amazed, and they both ignore her.

"You're the one who irons his dress pants before going on a hike," Maison shoots back. "You can actually control that one, that's far worse."

"Just because I have class—" Gurlien starts, but Delina laughs at that out loud, "— doesn't mean I'm weird."

"You're the one who was camped in an abandoned cabin," Delina chimes in, and Gurlien wrinkles his nose at her. "And you keep a gun on a side table next to a couch."

"You dropped your entire life because of an insane letter from your mother," Gurlien points out, which is fair. "For all you knew, the cabin might not've even existed."

"Yes yes, you're all strange," Chloe calls out, where she's pressing her fingertips against the metal of the door. "Wanna help me with the locking pins?"

All three of them look at each other.

"I always help," Gurlien says, as if that could get him out of it.

"I wouldn't know what to do," Delina says, but tromps over to join Chloe by the door, and Maison watches her like a hawk, all traces of fun and friendship immediately gone from his face.

She misses it. He's never one to make friends easily.

Chloe hands her an honest-to-god lockpick. "I'm gonna

transform this into a four-pin lock, so you can hold it open once I do. You know how to use this?"

"Definitely not," Delina responds, but Chloe's already turned back to the door.

The air shimmers around the lock, and...absolutely nothing happens, but a satisfied smile still sits on Chloe's face. "Here," she says, grabbing the lockpick back and jimmying it into the lock with a click, then holds it at an angle. "Hold here."

Delina does, and Chloe immediately starts poking the lock underneath it.

"This way, it's easier to transform them back, so if someone does come back, they won't know I've been here," Chloe says with a grin, her eyes alight. "That way, any alarms don't sound as easily."

"Is that how you broke out of Toronto?" Delina asks.

"You broke out of Toronto?" Maison interrupts, stalking closer. "How?"

Chloe gestures towards the door, one handed, "Exactly like this."

Maison crosses his arms over his chest.

"Look, it's their fault for training me to be a tomb breaker, then put me in a magical locked tomb," Chloe replies, but she's still smiling, like doing this is the best thing ever. Like she's the most alive by prodding this old, dusty door.

"Nobody's done that," Maison says, his eyes narrowed.

"Nobody they told you about," Chloe shoots back. "They don't exactly advertise." She digs her shoulder against the door, and another lock clicks, swinging the door open to reveal a grand locking mechanism, like a bank safe, and she rubs her hands together. "Thanks, Delina, that's exactly what I needed."

"I literally did nothing," Delina replies, but still deposits the lock pick into Chloe's outstretched hand.

"Welcome to my life," Gurlien says, but he too looks excited. "Any dead in there? What, I want to know now instead of when you get it open."

Delina blinks at him, then looks towards the dusty safe lock, and lets herself think.

The thick metal of the door blocks out most, but beyond a few faint stirrings of dead bugs —died of hunger, the pains still echoing through their husks—nothing.

"Bugs, I think," Delina replies, even though she's pretty damn certain of that. Better to couch it in maybes to not disappoint.

Maison side eyes her at that, like he can tell, even though his eyes are their normal grey.

"Oh those are fine," Chloe replies, then tugs on the lock wheel, giving it a preliminary spin and listening.

"How did you avoid the locking pits," Maison asks, and it takes Delina a second to realize this is still about Toronto. "Those are specifically to thwart lock breakers."

Chloe glances at him, but it's clear she's only half paying attention. "I'm smaller than everyone they designed it for," she replies idly. "I broke into the wall instead and walked sideways through it."

Maison stares down at her, then over at Gurlien. "You two are definitely weirder."

With another toothy grin, Chloe jerks the wheel of the lock again. It crunches, before the door creaks open, slow.

A quick glance at the lock shows that it's still intact, but instead of metal bolts, they're made of clay, soft and moldable.

"That was faster than the last three lock bunker,"

Gurlien says, checking an honest-to-god pocket watch. "You're getting better."

"Thanks!" Chloe replies sunnily, then pokes at the soft clay of the bolts. "Tried the bolt change instead of the socket. I think it'll work on everything but electric."

Maison raises an eyebrow. "You've been timing her?"

"Of course, I got to practice somehow, don't want to lose my touch," Chloe replies, then shoulders the door open further, pulling a flashlight out of the backpack.

A single lightbulb, long ago cracked, hangs at the top of the low ceiling, and everything else is coated with grime. The air is still, unmoving, and specks of dust hang in the beam of the light.

"Oh, it wasn't even properly sealed," Gurlien scoffs. "Too much dust."

"Why don't you buy a bunch of locked boxes on eBay or something?" Delina asks, drifting towards the shelving. A bunch of ammo boxes with their hinges rusted sit, cobwebs in between.

"That's not a real challenge," Chloe says, nudging a cracked plastic barrel with the toe of her boot. "This guy sucked at setting up a bunker, damn. The good ones are fully sealed, no decay or anything."

It's so fully surreal that Delina glances up again at Maison, who's frowning thoughtfully at the single room, poking through the shelving. The ceilings so low he hunches, just a bit, and his neck aches.

"Remembered to pack nudie mags," he says, holding up a Playboy magazine from easily the mid-nineties. "Classy."

"Any of that ammo nine mil?" Gurlien asks, and Maison shakes his head. "Damn, that's getting expensive."

"That's because you're bad at shooting. Have you ever

actually hit anything?" Delina asks, and he gives her a thin-lipped glare. "Seriously, you're bad at it."

"Right, you lived in Arizona, you'd have opinions on that," Gurlien replies. "Though that would probably be incredibly distracting if you ever actually killed someone. Frederick, can Necromancers kill anyone?"

"Don't call me that," Maison replies automatically. "But yeah, they should be able to. What they can give..."

"They can take away," both Chloe and Gurlien chorus, then Gurlien makes a face. "Oh that's dark for Necromancers."

"Thanks," Delina chimes in. "What would that mean for Chloe?"

"Oh, I just reverse the changes, it's super simple," Chloe responds. "It's a top tier alchemist trick, like day one."

"Probably day five," Gurlien corrects.

Chloe shrugs, piecing through the dusty shelves, giving Delina the big impression that she didn't exactly care what was in the bunker, just that the door was locked. "Oh, hey, a birth certificate, that'll be useful."

"What?"

Chloe flashes it at Delina. "Official documents are much easier to change from other official documents, so if we need a new identity this'll help." She pauses, her brain skipping. "Did your mom leave you any new identities?"

"Oh my god," Delina says, as deadpanned as she can, crossing her arms. "How would I know?"

"Probably," Maison mutters. "What, she had like five."

"There are safes in most of the properties she left you, there's a high chance there are a few new identities somewhere in there," Gurlien replies. "She did too much to ensure you had some safe places to exist, there are almost certainly things we don't know."

It's officially too much for Delina, once more, so with a nod to Maison she turns on her heels and walks back into the muted sunshine of the forest.

The breeze hits her face, cool and welcoming, and Delina sits her ass down on a log, wrapping her arms around herself.

She's going to have to deal with everything from her mother sooner or later. Every technicality, every location, every house she doesn't need and every bit of magical lore and research to be found within.

After all this drama, it's still going to exist, and she'll have to deal with it.

It's way more daunting than it should be.

The hinges of the door creak, and Maison follows her out, squinting in the sunlight.

She waves at him that she's okay, but he steps out anyways, sheltering his eyes.

"You alright?" he asks, and no she's not, but she shrugs. He rolls his eyes, then sits on a rock across from her. "You're still a shitty liar."

"I didn't even say anything," she protests.

"Yeah, you didn't need to," Maison says, rubbing his scruff. In a few days it'll be a proper beard, and she's not sure how she feels about that.

"Is it always like that?" Delina asks, gesturing towards the bunker at his blank face. "Magicians breaking into things, all that weirdness, inherited properties?"

"God no," Maison says, stretching his legs in front of him, briefly distracting Delina from the conversation. "Well, magicians all have really flexible morality, that's true, but most are more like normal people with just weird jobs."

"Oh, I just got lucky," Delina says, and he wrinkles his nose at her. "Great."

"Well, at least you're wealthy now," he says, then makes a face. "I mean, that came out wrong. At least you don't have to work anymore?"

She doesn't know what she'd do with herself without work, but she shrugs again. "It's weird," she starts, slow among the birdsong and the still glittering frost, "to think about what it's going to be after I figure this out."

His eyes linger on her a bit too long,

24

After that, Delina gets complacent.

Oh, sure, everything she does still has the edge of lurking danger at the back end of it, but even that becomes a bit normal.

Expected.

There's no new sign of the College, nothing to indicate to them that they're at all looking for them. No new demon threats, no new dangers in the world around them, and even the dead bird outside of the cabin lessens over time.

Instead, Delina gets to relax. Let her shoulders come down a bit, lean more into the thought work of the magic, into the practices and information. Chloe works with her on basics of defense, Gurlien grills her on histories and theories, and Delina gets a more comfortable grasp of how her mind works with the added sense of...all the dead.

She and Maison skirt around each other, caught between the awkwardness of the reveal of the bond and the itch inside her chest to make sure that the patchwork healing stays true. He paints a lot, and the small carved table is more often filled with drying scraps of paper than not.

Sometimes, it's hard to even think about him.

But they fall into a rhythm, just like Delina does with everything in her life. Of careful emotional distance, of not talking about their past. Of moments of connection and smiles that sear through her and immediately remind her of what they had, leaving a bitter taste in her mouth. Of him watching her like a hawk whenever she does anything with her magic, and of her pretending to not notice.

So when she has the chance to drive alone, actually alone, all the way back to deal with the rental car, she does.

It's a peaceful drive over the frost encrusted mountains and into the farmland below, much better in sunshine than the midst of the night. Where instead of the anxiety of her mother's letter, she has something actually approaching knowledge of herself.

She secures the rental car at the sketchy location for another month, figuring after that she'll be in a stable enough place to figure out buying a car. Or, somehow, getting back down to Arizona and driving her beloved car back up.

She can't imagine Maison liking that one at all.

On her way back, the Wight stands on the side of the road, just outside the trap, and Delina stops the car again.

"Yeah?" she asks, when the short woman does nothing but stare at her for a few seconds.

"People were looking for you," she replies, finally. "On the other side of my territory, off the mountain and into the woods."

Delina swallows. "Thank you."

"I don't want them there," she continues, with a critical eyebrow raised. "Ask your friend with the glasses how to throw them off the trail."

And with that, she disappears.

"Both of them wear glasses," Delina mumbles, getting back in her car.

PREDICTABLY, nobody likes that piece of information and Gurlien and Chloe immediately set out in the car to reach out to a contact, leaving Delina with an exceptionally antsy Maison.

"You can paint," Delina points out, after he paces by the window for the third time.

"Or I can put an additional level of protection around the demon circle and make it even harder to find the place," Maison says, bouncing on his toes.

Delina eyes him.

"Put some sort of befuddling spell on the road, so unless someone knows how to get here, they won't remember why they're coming here, or some sort of alarm so we know when cars are on their way or people walk over it," Maison continues, twitching the floral curtains. "You can go hide in the basement, it'll be safer."

She shuts the overlarge textbook with a snap. "I'm not hiding in the basement."

"It'd be smart," Maison argues, and she stands, sticking her chin up. "Make sure anyone looking would miss you."

"How long have you known me, Maison?" Delina asks, dipping her voice down low, and he blanches. "Have I ever come across as a person who wants to hide?"

"No, but it'd be for your safety," he says, but she can see in his face he knows it's a losing battle. "There's a chance they'd be on the lookout for my brand of magic and come running."

"No," Delina says, squaring her shoulders at him.

He crosses his arms.

"You can take it as an opportunity to train me," Delina points out. "I'm not some helpless person with no idea of this magic anymore, make the time useful."

"It'll be boring and difficult for you to do," Maison protests, but he's reaching for his jacket again.

"I don't care," Delina declares, grabbing her own sweater.

THEY WALK along the long gravel road, and the mist is so thick she can barely see the trees that line both sides, until they come to the burned in line of the demon circle.

"You don't know the runes yet," Maison says, and it's the first words he's spoken to her the entire walk yet. "And Necromancy isn't the best at that anyways."

"Still don't care," Delina replies, churlish.

A ghost of a dimple appears on Maison's chin, before he shakes his head. "When doing this, you'll need spray paint. I don't, but watch."

He reaches over to her and taps her arm, and the world blooms in gold.

Just like it did when Maison was killed.

Swallowing hard on that memory, Delina nods.

With the gold in her vision, the demon circle blazes in a brutal crimson, the air wavering with the heat of it.

"Do you always see the world like this?" Delina asks, once she gets her voice back.

He eyes her sidelong. "Mostly."

"So why'd you step into the demon circle on the porch?" Delina asks, hugging herself against the chill of the mist, even though she can swear she feels the heat from the circle. "You had to have known."

"The entire house was one large beacon of bullshit," Maison grumbles, looking out at the demon circle. "Your mother was a lot better and more subtle than Chloe will ever be, so it was hidden among general protections."

It makes some sort of sense.

"And I was a bit more focused on getting you out," Maison continues, nudging some gravel with his feet as if testing it. "I thought you were kidnapped, I thought they might be hurting you. Remember the bond thing?"

Like she could forget.

"I could just tell you were upset the entire time. I thought I would be able to come in guns blazing and get you out and then deal with anything afterwards." He sweeps his feet across the gravel, clearing a small pathway to the dirt underneath. "I miscalculated."

Delina snorts. "That's an understatement."

"Thanks," he snips back. "All I knew is that you disappeared, your dad didn't know where you were, you were upset, and I rolled up to the house and it's covering in intense magic."

"My dad knew," Delina replies, and he narrows his eyes. "Of course I went to him first. He told me everything."

"Of course," Maison mutters, then clears his throat. "He's a lot better at lying than I gave him credit for, then."

"He had kept something for my entire life for me to test when I asked him about it," Delina says, not quite sure why she's still needling him. "A pager, of all things. Touched it with my thumb and it shattered."

He blinks at her, then back down to the road. "At least I wasn't the only one who miscalculated," he says, "the documentation on him was that he hated all things magic because of what it did to you."

"No, he was fine," Delina replies, then gestures broadly at the cut of dirt he's revealed. "What are you going to do?"

He watches her for a long second, before his eyes flash red, and before she even has time to think, both of his fists are full of magic.

Delina flinches back, it's too close to Korhonen and his attacks.

Maison's face softens, like he can read her mind. "I'm not gonna hurt you." His voice is gentle, and it's suddenly like they're back in the condo in Prescott and he's talking her through a depression spike. "I will never intentionally hurt you."

"I know that," Delina says, then swallows.

"I'm going to use this to cut into the ground," he says, his eyes still unreal, and the hair on the back of her arms raises. "Then carve in the runes. Here."

Just like before, he dumps some of the magic into her hands, and a jolt goes up to her shoulder.

"Do this," he says, pulling the remaining magic in his hands between them, until they stretch like a dough.

She imitates his motions, and her fingers tingle.

"Don't aim this at someone or something you don't want to hurt," he warns her, and she nods, before he snaps the stretched-out magic into the dirt in front of him.

Gravel sprays up, and a vivid red line stains the ground, precise.

He gestures her over, a hand clinically on her hip,

arranging how she's standing, and her breath sticks in her throat.

"Here," he says, then, gently, stands behind her, a hand on each of her wrists, guiding her into the motion, solid against her back.

She leans against him for a split second, cozy and comfortable, until she realizes what she's doing and straightens.

He clears his throat, then spreads her arms a bit wider. "When I snap your arms down, release the magic, just like you did before with the threads, but this time try to place it in a straight line."

"That's it?" Delina asks, and he's warm against her, her heart pounding.

"No, I'll activate them after, that's the complicated part of this," he says. "It'd take a bunch more training before you can do that part. Ready?"

Delina swallows again. "Sure."

Like the one time he tried to teach her to paint, he guides her arms down, fast, and she lets the magic slip out of her fingertips with the motion.

It sends another jolt through her, and he hisses, as if he could feel it too, before he releases her and steps back.

A thin line of red glows on the dirt, much wavier and less precise than Maison's.

"Oh hey, I did it," Delina says before she can think of something more clever. "Look."

"Does all magic feel like that to you?" Maison asks instead, shaking out his hands as she nods. "Jesus Christ."

"What now?"

He stares at her for a few seconds, then shakes his head, as if clearing his mind. "They should have never sealed you away."

She bites the inside of her cheek to stop her retort.

"Literally they could've just kept you away from Frisse and actually train you," Maison starts, his face twisting in frustration, "and they'd have a powerful necromancer at their use and you'd have a grasp of these things."

"Well, they didn't," Delina says, smarting a bit.

"No," Maison almost cuts her off, "this is not on you, this is on them."

She eyes him, then down at the cut of red in the ground.

"They did the most convoluted system of keeping you ignorant, they arranged your entire life, when literally all they had to do was train you. That's it. It would have been the easiest thing, you would have grown up knowing about yourself and your power, and we could have met without secrets." He turns his eyes down to the red mark she left. "Instead, we have...this."

"What, so you could've met me while in the college and wouldn't have had all the pesky betrayal to worry about?" Delina asks, and he straightens, folding his arms over his chest.

It might've been a bit of a cheap shot.

"Are you asking if it would make my life easier? Cause that answer is yes," he says, voice clinical, and she hates it. "Yes, then I wouldn't have had to lie all those years and we could've actually been honest with each other. Yes, then they wouldn't have used my mom to literally make me afraid of my own relationship failing, and that would have been easier."

Delina shrugs into herself. "I'm still having trouble getting over it."

It's honest, too honest, and her face twists the moment the words are out of her mouth.

He stares at her over the vivid red lines in the ground,

his mouth unhappy, before he squeezes his eyes shut. "How can I fix it?"

It's such a stark question.

"I want to fix it, how can I fix it?" He stalks closer to her, over the red lines in the ground, and the hair on the back of her neck raises. His voice dips low. "Tell me there's a way to fix this."

Her mouth goes dry, and she stares up at him.

"Because I will," he continues. "I swear I will."

"I don't know," she breathes, and her heart pounds, every part of her body suddenly aware of him, of how close he is.

They had always had chemistry, and she can't forget that.

"I don't know," she says, clearer this time, lifting her chin, attempting to project some sort of control in the situation, even though her hands tremble. "Maybe start by actually teaching me what to do with this?" She slashes her hand towards the red mark in the gravel.

He leans back, and she's not sure if it's disappointment or relief in his eyes.

"Will you be able to use this with the defenses?" Delina asks, after a long silence in the mist.

"Yes, Delly, yes I can," he says, still frustrated. "This is something that way more advanced people have cast far worse, and you managed something like this with your first try."

She nods at that, unsure what to do. "So when you expected me to be useless in this, you didn't expect this?"

Finally, there's a hint of a smile, just a hint, beyond the frustration. "Serves me right for underestimating you," he replies, then shakes his hands out again. "Training you is gonna be intense."

She likes that he's talking about that, despite all the strangeness. "I'll have to knock you on your ass in the forest some more."

He bares his teeth at her in a grin, surprising her, before the expression fades into something more clinical. "The next part is demon magic, not human. Watch."

She nods once more, stepping back.

He eyes where she stands, then, in between one blink and the next, twists the magic in his hands over the red marks on the ground.

Power surges up from the marks, engulfing his hands, and her breath catches in her throat as he deftly, somehow, writes with it in the very air, red and black shimmering in the mist. It coalesces, solid, a warping smoky wall of magic, impenetrable to anything she can see.

All in all it takes only a few seconds, but the power reflects in his eyes and, for a split second, her heart jumps.

This is the Maison her mother called vastly powerful.

Until he smiles at her, releasing the magic in his hands, and abruptly she stops seeing the shining gold, and there's nothing in the air. Nothing but the uninterrupted mist and the chill.

"Alright," Delina says, unnerved.

"Anyone who doesn't know exactly where the cabin is will cross this line, get confused and turn around," Maison says, dusting off his hands and examining his now-invisible handiwork. "Unless they're specifically on the lookout for this, it'll work, and this is an obscure one."

She swallows down the sudden adrenaline in her system. "Okay."

25

The next day dawns full of frost, sparkling in the weak morning sunshine, and Delina throws on the magicked jacket once more and tromps outside, her chipped mug of coffee warming her hands.

Sure, they got frost in Prescott, but not like this. Not where every surface glitters with crystals, where every spruce needle catches the light, and the dead bird is...less.

She's not sure if it's because she's getting better or if more time has passed, more bugs crawling, and the hint of moss somewhere along the bones.

Even still, she finds herself wandering over to it and staring down at the small carcass anyways.

It's...just a bird. There's the puncture wound, with white bone exposed and shimmering with frost. The black feathers shine, and the eyes are beady and frosted over.

Some bug has been eating at the torn flesh around the wound.

Delina crouches next to it, not touching, but picks up a stick to prod it.

Cold still echoes through it, cold and the last remnant of

terror, but less of the gut punch than it was before. There's something...there...though, and it itches at the back of Delina's mind, next to the certainty that she could make it fly again.

The ethics of being able to bring something back from the dead are mind boggling, and for a few moments it weighs against her, crouched there in the early morning frost. That somehow with her mother's letter, she became some sort of wretched arbitrator of life and death. That whoever around her could possibly be raised, based just on her whims.

She wanted to be powerful, but not quite like this.

Carefully setting the stick aside, Delina backs up, until she can sit on a wood stump and still stare at it.

Of course, bringing back this bird would be a bad idea. Would still signal to the demons in the area, and even though they couldn't get through the trap without Chloe, they could still wait.

But there's something in her own bones that tells her there is something else she could do with it.

"I wish I could fix this," she whispers to the dead bird in the still chilly air, but of course there's no response.

Someone to sort out what she's feeling, what she's sensing, and what she could actually do.

Of course, she could go and wake up Maison, but that too sounds like a bad idea. When he's been so uneasy sleeping, to disrupt feels a bit too cruel.

So instead she stands, breathes out, and tries to reach for the ribbon of magic that she knows flows through the area. It takes three tries of squinting through the frosted trees, before she glimpses it, knotted around some bushes. It's golden, still, and the entire world sheens with that same gold when she looks at it like that, but no matter how hard she tries, the magic won't fall into her hand like it did with Maison.

Sure, her fingers tingle each time she passes her hand through it, but it's still tantalizingly far away from her grip.

From the stories Gurlien has told, the other Necromancer is able to do all sorts of things. Use someone's death to bind a demon, control a demon, blast through their defenses.

And she's the peaceful one.

With the anger in her heart, right below the hurt and the indignantly of all of this being kept from her, Delina doesn't want to be peaceful.

Not when she can still feel the slump of Maison, the moment after the attack hit him, every time she closes her eyes.

A bird twitters in the branches above her, and when Delina glances up, there's the faintest outline of gold where it fluffs its feathers, its heart beating and its lungs still working.

It's cold, too, but there's a sort of joy inside of it, at the singing it's letting out, at the sharpness of the air inside. It doesn't hate the winter, not like she would have thought.

And despite that joy, despite the life above her, Delina's eyes fall back towards the dead bird.

It shines with the same gold as the ribbon winding through the property.

"Okay," Delina murmurs, raising an eyebrow at it.

If the other necromancer used something dead to stop someone, to bind someone, then there's nothing to stop Delina from at least attempting it.

At this point the smart thing to do would be to go get someone else to watch her, to stop her if she did something stupid. But Gurlien would lecture at her, Chloe would chatter, and Maison...

...Maison would probably tell her to stop before she tried, if the last week is any indication.

"Yeah no," she mumbles, then softly treads over to the dead bird.

It took a lot of conscious effort to raise Maison, a lot of thinking real hard about repairing the damage, about making sure everything is in place correctly, so this time she blanks all of that from her mind. Blanks the idea of stitching the frozen skin back together, of starting the lungs and heart, and just lets herself...think.

Slowly, she settles her hand on the dead bird, on the soft feathers, and instead of the injuries, instead of the clawing need to grasp and bring back, she concentrates on that shining gold inside of it, until it tangles within her fingers, more real and more solid than the strip of magic ever was.

Careful, she stands, and the coil of gold remains in the palm of her hand, leaving the dead bird.

And just like that, she can no longer feel the death in front of her. There's no more gut punch of awareness, no more itch under her skull, no more snapping of her attention.

"Oh," she murmurs, staring at the glistening gold.

The plastic door to the cabin slams open, and she doesn't need to turn to know it's Maison, clambering out onto the frost with just his socks over his feet.

"What did you just do?" His voice isn't accusatory, just very, very confused.

She glances over at him, and he's clearly in his pajamas, his hair sticking up in the back. "Go put shoes on if you're going to be out here."

He blinks at her, then down at the gold in her hand, then back up at her, uncomprehending.

His toes are already cold, obviously.

Delina sighs, then, cradling the gold, she walks back towards the cabin.

He doesn't move, his face bewildered. "What did you do?"

"I don't know," Delina says, then shoos him back into the cabin with her free hand. "Did I send up a demon flare?"

Slowly, he shakes his head, and she follows him in, and the cabin is a cocoon of warmth after the sharp chill of outside.

The gold in her hand pulses.

At the stove, Chloe drops the spatula. "What is that?"

Gurlien idly looks up at them, at Maison's confused face and Chloe's shocked, before narrowing his eyes at Delina. "Did you do something?"

"Yes, yes, she did," Chloe responds, her eyebrows raised, leaving whatever it is on the stove and crossing over to peer at Delina's hand cradling the magic. "I don't want to touch that."

"It's from the bird outside," Delina says, and Maison flinches, his face pale. "I didn't bring it back, I think I...took away the potential from it."

Chloe backs away from her, but Gurlien springs up from the couch.

"You took the life energy from a dead creature and are now able to hold it?" Gurlien asks, sharp. "Just by instinct, without coaching."

Delina nods, and the magic shifts ever so slightly in her hands.

"Shit," Maison mumbles, and he clearly is without coffee. "What the shit."

She throws him a look, and he's just staring at her hand. "Should I not have done this?" She asks.

This gets Maison's attention back up at her. "I..."

Delina sighs, crosses to the kitchen and swipes her free thumb on the coffee machine, then flops on the couch. Chance takes one glance at her before springing away and skittering under the bed in the other room. "Get some coffee," she says, as the espresso machine kicks to life. "I don't think this will go away."

Her instincts say it won't.

AFTER EVERYONE else has eaten breakfast and she's still on the couch, Maison sits back next to her, still staring at her hand, but his eyes are aware this time.

"Yeah?" Delina asks, raising an eyebrow at him.

"This is new to me, too," he says, and underneath his voice is a trace of panic, one that has her sitting upright. "Gurlien, any idea why this feels like a threat to me?"

"It's not a threat to me, it's just really weird," Chloe says, and she's still at the kitchen table, also watching her like a hawk. "Like looking at magic through a funhouse mirror?"

"I'm not threatening you," Delina informs him, but he shakes his head, like it's not what he means. "I was trying to hold the strip of magic to practice and this was...way easier to hold."

Gurlien sits on the armchair across from the couch, attentive, his face pinched, but puzzles over it. "Threat how?"

"I don't know," Maison replies, bewildered, and it's been a while since she's seen him this confused, even accounting for the drama she's put on recently. "I'm just...it's like staring at a sleeping snake."

"A snake?" Chloe says, skeptical. "I mean, I guess, it's a normal rope..."

Maison's already shaking his head again even before she's finished. "No. Like the..." he gestures to his head. "Like the hind brain fear of looking at a sleeping snake. You know it's dangerous, you want to react, but you freeze."

"I can take it back outside," Delina offers.

"No," Gurlien says, but he's a bit delighted, his eyes alight, which is weird. "It is a threat to you. To the demon side of you. Don't you get it?"

Maison only briefly glances at him, then back at Delina's hand, where the magic shifts again.

"The other Necromancer, she used a death to defeat the demon Terese, yes?" Gurlien starts, almost bouncing with excitement. "She controlled one demon and killed the other. Of course it feels like a threat to you. It's instinctual."

Delina and Maison eye each other.

"It's like reacting in fear to someone holding a weapon you don't understand," Gurlien continues. "Of course it matters who's holding it, of course it matters what they do with it, but it's absolutely still something you will just instinctively pay attention to. This is great."

Maison leans back, before rubbing his face. "Great."

Delina pokes the shifting magic in her hand, and it flexes as if it's a sentient thing. A thing that had abilities and wants and interests.

"Once I took this, I couldn't sense the bird anymore," she says, slowly piecing her words together. "So once I take this, I don't think I could bring it back."

"Grim," Chloe chimes in, but she drifts back to the stove for another serving. "So this is how Terese was conquered."

"I think," Gurlien replies, but his eyes are delighted still. "You just stumbled into one of the Necromancers natural defense mechanisms. I think."

Maison looks halfway caught between the eagerness and sheer discomfort of sitting next to her at this time. "And this means we can practice on some offense as well."

Delina pokes the magic again, it twines against her finger, kind. Like it recognizes her.

"Because if you snapped that in my face, I'm not sure what would happen."

"I'm more thinking she could tie it on your wrist and compel you. Or, you know, any actual demon. The theory is there, we have one possible occurrence, we can draw some conclusions, this is great."

For a few moments, Delina wishes that she could just sit here and enjoy the knowledge that she actually did something, to marvel at the sensation cupped in the palm of her hand, before she has to deliberate on what it's used for.

Instead, she lets it unfurl, keeping her grip on one part of it, so it drops like a length of rope, shimmering and glistening, and Maison flinches again.

"I'm not going to do anything to you," Delina tells him.

"I know, I know, it's just...so weird. So very weird." Maison shifts, and she's not sure if it's so he has a better look at the entire thing or if it's to get further away.

"Want me to take it back outside?"

For a few moments, she's sure he's going to say yes, and she regrets even asking. That she might've wasted the potential of the bird, that she might've removed any possibility, however remote, that she could've brought it back.

It must've shown on her face, for Maison's expression gentles.

"Or should I practice?" she asks, and it's better than

letting it waste, and the rope thrums in her hand as if agreeing.

"Practice," Gurlien replies quickly, and Chloe's nodding at the table.

"It'd be smart," Maison says, and his voice is definitely not the strongest, and he swallows. "You could try some minor offensive on me, and I can tell you if it'd be something to pursue, at the very least."

"I don't want to make you...compelled...to do anything," Delina says, echoes of their conversation at the brewery pinging through her mind.

By the look of him, he's thinking the same thing.

26

After a few minutes of everyone else getting on enough clothing to be able to tromp around in the frost and Delina keeping the magic curled back up in her hands, Maison sits down next to her on the couch.

Chloe and Gurlien are still in the other room, audibly arguing over some magic theory, but Delina just watches Maison through her eyelashes.

He's obviously steeled himself up.

"This is a good opportunity," he starts, his attention still drawn to her hand. "Don't wince away just because I'm uncomfortable."

"Don't act like I'm going to leave you and get you in trouble if you say no to something," Delina challenges him right back, and he blinks. "You're not being compelled to do things anymore."

"I'm not..." he trails off, then sighs. "Okay, do I want to do this? No. Do I still think it's a good idea? Yes. Happy?"

"Not terribly," Delina answers.

"There's even a big chance you won't be able to compel

me to do anything, human willpower is a massively different thing than demon willpower," he continues, crossing his arms. "There's an equal chance to it doing absolutely jack shit to me in terms of compelling."

It still sits poorly with her, so she narrows her eyes at the knot of magic in her hand.

"Then let's figure out some guardrails," she starts. "If I can compel you, if this practice works, then we should decide ahead of time what I can and cannot do to you."

He sits back, like it hadn't occurred to him.

"Like, say, you didn't want to do jumping jacks," Delina continues. "So I know so I don't make you do jumping jacks. You know, establish some rules so I don't make you do something you don't want to do."

His lips part, but he says nothing, staring at her.

"I don't want to just...make you do things, even if this is practice, you need to have some say in things," Delina says, softer, muscling through a strange shyness at the conversation. "Otherwise, you're just terrified and I just feel like shit."

He's silent, his eyes on her, and there's something dawning over his face, something close to wonder. Like his entire view of the world shifted in that brief, little conversation, and now he's looking at her through a completely different lens.

She shifts, and the magic warms in her hand.

"Nobody has ever asked me that," Maison says, after a long moment of silence. "That has never mattered to anyone."

"Well, that's shitty," Delina says, and Chloe tromps through the hallway and down into the basement for something, and she waits for her to be out of earshot. "So what are the guardrails? Give me something to work off of."

"Don't make me hurt anyone," he says, quickly, too

quickly, and of course she's not going to do that. "Don't make me blow anything up or rip up magic without repairing it."

"Okaaaay, got it," Delina says. "That seems like the bare minimum."

She gets a hint of a dimple before it disappears. "I don't know, don't embarrass me? I don't care about the jumping jacks."

"Okay, then tell me way before if I'm going to trip on something," she says, and he nods, his shoulders relaxing, and it feels...somehow normal. Like this is a conversation they should be having, far beyond the stakes and the surrealism.

That this is a conversation they should be having regardless. That it would be just as in place as on their comfy couch in Prescott as it is here in the cabin.

"I mean it with the weird demon bond thing, too," Delina continues, softer still. "I don't know how that works, but I don't want...I don't want you to be forced to do something you don't want to do because of it."

He ducks his head at that, as if she couldn't see the emotions flashing across his face all the same.

"If I had known about the bond before, I would have said that before," she says. "I don't like...I don't like the idea that you did things you didn't want to."

She's had just enough time to think about what that might mean for him to really, really need to say that.

He exhales, thumping his head on the back of the couch. "You never made me do anything I didn't want to do," he says, which is a relief, even if she had a sneaking suspicion that he would say that. "I will say this until the end of time, being with you was never difficult."

"Glad of that, but I would definitely tread carefully," she

says, letting her eyes drift down to the magic in her hands. "The whole...you had to be with me...it's not a great feeling."

Beyond all the lies, beyond all the faking, it's still awful to comprehend the fact that he couldn't just leave. That he was trapped, no matter how bad he might've wanted to leave.

His hand settles on her elbow, startling her out of the thought, and a spark crackles to his palm, though he pays it no attention. "Delina."

"Yeah?" she asks, still cradling the magic.

"I'm sorry," he says, voice dipping low, and she blinks at him. "I'm sorry for lying, I'm sorry for not immediately telling you the truth. I'm sorry for keeping it from you, I'm sorry about all the little lies I ever told you."

She stares up at him, and he shifts closer with just a spare glance down at the magic in her hand.

"You are, by far, the best thing to happen to me in my life, and I wish I never hurt you."

Words escape her, and she lets her eyes fall away to the familiar lines of his throat, to his chest, until she's staring back down and away.

"I wish..." he trails off, and waits until Gurlien disappears down the stairs into the basement as well, before he gently, ever so gently, lifts her chin up to him.

She freezes, everything warring inside of her.

Of course being this affectionate with him is a bad idea, especially after everything she knows. Of course she doesn't know if she can still trust what he's saying, if she can believe his words. Of course allowing this touch pounds against her heart, floods her veins with how bad of an idea it is.

But now she can see the red reflected in his eyes, can tell without even thinking that his heart beats just as fast as hers. That his feet are cold and his shoulder is just tight enough to ache and that a non-zero amount of his attention is focused still on the magic in her hand, like it's impossible for him to not dedicate a small part of his brain to the threat.

And he's still holding her chin up, despite it all.

Her lips part, and his eyes flicker down to them, louder than anything in the room.

"Delina," he says, and a question lingers in his tone, somewhere behind a trace of desperation.

It's a bad idea. It's all a bad idea. Him being here at all is a bad idea. Her sitting here and feeling the warmth of his touch and the fire in his blood is a bad idea. Her not immediately fleeing from this situation, her not using whatever defense she might have against him.

But instead, she just looks up at him. At his handsome face, creased with worry and a bit of fear as well. Like he's steeling himself up.

She's seen this before, with him. Seen the fear, seen the desperation, seen the want. Seen the almost critical vulnerability in his hesitations, in the barely there tremble of his hand.

It was there right before he kissed her the first time, all the way back in undergrad.

It's definitely a bad idea, but she wouldn't move away right now, sitting on that old floral couch with cabin beams high overhead, not if you gave her all the money in the world.

"I love you," he whispers, barely audible, and it zings over Delina's skin. "I know you don't believe me, but I love you."

And she's not sure if she leans forward or if he leans down, but their lips meet, and then she's not thinking anymore.

His hand gentles on her chin, tracing glimmers of fire, his mouth opening against hers. He's tender, he's careful, he's cautious.

Right until he's not.

She can't pinpoint the moment, but the hair on the back of her neck raises, almost a sense of danger, like catching a glimpse of lightning across the sky, the hint of a storm before it unleashes a torrent. A scrape of the stubble on his cheek, a tension across his shoulders, his tongue darting across her lips.

Her breath hitches, and he freezes, motionless against her. His hand still hot against her chin, his heart still pounding just as hard, before he pulls away, his eyes flashing red.

She doesn't move, and neither does he, still too close to be probable for anything else, until the telltale clomp of feet up the basement stairs sends both of them scooting apart.

"So in theory it'll be safe," Gurlien says, breezing into the room and completely ignoring the flush on Delina's face and the redness of Maison's lips. "According to the—"

"—very limited," Chloe interrupts.

"—research we have, this doesn't cause any active harm on demons that normal mind control wouldn't cause on humans." He gestures for them to get up from the couch, oblivious. "So don't make him harm himself and he'll be fine."

"Were you spending that time checking for the dangers of this?" Delina asks, after probably too long of a beat, and Gurlien nods, insistent. "Uh, thanks?"

Her heart's still pounding in her throat, her stomach still tight.

"Yes, yes, we wouldn't want to lose him as a resource," Gurlien replies, waving his hand, and Chloe rolls her eyes.

"Do you want outside or basement? Basement we have the extra traps, but that might neutralize it, and outside has all the variables."

"Outside," Maison finally says, voice a bit distant. "She's probably not going to be in a trap if she uses this in combat."

Gurlien nods, like he had anticipated that. "The magic still there?"

Delina glances down at her hand, where the magic shifts almost restless. "Absolutely."

"Later, you should try it with a bug and we'll see how long it lasts without getting incorporated back," Chloe chimes in, and after the conversation with Maison, Delina's head spins.

It's too fast, too soon, with the touch of his lips still against hers like a brand.

"Don't tell him what you're going to do ahead of time, we want him to try to resist without foreknowledge," Gurlien continues, and Delina locks eyes with Maison, just a bit, at that.

He nods, almost imperceptible, though his eyes are still wide.

So Delina stands, and the magic twists in her hands, almost as reflex, and both Chloe and Maison flinch in surprise. "Then let's do this."

27

It takes a few minutes more of Chloe and Gurlien's arguments before they agree on the perfect place for this test. It's barely more than a clearing, just the space between two trees, but it's secure enough that even Maison is satisfied that it won't be seen by any onlookers, magical or not.

"Are you okay?" Delina whispers to him, as Gurlien and Chloe take a few steps back and he visually steels himself.

She's still holding onto the coil of magic, and it pulses in her touch, vivid gold.

He nods, of course, and she raises an eyebrow.

"You need to tie it on his wrist, and pour intention into it," Gurlien says for what feels like the hundredth time. "In that intention, put the willpower that he'll follow your instructions. Frederick, resist her instructions."

Maison's eyes narrow, almost impossible to see, at the other name.

"Tell me if I'm going too far," Delina whispers.

"Same to you," he whispers back, quick. "I shouldn't have done that."

She doesn't need a translator to know what that is, not when he's still flushed despite the cold air.

"Stop panicking," she whispers, because she can feel his heart jackhammering away. "You're fine."

"Am I, though?" he replies, then flinches as she holds the magic between two hands, like a string to tie, before he narrows his eyes further and holds his wrist out to her, almost a challenge. "You want me to be honest, you need to be too."

So she locks eyes with him. "I'm fine."

He searches her face, for what she couldn't tell anyone with a gun to her head, before he nods.

Once more, she holds out the rope, silky soft in her hands. "Last chance to back out."

"Last chance for you as well," he shoots back, and she's changed her mind, she loves this competitive side of him.

"Nope," she says, popping the 'p' sound and, before she can psych herself out of it, quickly wraps the magic around his wrist and double knots it.

Immediately, he jerks, hand gripping down on hers. A gold flash echoes behind her eyes, sharp, her breath catching.

Her knees wobble, and his eyes reflect red at her, wide and panicked and...hungry.

"Where is he?" Gurlien asks, high pitched, and Maison gasps.

Gasps, drops her hand, and flickers away, appearing in the same stance, still recoiling, on the other side of the clearing.

"What—" Maison starts, then disappears again, appearing behind the tree, and there's terror across his face, horror written over his features, and he flinches back.

"Delina, what's going—" he disappears, reappears right next to her, suddenly too close, his eyes flashing red. "...on?"

He reaches for her and a gold spark snaps out, and Delina's head swims before he disappears, appearing a few steps away.

"Stop," she breathes, and he freezes, eyes flashing red, his breath caught in his throat.

His heart is pounding, rabbit fast, and everything about him is...different.

"Where is he?" Chloe asks, behind them, her voice breaking through the chill air.

"I'm right here," Maison says, panic reeding through his words. "I'm right here, what's going on?"

"You're okay," Delina says, then tosses a glance to the other two. "He's here, he's disappearing and reappearing, things are weird."

Maison straightens, and he's not in pain, per se, but his body is...weird. Off.

"You commanded him to stop, what did he stop?" Gurlien asks.

"I'm not, I'm not..." Maison disappears, but doesn't move away, appearing once more in the exact position, stuttering in place. "What's going on?"

Delina takes a step towards him, and he recoils, still in one place, holding his arms up.

"Stay there," he says, and if it wasn't for the fear in his voice, she would've disregarded them. "I'm hurting you, I'm taking from you, I can't stop it, I don't—"

Delina stares at him, as he gapes, before he stares down at his hands.

"Am I a demon right now?"

"Okay, that's new," Delina says, but he doesn't give her a smile. "It's okay, you're fine."

"What's happening?" Gurlien demands sharply. "Tell us—"

"You, shut up, let me handle this," Delina commands, pointing at them, and miracle of miracle he closes his mouth. "Maison, look at me!"

His eyes snap up to hers, like he's fully unable to stop.

Right. She can command him.

"Do you want me to untie it?"

He swallows, his Adam's apple bobbing. "I don't want you to come close to me."

"Okay," Delina responds, and she takes a deliberate step back, and his shoulders ease a bit on their tightness. "I need you to answer me, understand? Are you in pain?"

He shakes his head immediately.

"Tell me if I ask something you don't want to say," she says, and he nods unsteadily. "What do you see right now?"

"You," he replies, fast, like he doesn't even need to think, "just you, there's nothing else, I can't see the world, I can't see the trees, I can't see anyone, you're just...just you."

Delina exhales, and whatever happened that made her head swim is slowly clearing away.

"Can you control the teleporting?" Delina asks, and he blanches. "I think you were teleporting."

"I don't know," he blurts out, and he's scared. He's so scared. "Delly, I was hurting you—"

"Look at me," she says again, and he does. "I'm okay. Breathe."

He does.

"Command me to not hurt you," he says, voice lilting up. "Command me. Please."

"Whatever you do, don't hurt me," Delina repeats, and his shoulders slump. "Don't take from me, don't feed, whatever it is that was."

Behind her, Gurlien stirs, then grabs Chloe by the collar, hauling her back.

Good. Means he figured it out.

Figured it out, and Delina's still grasping at straws.

"Don't hurt anybody right now," Delina commands, and he nods, eager. "Unless my life is in direct danger, I guess."

That, at least, gets some relief from him, like she's saved him from a hell she doesn't quite understand.

There are tears in his eyes, actual tears.

She takes a tentative step closer, and he inhales, sharp, still stuck in one place.

"This made you a demon?" she asks, dipping her voice low, and the other two are far enough away that they have no hope of hearing. "All the demon powers and everything?"

"I think so," he says, small.

"Is me commanding you making you do things?" Delina asks, and he nods again. "Then I guess this is a success. This test."

He's still scared, more frightened than when he actually died, and her heart hurts at it.

"Will you let me untie you?" Delina asks, and still, he hesitates. "It'll stop the danger, it'll stop all these side effects."

His lips part.

"You won't hurt me," she declares, then, slowly, reaches out her hand to him.

Of course she's terrified, too, but the chill of the air doesn't hurt her skin anymore, all her muscles are relaxed, more than they have been in years.

He stares down at her, his eyes inhuman, and she can see the pulse in his throat. "You're beautiful," he says, almost marveling, but his voice breaks. "You're shining so bright."

"Thanks," Delina replies, before reaching towards his wrist again. "Will you let me do this?"

Slowly, he nods, holding out his arm.

It's a quick yank on the knot, the magic slithering away and disappearing into the ground, and he slumps forward, crashing into her.

"Oh hey, I got you, I got you," Delina says, getting her feet back underneath her, and his arms wrap around her, gripping her into a tight hug. "Woah, you're okay, you're fine."

And his body is back to normal, none of the off sensation, none of the creeping inhumanity.

Just his ragged breathing and his face pressed against her shoulder.

28

It might be a few moments, it might be an hour, but Delina can feel that Maison's feet have gone cold by the time she hears Gurlien and Chloe return behind them.

"So you got him back, that's good," Gurlien says, and a tremor runs through Maison's shoulders at that, still pressed up against Delina. "Can you explain what happened?"

Maison slowly withdraws from where he's clutching her, and his cheeks are wet.

"Gurlien, give it a moment," Delina says, and Maison scrunches his face, obviously pulling himself together. "That was disorienting."

"I'm not surprised," Chloe says, and that at least gets Maison to shake a bit loose. "You disappeared, that's disorienting for anyone."

He takes a deep breath, shaking out his hands, before settling his confident mask over his face.

Delina hates it.

"So the death in the hands of the necromancer is what gets you to go full demon," Gurlien lists out. "That doesn't make any sense, but it does explain why they were never able to get you to do it before." He looks over at Delina, critical. "You're okay?"

"I'm fine," she repeats, and she is. Nothing feels awful, nothing hurts.

"Even I saw that gold flash," Chloe says, muted, and Delina winces. "That could've killed you if he was a bit less skilled."

"None of that was due to skill," Maison says, finally, and even his voice is raw. "I couldn't control anything."

The words settle in the clearing like a bomb.

"Congrats," Gurlien mutters, finally. "You'll have to practice at something for once in your life."

MAISON REFUSES to let go of her hand, even when they're all inside back in the warmth, and Delina's not about to make him.

He hasn't spoken since the clearing, and he's shivering, even though his skin is warm enough that he should be fine, and that alone makes Delina shoo him into her bedroom and shut the door behind them, despite Gurlien's token protest.

"Sit," she orders, pointing at the bed, and he does, even though there's no compulsion behind her words. "Scan me. Do that energy reading thing you did before. See that I'm okay."

He just gazes up at her, his face pinched.

"Please?" Delina hazards, and there's a ghost of a smile, gone too soon.

"I'd rather not do anything right now," he says, wan, but he swipes a thumb across her palm. "I could've killed you."

She doesn't quite know how to rebut that, or how close she came to actually dying, so she sits next to him instead.

Ever so slightly, he leans against her, shoulder to shoulder.

"Good to know that I can't compel you still," Delina says, staring down at the baby blue carpet. "I didn't want that to last forever."

"It would only last until you took the string off," Maison replies. "It would've fallen off in eighty-two minutes."

"Precise," Delina says, and he shrugs, still against her. "Gut instinct?"

"Yeah," he replies. "It was just something I knew. I don't know how I knew, but I knew."

"Weird," Delina comments, half because it is and half because she didn't know what else to say. "Well...sorry for that whole fiasco. Definitely wouldn't have tried to pull the death if I knew that was gonna happen."

"If I knew that would happen, I would've been prepared, and would have told you to order me to not hurt you as soon as it was tied," Maison says, full of frustration, like this was a foreseeable event. Like they could've anticipated this. "If I knew, I would've made sure you couldn't get hurt, I would've attempted to control the..." he mimes teleporting with his hands. "I would've been able to actually do something."

"That's not fair to yourself," Delina says, and he sighs, rubbing his face. "If you haven't had access to a part of yourself your entire life, how were you to know how to control it?"

It's a bit too real for her.

"Okay, point," he says. "I don't like that I hurt you."

"I feel fine," she burst out, breaking the contact to face him, still sitting on the bed. "I feel fine, I got dizzy for like a second, but I'm not in any pain, I'm not even that cold."

"Of course you're not," Maison replies, as if that's the point. "What do you think Demons take?"

It's not something she's thought of before. "Energy, I guess?"

"They take pain," he says, and his voice breaks again. "They take pain, until the pain takes from your body and you die."

"Well, that's grim," Delina responds, then glances down at her hands.

Of course everything had to be complicated once more. Of course there couldn't be an easy part of her magic, there couldn't be an easy to process emotional moment. Of course her heart hurts at his upset, after all the drama, and she still wants to push herself to fix it, somehow.

And that's not even processing the kiss, right before all of this happened.

"All my life, they've tried to get me to go full demon, and you manage it by accident in an afternoon," Maison says, and it's barely past lunchtime so she rolls her eyes a bit at that. "How the hell is it that you're just blowing by all the metrics that have made up my entire life?"

"Do you think it was the necromancer or the bond thingy?" Delina asks, unable to stop herself from wondering which parts of all of this is because of that bond.

"Necromancer," he replies immediately. "Any necromancer—"

"What, all two of us?" Delina interjects.

"Any necromancer would've had the same response. I think." He sighs again, reaching out and pulling her hand into his again, and she's not going to deny him that comfort. "I feel like shit."

Before she can even help herself, she flashes a scan at

him. There's still a shiver running through his body, his head aches dully, and his stomach is roiling.

He doesn't flinch at that, just blinking through it.

"You'll be okay," Delina says softly. "No permanent damage or anything."

"How are you not scared by me?" Maison bursts out at that. "You should be, I dunno, running in terror and never looking back."

He still cradles her hand.

And there's a flippant answer, at the tip of her tongue, but she waits and lets that float away. Lets herself think of what may be the real answer.

"I don't understand," he says, after she's silent for too long.

"If we're being honest, it's probably because I didn't quite grasp the danger," Delina admits, and she hates saying that. "I just thought you were going haywire or something."

His jaw works, tight, and she runs her thumb along his knuckles. Like she used to do when he was upset about something, anything, back in their little condo in Prescott.

Then it was usually the neighbors, or a nebulous work 'thing.' Not a bout of spontaneous change in magic that resulted in him literally teleporting and then hurting her.

It feels just as right now as it did then, and that bubbles up an entirely different well of emotions.

"And you called me pretty," she points out, and he groans, rubbing his face. "That was nice."

"Delly, you were overwhelming," he says, now flopping over on the bed. "I never want any demon to see you ever, if that's what they'll see."

"You'll have to paint it for me," Delina says, and her heart beats a bit at seeing him on her bed.

It's all such a bad idea.

"The entire world was dark," he continues, still covering his eyes, as if the lack of sight would help him talk about it. "I couldn't tell where the trees were, what I was standing on, or what temperature the air was. It was like I just...stopped existing, and the only light I could see was you."

"Romantic," Delina comments, and he opens his grey eyes long enough to give her a dirty look.

Right. Because all of this familiarity and all of this connection and they're still exes.

They had made out even, still exes. He still lied to her, lied about her entire life.

"I meant literally," he says. "Like a physical light, and everything else in the world was dim."

She doesn't have a quippy comment for that, so she stares up at the ceiling, instead of him.

"You know they're gonna make you try to practice again, right?" Delina says, and he sighs again. "I'm gonna have to start keeping dead bugs on me to do that with, aren't I?"

He tilts his head over to look at her, and she's still sitting next to him, with him on the bed. "I won't blame you if you never do that again," he says. "I won't blame you if you never look at me, if you never talk to me again. You could have died, Delly, and I would have been the reason for it."

The sarcasm dies at the tip of her tongue, as she looks down at him. At the line of his jaw and his neck, at the rumpled undershirt.

There's self-loathing on his face, out of place, and she's not quite sure she's ever seen that expression on him before.

"Okay," she murmurs, and stands so she's facing him.

He sits up, immediately, and the desire to rest her arms on his shoulders and cradle his face hits her like a brick. To run her fingers through his soft hair, until he closes his eyes and leans into her.

"You're upset," she starts, quiet. "You're upset and that's okay."

He opens his mouth to respond, but she holds up a hand, stopping him short.

"Do you want me to never talk to you again? Or are you saying it out of self-sacrificing bullshit?"

He closes his mouth.

"I don't like the self-sacrificing bullshit," she declares, and there's a ghost of a smile on his face, almost there, and she'll take it as he stares up at her, still sitting on the bed, and her so close.

He reaches a hand out to her, tentative, settling it on her lower back. Like with just one tug in, he would pull her on top of him. Kiss her, overwhelm her, with her straddling him and him in control of all of it.

Of course, he doesn't.

For a few wild seconds, she debates pushing towards him, making the move herself. Debates grabbing his hair and kissing him herself, see what he does.

If this morning is any indication, he'd kiss her right back.

She could have it back, she realizes with a jolt, with his arm strong around her and he stares up at her, eyes grey and beautiful. She could have him, just as devoted as before. Face this new world of magic and the dead together, with him right next to her.

And because of the fucking demon bond, he would do it in a heartbeat.

His lips part, at something on her face. "Are you okay?"

"It depends, are you going to go more into the self-sacrifice bullshit if I say otherwise?" she asks, and risks brushing his hair away from his forehead.

"If I promise not to?" he asks, voice low, like he's reading into her mind.

"I'm just confused," Delina admits, and it's not the suave self she has in her mind, and for a few minutes she considers walking away from the conversation. "Things keep on changing faster than I can get a grip on them, and this is just one more of them."

She doesn't specify what 'this' is, and he swallows, his arm tightening around her back, and for a wild second she thinks he is going to do it, going to thoroughly mess up any sort of balance they've reached, and for a wild second she hopes that he does.

"We'll practice more," he says, instead, going for the obvious safer option. "It'll be too good of an advantage for you to have a full demon in power on your beck and call than to not."

Delina bites back the disappointment at that, and sees it mirrored in his eyes, so she pulls away, and his arms fall back down.

"Do you want to go get drunk?" she asks, and he blinks.

OF COURSE, the moment they peek their heads out of the room, Gurlien makes them sit on the couch and walks Chloe through a barrage of diagnostic spells that do nothing to Delina but make her nose itch.

All they tell anyone is that Maison is, indeed, back to normal and Delina is a little lower energy than she otherwise would be.

All things she could have told them.

All things she could have told them, and Maison's gaze

on her is heavy, lingering, until she abruptly stands from the tests, her heart beating too hard in irritation.

"Am I in any danger if I go have a fucking drink?" she asks, probably sharper than is polite.

"It's like...three PM," Chloe starts, which isn't helpful, before she cranks her head to look outside. "And it's either going to rain slush or snow tonight, that's not gonna be fun."

"It snowed in Prescott. Sometimes." Maison also stands, shaking out his hands, like the scan affected him way more. "You said there was a dive bar?"

Gurlien narrows his eyes at him, then at Delina. "Just because you saw her as a demon doesn't mean it's a good idea to sleep with her again," he says.

Delina closes her eyes. "Look, I did a weird death thing and now I want a coping mechanism."

"Alcohol's not a great one," Chloe says, but she's already reaching for her bag. "Dive bar?"

"Dive bar."

29

When Delina had imagined going and getting intentionally drunk with her ex-boyfriend, she hadn't anticipated the entire group going along.

The dive bar is far cry away from what Delina would consider adequate, but beggars can't be choosers and there's a giant tacky mural on one wall and dim enough lighting that she can't see the circles under Maison's eyes.

Chloe orders a round of 'the special' for them, and all four of them crowd around a standing booth.

Unspoken, Maison presses his side against hers, and she's not about to begrudge him that simple comfort. It's nice, the physical contact, and she never quite realized how much they always touched until all the casual gestures were gone.

And if she leans into it a bit more, she's not going to admit it.

Nobody's talking, as Chloe comes back precariously balancing the four drinks. They're fluorescent green in tall glasses, and the dim lighting does them no favors.

"First time we got these Gurlien got so drunk he applied for law school," Chloe breaks the silence, as they all stare at the drinks. "Only stopped because none of his actual degrees could be found in the system."

"Thanks, Chloe," Gurlien grumbles, before picking up the drink and sipping it. "It was two weeks after I got kicked out."

"And your first thought was law school?" Delina asks, not quite containing the courage to pick up the drink, not with Maison still pressed against her.

"One of my degrees is an equivalent," Gurlien says. "The other is Biofeedback based, and med school seemed worse than law school."

This thaws Maison a little, and he raises an eyebrow at Gurlien. "You went through twice?"

"So the College does actual Degrees, weird," Delina says, still staring down at the drink. "I thought it was a 'school of thought' sort of college."

"I liked school," Gurlien says, almost plaintive. "I liked the research, I liked the clear and achievable goals, and I liked that all that mattered was your brain. It didn't matter how social I was, it didn't matter how awkward I was, it was just learning."

"Mine was technically in logic puzzles," Chloe says, and she, too, is staring at the drink with some trepidation, despite the fact that she's the one that ordered them. "But that's just a fancy term for breaking into things that other people had locked. They really thought I'd be useful for them."

"I was definitely not given a choice and it was demonology," Maison replies dryly, and it's so close to his normal personality that if it wasn't for the tremor that still ran through his shoulders occasionally, she would think he is better. "Then it was research, then..."

"Art classes after work?" Delina asks, and he nods.

"So if you weren't born in the college, you would've just done art school?" Chloe asks, honestly curious.

"Pretty much," Maison says, before he shifts away from Delina long enough to grab the drink. "What the hell is in this?"

"Something green," Gurlien replies sarcastically. "Some mixer. Probably vodka."

Maison stares down at it, then, in one go, downs the entire drink.

"Alright," Delina says, as he coughs once. "So tonight's gonna be like that?"

He sets the glass down with a thunk, and looks to her like she's the only person in the building. Like the sleepy bartender and the lackluster locals and the other two people at their very table no longer exist.

"You're the one who offered to get drunk," he points out, and she lifts her chin, not about to back down at that.

There's still the hint of a tremor running through his shoulders, and his throat is tight against her scan.

"Fine then," Delina says, then pounds her drink in one go, and it burns far more than it should, and is somehow not sickly sweet.

She sputters the burn all the way down her throat.

"Yeah, these aren't nice," Gurlien says, but both of his eyebrows are raised well above his glasses as he gingerly sips from his glass. "So Delina, how many dead are around here?"

"Ew," she responds, then lets her eyes flutter shut.

There's a dead mouse in the walls of the building over, all but a skeleton now, just the vaguest of pulls behind her gut. There's a trail of dead ants in a pipe behind the bar—ew —and some dead moths under the heater next to the door.

"Bugs," Delina responds, which seems to be the way things are right now. "Dead bugs seem to be everywhere in the world. And bones of a mouse in the next building."

Gurlien shakes his head, like it's still amazing. "One of these days you're going to unintentionally solve a murder and then things are going to be real weird for you legally."

A tremor winds its way through Maison at that, and she tucks herself closer to him.

"Wouldn't hold up in court," Chloe reminds him.

"I'm not saying as a court witness, I'm saying as a she's gonna stumble on some dead body hidden in someone's walls and blurt it out," Gurlien replies, which isn't better.

Chloe sets her drink in front of the two of them. "I'll drive tonight, enjoy." There's a hint of mischief in her eyes. "Make sure someone doesn't blow anything up."

"I don't blow things up," Maison says, instantly, and there's years of exasperation in his tone. "Why does everyone always think I'm going to blow things up?"

"It's the demon," Gurlien replies immediately. "Did you see the fight spot where they took down Terese?"

Maison shakes his head, still screwing up his face.

"Oh, it's brutal," Chloe chimes in after getting herself a normal soda from the bar. "So much demon junk, so much Necromancy, even I could tell. Like it's haunted."

Delina resists the urge to slink back. "That's where my mom died?"

They fall silent, before Gurlien nods.

"Wild," Delina replies blandly.

"Terese also killed off an entire few acres of land off of the coast near Bellingham" Gurlien says, obviously skittish that close to someone showing emotion. "Just...everything dead. Plants, dirt, everything."

Maison's hand settles in the small of Delina's back, a tentative connection. Like he's testing the waters.

She leans against him, just enough to be noticeable, and her skin tingles at that little touch.

"Do you want another?" Maison asks of her, voice low as if it's just for her.

"Not of these," Delina retorts, and there's a ghost of a smile on his face, something halfway between tentative and scared. "Get me something that won't burn my taste buds."

Maison pushes away from the table, and the moment he's arguably out of earshot both Gurlien and Chloe lean in.

"Are you sure this is wise?" Gurlien asks. "Is he okay enough for this? He did some dangerous shit today, is getting him drunk the best course of action?"

"I mean probably not," Delina says, but there's a worm of irritation in her now. "But he got scared, some sort of stress relief sounds like a good idea."

Chloe watches her, face solemn, sipping at the soda. "He meant emotionally."

"No, I didn't," Gurlien protests.

"You two have been weird," Chloe continues, and if it wasn't such a true observation, Delina would weigh being offended. "One second I think he's about to run away, and then I think he's about to write poetry for you, and you look like you're caught between ignoring the fact that he exists and making out with him. Is getting drunk really a good idea?"

It's a good point, but it doesn't do a thing for all the emotions welling up in her, mixed with the burn in her throat. "It's not like it's any less confusing for me."

"That's fair," Gurlien says, begrudgingly sipping the vile

green drink. "It's not like too many people are in such dramatic circumstances with their ex all the time."

"Remember you and Richard and Tina, though?" Chloe says, and Gurlien groans, thumping his head down on the table. "You were banging both of them well after you broke up with them and were so scared they'd find out." She gives Delina a hint of a smile, some sort of rescue. "They both already knew, it was a big giant nothingburger and Gurlien stressed about it for months."

"Oh my god," Delina deadpans, as Maison slides back in next to her, handing her a martini. "We're discussing Gurlien's romantic mishaps."

"Is this about Tina and what's his name?" Maison asks immediately. "That was hilarious."

"How did you find out about that, that was only three years ago?" Gurlien says.

"Monthly trip," Maison replies. "I'm fairly certain even my mom knew."

He swallows at the mention of his mother, before blinking through it.

There's still so much about him that Delina doesn't know. And now, one drink still burning in her stomach, she wants to know more.

"So it's a small community," Delina starts, and they all three nod, "everyone know everyone else? Rumors go crazy?"

"Like you wouldn't believe," Maison answers, this time sipping the glass of whatever whiskey he got for himself, gamely leaving the green drink in the middle of the table. "Everyone knew everyone else's business. Everyone commented on each other's business, knew the assignments, everything."

"That's why your mom was an outlier," Gurlien says, as if

eager to get it off of his gossip, pointing to Delina. "She kept herself and her protégés separate. We didn't know Alette was a spell weaver—and a ridiculous one at that—until she was far into her teens."

"And that Axel could change his appearance," Chloe pipes up, and Delina raises an eyebrow. "He had such a grasp of his alchemy he could literally change his face, and we didn't know until he was already an adult."

"Do you think they'd talk to me?" Delina asks, and Maison's hand traces a design on her back, threatening to derail her mind. "Or are they angry at my mom, too."

"That's why I've been calling them every few days," Gurlien grouses. "They don't like me."

"Not you, but me," Delina asks, forging on. "I call them, completely unknown number. Or show up wherever they are at their doorsteps. Get their help with Maison's mom, hide with them."

Gurlien and Chloe glance at each other, and one of those long wordless conversations ensues.

"While Axel is generally outgoing and friendly, I'm not sure how well your cousin would react to seeing you," Chloe starts, and Delina flinches.

"What do you mean, cousin?" Delina blurts out, and both of them blanch. "I have a cousin?"

Neither of them say anything, so Delina turns and gapes at Maison.

"By marriage," he replies, and there's the hint of a flush across his cheeks, the flush he gets when he drinks too fast. "Your mother remarried a few times, one of them was to Alette's uncle, I believe."

At least he's giving her an answer.

"And nobody thought to mention the fact that this person we're trying to reach is my cousin?"

"Honestly, I thought they did already," Maison says, and his face is open, open in the way it rarely ever is. "They were already throwing around her name, I thought..." he shrugs, still not moving his hand from her back. "I think you two would've been actual cousins for all of a year and a half?"

"Alette still called Frisse her aunt," Gurlien says, which isn't helping his case. "But I've mentioned you in the messages."

"Which they might not even be listening to," Delina deadpans, then takes a large drink of the martini for courage.

It, too, burns on the way down.

"Is every drink here just shitty?" Delina asks, and both Chloe and Gurlien nod. "Okay, how far away do they live?"

"They're a three-hour trip," Gurlien all but mumbles. "You have to cross the border."

"I can make you a new passport," Chloe says, not quite helpfully. "It might take a few days to a week to get it right, but it should be possible."

"Fine, make the passport and I'll drive myself—"

"—and me," Maison interrupts.

"And Maison up to Canada and talk to them," Delina says, staring down at the martini, even more of a knot in her throat. "She knew my mom."

The other three exchange glances, before Maison grabs his whiskey and shoots it back.

"She was practically raised by your mom," Maison says, after a cough. "So you're prepared."

"Great." Delina takes another large gulp of the martini.

"She tore down the demon protections on the compound," Gurlien says, and his face is a bit pale. "To fix the ley lines going through, so you won't be safe."

Maison straightens, squaring his shoulders, and stares Gurlien down.

"Or, you could take your overpowered ex-boyfriend there and he'll protect you from eighty percent of everything that could happen and probably scare the shit out of Alette and Axel and they might sic their necromancer on you," Gurlien says sarcastically. "That'll be a great show of force, and that compound was left to Alette so she could legally throw you out."

"Gurlien, stop," Chloe says, elbowing him and rolling her eyes. "Don't be a dick."

Gurlien gestures to Maison, like he started it.

Even though Delina's shoes stick to the floor, she shifts away, downing the martini. "Here I thought we were done with the big dramatic reveals."

She knows it's not smart to be this reckless with alcohol, when it's been this long since their heyday of undergrad, but she lets Maison put another martini in front of her, lets the conversation relax a bit.

Lets herself lean against Maison a bit more, until his arm is around her waist and she's all but resting her head against his shoulder, warm. Lets herself laugh as Gurlien and Chloe snipe at each other, as Maison and Gurlien trade stories like actual friends. Lets her mind wander away from the drama, away from the fear earlier in the day, until everything is just a bit softer and kinder.

Until everything almost feels normal once more.

30

At one point, after Gurlien and Chloe devolve into some lengthy conversation about some theory or another, Delina lets her head tilt up to Maison.

"Are you okay?" she whispers.

He's what she would call 'loosely drunk.' It's the state right after tipsy for Maison, where his cheeks redden and any tension in his shoulders relaxes.

She gets a brief glimpse of his dimple before he nods down at her, hesitates, then sighs.

"I'll be okay," he replies, his voice as warm as the arm around her waist.

"Good," Delina declares, and he smiles again, and it's so close to the comfort they would share before all of this. Before the letter.

But it's after a day where he kissed her, where she saw him in his full demon power, and a day where she had pulled death from a creature and used it.

"Are you asking me because you want to know or because you're used to asking?" Maison asks, turning and facing her, his other hand going to her waist so she's in some embrace.

That's right, this stage of drunk for Maison is also where he asks the too-honest questions. Where he dives into deep conversation he wouldn't otherwise venture into.

That didn't change, just because she now knows more about him.

"Well," Delina drawls, because it's a fair question. "Probably both."

He weighs her answer, his arms still around her.

"And you're still acting upset, and I don't want you to be," Delina continues, and there's the self-preservation part of her that wants to keep it all secret, keep all the soft parts of her out of the light.

But the lights in the dive bar are dim and multicolored, washing them in colors too weak to be neon.

Out of the corner of her eye she sees Chloe check in on them, then obviously direct Gurlien into conversation with her, facing away from the table.

So she hesitates, licks her lips, and the tips of her ears burn out of some strange amalgamation of embarrassment and nerves.

"Maybe I care, still," she says, after too long standing too close, every inch of her skin hyper aware of the points of contact between them. Of the weight of his arms around her, of the barest hint of where her chest leans against him. "Despite all the...complications."

Maison's face softens, his eyes flickering down to her lips, and her gut tightens.

Maybe it's the warmth from all the alcohol, maybe it's the kiss from earlier, maybe it's all the magic she's been doing, maybe it's that bullshit demon bond, but whatever they have between them abruptly floods through Delina, her heart in her throat.

She still wants him. Wants this. Wants the hugs and the soft embraces and the casual contact. Wants the drunken questions and wants the painting and the arm around her waist when she's just standing there. Wants the power, the panic, and the overprotective paranoia. Wants to see him look at her like he did before, and like how he did on the forest floor when she was the only thing that could control him.

It takes her breath away with a punch, before he recoils back, his eyes flashing red.

Delina freezes.

And all the hair on the back of Delina's neck raises. Something's off, something's wrong, and the very magic in the air constricts around her.

Chloe grabs Gurlien's arm, turns him back to the two of them.

"What's going on?" Chloe whispers, and her eyes are wide. "Something's going on, what is it?"

Gurlien looks between the three of them, fast. "Frederick, what is it?"

"I don't know," Maison says, deliberate, every syllable distinct. "Something is...off."

Delina forces herself to take a breath, the sudden tension like dousing herself in water.

The one other patron at the bar tosses a twenty to the bartender, then leaves, as if something's chasing him.

Leaving just the four of them and the bartender in the room.

The bartender watches them, and Delina can see the whites of his eyes. "Everything okay over there?"

He's sweating, too, and Delina can sense the single drop of sweat dripping between his shoulder blades.

She can sense that, she can sense the ache still on Chloe's neck, the sharp pain in Gurlien's wrist—worse than usual—and the sudden tension along Maison's jaw.

All without thinking.

Maison swings his glance down to her, and his eyes reflect back. "Delina?"

"I..." she trails off, her mouth suddenly dry, her skin cold where it was perfectly warm only a few seconds ago. "Everything is..."

There are two people outside the bar, between her and the skeleton of a mouse, and even though she couldn't see it, even though she couldn't touch it, it's like she could grab it with her mind.

The two people are...

One, the smaller of the two, seethes with an angry, chaotic sort of energy, half sour and half bitter. Their skin hurts, their lungs hurt, their bones hurt, their thoughts hurt. Everything about them is pain, brutal and violent against Delina's awareness, and they're furious about it.

The other...her scan slips off of, slithering away from him, as if the very essence of herself cringes away.

She grabs Maison's arm, unsteady, the tipsiness from before now horridly sitting in her gut.

"Someone's coming, they're outside, someone—"

The door to the bar slams open, skittering off its hinges, and the power slams off.

"Shit," Maison's arms tighten around Delina, swinging her back, the drinks on the table wobbling.

The bartender yelps in surprise, and there's nothing, no movement, the very air choking down Delina's throat. Not a stir of wind through the bar, nothing.

Until the bartender flicks on the flashlight on his phone, shining it towards the door.

The woman—she's the smaller one, she's in so much pain—squints against the light, throwing up an arm to shelter her eyes, recoiling back, until she thumps into the person behind her. She's petite, smaller than even Chloe, and one side of her auburn hair has been shaved to the skin, the other shorn harshly at her chin.

There's something around her throat, and it takes Delina half a breath to realize it's not something physical.

Behind her is Korhonen, and even before the flashlight beam hits him, the oil-slick drenched in cold sensation washes over Delina.

Immediately, Maison kicks over the table, sending the glasses shattering to the floor, and Chloe yanks Gurlien over, out of the way. Delina ducks behind the table, her heart pounding.

In the dim light of the flashlight, still held by the befuddled bartender, Korhonen points a lazy finger at him. "Kill the witness."

The woman grabs at the air, clenching her fist and yanking, and the bartender's neck snaps.

Just snaps.

The death punches through Delina, and she reels back, her butt thumping onto the floor behind the table, gasping.

For a few brilliant seconds, all she can see is the death, sharp against her awareness, closing around her throat.

Before the light from the phone clatters to the bar top, casting shadows through the entire bar, and everything stills.

"Good job, Frederick, at keeping some life insurance around," Korhonen says, as Maison crouches next to Delina, his eyes wide. "We weren't sure if she'd bother to bring you back."

"Where is she?" the woman asks, her voice high and lilting, and goosebumps prickle at Delina's arms. "I could tell she's here, where is she?"

Maison settles a hand on Delina's collarbone, keeping her down as she gapes at the death clouding through her mind.

Dimly, she sees Chloe crouching behind another overturned table, her bag in her hand, and Gurlien pressed against a corner in the wall, just barely out of sight between the corner and a broken pinball machine.

"Capture the demon and the necromancer if you can, and dispose of the rest," Korhonen says, still casually, as if he's ordering a drink from the now limp bartender, when the body is still warm. "Have fun."

All Delina can see is the shadow of the two of them, and the woman straightens, lifting her chin.

"Delina, demon," Maison whispers down at her, and Delina squeezes her eyes shut, in some attempt to block out the death still drowning out every other sensation. "I don't know how they can see her, but that's a demon."

She nods at him.

There's death in the bugs on the floor, death in the room with the bartender, and the mouse one building over, and Delina breathes out her nose and concentrates on the closest one.

A bug, some sort of moth, desiccated by time until it's almost dust, but the glimmering sort of gold still tugs behind Delina's stomach.

It's worse, doing this while her head still swims from the shots.

A snap of magic cracks out, harmlessly splintering a chair on the other side of the room, away from all of them.

Like the woman—the demon—can't see them.

In the dim light of the flashlight still on the bar, Maison's brow furrows, like it doesn't make sense to him either.

But they can't just wait for this demon to find them, to slowly destroy the furniture until they're revealed, and she sees Chloe come to the same conclusion at the same time, locking eyes with her.

Chloe nods, then gestures with her chin to Gurlien, who shuts his eyes as if steeling himself up, taking his phone out of his pocket, like that can do anything.

Inhaling, Delina glances up at Maison, then lets her eyes fall to the dead bug. She doesn't know if he can see it, if he can tell what she's going to do, but he's spooling up the magic in his hands, as if gathering ammo.

She'll need cover, she'll need distraction, the nearest death is still in the demon's eyesight. It's a horrible calculation, settling heavy in her stomach.

"Something's wrong with her," Maison breathes out, brows furrowing. "This is wrong."

It's wrong on many levels, but she's not going to doubt him right now.

Maison twists more of the magic between his fingers, eyes reflecting red in the dim light, a detached expression settling over his face, and she hates it. Never wants to see it again. Wants to give him a life where he doesn't have to think of violence, doesn't have to make the decisions to defend her like this.

Then, his face screwed up, Gurlien steps out of the corner.

"How'd you find us?" Gurlien asks, and the magic cracks against the drywall next to his head, the shadow of the demon pivoting to face him.

Gurlien jerks his hand up, the flashlight on his phone shining directly into her eyes, and she recoils back once more.

An opportunity.

Before she can doubt herself, Delina lurches towards the dead bug tucked under the table, and her fingertips graze it just enough that she pulls it towards her, pulls the little coil of gold into the palm of her hand.

It's only her second time doing it, but it surges through her with the 'rightness' of the sensation.

In a flash, Korhonen snaps magic out towards her, vicious, and Delina ducks before it hits her, scrambling back to the shelter of the table, cradling the death in her hand.

Because it's not just a demon, it's him, too.

And all around her, everything spurs into motion.

Chloe chucks a bicycle chain from her backpack out at Korhonen, and midair it transforms, the air blurring around it, until it strikes Korhonen in the shoulder, drawing vicious lines of pain down his arm.

Gurlien kicks a chair towards the demon, who flicks it away with a wave of her hand, still squinting against the direct light.

Maison stands, whipping the magic in his fist towards the demon, catching her in the stomach, and though black blood sprays, she just staggers back before straightening.

The demon's eyes snap onto Maison, and panic bleeds into eagerness and mixes with the pain all around her. "You're one," she breathes, standing perfectly still, like blood isn't still oozing out of her gut and Gurlien's light isn't still directly into her eyes.

Maison blanches, before raising his hand and deflecting another stab of magic from Korhonen that crackles against the shield.

"You're one of me, you know—"

And whatever leash it is around her neck tightens, Korhonen yanking back, and her hand comes up and scrabbles at her throat.

It lasts for just a few seconds, before the demon clenches her fist and the tables on both side of her...detonate. A shard slashes across Maison's face and he staggers.

Delina's ears pop and the warping gold bubble blasts brilliant against her awareness. Splinters of the tables float in the air, and the demon's clothes flutter.

The table in front of her cracks, and for the first time, she locks eyes with the demon.

Her eyes reflect the light, unholy, and a pained hunger flashes across her face in the light of the golden bubble.

"Necromancer," she breathes, seething through the pain, reaching a hand out to her.

Despite everything else, the hand is tiny, petite, like it should belong to someone with a soft job.

Like the body doesn't match the person wearing it.

Between that and a blink, the demon's in front of her, fist closing around Delina's shirt, yanking her upright.

There's a single flash of gold, and a remote part of Delina realizes it's from her, her knees buckling.

Another pop, and the gold bubble encircles them.

There's noise, of course, from outside the bubble, muted and distant, and Delina can't see through the warping gold threads out.

And her feet are numb, all sensation gone, like they've been wrapped in wool.

And it's just her and the demon in the bubble, and from within the leash around her neck burns, a twisting pain.

"How are you alive?" the demon whispers, as Delina gets

her feet underneath her, confusing with the lack of sensation. "That kills people, it kills everyone."

There's a jerk on the leash from outside the bubble, and the demon's head snaps back, before struggling against it enough to stare at Delina

But there's no more flashes of gold from her, despite the fist still around Delina's jacket collar.

"I don't know," Delina whispers back, and the demon blinks rapidly, like there's something she's not understanding. "You need to let me go."

Her fingers tighten, and there's a blast, something rocking the bubble from outside, but beyond a quick blink towards the wall, the demon doesn't react. There's blood, viciously black, still seeping from her gut, but she pays it no attention.

Another jerk of the leash.

"Do you want to be controlled by that for forever?" Delina bluffs, and the demon's eyes light up. "I can take it off, I can figure out how."

"They've trapped me in this," the demon breathes, almost too quiet for Delina to hear. "I'm trapped and I can't switch out."

"We'll figure it out," Delina says, shifting the death in her palm, her heart pounding. "You saw those two other people out there? They can help."

A side eye outside of the bubble, so at least the demon can see out. "It's an alchemist and a dud."

"The alchemist is powerful," Delina says, completely unsure if she's actually telling the truth or not, but not willing to stop the conversation, not when she might talk her way out of it. "The dud is brilliant, he has the most knowledge of all of us, he'll know exactly what to do. And the Half Demon—"

"He's just half?" the demon interrupts, her brow furrowing in horror. "He's not trapped, he's just half?"

"He could help," Delina replies desperately, tugging at her collar, but the demon keeps it in her grasp, tight. "Help me and we'll get you free."

She doesn't know if she can, but the bluff is enough.

"How did you find us?"

The demon breathes, as if weighing her options. "He had me track the demon," she says, throwing a nod outside of the bubble. "He threw up a flare, I tracked him down, he's glimmering with demon power."

Delina swallows, then nods. "Does anyone else know we're here?"

There's a moment, then the demon grins, baring her teeth. "No." For a blink, there's no red in the demon's eyes, revealing startlingly normal brown eyes, before the leash jerks back and another flash of gold blasts through Delina.

Her legs go out, and the fist around her collar is the only thing keeping her upright.

"He's making me," the demon whispers, half choked from the leash. "I can't stop him."

The death's still in Delina's hand, and without any finesse or real plan, Delina swings her arm and smashes the cord of power against the demon's face.

The demon shrieks, a high pitched, shrill sound, dropping Delina in a heap on the floor, the bubble collapsing around them, splinters clattering to the sticky tile.

Delina gasps, air fire down her throat, and all other noise slams into her.

Someone's screaming, the neon lights are back on, flickering, and there's a gash across Maison's face, a bright line of pain, but he drops his shoulder into the demon and they both drop to the floor.

Gurlien's huddled over Chloe, there's blood there too, and—

Korhonen hauls Delina upright, spinning her so she's facing the room, pressing a hand against her neck.

Dimly, she knows it should hurt, but nothing does. It's hot, so hot it should be painful, but nothing registers.

It's the same as what he did to Chloe, the same move, everything.

"Frederick, stop," Korhonen says, jerking Delina back.

Maison freezes, and the demon shoves him away from their scrabble, panting.

She's still in pain.

"Get up," Korhonen commands him then, as if to punctuate it, shakes Delina.

It should hurt.

It still doesn't.

"You still like this one?" Korhonen says, as Maison slowly climbs to his feet, raising his hands, his eyes wide. "Maybe I'll throw her in the cell with your mother."

There's so much dead in the room, the bugs, the brilliant line of the bartender, the ants in the aftermath of the bubble, and Delina can't grasp any of it, can't reach anything.

Korhonen himself is mostly unharmed, wound on his arm barely distracting him. His heart pounds, harder than it should, like he's scared. Like he's extending himself with this entire thing. Like his mind is racing and he's only a few steps away from losing control of the room. Of the demon.

There's even a trail of sweat down his back, itching at his nerves.

She's not usually this aware of it all.

"Do you want them to live?" Korhonen says, nodding to

Gurlien and Chloe, not taking his eyes off of Maison. "You want them to get out of here? Tell them to leave."

Maison swallows, and she can see his Adam's apple bob at the motion.

The demon rolls into a crouch, her eyes reflecting the light back, and her lips are pulled back into a snarl. There's a burn, vivid and angry, across her cheeks where Delina grabbed her with the death, and the skin flakes from it.

Something trickles down Delina's neck, and with a jolt she realizes it's blood.

Whatever he's doing, whatever sensation the demon stole away, it's enough that she could bleed without feeling it.

Maison locks eyes with her, eyes still wide, some sort of calculation still flying through his brain. "I'll go with you if you don't hurt her."

Fuck that.

If Delina could control her legs enough, she'd kick out, but as it is she just manages a somewhat feeble twitch, and Korhonen shakes her again.

Korhonen's panicking, she can feel the acrid chemicals flooding through him, almost taste the bile in the back of his throat. He thought it'd be easy.

And his hand is still on her, providing her a direct line of all of his sensations, with just a thought.

With the dead bartender still almost blinding her, almost crowding out all of her ability to see, all she'd have to do is grab his hand and jolt him back. Socket the bones in his neck, smooth out the spine, and shock his heart back to beating.

She inhales, past the almost rabid want to give the life back.

"Wait," she mumbles, everything coming out mealy

mouthed and weak, and Maison blanches, flinching towards her, as Korhonen pulls her away.

If she could give someone their life, she could take it away.

"You'll come with me?" Korhonen says, ignoring her words, directly at Maison. "Without a fuss, anything?"

Still pale, still looking at Delina, Maison nods, clearly panicking as well.

"No," Delina fumbles out, and Korhonen clenches the hand tighter on her neck. Every vein in his palm, the blood pumping through it, the nerves firing through his skin.

And Maison looks like he's about to accept a death sentence, just to save her.

"Nope," she says louder, then, squeezing her eyes shut, tries to reach out and grab that life power coursing through Korhonen. To twist her mind around the nebulous sense she has of him, twist around it and pull.

Nothing happens. At first.

Then, with a gasp, the hand tightens on her neck, and everything goes to shit.

Pain blooms, brilliant, through her neck and her chest, and with one sudden motion Delina can feel her legs, gets her feet back underneath her, though her knees are still weak.

So she pulls on that nebulous power again, still on the hand on her neck, as hard as she can.

The skin on his palm blisters black, then peels back, and the nerves abruptly die, one by one, and Korhonen lets her go.

She twists, he's clutching his hand in horror, panicked, shaking.

His eyes snap up to hers, blue and brilliant, before he screams.

Screams, like the sound is torn out of him, and all the hair on the back of Delina's neck raises. Screams like a child, like the very air is stolen from his lungs.

The skin flakes off like sheafs of paper, black spiraling up his arm, revealing muscle and sinew, before that crumples to dust.

Delina staggers back, and Maison grabs her, steadying her, pulling her away from Korhonen, away from the terror and pain.

The black reaches his shoulder, and completely silently, caves in his chest, and the lungs crumble into nothing, and Korhonen slumps back, dead before he hits the floor.

Then it's just a few small twists, and the black flakes over the rest of his body, until all that's left is a body shaped pile of dust.

And then.

Stillness.

31

Tremors wind through Delina's body, and she's shaking. She's shaking, her hands are shaking, her teeth are shaking.

Maison drags her back a few more steps, like the dust could reach out to her and catch her in it, too.

"Oh my god," whispers Chloe, and she's in pain, all but forgotten with a stab wound through her shoulder. She climbs to her feet, her face pale, clutching the wall for support.

The demon's eyes are wide, staring down at what's left of Korhonen, before she recoils in horror from Delina.

"We need to get out of here," Gurlien says, breaking the silence, absentmindedly reaching down to help the demon up. She clutches at his arm, then shoves away from him, her eyes red.

"What did you do?" the demon spits out, and Delina can taste her terror mixed in with the pain. "What did you—"

With a jerk, the leash tightens around her throat, yanking her back. She claws at her throat, her nails drawing lines of black blood, before she abruptly disappears.

Disappears, and going with her all possibility of helping her. Of getting rid of the control.

Delina swallows and, still shaking, turns to Maison.

He's pale, so pale, the blood on his cheek brilliant.

"We need to go," he says, his voice strangled.

"I should bring him back," Delina says, pointing to the bartender with a shaking hand. "He died, he didn't need to, I should—"

Maison steps in close, even though she can taste his fear. "If you try one more thing you're going to die," he says, voice dipping low. "We need to get you out of here."

THEY BANDAGE their wounds back at the cabin, and Delina all but falls onto the couch, her head thudding.

"How did we see the demon?" Gurlien asks, after a few long moments of cleaning out splinters from Chloe's shoulder in silence. "I can't wrap my mind around it."

"That's what you can't wrap your mind around?" Maison shoots over, holding a wet paper towel to the cut on his cheek.

Gurlien looks up enough to give him a glare. "The other things have explanations. She went offensive, you tried to sell yourself out at the first opportunity, but I do not understand the demon."

"She said she was trapped," Delina says dully, as Maison squares his shoulders at Gurlien. "We were about to be able to help her."

"Ow," Chloe mutters, as Gurlien pulls another bloody shard of wood out of her shoulder. "We wouldn't have been able to."

"I was...I was bluffing," Delina says, and her hands still

shake, no matter how hard she stares at them. "I was trying to get her to stop—could you guys hear what I was saying?"

"Enough of it," Maison mutters, ducking his chin down.

"Yes, maybe don't promise a demon things you don't know are possible," Gurlien says, and behind all the bluster there's a very real fear.

A fear of Delina.

"I was...I was trying not to die, okay?" Delina snaps, and they all turn to her. "I didn't know what to do or what to say?"

"And then you got out and immediately went all Indiana Jones and the Temple of Doom on Korhonen?" Gurlien says.

"That's the wrong movie," Chloe chimes in, small through the pain of the wood fragments still in her shoulder.

"I didn't know that would happen like that," Delina says, quieter than she likes, and another tremor quakes through her shoulders. "I thought I could get him to let me go, I didn't..."

Suddenly, bile climbs up her throat, and she leans over, putting her head through her knees.

"I didn't know he would die! I didn't know, I didn't..."

Too many things had happened that day.

Too many.

The cabin is silent, and Delina just breathes through her nose against the nausea, tears crowding into her eyes.

"You're still hurt," Maison says, gently sitting next to her, pulling back the collar of her shirt, where she swears she can still feel the echo of Korhonen's hand gripping her. "Process this tomorrow, we need to take care of you."

"No, processing now would be good," Gurlien interrupts, and Delina's eyes prickle. "We killed the top battle mage, their demon escaped, this is going to escalate!"

"Shut it, Gurlien," Chloe mumbles.

"No, I won't shut it, this is bad!"

Delina glances up to see Gurlien throw up his hands, the fear twisting to frustration.

"I'm tired of pretending that this isn't bad, that every new thing isn't some horrible revelation, and that I'm supposed to be normal after all of this! We saw him die! He literally crumpled into dust! We're not gonna be okay after this!"

Gently, Maison rubs between Delina's shoulder blades.

"A demon was told to dispose of me, if Chloe was three inches to the right that wood shard would have gone through her throat! Delina almost got zapped to death by a demon, and you—" he jabs his finger at Maison, "—you just gave up so quickly!"

"He had her by the throat! She couldn't stand!" Maison says, and Delina can feel his anger like it is her own. "I was trying to buy time! I didn't want her to die!"

"Thanks," Delina breathes out, her mind still flashing to the horror on Korhonen's face as the skin peeled off his hand. At the bones disintegrating, at the dust falling from him.

"And still your first thought was to give up. To go back to them. To go right into the situation you just got out of, except worse." Gurlien paces in the small living room, and Chance the cat pokes his head in before skittering away.

"Not sure if you noticed, but there was a full demon there, and I wasn't exactly winning that fight," Maison bites out, his hand stilling on Delina's back.

"And the demon, who nobody will explain to me," Gurlien finishes, crossing his arms. "How could we see her? Did you know her?"

"There was a thing around her neck," Delina all but

mumbles. "It was controlling her, she didn't want to be there."

Chloe clears her throat, picking out another shard of wood out of her own shoulder, and it turns Delina's stomach all over again.

"I think we should abandon the cabin," Chloe says, and everyone abruptly shuts up. "Go somewhere else. They know we're nearby now."

"The demon said nobody else knew," Delina replies, because this, at least, can distract her mind from the horror, from the skin flaking away like burned paper. "Said she tracked Maison, not me."

Chloe watches Delina, her brown eyes serious. "And now they know how to do that. We should run."

"I don't want to leave the demon circle at this moment," Gurlien says, like the conversation is distracting his mind too, derailing it from the conflict. "We go anywhere else, they now have a sniffer dog out there waiting for us to pop up."

"She's not a dog," Maison shoots back, immediately standing up. "She wasn't there because she wanted to be."

"That didn't stop her from almost killing Delina!" Gurlien says. "That didn't stop her from blowing up the bar, from fighting you, from disappearing the first moment she could! She's probably back there now, telling them where we are and how to get us for more of the Necromancer!"

"Calm down," Chloe says, softly, but her gaze is hard. "We can create the demon circle again. We'll pick the next property on the will."

"I'm not leaving," Delina says, and once again, everyone falls silent to look at her, so she sits up even though her stomach still churns. "The demon can't get us in here, and she might not even want to tell them where we are. For all they know, Korhonen took a demon out of whatever prison —" Maison flinches at that, "—and he didn't come back. They might not even know why."

"You can't seriously be taking the demon's side in all of this," Gurlien replies, turning to sarcasm that obviously masks some fear. "You were a few random zaps away from being dead because of her."

"And she didn't even want to be there!" Maison all but blows up, and it takes Delina a few seconds to track that he's still a little drunk, despite all the action and magic. "She was obviously just another victim."

Gurlien scoffs, and Maison's shoulders tense, his arm pulling back, and—

Delina catches his hand, right as his hand clenches into a fist.

"Sit down," she orders, and they both stare at her. "No, both of you. Sit."

"Thank you, Delina," Chloe mumbles, as they sit on opposite sides of the couch.

"Anyone who wants to leave, can leave." The very thought of it turns her stomach, along with the alcohol and the horror. "I'm staying here, it's my cabin, they don't know exactly where it's at. That means it's safe."

Chloe ducks her head down.

"The two of you are probably safe to leave, they're not tracking you," Delina says, pointing to Chloe and Gurlien. "But we can't make a decision right now, not while..."

Not while the bone crumbling away sticks in her mind.

She swallows, hard. "Maison, do you think she could track us down here? To this cabin? Even if they forced her?"

Gurlien scoffs again, but quieter this time.

"No," Maison replies, staring hard at Gurlien. "She can't see beyond the demon circle and couldn't get in."

"Okay," Delina says, and her voice wobbles. "Then I'm staying, at least until tomorrow."

"We should plan for tomorrow," Chloe murmurs, like she doesn't want to contradict Delina, but wants to be anywhere but in the room at the moment. "We should have a plan in case they knock on our door."

"Not a bad idea," Delina says, but the horror rises up in her stomach again.

She killed someone. Someone who was previously alive, and no amount of necromancy could bring back the dead like that.

She swallows it down again.

"I'll sleep out here," Maison says, and Gurlien squints at him. "If they come through the door in the middle of the night, they'll deal with me first thing."

"Or you'll just give yourself up at first chance," Gurlien shoots over. "Whoops, welcome in, have my ex without a fight, the other two sleep over there, leave the cat alone if you can, I'm just gonna go with you and back to my cushy life where everyone believes I'm a prodigy and—" He cuts off, abruptly swallowing, before he buries his face in his hands, breathing raggedly.

Without the yelling, the silence churns in Delina.

Delina glances up at Maison, and instead of the anger, there's something else on his face. Something between pity and resignation.

Chance the cat pokes his head around the corner again, at the sudden quiet. At Chloe, holding a damp towel to her shoulder with a pale face, at Gurlien, not looking up. At Delina, who probably doesn't look that great either, and Maison, who's still bleeding from the cut across his face.

Maison shifts, and instead of any punch or any violent motion, just clasps Gurlien on the shoulder.

Gurlien flinches, but doesn't open his eyes, before he relaxes, exhaling.

"We're not giving up," Delina says, and each time she speaks, she just hears the shriek from Korhonen, before his lungs caved in.

"Yeah," Gurlien says, voice weary, before he rubs his eyes again. "Sorry, Maison."

"I get it," Maison says, though his jaw is tight, before he shifts away until he can lean against Delina. "You should absolutely eat something before you try to sleep."

As if sleep is something that'll happen at this point.

"Don't really think I can keep anything down," Delina attempts at a joke and immediately regrets it, everyone suddenly staring at her. "I...I killed someone? I've never done that? I think I'm still drunk? I don't..."

Chloe tromps over to the kitchen and comes back with a chocolate bar, shoving it in Delina's hands, before she sits in front of Gurlien, handing him the tweezers and pointing at her shoulder. "Fix please."

"Yeah, okay," Gurlien says, still a bit numb. "Sorry."

Chloe nods, yanking down the collar of her undershirt, so he can see the mess better.

This close, it's a bloody pulp and Delina can see what might be a muscle.

"Should you go to the hospital?" Delina asks, and Maison takes the chocolate bar from her, opening it for her.

"They're absolutely going to look at the hospitals," Chloe says, grim. "I've had worse, I'll get better."

Another silence descends on the cabin.

"Well, at least now we know I can fight," Delina attempts at a joke, even though the horror still crawls under her skin. "I'm not just...helpless."

"Jesus Christ," Gurlien mutters.

DESPITE THE EXHAUSTION, despite the ghost numbness that
steals over her if she's not thinking too hard, despite the now
acute hangover, Delina can't sleep, tossing and turning in
the giant bed, alone.

Oh, she's not alone at being unable to sleep. Maison's
sitting up on the couch in the other room, back rod straight,
the cat curled up on his lap. Chloe's down in the basement,
next to the dead fly, on one of those rolling chairs. Gurlien's
awake in his room, pacing the small distance, back and
forth.

She's not sure the last time she's felt so tired, but closing
her eyes just brings back an almost unnamable sort of
terror, so she peels herself off the bed, clutching one of the
blankets around her shoulders to ward off the chill, and
kicks open the door to the living room.

Maison's not surprised to see her awake, that's for sure,
but he doesn't get up, the cat too nestled on his lap.

Delina blinks at him in the dim light, before grabbing a
water from the kitchen and joining him on the couch.

He shifts, just enough so she can curl her legs underneath herself, tugging the blanket around her.

It's quiet, beautifully quiet, before Maison breathes out,
pointing towards the window. "It started snowing a bit ago,"
he whispers, and through the gap in the floral curtains,
there's just a hint of falling snow.

"Will that affect the demon trap?" Delina asks, but he's
already shaking his head. "Oh."

"If anything, it'll make it less visible to normal humans,"
Maison says, and there's something sad on his face. "Just
uncrossable for demons."

"That's good," Delina says, and Chance the cat yawns,

stretching out his paw just enough so he touches Delina's knee. "Have you...have you had to kill someone before?"

Maison swallows, then nods.

"Does it get less weird?"

He shakes his head, firmly, before he equivocates. "Less weird, yes. Less awful, no."

"Who did you kill?" Delina asks, almost desperately, the need for some sort of knowledge tugging at her. "What did they do?"

Maison stills, and in the dim light it's as if he's carved from stone. "Try to kidnap you," he says, and his voice is strange, foreign. "A splinter group from the East Coast, they weren't...they weren't going to keep you alive."

"Grim," Delina says, tugging the blanket tighter.

"You did a good job, at least," Maison says, still soft. "Didn't hesitate from what I could see."

"Not helpful," Delina says, settling deeper in the couch, but the loneliness is a bit less severe, out here. "Would you really have gone with them?"

Maison breathes out, shutting his eyes. "If it was the only option to keep you safe."

"I don't like that," Delina says, and he shuts his eyes further, scrunching his face down. "Don't, okay."

He doesn't say anything, and in the dim light, Delina lets her eyes fall shut, the blanket wrapped around her shoulders, the only sound the purr from the cat.

32

T he next day is full of tension. Of planning and packing. Of scanning the trees around them, looking for surveillance.

Only in the afternoon, when the sun is just barely beginning to turn orange over the trees, does a loud alarm blare through the cabin.

"Satellite phone?" Chloe asks, her brow furrowing. "Nobody calls that."

"Only the forest service calls that," Gurlien corrects, but he clambers to his feet from where he had been feverishly leafing through paperwork, pulling out the brick of a phone from the drawer.

There's no display to read numbers off of, so they all stare at it a beat before Gurlien presses the button to answer it.

There's a pop of static, loud, before a click.

"Yes?" Gurlien asks, crossing his arms and locking eyes with Chloe.

It is their hideout after all that is at risk.

There's another pop, like the phone is connecting to

another satellite, before a woman's voice filters through, garbled and staticky.

"Frederick?"

Maison stiffens, as all eyes snap to him in the small cabin, even the cat, but he doesn't say anything.

"Frederick, they told me to call you." The voice is trembling, even through the tenuous connection. "They said to call this and see if you're alive."

His jaw tightens, and he rubs his face, before shaking his head at Gurlien.

"Sorry, ma'am, I think you got the wrong number," Chloe says, leaning forward and putting on an immaculate British accent. "Are you okay?"

"No, this is the number they gave me," the woman replies, and through the connection, there's a desperate tone to her words. "They said he would be here if he was alive. Please."

Chloe gapes over at Maison, who's as still as stone. "No, ma'am, this is a rural number, I'm so sorry."

"Please, they told me they'd hurt me if I don't find him, is he there? Is he alive?"

Maison crosses his arms, and shakes his head.

"No, nobody here by that name, sorry." Chloe trails off, and Maison grabs the phone and snaps it shut, cutting off the call.

"That was a trap," Maison says, his voice tight.

"No shit," Chloe says, higher pitched. "They know where we are, they're going to come, we need to get out."

"That was your mom?" Delina asks, and they all three stopped to look at her. "Would they actually hurt her?"

For a brief moment, she thinks Maison's going to shatter, but he just nods. "She doesn't call me Frederick if she needs me. That was her signaling me to not rise to the bait."

"But they'll hurt her?"

He locks eyes with her, and she would do anything to not see that expression across his face ever again. "Probably."

"Jesus Christ," Gurlien murmurs.

"Do we need to finish packing? Do we need to run right now?" Chloe interrupts, scrambling up to standing. "If they know our satellite phone they can find us so easily, they could just walk right up and knock on the door, why the call?"

"They think that whatever they do, I'll counteract it, so they want to know if I'm still alive," Maison says, his voice dead. "They don't want to ambush you if I'm in the building."

"So they think you might be and Korhonen didn't get to report back, but they're not sure, which means they don't have drone footage that could see through the windows," Gurlien says, but he's almost vibrating with nervous energy. "If we leave now, they might have the roads blocked off, they might have something in place, they might—"

Not even bothering to stick around for the rest of the talk, Maison turns on his heel and strides into the room he's been staying in, shutting the door behind him with a click.

Gurlien gapes at him, then shuts his mouth, then opens it again. "Chloe, we need to pack, get the research and I'll get the components," he says, grim. "If they don't have something in place, they will fast, and we need to beat them to it."

"We don't have room for all the research, we have two extra people, we need..."

They squabble on, discussing what parts of her cabin to divide up, which parts of her mother's precious research to leave behind for these people who had tried to keep her ignorant. Try to make plans for something they don't know.

Delina pushes herself up to standing, and they both look at her.

"Make preparations, don't take any of my mother's stuff, and don't leave yet," she orders, and it's bizarre, giving edicts for something like this, when pretty much everyone else is better suited to leading them than her. "They might be guessing, and no movement would be more confusing than not. They're expecting you to run."

With that, she glances to the door that Maison disappeared to, and, with confidence she certainly doesn't feel, walks towards him and closes it behind herself.

The click of the door is loud, far louder, in the tiny room.

There's a small bed tucked in the corner, and the baby blue carpet is dusty with disuse. There's a single bare bookcase with Maison's paintings from the last few days drying on one of them, and a small suitcase leans up against a bedside table.

And Maison's sitting on the floor against the bed, his head in his hands.

"What do you want?" he asks, muffled behind his hands.

Delina would've absolutely greeted him the same way, so she dismisses the offense with a shrug, folding herself up so she's sitting next to him.

He doesn't move, and for a long moment she just sits next to him, listening to him breathe.

"You don't have to talk me through this," Maison says finally, after the moment of quiet stretches on, twisting and warping her perception of time. "I've dealt with this before."

"That sucks," Delina says baldly, and he lifts his head enough to look at her, really look at her. "I'm sorry."

"I know you didn't do anything for this," he mumbles, and there's actually wetness around his eyes. "They would've still made that call if you didn't bring me back, they would probably still hurt her if you didn't bring me back, and I would still be unable to do a damn thing about it if you didn't bring me back."

How many times did he struggle with this, with her blithely unaware next to him?

"Do you want to go to her?" Delina asks, and he makes a small noise in the back of his throat, something close to pain.

"I can't," he says, miserable, and he lets his head thump against the bed. "I can't and you know why."

Because of her. Because of that bond he described. Somewhere along the line it turned into a chain around his foot, anchoring him to her.

"All I can do is sit here, hope they think I'm dead, and hope they let my mom go sometime. I leave you, they'll kill you. They'll storm this place and shoot their way in and you'll be the first shot." He squeezes his eyes shut. "If they don't get you, the next time you slip up, a demon will. I can't do a goddamn thing."

"I'm gonna take it that if I say you don't need to stick around it's not gonna help?" Delina asks, and he shakes his head. "Then we go to them."

For a moment, she thought he misheard her, before he sits up straighter. "Delly, we can't."

"Why not?" she asks, and she doesn't truly know what she's saying, not really, but him sitting here in misery is equally not an option. "You don't want to leave me alone, we can't just let them hurt her, we go to them."

"Again, they could just kill you," Maison says, his voice rising in pitch.

"You don't think they would like to have someone who can bring people back from the dead in their possession? Like what Korhonen said? He brought out an entire demon in order to try to capture both of us." She challenges him, twisting so she's seated cross legged in front of him. "Let them think they can cheat death, get your mom out, then we run. All three of us."

He stares at her, then rubs his face. "It won't work."

"Why not?" she says again, as impish as she can, and it almost pulls a hint of a smile from him. "It'll require planning, but they're not expecting me to just go to them, it'll catch them off guard. We can go in, save her, then you don't have to sit here and worry about her."

"It's a lot more complicated than that," he says, which is expected, but his shoulders loosen, just a bit, and if she can get him out of this misery for a few minutes, then the conversation will be a success. "Nobody can just waltz in and ask for what they want."

She shrugs, which succeeds in drawing a smile from him as he shakes his head at her.

"Delina," he starts, "even if there was something we could do, we couldn't do it without more information," he says, and she can just feel his heart breaking just by sitting next to him. "If they think I'm going to do something, they're going to move her, they've done it before."

"When my dad broke his ankle?" Delina asks, and he nods.

"So even if I wanted to go burst in there, guns blazing, I...couldn't. I would need more information, we'd need to hack into their systems, we'd need to break in - which is incredibly complex by the way - and then we'd have to find her, all while they're on the lookout for us." He thumps his fist against his leg, a stark contrast to his calm words. "We can't just go in right now."

"Okay, so maybe tomorrow," Delina says, and he smiles,

briefly. "Or the next day, my offer doesn't expire just because a few days have passed. It's not the worst idea."

"We need more information, and that will take days."

"Then we will get it," Delina protests.

"And if they spot movement from this area, they're almost certainly watching in some way, then they'll do worse, so we're literally stuck. Maybe Chloe and Gurlien can leave, they'd be sitting ducks if that demon is out there and they cross the circle, but we're stuck."

"I feel bad about that," Delina says. "I pretty much showed up on their doorsteps and blew up their lives. Nobody expected me."

"Nobody ever expects you," he says, and she's not sure if it's a compliment or not. "You're the singularly most confusing person I've ever met, and I've met some weird as hell people."

"You know, I think I believe you on that," Delina jokes, and they briefly, ever so briefly, share a smile. "Before this last...however long..." her mind refuses to believe that it's only been maybe a few weeks. "I would've laughed at the idea that your graphic design company had weird people, but apparently you know like vampires and shit."

"Vampires aren't real," Maison says, then pauses. "I think."

"You're apparently half spooky, so who knows."

That was a mistake, his smile fades at the remembrance of the situation they're in.

"Delina..." he starts, then squeezes his eyes shut again. "I appreciate the offer for help, you are under no obligation to do so."

"I know that," she replies, crabby, before she reaches out and grabs his knee, in a motion of confidence she doesn't fully feel.

A spark crackles from her hand to his jeans, and he flinches.

"I know that doesn't hurt you," Delina says, as if chiding him would make this any better. "I don't care if you want my help, I don't even know if I can help, I just don't want you to think you have to do it alone."

He looks at her, really looks at her, his lips turned down in a frown, his eyes pinched, and she makes herself meet his gaze. Doesn't turn away from the awkward, doesn't turn away from the creeping sensation that she should still be angry at him, doesn't turn away from the fact that she's not.

Finally, his lips twitch, and it's not a smile, not quite, but still, she's relieved.

"You're giving me a lot of mixed signals, Delly girl," he says, his voice deep and a little raw. "I can't figure out where your head is."

She gets the question.

"You ran away, you broke up with me, you saved my life, you're concerned with me, and now you're offering to put yourself in danger for me. Not for me, but for my mom, who you've literally never met." His hand settles over hers, still grasping his knee. "And I think you're trying to make me feel better?"

"Trying," Delina admits, and he gives her a soft smile at that. "Not sure I'm succeeding."

"Why?" His voice beaks, just a bit,

Because her heart hurts at the idea of him sitting here alone. Because she can tell he's upset just by his shoulders and the lines between his eyebrows.

Because he's held her through years of her depression, her helplessness at the rages of her own mind. Because he held her behind him when faced with someone there to end her, took the shot meant to kill her.

"Because five years, I guess," Delina admits. "If you want honesty."

Gentle, telegraphing his motions, he reaches up and cradles her chin. They're sitting so close to each other that her hip is pressed against his, her side against his.

And he's searching for something in her eyes, something in her expression, and she doesn't know what, so she just focuses on breathing, on making herself an open book for him to read.

"Honesty?" he asks, and she nods, of course. "Do you remember the Christmas we went to the town square lights? The first one?"

Of course she does. Prescott goes all in on Christmas lights around the courthouse, and the first year they went it actually snowed, leaving magical drifts of white with the lights twinkling through.

She had also just recovered from a bad bout of the flu, and had practically clung to him all day long, stubborn in the want to see the lights but utterly exhausted.

"And we went to the pizza place afterwards and it was so full and so warm? And they had the lights dimmed down so everyone could see the snow and the decorations outside?"

She doesn't know how this relates to any of their conversation, of his mother being hurt and the confusion between the two of them. They had gone to the lights every year after that, too.

"We were crammed in that tiny booth, there were people everywhere, and then you rested your head against my shoulder," he continues, and he gently pushes a strand of her hair behind her ear. "That's when it stopped being about my job to keep you happy, that's when I started wanting to make you happy."

That was well over four and a half years ago. They had been dating for maybe three months.

"With your head on my shoulder, with the noise and the dim lights and too many people, I felt myself crumble into love with you. You were so tired, and with just that little touch all my ideas of keeping a professional distance with a professional amount of affection just...evaporated." He gestures something flying away. "I never wanted to leave that moment."

"Oh," Delina says, soft.

"I still don't," he finishes, his voice so quiet she can barely hear him. "And now you...know. About me, about my parentage. About your mother and about all the lies. And I still don't want to do anything that would lead away from that peace I felt in the pizza parlor, staring out at Christmas lights. You were complaining about being too warm and making jokes about how many people were there and every word out of your mouth was the best thing I ever heard."

He ducks his head, as if this takes so much out of him to tell her, and his words hang in the air between them.

And it's on her to respond.

"More honesty?" Delina asks, and he nods as well. "I don't know if I'll be ever able to trust you again, fully. But I want to try."

Her heart pounds in her chest, and his face breaks.

"Delly..." he trails off.

"You are so not allowed to keep secrets from me anymore," she declares, as imperial as she can. "And that includes any details on how I can help with your mom."

He tugs her into a one crushing, heart breaking hug. The sort of hug where he clings to her, as if she is a life raft in the middle of an ocean, like she's the only thing that can keep his head above the water while he desperately treads.

She wraps her arms around him and clutches tight back.

His heart beats, loud and fast, and his arms tremble around her, like he's so scared of hurting her but can't hold any less tight, and she smushes her face into his chest.

"I don't ever want to lie to you again," he mumbles into her hair, pressing his cheek against the top of her head. "I don't. I don't."

They're still sitting on the carpet in the room, with his paintings spread over the bookcase and his small suitcase is leaned up against the bedside table, and it's so far away from the peace of Prescott. The air smells different, the frost creeping along the window is different, the brilliant green of the trees under the snow is different.

The knowledge they have is different.

Instead of just her boyfriend Maison, who paints and bakes cookies when he's stressed, who works with graphic design and likes her dad, it's Maison who put his life on the line for her. It's Maison the half-demon, whose artery broke and spilled blood throughout his body. It's Maison who is half terrified of her, of the problems her powers create. It's Maison who's spent almost every day in the last five years utterly stressed for her safety, who bent over backwards to make her happy.

It's Maison, who also misses his mom.

"I'm not gonna let you keep me away from helping you," she mumbles back. "You're gonna have to accept that, too."

His arms briefly tighten, before he pulls away, and that's all the warning she gets before he grabs her chin and kisses her.

They've kissed hundreds of times. Thousands, probably, over the last five years, but none have ever felt like this.

His lips sear against hers, as if he could consume her through just the act of passion. Like it's every bit of his willpower to not escalate, to not overpower her. His hand on her chin is hard, firm, keeping her in place, so even if she wanted to pull away, she couldn't.

She doesn't want to.

She arches her back, pressing against him, throwing her arms around his neck, tangling a hand in his soft brown hair. Every line of him, every touch, burns, blazing through her and any anger and frustration and leaving just...this.

He makes a note in the back of his throat, a soft, needy noise, and she opens her mouth to his, and he takes it. Greedily, like they've never kissed before and he will never get another chance again.

It sings through her blood, lighting a fire in her stomach, and she breaks the kiss just long enough to straddle his thighs, then grips him by the hair and pulls him back in.

He relents, happily, pulling her closer, a hand at the small of her back, holding her there, relentless, and she bites his bottom lip, and he groans, just like he always does.

It's not enough. It was everything, and then, suddenly, it's not enough, and she scrabbles to pull up her shirt, bare her skin so more of him can touch her, so his hands can circle her skin and warm her touch and—

Loud, a spark crackles from her hand.

They both jump, their lips breaking apart, and his eyes glow red, wide.

"Did you mean to do that?" he whispers, and his lips are wet.

"I still don't know what that is," she whispers back, gentling her hand in his hair, resting her forehead against his.

He grins at her, the sort of smile that takes away all of her fears and her stress, blowing them to the wind, and she smiles back, all sorts of foolish. "I don't either."

"Weird," she whispers, pressing a small kiss to his lips again, in between words. "Here I thought you might know everything."

"I wish," he responds, holding her tight against him, and it's so breathlessly easy, it's so breathlessly simple, sitting here straddled on his lap. Like she never left, like nothing ever happened between them. Like it's home.

She kisses him again, and his stubble scratches against her, his hands gripping her hips in place, his thumb brilliant against her skin, until—

The alarm blares through the cabin, and they jolt apart.

The satellite phone.

His eyes still glow red, and his cheeks are flushed, but his face sobers as they dimly hear Chloe answer it again, and the same woman's voice asking for Frederick once more.

And here she is, straddling him with her shirt off.

"Oh," she whispers, pulling back, reaching for her shirt, and he hands it to her where it fell next to his bed.

"Yeah," he whispers back, briefly squeezing his eyes shut, breathing in deep, getting himself under control. "They're not going to stop."

She shrugs her shirt back on, awkwardly climbing off his lap, and he rubs his face.

"Let's go back out there and plan," she says, hoping her voice is steady, "and we will continue this later."

He blinks up at her, like it's the last time he'll see her face. "I'll hold you to that, I will," he warns, and it tugs a smile from her, almost against her wishes, as he flattens down his hair from her mussing and adjusts his jeans.

It's just as familiar of motion as he always did, before he climbs to his feet, offering her a hand up.

This time, she takes it.

33

They have his mother call three more times that morning, but she never calls him by the name Maison, and they never deviate from Chloe's British accent.

It's awful and Maison's face twists each time hearing her voice, and Gurlien gets more and more frantic. He's packed three bags, all neatly placed by the plastic front door, with a tote bag of books leaning against them.

Chloe's just packed her backpack.

They had all agreed that showing activity in the cabin during the day would be bad, but that hasn't made them any more likely to relax anytime soon, and Gurlien keeps on twitching the floral curtains open to peek out at them.

Instead, all four of them are trapped in there together, and it's not helping anything.

"I still think we should draw up the schematics of where she's hidden," Delina drawls. "There has to be a way in there."

"There's not," Gurlien replies, screwing up his face in frustration at her. "Tell her there's not."

"There's not...that we know of," Maison replies, and Gurlien makes a crude gesture at him, almost upsetting the cat sitting on him. "She's probably not even at the Atlanta base anymore."

"What, do you think they'd take her to LA or to the Toronto location?" Gurlien replies, sarcastic. "Because all of those are so easy to break into."

Chloe makes a noise, a small noise, but it's enough to draw everyone's attention, and the mint box in her hand turns into a blob of plastic once more.

"Yes?" Delina asks, and Chloe blinks up at her, then over at Maison.

"They have a demon center at the Toronto location," she says, small. "A lot of their research is there, a lot of demon defenses are there."

Silence descends over the room, and Delina twists, breathless, to look at Maison.

His expression is as if stone.

"They had stasis holding cells designed to keep full demons at bay," Chloe continues, and she hunches her shoulders in on herself. "And everything in between."

"Yes, that's where Dr. Frisse stole the idea of the Terese project," Gurlien says, as if he's trying to be dismissive but failing. "They have a thousand failed vectors of that experiment in there, it's ghastly."

"If I was trying to keep a Half Demon out of somewhere, I'd go there," Chloe says, but she's frowning at the very idea of it, and Delina starkly remembers the scars on her ribs. "Or trap a necromancer."

Gurlien sits up, jolting the cat from its perch. "Frisse has three condos in that city, they only know about two of them."

Maison's face twitches. "That's a lot of conjecture," he

warns, but there's a small light of something approaching hope in his eyes.

"I'm gonna...I'm gonna make something," Chloe declares, then throws a look at Gurlien. "The extra laptop, I need it."

"Are you going to wreck it?" Gurlien asks, but he's standing, already in motion.

"Maison, with your permission, can I make a tracker for the satellite phone?" Chloe asks quietly. "It should just be on our side, but there is a chance they'll be able to tell."

Maison freezes.

"I want to confirm at least the zip code they're calling from," Chloe continues, "that could help us with the location."

Slowly, Maison nods, as Gurlien comes back with the laptop.

"How big of a chance?" Delina asks, standing and stretching her legs. "You said there's a chance, how big of one?"

"If she does this correctly, about point seven percent," Gurlien says, clattering the laptop onto the table. It's an old laptop, bigger than most of Delina's college textbooks, and she'd be shocked if it could actually connect to the internet anymore.

Delina paces into the kitchen, crossing her arms, but Maison's still. Pale.

"How often do you not do this correctly?" Delina asks, if Maison isn't going to.

"Well, I've never done this particular conversion," Chloe replies, turning over the laptop and taking a screwdriver— that was just a mechanical pencil, Delina belatedly notices —to the underside of it. "But electronic conversions are mostly all the same and mostly deal in intent. I just need to figure out exactly how to do it."

She pops the casing off, showcasing the innards of the laptop, and despite occasionally having to function as IT for a group of older coworkers who can't fix printers, it's over Delina's head as well.

"Take your time," Gurlien mutters, staring hard at the laptop as well. "Remember, the closer to use, the better."

"Right," Chloe says, and they both bend their heads over the laptop, and she converts a fork to another screwdriver with just a twist of her fingers.

It takes Delina a few seconds to notice, but somewhere in that mess Maison has lifted his gaze to her, and held it, somehow even more terrified than he was before.

If he hasn't ever had a chance to even allow himself to think about getting his mother out, this must be a thorny knot of emotions and confusion.

"We're going to figure something out," Delina informs him, quietly, pacing to stand next to him. "Even if this isn't it, we'll do something."

Gurlien briefly glances up at them, then back to helping Chloe dissect the old laptop.

Maison rubs his face. "It's a bit hard to believe."

"This is just information gathering," Gurlien says, still bent over the laptop. "This isn't a for sure thing, this isn't even a plan. This is just us getting the info we might need to make one."

It's a surprisingly adept thing to say, and Maison breathes out, closing his eyes just long enough for the cat to jump on his lap and meow loudly.

"This also gives us a way to evaluate if we truly need to split and run," Gurlien continues. "So it's not just helping you, if you're going to be weird about that."

"Thanks," Maison says, probably aiming for sarcasm but missing it completely.

"Can you use parts from that to scour for drones or something?" Delina asks, and they all blink up at her. "It'll help us know if we're truly under surveillance or if it's just the phone."

Chloe sets aside a chunk of plastic that may or may not have been a graphics card at that.

"This will take a few hours," she warns, and there's some tension along her face, tension that's not usually there. "I'm slow with electronics, but I'll get there."

"I don't know why, but that makes sense," Delina says, and gets a wan smile in return. "Did my mother leave behind binoculars?"

TURNS OUT SHE DID, deep in the basement, and Delina's skin crawls at the sensation of the dead bug, but she strides past it, holding her head high, then enlists Maison's help to climb in the attic.

"Even we've never been up there," Gurlien calls out, still working with the laptop. "No guarantee it's at all safe."

By the look of the outside, it'll be small, but a few windows still peek out to the setting sun outside. If the cabin had been normal, Delina would have pegged it as the sort of attic that someone stores Christmas decorations and luggage in.

"You mean they have a tomb breaker and they never tried to go into the attic?" Delina whispers to Maison as they drag a chair over for easier access.

"It's not locked," Maison points out, his face still pale. "No interest if it's not locked, it's not climate sealed so there's no way Dr. Frisse would store research, there's no obvious magical trace of anything."

He stands on the stool, testing the seal of the hole in the ceiling door, exactly like he did the times they helped her dad decorate.

He had always been so excited to do so, and now she knows it's because he didn't have that in his childhood.

The door pops open easily, and a small rain of paint dust falls into Maison's hair, and he blinks at her, at the almost comedy of the moment, before he climbs off the chair and offers her a boost up.

"No, you're not waiting in the sitting room as they try to figure that out," Delina says, and the corners of his lips tip upwards. "Come up here and help me try to spy on any mysterious drones."

"You would be a horrible spy," Maison says, boosting her up so she can push herself into the attic.

It's a tiny room, barely tall enough for her to stand, and even more of the floral curtains hang over the small window. Sheets are thrown over a pile of things, and dust covers those.

It smells fresher than most attics, but that's not difficult to do.

Behind her, Maison climbs up, then blinks wildly at the small room.

"This may be the most normal room in this cabin," Delina says as he pulls himself in.

"Nothing dead under those sheets?" he asks, and she shakes her head. "Though you'd probably have complained about that already if there was."

"Absolutely," Delina replies, before she twitches the curtains aside.

In the attic, they're not quite above the trees, but the

vantage point is excellent. With the binoculars, she can see all the way down the winding gravel driveway, to the proper street, and even the spot where the tree had fallen, now fully dusted with snow.

"Neat," Delina says, impressed, before handing the binoculars to Maison. "Take a look."

He doesn't take them, instead frowning at one of the piles of things right next to the window, before he whips off the sheet in another cloud of dust.

Revealing a sniper rifle and a spotting scope, helpfully set up to be pointed directly out the window. The rifle gleams, all sleek metal and hard plastics, and it still smells a bit of oil.

"Of course," Delina comments, out of a lack of anything else to say. "That's logical for my mom to have."

"Congrats, you inherited a sniper's nest," Maison says, and there's a little more color in his face, though his brows are furrowed. "She could literally strike people with magic, why would she need a sniper rifle?"

"Greater distance?" Delina offers, and he shrugs idly, like that doesn't quite make sense in the context. "Maybe it came with the place?"

"Doubt it," Maison says, skirting around the rather impressive rifle and adjusting the scope instead. "That's... illegal in a lot of states. Probably Washington, too. Definitely in Canada." He pokes the edge of the rifle, like he could determine something from it by touch, and his eyes gleam red for a split second. "She maintained it, too. Last touched it about a year and two months ago."

Which would've been right before her mother died. Somewhere in the middle of the Terese disaster, somewhere between apparently running around all of Canada and finding another Necromancer and getting dead, her mother found the time to come up to the cabin and oil the gun.

"Right," Delina replies, casting a critical eye to the rest of the room. The gun definitely adds more questions than it answers.

Below them, in the sitting room, the satellite phone rings again, and Maison flinches, his shoulders locking up.

They don't answer it this time, just letting the number ring out.

"Well, this'll be useful in defending this, I bet," Delina says, forcefully, and his eyes swing up to her face. "If we get, I dunno, ambushed or something."

"If we get ambushed, you're hiding in the basement," he replies automatically.

"I can almost guarantee I'm a better shot than Gurlien," she says, pitching her voice a little louder in case he can hear her, and it gets another hint of a smile from Maison, as the phone finally stops ringing. "We'll figure this out, don't concentrate on the phone."

It's far easier said than done, but he turns his attention back to the scope, pointing it out the window, adjusting it, and she lets him. It's a good distraction, at least something he could do with his hands.

If the kitchen table below wasn't covered in laptop guts, she'd tell him to paint.

"Got it," Maison says, still splayed out with the scope. "Drone, other side of the confusion spell."

The hair on the back of Delina's neck prickles. "Can you shoot it down with this thing?"

He gives her the barest of glances. "I don't think I'm that good of a shot." He fiddles with something on the scope, narrowing it in. "They're definitely watching, we'll have to wait for nighttime to leave."

Instead of reacting, Delina glances to the other small window, facing the back of the property, and the large sheet covered pile in between her and it.

Climbing over it without knowing what it is sounds like a horrific idea, so she tugs off the top of the sheet.

Revealing a crib.

Delina stills, her breath catching in her throat.

It's painted a soft pink, though the paint has peeled and chipped, and her name is carved into the headboard. There's a blanket, color faded by time, with a ribbon edging, neatly folded on the bottom, and a single stuffed animal in the corner.

"What?" Maison asks, glancing up from the scope, then making a small sound at the back of his throat. "Oh."

The crib would only hold a newborn, it's so tiny.

And it's so obviously unused, despite the passage of time.

Delina traces a fingertip over her name. It's carved by hand, with a chisel, with a care and skill that far outpaces any woodworking skill her own father had.

Maison reaches a hand out to her, but she doesn't move.

There's so much care in this little crib, that her heart aches. It's deliberate, there's no way in interpreting it as something to be thrown away as a casual motion.

"Wow," Maison murmurs behind her, his hand settling on the small of her back, gentle, before he too touches the carving of her name. "This wasn't done by magic."

She hadn't even thought that, but her breath hitches again, and with a quickness she didn't know she had in her bones, flips off the rest of the sheet in front of her.

There's a small pink table, carved for a toddler, with flowers painted on the edges. A tiny bookcase, a car seat, and a photo album.

Maison and her glance at each other just long enough for her to glimpse the seriousness in his gaze, before she sits, cross legged on the floor of the attic, pulling the photo album towards her.

The spotting scope forgotten, Maison folds himself next to her, as her hands shake to open it.

It's incongruently frilly, in the way that was popular when Delina was born, with pastel pink fabric and lace on the front, and her name stitched on.

The first picture is of her father, smiling widely, standing next to a largely pregnant woman, who's jawline echoes Delina's own, and who's eyebrows match hers.

Her mother.

She has darker hair than Delina, and the makeup is a couple decades old, but her blue eyes are bright and her cheeks are round from grinning. She holds a hand over the belly, protective, and her other hand holding Delina's father's shoulder.

It's a casual portrait, the type taken by a friend at an event, and the only photo Delina's ever seen of her.

"Oh my god," Delina murmurs, and Maison rubs between her shoulder blades.

The next picture was of the two of them at the same event, laughing, the picture blurry, but her dad's scrunched up face is as familiar as they come.

The next is at a baby shower, pink balloons everywhere, and her mother glowing, a large group of friends crowded behind her, everyone beaming.

In the background, grinning just as proudly, is Korhonen, wearing an outdated suit and having much more hair.

"Oh, I know them," Maison says, pointing at another couple, all decked out in early nineties finery, and their faces are completely unfamiliar. "Two demonologists, they wanted to train me to be an assassin."

"You'd be a terrible assassin," Delina replies automatically, unthinking.

"That was the conclusion they came to," Maison says, then points to another person, younger than the rest, also smiling. "That was my third-grade teacher, I think."

"Oh my god," Delina says, but her eyes keep on straying back to her mother. "These were literally her work friends before..."

Before whatever experiment it was that she had put on Delina. Before whatever sanctions they put on her, before she scared everyone. Before whatever insanity she had gone through.

The man who literally tried to kill Delina attended her baby shower before she was born.

And now he was dead at her hands.

Swallowing another lump, Delina turns the page.

There, a picture of her mother lying on a hospital bed in a medical gown, her hair messed up, holding a sleeping newborn to her chest. Underneath, written in pen, the words 'Delina Joyanna Frisse, born at 8:49 AM.'

There's a handcuff on her mother's wrist, locking her to the bed.

Baby Delina was tiny, red-faced in her sleep, smaller than she should be.

The oldest photo of her Delina can remember is when she's much bigger, healthy and chubby, in her dad's arms.

Delina rubs her face. After all the emotions of the day, after the phone calls and the breakdown sitting on the floor with Maison, everything is just...wrung out. There should be more feelings, there should be more sensations welling up inside of her, but instead she's just...tired.

"Oh, you were so small," Maison whispers. Somewhere around year three of dating, her father had shown him all of the baby pictures they had just to embarrass her, and all of them were far healthier.

"I guess I really do look like my bio-mom," Delina says, though the words don't seem real. "People keep saying that."

She turns the page, the handcuffs sticking in her mind.

There's a badly scanned copy of Delina's first grade class photo, with Delina circled, then a copy of her Junior High Graduation picture where she's grimacing around braces while shaking her principal's hand. None of them are the original, she must've pulled them from somewhere, been passed them.

There's a cutout newspaper article of high school Delina competing in the Model EU, her frustration of it clear even in the black and white photo. There's a pristine copy of her prom photo, where she went with a bunch of her friends and thought that she looked good in neon orange for a dress.

All little bits of her life, hoarded into this one photo book.

Maison doesn't say anything, just keeps his hand in between her shoulder blades. He's had a hard day too, should be much more emotional, but here he is, quietly supportive, as they sit on the floor of the attic.

"There's no way they knew about this book, did they?" Delina asks, and he shakes his head. "They told me she had no interest in me. My whole life."

He swallows, then gestures down at the picture from her prom. "I'd say she did."

Delina squeezes her eyes shut, briefly, against the muted light of the windows, then to him, half desperate. "Do you want to go downstairs? I can look at this later, I don't need to right now, now when we're trying to save your mother, it's insensitive..."

He tucks a strand of her hair behind her ear, tender. "You mean go downstairs and hear the phone ring over and over again that has my mom telling me in coded language to not come save her when that's exactly what we're trying to do?" he asks, which is fair, though his voice trembles a bit. "And not be able to do anything until Chloe, an alchemist who specializes in ancient equipment and stone locks, tries to create a phone number tracker on a satellite phone from a laptop that hasn't worked in probably five years?"

"That's unfair," Delina protests, but he shakes his head. "At least it's inorganic?"

"I guess," he says, before leaning against her, just a solid pressure against her back, and she takes a brief moment to check his breathing, his lungs working as they should, his heart sending electrical signals to his brain, everything fine. "So I can be up here and possibly uncover more sniper nests and look at embarrassing pictures of your childhood, and that sounds far better."

She huffs out a wet laugh, and she's not crying, not exactly, and he offers her one of his heartbreaking smiles, then turns the page for her.

To three mugshots of young men, one of them Maison, five years ago.

"Um," Delina says, peering at them. Maison's obviously uncomfortable in them, looking away from the camera, and his hair is short, how he kept it for the first month of knowing each other.

Underneath his picture reads 'Frederick, half-demon.'

The other two young men are similar in type to him, and underneath theirs reads 'Lutes, forgery specialist' and 'Devin, trapper.'

Delina raises an eyebrow up at Maison, and the expression he wears now mirrors the one in the pic. "Is this my mom's research on possible boyfriends for me?"

"Looks like it," he replies, shifting. "Really? They wanted to send Lutes to you? You would've hated him, absolutely hated him. He was a snobby asshole."

Lutes does in fact look like he'd sneer at drinking beer in a rural brewery.

"Devin at least is good looking, but he would've bored you inside of a year," Maison continues, like she actually had any say in this, like she was the one considering them. "But Lutes? No way."

"Before you found me, we tried to get into the city for cell connection, so I could pull up my Facebook," Delina tells him, and it's so long ago, after everything else that happened. "So they would know which one you were, because they didn't know your code name and they wanted to know how to defend this cabin." She gestures down at the book. "All they'd have to do is look at this book sometime in the year or so they've been here and they would've known."

He stares at her for a long second, then shakes his head. "Oh my god."

"Literally could've avoided the whole tree thing, and I was about to go into the trap when you got there. You would've missed us completely, we would have come back to find you in the demon trap and my door wrecked."

"I would've been able to tell you weren't there," he protests, but his eyes are crinkling up a bit, like he gets the joke as well. "Good lord, you would've passed me in the car on the street."

"That day would've gone differently," she says, then turns the page.

It's a picture, obviously printed on flimsy paper from her

Facebook page years ago, of the two of them. His arms around her, his smile cheesy, and she's pressing a kiss to his cheek for the camera. It was right after they graduated and had gone on a trip to Colorado together, and they had both hiked too much and eaten way too much barbecue before crashing at a hotel and doing nothing but sleep for a few days.

And it's the last page in the book, the rest blank, as if her mother had kept on intending to fill it with more pictures from afar for the rest of Delina's life.

It's so few pictures it's heartbreaking. So many obviously received in secret, hidden in the attic of this cabin, where the sniper's nest would distract.

Delina closes the book as softly as she can, gentle with the pink frilly cloth covering, and sits there.

"Wow," Maison says, voice hushed in the still attic air, and he leans against her side, a solid pressure.

"Yeah," Delina replies, and there are tears, close by, but not quite to her eyes yet. "My dad didn't have any pictures of her."

Teenage Delina had asked for one, in the midst of a depression spiral fueled by school stress and a lack of friends, but her dad had none. Not even one secreted away, like he had the pager.

"I met her, once," Maison starts, and she twists to glance at him. "Before...before I knew you. I was sixteen, and she wanted to survey all the 'viable demon projects.'" He grimaces, and she gets why he didn't tell her earlier. "She wasn't terribly impressed with me, as a project goes."

"From what I know, that's probably a good thing," Delina replies, but there's still so much emotion, so many things in her chest that she cannot give name to. "What was she like?"

He visibly weighs his words. "Cold," he says, finally, and

it's so different from the pictures in the book on her lap. "You could just...tell that she wasn't satisfied with her life, that she wanted to be in control of more."

It's a somber view of someone who died at the hand of one of her experiments.

"At the time, I was..." Maison shrugs, obviously uncomfortable. "Temperamental? Not the best at control?"

"You were sixteen," Delina says flatly.

"And everyone thought that by then I would be teleporting around the globe but my grip on demon magic is faint at best," Maison says, before glancing back up out the window, as if a task would make him feel better. "It wasn't a great time for me to try to impress someone, that's for sure."

"I wasn't impressing anyone at sixteen, I can assure you that," Delina says, before her hand smooths over the fabric book again. "I can't believe she made this. I can't believe she kept this."

Maison doesn't look at her. Instead, he's looking at the crib, at the side table, at the room at large.

"She...she really wanted me."

There's a moment of quiet, before Maison wraps his arms around her, pulling her into a hug, and she presses her face against his chest.

When this is all over, when everything's figured out and she's settled, she's going to cry. She can feel it, can feel the pressure, detached from herself, in the background. It's not immediate, it might not even be until she fully relaxes again, but it'll happen and it'll be an ugly cry.

After they figure out if they need to hide away, after they rescue Maison's mom, after she figures out some place to live and exist outside of the College's control. After they help out Chloe and Gurlien, after they assure everyone's safety. After the threat to her life, after they figure out how she can get a grasp of her powers without calling someone down on them.

After everything.

"If we have to run from this cabin, I'm going to take this book," she says, and feels him nod against her.

"I wish I could teleport," Maison says, and she pulls back enough to raise an eyebrow at him. "It's...the basics of demon magic, and one that's always been locked to me. But...it'd be damn useful right now."

She cracks a smile at him, at the ridiculousness of the sentence, at how wistful it is and how utterly true that it would be incredibly useful at the moment. "There's still the dead bug in the basement if you really want to," she informs him, and he rolls his eyes.

The emotions recede, somewhere back into manageable levels, until she's able to breathe without the knot in her chest.

Before the phone downstairs rings again.

This time, there's a pop on their end on the phone, and Maison stiffens again, pulling away, his eyes ablaze in red.

"Wha—" Delina starts, before Maison puts a finger up to his lips, gesturing for her to be quiet.

Another click and Maison slowly unfolds himself, silently opening the attic door once more.

Same woman's voice. "Frederick?"

Chloe hisses through her teeth. "Ma'am, do you need us to call the police?" Still, even with her words, there's a note of triumph in her voice. "If they're going to hurt you, I'm sure the police can help."

"They can't get to me," the woman says, and for the first time, something steely enters her voice, like the pitiful pleading is an act. "Tell me where my son is."

"I don't know any Fredericks," Chloe says, and Maison

quietly drops himself from the attic, landing lightly on his toes. "Sorry, ma'am."

This time, the line goes dead on their end.

Maison reaches up to help Delina down, just in time to see Chloe leaning back, her eyes alight.

"I got it," she says, then swallows. "Toronto."

Gurlien twists to glance at their packed belongings, then back at the table, at the gutted laptop, then up at Chloe. "See, knew you could do that. The electronics didn't have a chance against you."

Maison exhales, then shakes out his hands, and Delina catches a glimpse of red in his eyes.

Chloe scrubs her hand through her hair, and she's sweaty. "That fucking sucked."

"Any surveillance?" Gurlien asks, and Maison nods his head. "The demon trap still there?"

Delina thinks of the burning, warping trap of red through the white snow. "Still pretty vivid."

"If we're going to leave, it should be tonight," Maison says, and despite the command in his voice, his jaw tightens and he shakes his head, like he can't believe what he's saying. "Are we really thinking about doing this?"

"Yes," Delina interrupts, almost before he's finished talking.

Gurlien and Chloe look at each other, having another one of their long conversations with just glances.

"It'll take more planning," Chloe says, finally, her face twisted. "I know it like the back of my hand, I can get us through most of the traps."

"And I'll be able to identify and explain the ones you don't know," Gurlien says, before he sighs. "Yeah, fuck them. Let's figure out how to do this."

34

They leave the cabin in the middle of the night, piling half the research into the ratty little sedan and half into Chloe's car.

Delina brews enough espresso shots for them to stay awake all night, and shoves the photo book into the trunk of the car, even though they're short on space.

She puts the dead bug in her pocket, still in the plastic pill container, breathing past the sensation.

If that demon is waiting for them on the other side of the barrier, she wants to be prepared.

Chance the cat jumps into Gurlien's lap in the car, curling up like it's the couch, so Chloe runs back in and grabs the remaining cat food before they're all off, the tires crunching through the snow.

Delina twists to watch the cabin disappear between the trees, her heart caught in her throat.

"You'll be able to go back," Maison says, even without looking at her as he drives away.

Delina swallows that down, but doesn't look away until even the gravel driveway is away from her view.

"This is gonna be bright," Maison mutters, cranking down his window, staring at the drone sitting idle on one stone.

Delina twists back in her chair, just in time to see him clench his fist and yank, before the drone explodes into a million sparks.

She blinks at it, and in a moment they're past.

"They'll know that was one of us," she says dumbly.

"And now they'll have no footage," Maison says, succinct. "I'm fine with that."

Halfway down the street to the main highway, Maison leans across her and pulls out her burner cell phone from the glove compartment, not breaking his eye contact with the road.

"Wanna text your dad?" he asks, and Delina perks up. "We're leaving here, you can throw the phone out the window afterwards, they won't know where we're going."

"He's gonna be asleep," Delina warns, but cradles the phone anyways. "He's gotta be worried out of his mind."

She clicks on her phone as they drive through the dark, and the silence gets filled with beeps.

DAD (10:21 AM): Maison stopped by.

DAD (10:39 AM): I told him you were helping a friend, tried to get him to stay a few hours, he wouldn't. Stressed out of his mind, he will definitely track you down. Stay safe.

Then, a few days later:

DAD (3:20 PM): Had some of your mother's old friends stop by. Told me you were missing. I acted surprised and worried. They're gonna catch on.

DAD (3:22 PM): Stay safe, love you.

A few days later:

DAD (8:00 PM): They just told me Maison died. Are you okay?

"Oh wow," Delina murmurs, scrolling through the filtered texts, and Maison side eyes her from the driver's seat. "They told my dad you died."

Maison frowns, then sighs. "Makes sense, it's what I'd do in their situation." Another side eye. "Are you gonna tell him I'm alive? We have to believe they're monitoring his phone now."

Delina stares down at her phone. "My dad really did like you."

"It was nice having a normal dad around," Maison says, a bit sad. "I think I talked to him about more mundane things than anyone else."

It's true, she knew that Maison would occasionally go and get advice from her dad, but knowing what she knows now just makes it a bit worse.

That his mother was locked up, his other parent generally unavailable, and he was completely cut off from any aspect of community he's ever known.

DAD (7:22 PM): Hope you are well. They've increased their spies around my house. Brought a woman with a half-shaved head around, she was not all there, her eyes were weird. Stay safe.

Then, one day ago.

DAD (3:01 PM): they told me you're killing people now. I don't know what's going on, but please be safe.

"Great, they told him I killed Korhonen," Delina says, the familiar bitterness rising up at the mere mention.

"He'll still love you," Maison murmurs.

DELINA (11:45 PM): Hey Dad, I'm doing well, the cabin is beautiful and the woods are glorious. Mom really left some surprises for me, I'll visit soon.

Of course, the text sends, and doesn't immediately click over to read, which means he's fast asleep.

Delina cradles it for a few minutes longer, then rolls down the window and chucks it into a particularly gnarly blackberry bramble and watches as that, too, disappears through the mist.

In the silence, Maison reaches over and grabs her hand.

THEY PULL up to another property of her mother's around 4:30 AM, an apartment in a row of other, unremarkable apartments in an otherwise unremarkable mid-sized city.

Chloe gets through the lock on the door with barely any thought, and Maison disables the single magic snare left behind with very little trouble.

The apartment is way more utilitarian than the cabin, no personality to be found, like Delina's mother never bothered to break down the display furniture that came when she purchased it. No books in the bookshelves, no food in the cabinets, no dead bugs underneath the sinks.

There's two bedrooms, a dusty looking couch, and one of those massive bean bags that were in fashion a few years ago. Without even saying anything, Chloe flops over onto the bean bag, and Chance the cat curls up with her, both of them falling asleep so fast Delina is briefly, briefly jealous.

"Yeah, the cat meowed the entire drive," Gurlien mutters, before turning on his heel to the smaller of the bedrooms.

Delina's eyes have gone crunchy somewhere after hour two of driving, and Maison's face is pale with exhaustion.

Inside the room, magic blazes up, and Delina's breath catches in her throat, before she relaxes.

Nothing happens, the magic licking against her feet, and

Maison gives her a sharp glance, before staring down at her feet.

"That's not a danger spell, it's a notification," he says, narrowing his eyes before rubbing them. "It'd be to let your mom know someone was here."

"Huh," Delina says, peering down at it. "So who does the notification go to now that she's...dead?"

"Nobody," Maison says with a sigh, and exhaustion eats at him, she can feel it. "It's...it's a useless spell now. Just alive enough to show up on the carpet."

The carpet itself is the beige type found in most rental properties, completely unremarkable.

"The bed has an anti-dust spell," Maison mumbles.

"Good," Delina says, then flops over on the bed, holding her hand out to him to join her.

They hadn't spoken much on the drive, both too full of jangly nerves to carry on too much of a conversation, but Delina can read the apprehension on his face as clearly as if he had spoken it.

"Unless you want to crash on the couch or split a room with Gurlien," Delina says, which breaks him out of it enough that he rolls his eyes, shucking off his flannel shirt and kicking off his shoes.

Still tentative, he crawls under the comforter with her, and...

...and they hadn't slept in the same bed since the night she brought him back from the dead.

Immediately, she curls up against him, and he throws his arm over her, tugging her in close.

Like nothing had ever happened.

He breathes in, deep, a tremor somewhere in there.

"Is this okay?" Delina asks, after a long moment of

silence, but him wide aware against her. "It's been...a bit of a day."

"Yeah," Maison says, and his voice is a little rough. "Yeah, it has been." As if to punctuate his words, he pulls her in tighter.

They had agreed to sleep in, to leave mid-afternoon and travel mostly at night, but the strangeness still pulls at Delina.

Of sleeping in yet another strange bed in another strange place. Of the noises and creaking in the apartment, of the still softly glowing magic.

"When it's safe, I want to go back to the condo in Prescott," Delina starts, speaking into the quiet of the room. "Not permanently, just to find some of our things."

"Definitely not permanently," Maison mumbles against her hair. "But. Yes."

"Get your art supplies, get my things, then..."

"Then we'll figure out which of your properties we should visit next," Maison continues softly. "Tour around in them, find the best views."

"Yeah," Delina says, and sleep tugs against her, finally, pulling her breathing deeper, weighing at her eyelids. "We'll figure it out."

SHE WAKES BEFORE EVERYONE ELSE, and a quick scan shows the cat still curled with Chloe on the bean bag, Gurlien still fast asleep on the extra bed, and Maison still breathing deeply against her.

It's close to perfect.

So she just breathes out, blinking into the room.

Instead of the floral curtains, there are blank slats,

sending long shadows on the white walls in the midafternoon sunshine. They're still northern, they're still in the United States, but a brief glimpse of blue peeks through the window.

"Delly?" Maison mumbles, still holding her close, voice raspy with sleep.

"Yeah, I'm here," Delina whispers back, turning in his arms until she faces him.

He gazes at her from underneath his lashes, and they're so close she can see the faintest of freckles across his nose.

He doesn't say anything, just watches her in the shadows of the blinds.

The condo in Prescott had blinds like this, and for a few moments, she could swear they were back there.

"I didn't think I would ever wake up like this again," he whispers, voice so low.

Delina didn't think so either.

"I know we'll have to get in the car and drive more today, but..." he tightens his arm around the middle of her back, an almost unconscious motion. "I don't want to leave this."

It's nice, sleepy words, spoken out of some quiet want for contentment, and she gets it. She gets it so strongly that every part of her is almost to tears with the idea of having to leave the bed.

His eyes flicker down to her lips, then back up to her, serious. "May I kiss you?"

She blinks at him.

"Look, I kissed you before you were ready, and—"

She presses herself up to him, kissing him, opening her mouth to him, and he responds with a startled sound, his hand sweeping to her lower back, under her shirt and to the too untouched skin beneath.

A crack sparkles from his fingertips to her skin, and he pulls away.

"That's new," Delina breathes, and he smiles at her, heartbreaking and beautiful, before he kisses her again, stronger this time, biting on her lower lip.

It sends a trill down her skin, and she shivers, even though the air inside the apartment is more warm than not, so she pulls up at the hem of his shirt until he leans back long enough to pull it over his head.

He grips her chin, keeping her in place, and her skin tightens once more as she splays her hand over his abs.

He's still wearing his jeans—he slept in them like an exhausted moron—and she lets her hand go to the button to the fly, raising an eyebrow at him.

He raises his right back, before grinning.

Before she has any real idea of what's going on, he flips her over, until he's on top of her, legs bracing hers.

She squeaks in surprise, before he grips her chin again and presses a bruising kiss to her mouth, insistent.

"We're going to have to be quiet," he whispers, lips brushing against hers.

Inhaling, she kisses back. He's usually not this strong, preferring her to take the lead, preferring her to make all the large actions. Making sure she's in control.

But not this, and it sends another shiver down her back.

Another raised eyebrow at her and his eyes glint, ever so briefly, red.

"What are you doing?" She breathes, and she's not sure she's ever seen him quite like this. "Your eyes..."

He doesn't answer, kissing her again, before pulling back enough to help her pull off her sleep shirt and pressing his lips against her collarbone.

"You're beautiful," he whispers, a soft caress of words, his mouth moving against her skin, his hands sweeping downwards to the hem of her shorts.

It's all of the sudden so much, and her breath catches in her throat with the sudden need.

Kicking off her shorts, she grabs his hair, twisting her hands in his soft locks until he breathes out, halfway between a sign and a moan, arching the column of his neck.

He's still wearing far more clothing than she is, and she pushes his jeans down until she can grab his cock, hard and heavy in her hands.

He makes a choked off sound in the back of his throat, and she raises her eyebrow at him.

"I thought you said we have to be quiet," she whispers, and he grins at her, wide, a spark in his eyes, and before she even knows what's happening, his hand slides between her thighs.

It's been too long, and she has to muffle her own noise of need as he presses the palm on his hand against her clit.

He's always known how to make her scream, and now she can't.

"I've wanted to do this every day," he whispers, as she squirms in his touch. "Wanted to undress you, to see you beneath me again."

"Not fair," Delina pants out, and he's holding her down, his legs pressed against hers, and she's never felt so wonderfully trapped as he lazily circles a finger over her opening.

He presses another kiss against her collarbone, then slips his finger inside her, and she jolts against him.

"Wanted to see you fall apart," he murmurs, curving his finger just right, until heat starts to pool inside of her. "Wanted just you, just like this."

A small remote part of her finds it somewhat unlikely, with all the change and drama and strife in the last few months, but she shrugs that off, arching her neck up at his touch.

It's almost too much, and the moment she thinks she's about to break, he shifts, pulling away, and a gasp wrenches out of her throat at the sudden lack.

"You're beautiful," he murmurs, his hand spreading over her chest, whisper gentle, and she shudders at the almost touch. "I can't believe..."

Before he can finish that sentence, she kisses him again, as if she can compel him to do more with just her lips. As if the last month between them just made it stronger, made her able to control more.

It almost derails her thought, before he presses her back against the mattress with one strong motion, forcing her legs apart.

Her breath hitches, and he pauses, perilously close to her, his eyes flashing red for a split second. A split-second check in, like he could tell something that way, like he's been checking in on her the entire time and just now she's able to see it.

"Fuck me," she whispers to him, and his brows flash up, before he grins and thrusts into her.

This time she does gasp, loud, before he covers her mouth with his hand, and the gasp dissolves into a giggle.

"You still need to be quiet," he whispers back, laughter at the edge of his voice as he, almost lazily, fucks her. There's a smile hidden in his eyes, the dimple on his chin, and she resists the urge to pull his hair again, to control the rhythm.

"You need to not surprise me then," she whispers back, breathless, heat pooling behind her stomach. "I was fine before you surprised me."

He grins at her, wide, a glimmer of mischief in his eyes,

and she knows, she just knows, that he's absolutely going to make her break.

But not if she makes him break first.

She twists her hands up and into his hair again, pulling sharply, and he moans, just slightly, barely audible, still thrusting into her.

So she rakes her fingernails against his scalp, sending goosebumps down his arms.

"Delly," he warns, and she grins back.

This isn't how it usually is for them.

Usually, sex is...comfortable. Great in its comfort, great in how predictable it is, great in how they could always improve each other's mood through it. Great in how much she can count on it, can know that it'll always be the same.

This...there's some spark in there, something she doesn't quite understand. Some strange thrill of danger, beyond the worry of being overheard. A newness, something a bit more raw between them.

Even their first time together hadn't been this vulnerable.

He must see something in her face, for he stills, and for a split second his eyes gleam red at her. "Everything okay?" he whispers, his hand falling to the small curve of her hip, to the tender skin there.

Even the check in has a different weight.

She nods, words vanishing from her mind, and his next thrust pulls another small gasp out of her.

He hmms, his voice low against her, and another thrill goes down her back. Another small sense of danger, of risk.

"Are you getting into your head?" he murmurs into her ear, because of course he knows how to recognize that.

Even with the strangeness, he still knows her.

She nods again, ever so slightly. "Don't stop." Her voice is breathy despite herself, and her blood thrums with the need of his touch.

"Of course not," he murmurs, hand smoothing over her skin, before he grins, a hint of mischievousness in his gaze. "You could always compel me if you needed."

"Oh fuck off," she blurts out, too loud, and he laughs, something genuine and real in the sound, before his hands come up and grip her wrists, holding her in place.

It's another spark of danger, this one delicious.

Cause she knows him now. Knows what he's capable of, knows the depth of his devotion in her. Knows what it means for a Half Demon to hold her down like this, how much power is in his hands.

He thrusts again, carrying all thoughts away from her, and she arches her back.

"Because all you have to do," he says, still low and close, "is merely ask and I will do whatever you want."

And she knows that now, too.

35

After, she lets herself rest her head against his chest, hearing the strong beating of his heart, as the afternoon sun fills the barren apartment with warmth.

There comes a point, where she can practically feel Maison's mind kick in, and while he doesn't really tense, he sighs, his arms restless around her.

"What?" she murmurs, not willing to let herself get uncomfy.

"Someone just broke the confusion spell on the cabin," he says, and she blinks up to him. "I put an alarm on it, so I could tell."

"So they know we're not there?" Delina asks, stretching out against him. She should be more scared, she knows that, but right now she...can't.

"Or they will, soon. We should probably get up," he says, his hand tracing shapes on her bare back. "Figure out the next move, the next stop in this."

He's right, but she just snuggles harder against him.

"I don't know how many of the properties they know about, just Gurlien does, but we should...not stay in place."

She draws away, sitting upright, and a frown tugs on his lips at the lack of contact. "They're not awake yet," she says, finger combing through her hair with a nod to the door. "We'll need to get food."

He sits up as well, still bare chested, completely derailing Delina's train of thought for a few moments, before he obviously steels himself up.

Delina raises an eyebrow at him.

"When we have a break, when we get a chance, I want you to practice tying me with the death again," he says, and he's so handsome in the late afternoon sun through the slatted blinds. "If they catch up with us on the road, I want us to be prepared."

"That'll be your choice," Delina says, and the ghost of a smile traces over his lips, barely there. "I meant what I said about your wants."

"And I," he says, letting his hands fall to Delina's hips, the skin there still sensitive, "want to have the best chance at keeping you safe."

"Then we'll find a way to practice." She rolls out of the bed, and he gazes up at her with hunger in his eyes, as she rummages through her bag for a top and some jeans. "Think we can safely sneak out for breakfast?"

"Without waking them? Unlikely," Maison replies, pulling his shirt on, before his face twists, suddenly, and he jerks the closet door open.

Inside, glowing softly, is a safe.

Delina peers at it, halfway through wiggling into her jeans. "Is that gonna be dangerous?"

Maison sighs, rubbing his face and sitting back down on

the bed. "It's another biotrap. I'm gonna assume it's for you again."

"What?" Delina asks. It's a normal looking jewelry safe, as much as safes could be normal, the strange glow notwithstanding. "But I already went through the one, why would there—"

"I have to assume she left more than one, I guess," Maison says, then sighs again. "She was insane."

"Right," Delina says, then takes a cautious step towards the safe before Maison stops her.

"Don't touch it until I can get Chloe and Gurlien's opinion," he mutters, all trace of the softness gone. "I don't want to be wrong and set off traps your mom left behind."

AFTER A BREAKFAST of power bars and lukewarm energy drinks, Maison corrals Gurlien and Chloe in to look at the safe. Or, rather, for Chloe to look at it and sketch out the types of the runes for Gurlien to identify, and the cat batting against Chloe's pencil at every motion.

"It's definitely a biotrap," Gurlien says, when Chloe finishes working with him on the runes, and Maison rolls his eyes. "Doesn't say for whom, so we can't confirm it's for you."

"I gathered that, what is it a trap for?" Maison asks, shifting to peer at it. "It's not like the other one."

Gurlien props his elbows up on his knees, because of course they're both sitting on the carpet next to the safe, and gives Maison one of his expertly bored expressions. "However do you mean, Maison?"

Maison crosses his arms at him.

"Details are helpful," Gurlien continues.

"It doesn't...feel like the other one," Maison says, begrudging, and Chloe cracks a smile, like this is some long running joke. "The other one, completely obvious what it's for. This one, not so much."

"If I had to guess, it's to destroy or transform anything inside," Chloe says, peering at it with something approaching eagerness. "So only certain people can get inside, a lot of people do them with safe boxes, so if other people get access to them, they're useless. I saw one guy who made a safe that transformed everything into useless teeth if anyone but him opened it."

Delina blinks down at her. "So this sort of thing is your jam, right?"

"Right," Chloe says, before her grin fades. "We probably don't have time for me to properly break it, do we?"

"Not with the biotrap," Gurlien says, still narrowing his eyes at Maison. "Think Delina would be biologically similar to Frisse to get it off?"

The question is directly to Maison, who scowls.

"That's all about how good of a spell caster they are," Chloe says clinically, peering at the box. "Most people don't have that level of control in their biological markers, but Frisse probably did, but also Frisse might've wanted her daughter to have access, so it's really a toss up." She taps the floor next to the safe, and it glows a bit stronger.

"I mean, I could try," Delina says, and Chloe at least looks like she's considering it. "It probably wouldn't harm me, right?"

"Probably isn't good enough," Maison replies.

"If I had time and some lead gloves, I'd do it," Chloe volunteers, before she smiles, impish, at Delina. "She left this place to you in the will?"

"Yes," Gurlien replies for her, because he's the one who

has the entire will memorized. "So it would go to reason that it'd be safe in theory, but—"

Before Maison can stop her, Delina steps up and presses her palm against the top of the safe.

There's a pop, close to the sound of a jar being opened, and a sizzle against Delina's skin, barely there before a plume of smoke puffs from the cracks of the safe and the door swings open.

"Aww I couldn't even unlock it," Chloe says, as Maison grabs Delina's hand, peering at it.

"I'm not hurt," she says, though her skin tingles a bit, completely unmarked.

"No, she just put a tracker on you," Maison grumbles. "So she'd be able to track anyone who tried to open her safe. Insane."

"It's not the most insane thing she's done," Chloe says, before gingerly creaking the door open.

Inside is a six-shot revolver, three cases of bullets, and some paperwork.

"Why'd she need guns?" Maison breathes, rubbing his face. "She was super powerful, why the hell would she ever keep guns?"

The revolver shines as if new, the pristine mother of pearl handle all but shimmering in the late afternoon light.

"I take it I'm gonna just find these at all of her properties?" Delina asks, and all three nod, even as Gurlien and Chloe piece through the paperwork. "I didn't even keep a gun in Arizona."

Gurlien sets half of the paperwork aside, then hands some to Chloe. "Can you transform an already fake passport?"

"Psh, easy," Chloe says, before flipping through it and showing it to Delina.

"Good, cause there's about a dozen in here," Gurlien says, and Delina cranes her neck to look at all of them.

Most are for her mother, some with brown hair and some with hair gone dramatically gray, all with the same severe expression on her face, all with different names.

There's one for a pretty dark-haired woman with brown skin and a long braid, her eyes alight with intelligence, and one for an impish young man with skin as smooth as glass and creepily symmetric features.

"Axel and Alette," Gurlien supplies. "He doesn't look like that anymore, when he lost his magic, he reverted to his actual appearance."

"Huh," Delina says, then pulls out the beautiful leather holster for the gun, oiled and glistening.

Runes are carved into the very leather, decorative and looping, almost a cursive, and Maison swears under his breath.

At her look, he shrugs. "If she had been less insane, she would have been the mind of a generation."

"Yeah, this is intense," Chloe says, peering at it, then down at the passports. "She put a ton of protection on these, I'll have to break them piece by piece to use them."

"Two days?" Gurlien guesses, and she nods. "Do it while we drive. Maison, you drive with Chloe while she does that, I'll tutor the rune breaking to Delina today."

Maison crosses his arms over his chest and stares down at Gurlien.

"I'm a better teacher than you on that and you know it," Gurlien shoots back, dusting himself off and standing up. "And Chloe'll be giving off crazy flares while doing those, you can actually mask those."

36

They pull off at an abandoned rest stop right after sunset, when the sky still glows faintly dark blue, and snow drifts crunch underneath Delina's boots.

By now, she's heard of a thousand different ways to break runes and heard the cat meow about as much, so she bounces on her toes once out of the car.

There's an ache in Maison's shoulders, but he holds his face carefully impassive as he shakes his hands out. Chloe's head is pounding from the passports, and Gurlien is about to tear his hair out at how slowly Delina's learning.

The need to do something she's actually good at itches underneath her skin.

"Death practice?" she asks Maison as soon as he confirms there's nobody else at the rest stop, nobody hiding in the bathrooms. "There's a deer about ten feet into the woods."

"Good lord," Gurlien mutters. "Can't remember a rune larger than a penny, can pinpoint a dead deer in three seconds."

"Put it into a spreadsheet, maybe I'll remember them that way," Delina snips back, and to her horror, Gurlien looks like he's actually considering it.

Maison coughs out a laugh, before turning around and facing them. "I once put the bill paying rotation into a spreadsheet so she'd pay attention, and it worked."

"Only after I completely redid it," Delina shoots at him. "It was horrible."

Gurlien covers his mouth with his hand for a brief second. "You know, occasionally I forget that you were just completely normal."

"Rude," Delina says, before glancing up at Maison.

Maison's jaw twitches despite the joking, but he exhales out his nose, reaching out and letting his hand rest on Delina's arm.

"I'll command you not to hurt me immediately," Delina says, leaning into the touch, into the comfort.

It's only been a few hours since she saw him.

"Command me to do something specific this time, too," Maison says, shaking out his hands again, and it's enough permission that Delina ventures off the little pathway, directly towards the dead deer pulling beneath her gut.

It's been dead for a while, half its rib cage gone, broken off by scavengers, and the eyes have rotted out of the skull, but the thread of gold remains the same.

There's snow in its chest cavity, pillowed and soft against the remnants of its lungs. One of its legs is snapped, from before it died, crumpled beneath it.

It's so involving that Delina barely hears Maison tromp up behind her until he rests a hand on the small of her back.

"It broke its leg then starved to death," Delina informs him, and he twists his face. "I wouldn't want to try to bring it back, it'd be too much."

"Yeah, definitely don't do that," Maison grumbles, but the hand on her back is gentle. "I want to see you actually pull it."

She quirks an eyebrow at him. "Last time you sprinted outside in your socks." But at his slightly embarrassed shrug, she crouches down next to the deer, poking at the frozen skin.

Bugs had long ago crawled over it, sending phantom prickles across Delina's arms, but instead she just breathes out, focusing on that single thread of gold, until it twists its way into her hand, falling into her palm like links of a chain.

Maison flinches, but the red in his eyes flash as he's watching her. "That's insanely spooky," he tells her, then shakes his head at her grin. "You're going to scare the shit out of people in Toronto."

"Good," Delina says, then spreads the magic between her hands. It's more than the dead bird, scalier, warmer. Less happy to see her.

"Objective is to control Maison enough to blow up a tree," Gurlien says, as if it's a completely normal sentence. "Don't tell him which tree, just use your willpower."

Maison rolls his eyes, the hint of a dimple appearing, before he holds his hand out, and despite all his bravado the tremble is back in his arm.

Delina cocks an eyebrow at him, much like she did earlier that day, and he nods.

"You're not going to hurt me," she declares, quickly looping the magic around his wrist and—

He clamps down his hand on hers, but no gold flash echoes in the woods around them.

"You're good," Delina whispers, and his eyes reflect the light back to her, startling so as he searches her face, the sense of his body being off bugging at the back of her mind. "See?"

She reaches her other hand out, cradles his face, and he exhales, his eyes wide.

"You're beautiful," he whispers back, his voice breaking, and in between one breath and the next, he teleports away, behind a tree, then appears behind her. "Why—"

"Stop teleporting," Delina whispers, and he stops, immediately, turning back to her, and the hair on the back of her neck raises. "We'll work on that later."

"Okay, he disappeared again, that's still spooky," Gurlien speaks up, and for a split second Delina had forgotten all about the two of them. "Everything good?"

"Yeah," Maison says, before shaking his head the moment they don't hear him. "Oh this is weird."

"He's fine," Delina calls back.

In the twinkling dusk, where the setting sun settles softly on the snow, Delina watches Maison with sharp eyes as he draws in a breath, like testing the very air around him.

His throat bobs as he swallows, before he focuses back on her, his eyes narrowed.

"I can tell that other demon took from you," he says, voice carefully controlled, and Delina raises her eyebrow at him. "That was days ago, why can I still tell?"

He stalks close to her, and a shiver goes down her back, but she lifts her chin instead of reacting.

"She doesn't get to touch you again," he breathes, and there's almost something akin to a growl behind his voice.

That's new.

Delina's other eyebrow joins the raised one. "Noted."

"I mean it," he warns, and she believes him, though her heart kicks up a beat. "I'll kill her if she does."

Considering he wanted to help her back at the bar, it's an...interesting change of heart, and her stomach tightens.

"Obviously," she says, and finally, there's a twitch of a smile against his lips. "I don't want that either."

There's a long moment, where he stares at her, his eyes flickering over her face, like he's tracing a thousand different things over her skin, before Chloe clears her throat and they both startle.

Both Chloe and Gurlien give her matching, profoundly uncomfortable expressions. The cat sits languidly in Chloe's arms, like it has absolutely zero issues being held through the forest.

"The tree?" Chloe asks, and Delina's not entirely certain how much she's able to perceive, how much of the back and forth.

Maison steps back, shaking out his hands, even though he's not feeling any discomfort. "Just willpower, no verbal," he says, like he's reminding himself more than her. "Just instinct."

Gurlien had repeated it in overwhelming detail during their drive, and Delina's fairly certain she has the concept down, but it's...different. With Maison like this, so obviously in the palm of her hand, invisible to everyone else and yet brimming with power.

She inhales. That's what it is, that's what the off sensation of his body is. He's full of power, overflowing with it, bleeding into the ground below him and the forest floor, over the dusting of snow and the moss, the dead leaves, the dirt and the worms and the decay.

And she, in theory, should be able to control it.

Maison's face twitches, like he could absorb her thoughts and experience them as well like this.

Who knows, maybe he can.

Before she can psych herself out, she lets her eyes fall on a tree. There's a bird's nest on it, empty and cold, and the sap moves sluggish through the core of the wood. Frost glitters along the needles, weighed down by the snowfall.

So she reaches out through the nebulous tether between her and Maison, and he jerks in response, like she grabbed him with a brand and...points.

He jerks again, and the tree explodes.

Just explodes, showering them with splinters too small to hurt, needles flying everywhere. The snow, so previously weighing down the branches, powders through the air, catching the dying rays of the sun and shimmering.

For one beautiful, heartbreaking moment, it's perfect. Just power and carnage and...hers.

The cat yowls in Chloe's arm, and pain blooms in the back of Delina's mind as he digs his claws into Chloe's shoulder. Gurlien grabs Chloe, pulling her back with his bad hand, sending an ache down his wrist.

And Maison's still, so perfectly still, like he's been carved out of the very stone underneath the dirt.

"You okay?" Delina calls back to Chloe and Gurlien, but none of the trees hit them, just a small dusting of sawdust coloring their hair.

Both their eyes are wide, panicked, but Gurlien nods, swallowing.

"And you?" Delina asks, but Maison's motionless, as if he's not even breathing, his eyes full of light. "Maison?"

There's a beat, a moment, before he stirs, blinking, his lips parting.

"Is that what it's supposed to feel like?" he asks, wonder behind his voice. "Is that..."

"No idea, are you okay?"

He blinks over to her.

"Any other tests needed?" Delina asks, the back of her neck prickling once more. There's something wrong here, some sort of danger she's not fully realizing, and despite the hours spent in the car, she's itching to get back to relative safety.

Gurlien opens his mouth to reply, then closes it, shaking his head.

"Okay, Maison," Delina turns back to him, and he's so still another shiver goes up her neck. "Time to go; something's wrong."

He tilts his head at her, and the single motion is inhuman.

"Okay," Delina breathes, and he reaches his hand out to her, all at once a familiar and so foreign of an action. "Maison..."

The hand reaching out to him is the one she tied the death around, so she lets her fingertips trace on that golden ribbon on his wrist, and he shivers.

"You're not in danger," he says, voice almost disgruntled, and it, at least, is familiar.

"You can tell right now?" Delina asks, and he inclines his head in a single nod.

"Nothing here will harm you."

She narrows her eyes at him, still letting her fingertips rest on the golden chain, which twists under her touch, almost responding to her in the chill air. "Is this," she starts, and even with that little contact, goosebumps raise on his arm, "something to do with that bond?"

They still hadn't really talked about it.

"Yes," he says, voice low, and she believes him.

Before his breath hitches, and his hand clamps down on hers.

Around her, the world alights ablaze, his power a brutal red, so bright she can't see anything else around them.

She gasps, the air ripped from her, but...

Other than her heart pounding, she's fine.

She takes a moment to breathe, to calm herself, before she tilts her head back up to Maison.

An expression of intense concentration filters over his face, his eyes narrowed, like he's listening to a wind that only he can hear.

"What is it?" Delina whispers, as if the very magic around her can eavesdrop.

She can't see Gurlien and Chloe, can't hear them, nothing.

Maison's hand gentles on hers, before his eyes flicker down to her, reflecting the light back to her.

Quicker than it happened, the magic falls away, revealing the twilight forest. In a perfect circle around them, all snow and frost is melted, the very pine needles steaming.

He exhales, a slow, controlled sound. "She did another scan," he says, voice remote. "I masked us."

Delina blinks out at the circle around them.

"Alrighty," she says, then slips her finger underneath the rope, untying it with a jerk, and the coils slink off his wrist, slipping into the forest floor.

Maison jerks, blinking hard, and all the normal sensation she gets from him floods back in one motion.

She takes a step back, letting him shake himself back into his body, letting his eyes track over to the destroyed tree, before back to her a little wild.

"That was you masking me?" Delina asks, after a long moment of him staring dumbly at her.

"I..." he shakes himself again, like ridding a particularly strong thought from his mind, before he rubs his face. "Yes.

They had her looking for demon activity. Generic scan." He looks past her, at Gurlien, his face grim. "They have that demon doing blanket scans right now."

Gurlien and Chloe glance at each other. "Did they find us?"

"She felt there was a demon here," Maison glances down at Delina. "I showed I was alone."

It's all very remote, all very far away, but still, Delina shivers.

"Congrats, you certainly were able to destroy the tree," Gurlien calls, now gripping Chance hard as the cat tries to wiggle its way inside his jacket out of fear. "Feeling better this time?"

Maison tears his eyes away from Delina, still shell shocked.

"Well, he didn't hurt her this time," Chloe says, and she has a fresh rip in her sweater from the cat. She picks at it idly, but her eyes are still sharp. "No gold flash or anything."

Maison exhales forcefully. "No, I didn't."

Delina can't tell, not quite, how he is, now that his nerves are jangling and his eyes are back to normal, and with a sinking feeling she realizes that it might take years to figure it out. Years to fully understand what he's going through with each magic change. With each step into a power system that's been held away from him by the very nature of his biology.

So she tucks herself underneath his arm, pulling him away from the destroyed tree, from the spot of the scan.

He flinches at her sudden touch, before draping his arm around her shoulders, letting himself be steered away, though he cranes his neck to see the remnants of the tree.

37

They drive through the night, and in the middle of the night they stop at a single pump gas station.

Snow falls softly in the lone sodium light, and Delina hasn't seen the passing of headlamps in roughly an hour.

At some point, Gurlien had fallen asleep, the cat safely tucked inside his jacket, leaving Delina to her thoughts, so by the time they actually stop, her mind has well and truly soured on itself.

It's almost remarkable that it took so long for her mind to do so.

A small part of her had thought, had hoped, that since it had been so long, that the reason her mind would turn on itself was because she knew she was supposed to be powerful and it had been locked away.

But instead, as the hours inched along, the pit of despair in her gut just...widens.

The stop is just a single pump, a vending machine, and a single restroom.

"This is grim," Delina says aloud, as she parks the ratty

little sedan under the light, as Chloe sketches her fingertips over the gas meter.

Gurlien jerks awake, and Chance gives a pitiful mew at the motion as Delina kicks the door open, standing up and stretching her back. Stretching, moving, anything to see if it'll knock loose the pit of awfulness inside of her.

Outside the tiny sedan, the world is...quiet. All sound muffled by the snow, no wind, no city noises.

No trees to rustle their branches, nothing but grass as far as she can see, now buried in the snow. No mountains, not even a rolling hill.

Just a barren emptiness.

"Eh, not that bad," Chloe says, somehow cheerful despite the still stinging cat scratches on her shoulder.

Maison steps out of the car, stretching his shoulders, face pale, before he narrows his eyes at Delina.

"What's wrong?" he asks, voice guarded, but still he bounces on his toes, as if he can move the inactivity out of himself.

He's not in any pain, according to the quick scan she throws at him.

"Nothing's wrong, I'm just wiring it to give us free gas," Chloe replies absentmindedly, tapping a fingertip against the screen.

"That can't be legal," Delina says, skirting around Maison's question as the snowflakes powder in her blonde hair, melting against her scalp.

"Oh, it's not," Chloe says brightly. "But there's no security camera here and I'm tricking the machine into thinking we're paying anyways."

Maison crosses his arms, leaning against the other car, raising an eyebrow at Delina.

Gurlien, by all accounts, just adjusts the cat in his arms,

resting his head back against the headrest and falling back asleep.

Delina stretches again, pacing towards the vending machines, and Maison immediately stalks over to her.

"What's wrong?" he repeats, as she stares at the truly dire selection of chips available at an unmanned gas station in northern Minnesota.

She shrugs, one shoulder. She's talked to him at length about this, he knows how to help, but...

...she had hoped that this reaction of hers would be done with after getting access to the biotrap.

And after they just reconnected, after just earlier that day, she doesn't want to show him that.

"Was Gurlien just an asshole?" Maison asks, throwing a glance at the obviously asleep Gurlien in the car. "What did he say, I'll talk to him."

Delina just gestures to her head, like that could explain everything. "Eh, he's been asleep for a few hours."

Maison narrows his eyes further, leaning against the vending machine, before his gaze clears with understanding, which is almost worse.

"I'm fine," she preempts.

"Delly," he starts, and she bites back a snap at that, "we'll switch cars, you'll drive with me."

"What, Chloe has to do her passport making and Gurlien is...definitely asleep again," Delina says, before sighing. "It's just my brain being mean, it's no big deal."

"Sure," he says, "it isn't. But that doesn't mean we can't make it easier on you."

In the single yellow light, with the snowflakes settling in his soft brown hair, she finds herself a little bit without words. Like the silence has stolen them from her, like the chill and the flatness of the world robbed her.

He shifts, staring out at the blank black nothingness around them, as Chloe starts the pump working and begins to fill the two cars.

"I thought this would go away," Delina says, hushing her voice to match the falling snow. "That I wouldn't be this way now."

"What, depression?" he asks, almost skeptical. "You've had that for what, since you were twelve?"

"Yeah," Delina says, staring again at the vending machine, before feeding a dollar bill to get a singular bag of chips. "Thought, with the biotrap and actually, you know, knowing more about myself that it'd go away."

She can feel his eyes on her, heavy.

"Plenty of magicians are depressed," he says, rubbing the scruff that still hasn't materialized into a full beard yet. "Magic has...very little to do with brain chemistry, near as they can tell."

It's logical, but it still smarts against her hope. "I just thought..."

Her voice breaks, and she screws her face up.

"Hey," Maison says, resting an arm around her lower back and tugging her in so that her head rests against him. "It's fine."

She sighs.

"You didn't know, you couldn't have known, it's okay to be disappointed," he says, tucking his chin over her hair. "But you don't have to be alone."

The vending machine clunks out the bag of chips, and in the snow and the silence, she wrestles with her heart to believe him.

"You would think, with all the weird advancements you guys have, with the changing faces and the free gas and the bringing people back from the dead, that there'd be something already solved." Her voice sounds whiny, even to her own ears, and she shuts her eyes against the snow. "I think I've been too busy since this happened to actually be depressed."

He says nothing, just leaning his cheek against her hair, like he always did back in their condo in Prescott, and she buries her face into his shoulder, for that brief little bit of comfort.

Comfort she's allowed to have.

"Wait," she says, pulling away just enough to read his expression. "Was the weird bond thing how you were able to know when I was like this?"

He opens his mouth to answer, then closes it.

"And here I thought you were just a good boyfriend," she says dryly, and he has the gall to roll his eyes.

"I can't, you know, pick out 'oh this one is depression' and 'this mood is pissed about the weather' and 'this one's because she forgot coffee,'" he says, and she squints at him. "Just general moods. I thought Gurlien was picking a fight with you the entire drive."

"Nope, just my brain," Delina replies, then breaks the contact long enough to grab the bag of chips. "I'm okay."

He huffs out something halfway between a sigh and a laugh, then follows her back to the car.

~

38

They don't stop until the sun has risen over the flat farmlands and Gurlien directs them to a lone cabin, hidden behind a windbreak of trees about three miles off the main freeway.

It's more of a shack than anything else. While the roof stands steady above them, the wind whistles through the slats in the walls and dust piles in the corners, soft and powdery.

"Wait," Chloe says, as Delina peers inside, and Maison puts out his arm to stop her from stepping inside.

"What is it?" Gurlien says, and the cat is now zipped up in his jacket, creating an odd bulge on his chest.

"Demon trap," Maison says, staring down at the bare baseboards, and Chloe nods. "And something else."

Delina shivers out in the wind. Snow still technically falls, a few snowflakes here and there, but the wind cuts through her meager jacket.

After the scan earlier, everything feels dire.

"This isn't Frisse's work," Chloe says, kneeling down in front of the open door, peering down at the boards. "Not entirely."

"Demon trap is," Maison grumbles, then sticks his head in just enough to shine a flashlight up to the roof.

A dazzling array of symbols sketch across the ceiling, spray painted on, the color vivid gold.

"That is," Maison continues, and Delina blinks up at it, at the dazzling, looping lettering.

From the tutoring of Gurlien, it's intense.

Chloe looks back at them, at the rising sun, and sighs. "Gurlien, where is the next safe place?"

"There's a hotel about ten miles back," Delina supplies, but the other three already shake their heads.

"Not for at least three more hours of driving, and I'd like to be across the border by then," Gurlien replies, and despite the fact that he napped the majority of the drive, he still sounds exhausted. "If it's Alette's work, she usually allowed for more back doors that a spell weaver could track."

Maison's still staring hard out at the shack, before he taps Delina's shoulder twice, and the entire thing blooms gold.

"Oh geez," Delina mumbles, rubbing her eyes. Gold is written into the walls, twisted into the wood slats, woven into the very being of the shack itself.

And alongside it, a warping red/black power glimmers, shining like fresh tar.

"Is that demon junk?" Delina asks, and both Chloe and Maison turn to stare at her in the biting wind. "There." She points, as if that could help anything.

Immediately, red flashes over Maison's eyes as he aims the flashlight towards it.

"Not exactly," he replies, voice pondering. "But it's not...not."

"Helpful," Gurlien snips, and the cat mrrs in agreement.

"Did my mom have any demon friends?" Delina asks him. "Cause to me this looks like working together."

"Just Terese before she lost control," Gurlien answers, then his eyes widen.

Chloe cusses under her breath, then, splaying her hand on one of the twists of gold, slowly starts to unravel it.

"Take down the demon trap first," Maison orders, and Chloe rolls her eyes, as if that's what she's already doing. "I can neutralize the rest."

It's almost sad staring out at the twisted magic, but the memory of the scan and of the fury of Maison's power sends another shiver up Delina's back.

"If this is where Terese has been hiding," Gurlien starts, his voice muted, "we don't know what happened to the...the body. The body was still alive."

Delina stares down at the dust piled in the corner, at the wind whistling through the cracks. "Hell of a place to hide."

The air above the gold threads shimmers, blurring, and Maison steps forward, confident, and sparks swirl around his shoes, burying themselves into the folds of his pant legs.

Delina's lips part, at the living magic, as Maison crouches down, rubbing the red and black strip of magic through his fingertips.

"Whoever did this is still alive," he whispers, like the very walls could hear them. "Not the demon Terese."

Gurlien shifts. "So the human side?"

Delina stills, staring at the red-black strip in Maison's hand. It's not the malicious glow from the other demon, nor is it the familiar power she now can halfway recognize from Maison.

"If this is the human side, then she's a lot more demon than you think," Delina says, even though she's far less than confident in that, but Maison nods along absentmindedly.

"But this suggests some form of cooperation, so it would be early in the...event," Maison continues for her, and a hint of a dimple shows on his chin. "And it's not...malicious."

He spreads the magic between his hands, and it glistens. Still off, still unreal, but it's malleable in his grip.

Still feels sick.

"Not that this isn't interesting," Chloe starts, and the demon trap unwinds with a snap, sending harmless sparks skittering across the room, "but this is some weird spell weaving."

"Weird how?" Gurlien asks, voice well and truly frustrated. "All I see is an empty shack."

Chloe just has a glimmer of mischief in her eyes, just the hint of something, before she cracks another bit of magic in her hand and the entire room...unfurls.

Before she can even think, Maison has an arm across Delina's chest, backing her out of the doorway, but Chloe stands, her hands on her hips with something close to satisfaction in her stance.

A rug rolls out, covering the bare wooden slates, and though the room doesn't grow, a couch shimmers into existence and a bed tucks itself into a corner. The lone fireplace, with broken bricks, rights itself, pristine.

There's a counter, a stove, and though there's no electricity that Delina can see, everything is clean and everything glows faintly with gold.

All four of them stare at the room, then Gurlien sighs, explosive. "Illusion spell?"

"Weird one at that," Chloe says, honest-to-god dusting off her hands. "But it's safe."

Maison doesn't budge for a long second, before his shoulders relax and he lets his arm fall away.

Gurlien pushes past them, unzipping his jacket and letting the cat jump out. Chance sniffs the rug, his nose twitching, before turning around and meowing loudly at them.

Slowly, Delina steps inside, and the carpet is plush against her feet, finer than anything she's ever stepped on.

Maison settles a hand against her back, but follows her in, breathing deeply. "Still sets my teeth on edge. Not malicious, it's not gonna hurt us, but..."

Chloe prods at the stove, and it does absolutely nothing.

"It's a place to stay," Chloe says, opening the cupboards, revealing them empty.

They had bought sandwich makings at the last town, so they won't go hungry, but Delina at least wishes there was some way of making a hot meal.

The wind still blows through the cracks, but it's warmer, somehow, and Delina just breathes out, then hesitates.

Something bothers her at the back of her head, so she crouches down, looking underneath the bed.

Of course, there's a box, clean and pristine, the metal edges glinting in the golden glow.

"Your mother was insane," Gurlien's saying, flopping over on the couch, and the cat sniffs along the arms, but Delina's ears buzz. "It's an abandoned shack, there's no reason for this amount of security."

"It's just the paranoia," Chloe replies flippantly. "Remember how bad the cabin was when we first got there?"

Delina doesn't reach out to poke the metal box, it's not the same sensation she got when looking at the locked safe at the last apartment.

"Delina?" Maison asks, crouching next to her, then peering under the bed. "There's nothing there."

"Oh, so it's something disguised that only I can see," Delina replies, and Maison raises an eyebrow at her, and she gets the strong sensation that he really wishes he could yank her backwards but he's restraining himself. "Or just necromancers?"

She straightens and everyone's staring at her again.

"It looks like a metal box, tucked underneath the bed," she supplies, as Maison pokes a broom handle at it, and it connects with a resounding thunk.

"Of course," Gurlien replies, as if all exhaustion has taken all of the doubts right out of him. "She would do that."

Chloe also crouches down, then shakes her head sadly. "I can't even see anything. No magical trace, nothing."

"Do you want me to drag it out?" Delina asks dryly, and Chloe's nodding but Maison's shaking his head before she can actually do anything. "Maybe after we sleep."

It still buzzes against her mind, but they all uneasily put it aside, dividing up the bread and peanut butter for a meager meal, before a quick but vicious argument of who's sleeping where before—full of suspicion and full of unrest —they all attempt to sleep.

DELINA WAKES, far earlier than she would want, to Maison shifting next to her, sitting up.

The two of them had pulled the short end of the stick, sleeping on the plush carpet instead of the twin bed, but she just blinks her eyes open as he straightens, his breathing light.

The sun filters through the planks in the walls, warming the air around them, and dust motes hang still around them, settling into the Maison's hair.

He's still, inhumanly so, before he carefully slides out from under the makeshift blanket, rolling himself to his feet.

Delina's lips part, but she stills herself from saying anything, as he scans the room, his eyes red, before he carefully, ever so carefully, pulls on his jacket.

He's moving as if he thinks that any sudden motion would draw attention to them. As if he has to in order to remain undetected.

He glances down at her, visibly startling at her open eyes, before he holds a finger up to his lips, then gestures for her to remain in place.

Delina rolls her eyes at him, sitting up as quietly as she can, and he rolls his eyes right back, before mouthing, "Stay here."

She props herself up to standing, just as quiet as he is.

There's no motion in the shack, not even the breath of the wind that had plagued them for most of the night, and Chloe and Gurlien sleep on, though the cat blinks idly at them from his place draped over Chloe's back.

Maison tilts his head at her, and Delina lifts her chin.

"There's someone outside," he breathes, leaning close enough that her heart jumps, close enough so the fabric of his jacket grazes her chest. "They're not approaching, they're not fighting, but someone's there."

Instinctively, Delina glances towards the slats in the wall, but it's too thin of a slice to see out of.

"I'm going to try to get a better look," he whispers, and his hand falls to her elbow, steadying her. "Stay out of sight."

Delina nods, though she raises an eyebrow right back at him, and he grimaces at her expression, before stepping silently towards the wall, towards the dust encrusted window mostly covered up by particle boards. He leans against the wall, next to the glass, tilting himself towards the line of sight, smooth and fluid.

It's a motion she recognizes at once. Anytime they went somewhere new, anytime they went over to someone's house, he'd position himself near the window, facing the room but casually able to glance out.

Yet another bit of him that she thought was an odd quirk but it's really him protecting her.

His shoulders are tight, but his face remains impassive, like he's just woken up and just wanting to look around. Like this is nothing.

She watches in fascination as Maison's jaw works, as if he's somehow talking without making any noise.

Though his face is serious, it's not afraid, so she creeps up next to him, peering out.

Among the crunchy dry snow and dead cornfield, stands a woman, staring unblinkingly at them.

She's striking, with short white-blond hair and pale eyes, like someone took her and sapped all the color from her, and the very ground around her swirls with some strange energy.

The colorless eyes snap onto Delina, and she raises her chin, mouthing something that Delina can't hear, but Maison hisses out a breath.

Even from this distance, the crawling sensation of intense pain washes over Delina, her stomach dropping.

This woman shouldn't even be alive, and Delina can tell with just a glance.

Still, she doesn't move closer to the house, just evaluating Delina, before she vanishes.

There's another moment, where Maison still stares out

the window, before he exhales, letting himself shift away from the window.

"Who was that?" Delina asks, though the hair prickles on the back of her neck.

"Terese," Maison whispers back, and it takes a moment for his words to register in Delina's mind. He sighs, rubbing his eyes, and in between one blink and the next, they're back to normal. "Well. I hated that, but she didn't want to fight, so that's good."

"She was in pain," Delina murmurs, and he nods, shaking out his hands. "How was she alive?"

"We should leave," he says, at full volume, and both Gurlien and Chloe startle awake.

"What is it?" Gurlien asks, and Maison shakes his head. "No, tell me, I want to know."

"We just got a visit from Terese," Maison starts, and both Gurlien and Chloe flinch.

Chloe stares blankly at the two of them from her place on the couch, before she springs into action, grabbing at her go-bag, scrabbling to shove her feet into her shoes. "What do we do, where do we go, how—"

"What did she say?" Gurlien asks, yawning blearily, but his eyes are sharp. "Is she still there?"

Maison's already shaking his head. "She backed down and left." With less urgency than Chloe, he rolls up the makeshift blankets that made up his and Delina's bed, his brows tight. "She rabbited the moment she saw Delina, I don't like it. She wasn't a demon, she didn't feel like anything I know, and I don't know how long she were out there before I woke up."

Delina's skin crawls, just barely, so she hugs herself. "Great."

"I don't know what called her to this place, I don't know what alarm we set off, I don't know."

Him and Gurlien lock eyes, before Gurlien swings himself up to standing. "Got it, let's get out of here."

"Should I grab the box?" Delina asks, and everyone hesitates, the three of them having a wordless conversation that goes over her head. "If only I can see it, that means it could be from my mother, right?"

"That's a risk," Gurlien says, crossing his arms at Maison, like Maison won the argument. "See if it's biolocked, but I wouldn't bring it."

Before they could change their minds or stop her, Delina crouches to underneath the bed, letting her fingers fall on the cool metal of the box.

It's just as inert as it was before, and she tugs it out, and nothing changes.

It doesn't open, it doesn't reveal itself to them, nothing.

And it's another thing she has to leave behind.

THE SUN IS JUST STARTING to set when Maison finally speaks on the drive.

"We should talk about what we might see in Toronto," he says, and Delina leans her head over to watch him, well and truly bored with the waves of dead cornfields out the windows.

"Well," Delina drawls, "I know there are locking pits, I know Chloe almost died getting out, and there are demon traps."

He spares a glance at her before returning to the road. "It's a prison. We're on our way to break into a prison, then break out."

Delina mulls over that, testing how she feels, like it's a piece of taffy that she can pull at. "And we have someone who's come out of it," she starts, "and you. And they don't expect me."

He hmms, drumming his knuckles against the wheel, and it's only years of knowing him that she can actually tell he's holding back.

"I'm..." he starts, then trails off, like he's halfway caught between despair and hope. "I don't want to bring you in there, I don't know if you'll be able to get out."

It's not some authoritative sentence, it's not some controlling statement, and his voice breaks in the middle.

She shifts, not reaching out and touching him, but watching him, and he glances at her again.

"We're doing something you've told yourself your entire life that you can't do, right?" Delina asks, and he nods again. "I get it, that's terrifying."

"And if we fail, I lose you. And my mom. And probably... probably any sort of freedom of my own." His words stop, and he frowns, like they pain him to admit out loud. "I don't want to run away now, but I..."

"But you kinda do?" Delina asks dryly, and he nods, so she shifts again, so she can rest her hand on his arm. "I'll just, I dunno, necromancer drain the life of anyone who gets too close."

It surprises a laugh out of him, and she grins.

"I love you," he says, risking another glance, the serious expression filtering over his face again. "I don't...I don't want to lose you."

She could respond to it, but all the words are gone from her, so she just lets her eyes drift back to the rows upon rows of dead corn reaching as far as the horizon stretches.

"I'm scared, too," Delina says, after the silence is as long

39

After a brief stop for Chloe to give them all fabricated passports and an even briefer stop at the border, they make their way through the labyrinthine skyscrapers of Toronto, to an unassuming condo in the near suburbs.

There's nothing to mark it as unusual, and it's so unprotected that Maison's extra uneasy.

"And, here we are," Gurlien says, after the third check over by both Maison and Chloe, searching for traps or guards or something, anything, and finding nothing. "She probably kept it unmarked so it wouldn't trigger any random scans."

It's…fine, in terms of condos in big cities. There's a bright blue tile backsplash behind the stove, and the ceilings arch up higher than practical. There's the same anti-dust rune, there's a collection of completely normal paperbacks from the last ten years in a bookcase and on the nightstand of one of the bedrooms, and a smattering of jackets in the hall closet.

There's less creeping exhaustion after this drive, more of

a slight electricity among the four of them, as they convene back in the modest kitchen. The cat sniffs along the baseboards, tail held high, before meowing pitifully until Maison picks him up.

"Oh neat, there's actually pantry stuff," Chloe says, pulling out a jar of spaghetti sauce and some curly looking pasta, the sort found at too-fancy of restaurants. "I think she actually stayed here some."

"The safe is in the linen closet this time," Maison mentions, and Chloe immediately perks up. "No magical signature, nothing. Just a normal safe."

"On it," Chloe says, leaving the food out on the counter and the pantry wide open, dusting her hands on her overalls. "What type of safe?"

Maison shrugs at her as she passes by, already down the hall.

"She actually put paperwork in a file cabinet," Gurlien says idly, digging around under the counter and pulling out a copper pan. "Stuff she normally keeps in her safe, so maybe she thought this place was more secure than it is."

"See, that just makes me feel worse," Maison says, before leaning on the counter still holding the cat, casual in a way that makes Delina immediately doubt it. "There has to be some trap, something."

There's a muffled thump from the linen cabinet, before Chloe swears joyfully.

Gurlien rolls his eyes, testing the sink. It chugs for a few seconds, before it blasts out clear water, the faucet obviously unused for quite a bit. "Surprised the pipes didn't freeze," he says, filling up the pot. "We had to do some maintenance on the cabin before the water worked, and even then it would've been impossible without Chloe."

"This condo block probably goes for a million five each,

they're not gonna let pipes freeze," Maison points out, as Delina pokes at the bookcase.

All the books are...completely normal. Bestsellers, mostly thrillers, some with pages folded over where her mother never finished it.

"How often did my mother visit Toronto?" Delina asks, letting her fingertips trail over the spines of the books.

"At least three times a year, sometimes more," Gurlien answers immediately. "Before Terese, even if she wasn't... accepted...she was still an expert."

"So some of the traps in the base might've been set by her?" Delina asks, squinting hard at the wood grains of the bookcase, like she can learn truths if she just stares long enough. "Or wards?"

Maison's jaw twitches. "Probably." Chance meows in his face, at the expression, and Maison lets the cat jump out of his arms and onto the sofa.

"They'd replace them after she died, almost certainly," Gurlien says, which eliminates that idea from Delina's mind. "Small chance there might be a few, only if they couldn't figure out how to write over them."

He sets the copper pot on the stove, and then his phone rings.

Delina and Maison stare blankly at him, as his brain obviously skips a beat at the sound.

"You kept your phone?" Maison asks, dipping his voice dangerously low.

"It's been off this entire time," he says, his brows furrowing together, digging it out of his pocket. "Only people around that would be if someone already held it and put a back door and..." He trails off, staring at it, then sighs. "It's Axel. Of course Alette probably put a back door."

Delina perks up, and Gurlien gingerly sets the phone on the counter, as it continues to ring.

"It's almost five AM," Delina points out. "Who would call you at five AM?"

"Would they rat us out?" Maison asks, still deadly low, and Gurlien's face twists, before shaking his head.

"They hate them more than we do."

Propping it up, Gurlien answers, flipping it to speakerphone.

"Axel?" he asks, crossing his arms, still standing at the stove. "Did you finally listen to my messages?"

There's a pop on the other end, and Maison flinches.

"No, but we got an alarm of someone at one of Dr. Frisse's old cabins yesterday," a voice filters through the phone, falsely jovial. "And apparently you were there as well."

Gurlien looks up, locks eyes with Maison. "So Terese is with you?"

"And you have a Half Demon and another Necromancer, you're keeping more secrets," the other voice says, clearly exasperated. "And the College tried to ask us about you, what are you doing?"

"What did you tell them?" Maison interrupts, and the other side goes silent for a long second at his voice.

"Obviously nothing," Axel responds. "What's going on?"

"I don't trust it," Maison says, loud enough that the other side of the phone has to have overheard. "How do you know…"

"Wait, if you've had Terese for however long and they're still calling her missing and dangerous?" Gurlien interrupts, like that's the important part here. "How…"

"Oh my god shut up," this time, a female voice, lightly accented, interrupts. "Gurlien, can you answer for once?"

Gurlien rubs his forehead. "Hi, Alette, we've been trying to call you for weeks." His eyes flicker over to Delina who's frozen at the bookcases. "Dr. Frisse's daughter is a Necromancer, she knows everything now, her boyfriend is a Half Demon and we're on a real misguided attempt to go free his mother from Toronto, any help?"

Silence on the other end, and Maison sighs.

"I've literally been trying to call for weeks to get some sort of necromancer advice," Gurlien says, and Chloe drifts back into the kitchen, her lock picks held loosely in her hands. "And apparently you two have been working with Terese? Or something? How?"

"She's not going to attack you," Axel replies, obviously grumpy, "drop it."

"Wait, Aunt Frisse's daughter?" the female voice asks, and it's so chaotic that Delina's head spins. "She was sealed away..."

"And now I'm not," Delina interrupts, and everyone falls silent. "Hi, cousin."

IT TURNS out that Axel is absolutely not willing to risk actually going out and helping them, but Gurlien and Alette spend too long on the phone discussing distractions, techniques, switching between English and French with a fluidity that makes Delina's head spin.

Her cousin, an actual family member who knew her mother and was actually raised by her mother, and Delina can't actually think of the things to say to her, so she leaves Gurlien and Maison to it, flopping over on the bed in the other room.

Her own mother probably slept in the same bed she's now laying on.

Her own mother might've set some of the same traps they're going to break.

Chance follows her into the room, jumping on the bed and curling up next to her, already purring.

Delina lets herself have a brief existential crisis, laying there on a far too comfortable bed, before a polite knock on the door drags her out of it.

"Yeah?"

Chloe steps into the room, briefly letting in the sound of arguing in French, before shutting the door back behind her.

"Don't mind that, they don't like Gurlien, which makes him even more defensive and dickish than he already is," Chloe says cheerfully, then raises her hands to show a plain wooden box. "Want some defensive charms?"

Delina lets herself push up as Chloe sits cross legged next to her on the bed. "Is it going to attack me?"

"No, just a bunch of jewelry in the safe," Chloe replies, popping the plain, raw pine box open. "All normal looking, all charmed for simple protections. Nothing fancy, nothing intense, just give you a bit of an edge."

Delina glances inside—all the necklaces are neatly coiled, the rings polished, and even a diamond tennis bracelet perfectly in place.

"I thought I should give you first dibs as, you know, it's your mom's jewelry," Chloe says, voice hushing a bit. "It won't do too much, but something."

Delina tentatively touches the coils of the necklaces, letting her fingertips play over the rings.

"That one I know she wore a bunch," Chloe says. "It's in a lot of her press materials."

"Why?" Delina asks, plucking a ring from its spot. It's the

most worn out of all of them, a few dings in the gold of the underside. There are a few stones, a bit small and too cloudy to be proper diamonds, but it fits neatly on Delina's hand. "Why would she need protection during press conferences?"

"I'm gonna go with paranoia as an option," Chloe remarks dryly. "And, you know, assassins."

Delina glances at it, holding it up to the light of the lamp by the side of the bed. It's a romantic idea that her mother may have left these to her that they fit so perfectly.

"Maison's probably gonna like a few additional charms," Delina remarks, and they're not her normal style, but she picks up the tennis bracelet as well, clipping it on her wrist. Those diamonds are of much better quality, glittering even in the lamp light, and Delina likes it less than the ring.

"The way I see it, any little bit is good," Chloe replies, her voice uncharacteristically grim. "It's your inheritance, but I think each of us should have at least one of these on us."

Delina nods, tossing her hair behind herself. "Obviously, I'm not gonna be stingy."

Chloe glances, then pokes around in the box, uncovering a pair of simple gold studs. "Here, these ones are good, they'll help bend any bullet slightly away."

Delina raises an eyebrow.

"Not all the way away, just, you know, less likely to hit an important organ, that sort of thing." Chloe nudges in the box, her eyes distant, like she can tell all the charms simply by the feel. "If I think I'm going to be trapped in there, I'm gonna run."

Delina doesn't need to be an expert to know what she's talking about.

"Gurlien and I have been going over it, I think we'll be

okay, I know the way out, I should be okay, but..." she shrugs, one shoulder, poking at a simple necklace with a heart charm. "I'm not gonna be trapped."

"I get it," Delina says, and Chloe glances up at her, quick, then looks away. "Do what you need to do."

"Well," Chloe starts, then scowls, "there's something I want there, it's not just me helping you, and going in with a group gives me a better chance."

"Got it," Delina replies, and despite the serious conversation, a smile tugs at her lips.

"It should be on the way, it should be in the evidence lockers, they haven't moved it from there. I have trackers on it," Chloe continues. "It'll fit in my bag, it's not going to weigh us down or slow us too much."

Chloe pauses, like she's expecting a blow back or something from Delina, who's absolutely not going to give that to her.

"It's my old research," Chloe says, finally, after a too long of break. "I had some...string of spells, some information I was working on decoding, for something that...means a lot to me."

Considering how Chloe's not one for ascribing emotions too much besides cheerfulness, the statement is weighty.

"How can we help?" Delina asks, though curiosity burns her to ask more. "Anything in particular?"

"Oh thank god, Gurlien says I should give up on it, he's gonna be so grumpy you agreed," Chloe says, leaning back, relief slumping her shoulders. "Maison thinks it'll be no big deal, but Gurlien's convinced that it's gonna be a disaster if we take the time."

Delina plucks out the necklace, clips it on. "Honestly, you break into tombs, any research they have locked away from you is probably terrifying and really, really cool."

It surprises a smile out of Chloe, before she pokes around more in the box. "Mind if I give the guys some of your mom's old jewelry? Gurlien's gonna hate it."

Delina can recognize a conversation change when one's given to her. "Go ahead, it'll be funny."

40

They sleep through the day, and by the time the night falls, Delina awakes to an empty bed.

It's dizzyingly close to how she would wake up when Maison started work early, and for a split second, she has to exhale through the odd torrent of emotions it piles on top of her.

They're in Toronto, she's sleeping in her mother's old bed.

With just a brief touch of her mind, she can tell that the cat is pacing in front of the one window, an odd buzzing sensation of excitement rumbling through him, and that it's only Maison outside the bedroom door.

Not Gurlien, not Chloe, just Maison.

Not even bothering to put on her pajama pants, Delina pushes herself up, wandering into the main room.

Maison's at the counter, furiously mixing together something in a baking bowl, a scowl across his face.

"Good morning," Delina drawls, and he almost startles from her presence. "What, I even scanned you, how can I surprise you?"

Carefully, he sets the bowl down, then rubs his eyes. "I think I only slept three hours."

Delina crosses to the stools sitting on the other side of the counter, hopping onto one of them. "Did you find... butter in the fridge? Was it any good?"

"No, Chloe went on a supply run," Maison says, then gives her a crooked smile, almost self-deprecating. "They wouldn't let me out, I'm too recognizable in this city." His eyes trail down her, where all she's wearing is one of his T-shirts. "They're both reaching out to contacts tonight, getting us some more information."

It's good knowledge to have, so she nods.

"Chloe's focused in on the traps, Gurlien's trying to find staffing levels and how to get as many people out before we go in," Maison recites, and there are circles under his eyes as he idly picks up the spatula again.

Delina's not the most adept at baking, but it looks like his oatmeal muffin recipe.

"Good morning," Delina repeats, a bit gentler, hopping off the stool and striding around the counter, sliding her arms around him. "I don't need immediate status reports, it's okay."

"Right, yeah," Maison says, his arm curling around her waist in return, before he tugs her in, pressing a kiss to the top of her head. "Sorry, I..."

Delina nods, and tucked this close to him she can hear his heart.

"Nothing's gonna happen tonight," Maison says, almost as if he's reassuring himself. "It's just fact finding and planning."

"And baking, apparently," Delina says, poking at the bowl, and he catches her hand, peering at the ring she slept with.

Of course he had inspected all bits of jewelry the night before, but still, it catches his eye.

"That distracting?"

"The lack of sleep is that distracting," Maison grumbles, but keeps one arm around her, just standing on the kitchen linoleum, the purple pinks of the sunset fading into the dark blue of a city night outside the one window. "The coffee machine here isn't nearly as good as the one in the cabin."

Delina lets herself lean fully against him, and it's...amazing. Reassuring. "Any way I can convince you to get some more rest?" she asks.

"Not likely," Maison mutters, awkwardly dumping in chocolate chips into the bowl with one hand, mixing as he goes, seemingly just as unwilling to let Delina go. "My mom's in the same city as me and I can't do anything about it."

"Yet," Delina corrects him, and he gives her another crooked smile. "You can't do anything about it yet."

"Yeah," he replies, still wistful, like the lack of motion is driving him crazy. "So I'm baking." He presses another kiss to the crown of her head, like that could give him strength, then unwinds himself to support the bowl.

The oven is preheating behind them, and there are even a set of well used muffin tins already out, dinged and everything.

"Do you think my bio-mom actually baked?" Delina asks, as if that could get his mind off of the impending crisis.

"Oh, absolutely," he says, grabbing on to the distraction and running with it. "There are too many actually used gadgets here. There's a kitchen aid, an actual kitchen aid, and it's been used so much the motor wobbles." He nods at one of the cabinets. "I thought about it, thought better of it."

They fall into one of their easy rhythms, where she helps him just enough with getting things around the kitchen, the easy patter of him baking and her chatting, and it's so close to normal that a part of her yearns for just... more of this. More of the casual contact of the two of them as if nothing ever happened.

But a phone in the other room chimes, just as they pull the muffins out of the oven, and Maison stiffens, his eyes flashing red for a split second, before he consciously relaxes.

"Chloe got us all burner phones," he says, dusting off his hands and meandering over to the couch. "So we can coordinate at least a little without being in the same room, and Axel talked her through making them impervious to dead zone runes."

"Well, at least they're willing to do that," Delina says, and he hands her a brand-new phone, the plastic cling still on the front. "I take it I can't text my dad?"

"No, but you can text your cousin if you really feel like it," he says, poking at a phone of his own. "Gurlien says the smallest shift will be there on Sunday night."

Delina has to check her phone to even see what day it actually is, between the travel and the driving. "Three days."

Maison sits down, hard, on the couch, and the couch has a dip in it, as if someone slept there many times. "Three days." He rubs his face, before looking up at her, almost beseechingly. "I have to wait for three days of this."

"Beats three days of driving," Delina says, then stands in front of him, resting her arms on his shoulders, and he tilts his eyes up to her. "We'll get through this."

"Three days of planning and three days of trying really hard to not get spotted in a city that almost certainly would recognize me on sight," Maison says, but he lets the phone fall to his side, an arm grazing down along her back, to her still bare legs. "Are you trying to distract me?"

"Absolutely," Delina replies, and he cracks a smile, just barely, and she yearns for more of the smile, more of anything to keep him looking at her like that. "Right now, right this moment, is there anything you can do about this?"

He shakes his head, and she winds her hand through his soft brown hair, and his eyes slip shut at her touch.

"Right now, is there anything you personally need to be planning for?"

Again, he shakes his head, slow, like he's spellbound by her. "I could be better preparing you," he whispers, as if someone could overhear them. "You still know so little."

She twists her hands in his hair, a little tighter, and he follows the motion.

"I'm not insulting you, I want..." he sighs, letting his hands grip the back of her thighs, completely at odds with his words. "You're beautiful, you're powerful, and you're entirely unskilled right now and it terrifies me."

"Are any threats going to walk through that door?" Delina asks, before a thought occurs to her. "Our entire relationship, I just thought you had anxiety, but it was this sort of thing, wasn't it?"

He nods again. "It's not anxiety."

"True," Delina says, gentling her grip and trailing her hand on his neck, across his jaw, tilting his face up to her. "Just me putting things together."

His lips open, but he doesn't say anything.

"What I'm saying is, we can try to relax in these little moments," Delina says, and his stubble along his jaw is almost a full beard, more than he's had any time she's known him, a pleasant scratch against her palm. "You won't be the most useful if you worry yourself sick."

He briefly shuts his eyes, then tugs on the back of her thighs until she falls forward, straddling him.

"You're making it awfully difficult to focus on it, Delly girl," he says, voice low, and she grins at him, impulsive.

"That's the idea," she replies, and his dimple briefly appears, before he grips her chin back and kisses her.

Kisses her like there's nothing else in the world, like there's no one else outside the walls of the condo. Like there's no bad news, nothing to worry about, no insane magic powers and dire things to break into, nothing.

She opens her mouth to him, and he sighs, deep in his chest, pulling her closer, gripping her thighs tight.

It's precarious, his touch on her skin, with everything still wrong in the world. Where she's not sure if they'll live through the next few days, where he's frightened about not being able to rescue his mother.

But there's the fire again, the spark between them, the same thrill of danger on his lips and openness in his hands.

"What do you want me to do," he mumbles against her lips, before tilting her head away and kissing down her neck, across her collarbone. "Tell me what to do and I will do it."

It's a little like a vow.

So she pulls the pajama shirt over her head, and he immediately presses a kiss between her breast, like he could kiss his way into her heart.

AFTER GETTING DRESSED and snagging one of the muffins, Delina curls her legs underneath her on the couch, tucking herself next to Maison.

His breathing is more settled, thankfully, but he throws

his arm around her shoulders, as if he could keep her safe just by sheer force of will.

"This'll be difficult for you, won't it?" Delina asks, after a long soothing silence, where the only noise is Chance chattering at the snowflakes falling outside the window.

He doesn't bother to ask for clarification, just nods, playing with the tip of her ponytail.

"I'd lock you up until it was done, but I can't figure out a way past the fire trap without the necromancy," he says wistfully, and she tilts her head up to look at him. "It's proofed against alchemy, it's proofed against demon powers, I just... don't think they've been able to proof against necromancy."

Gurlien had suggested so much, in the long drives.

"I can guide, I can protect you with my entire self, but I can't...I can't get us over that trap without you."

"You totally would lock me up, wouldn't you?" Delina asks, and he nods, fervent.

"If the choice is between pissing you off and saving your life, I'm gonna save your life every time," he vows, and she believes him. "I'll deal with you being angry later, when you're still alive."

"Hmm," Delina says, and he pokes her in the side at that reaction. "What, I'm still coming to grasp with the fact that I've had a bodyguard for years, it's weird to think about."

"It was a lot easier when you weren't a walking flare," he grumbles, but it's good natured, and he presses a quick kiss against the top of her head. "Inside the Toronto Base, with all the demon traps, might be the one safe place for you to raise more than one thing."

The thought strikes her, like a cloud disappearing in the wake of the sun, and she blinks through it. "Well, I hope I don't have to do too much of that," she says, but the idea is still way too alluring. "Besides, I'll be bringing those dead bugs to jack you up, not to raise them."

"They still bothering you?" he asks, almost lazily, despite the seriousness of the conversation.

"Bother isn't the right word, but they're easier to ignore." Chance the cat suddenly races across the couch, sprinting down the hall, then back, skidding in front of the window once more with a loud meow. "After...after this, think we can hide your mom with my cousin?"

"It could be a safe place to start," he says, and she can hear the same creeping hope in his voice, like he's almost too afraid to even think it. "I texted with Alette over there, she's terrifying."

Delina cracks a smile at that.

"She's apparently so enmeshed with the Wight community there that they view her as one of them," he says, like it's the gossip he would have of his work friends back in Arizona, and she loves it. "The Necromancer is dating—actually dating—an actual demon that she actually raised from the dead and I do not understand it."

This time, Delina pokes him in the side. "Think about that," she says at his faux outraged noise. "Think about that for one more second."

"Hey."

"So that's how she's safe," Delina says, moving along, and he nods. "So wait, I can get tips from her." She sits up, reaching for the cheap burner phone on the coffee table. "She knows how to use all of this, she can help—"

"I asked, she's never killed someone with it besides demons," he interrupts, then twists his face. "God, she's killed two. I can't even imagine that, apparently they all avoid her now because she's just so good at killing them."

Delina raises an eyebrow. "I definitely need to get tips."

She pulls the phone to her, and even flipping to the phone number entitled Alette gives her heart a pang.

DELINA (5:21 PM): Can I have the other Necromancer's number?

There's no immediate answer, but she props up her phone, her mind racing.

"So I can defend myself, so you won't have to be as scared," she says, and he rolls his eyes. "I can actually know some things, they all knew my bio-mother, and we can be safe. That's a win win."

"You're not going to be in danger of demons in the next few days," he replies, which she knows, but he takes the moment to stretch out his legs, before standing up. "Come on, let's do some actual practice, Gurlien and Chloe won't be back for another few hours. I want to drill you on the wards again."

Delina rolls her eyes, but stands anyways.

DELINA SENSES GURLIEN at the door a split second before he opens it, his wrist pain almost a signature.

"They're shoring up their demon protections, it's gonna be difficult," he says, before he even sheds his jacket, then pauses, looking at the relative disarray that Delina and Maison have caused by practicing grasping the magic that runs naturally through the condo. "Alright, didn't anticipate that."

"Which protections?" Maison asks, dusting off his hands. Chance the cat pokes his head out of the other room at their voices and gives a little meow, before wandering in and butting his head against Gurlien's leg. "Internal concrete or pathway?"

"Pathway," Gurlien says, then slings off his backpack, pulling out an honest-to-god scroll of paper. "I got a friend to mark where."

Maison straightens, squaring his shoulders. "Do you trust this friend?"

"Not really, but they'd rather die than ever seem like they don't know something, so the info is correct," Gurlien replies idly. "They're expecting something, but no prisoner transfers in the last week and a half."

"And now they know we're in town," Maison says, exasperated.

"No, he knows that one person is asking about protections and he doesn't know why so he's not going to say anything until he knows." Gurlien rolls out the scroll on the table, using the saltshaker to hold it down. "I told him I'd say more in a few days, he'll wait until after that has passed to say something. I 'suggested,'" Gurlien uses air quotes, "that it's for something interesting next month, I'm not an idiot."

Delina coughs out a laugh, and both of them glance to her. "No, don't look at me like that, it's hilarious."

"They're expecting us to be unaware of notation alarms here, here, and an underground demon trap here," Gurlien says, jabbing at a well-drawn map of a few blocks in what appears to be a suburb of Toronto. "Anyone unknowingly cross them that's even the slightest bit magic, camera in this building and this building snaps a picture."

Maison nods, already absorbed in the map.

"So the main thoroughfares, on the sidewalks and street," Delina says, then hesitates. "I hate to ask the stupid question, but does it extend through the buildings there?"

Maison gives her a sideways glance, the hint of a dimple appearing on his cheek.

"Through this one," Gurlien points, "but not this one. Congrats, you have easily identified one of the problems with small notation alarms. They're small and if you know where they are, you can avoid them."

"I'm more concerned about the demon trap," Maison says, tracing a fingertip where the now familiar circle is sketched on with pencil. "If we can't access the paint, we can't change it."

"Two options," Gurlien says, and Chloe slips in the door, clutching her backpack to her chest. "We send in someone ahead to take it down, or we find a different way in."

"That's past the lobby, that's past the first key lock, once we get that deep they're gonna lock down and they won't let anyone in," Chloe says, peering over Gurlien's shoulder. "Unless we plan on walking Delina in and offering her as a way to get access—"

"No," Maison interrupts.

"—then that won't work," Chloe finishes, rolling her eyes. "Obviously, we're not going to do that. That'd be the worst option."

"If we can do this entire thing without anyone knowing it's Dr. Frisse's daughter, that'd be ideal," Maison says, and it's only the conversation they had earlier that prevents Delina from reacting. "I'd much rather they think it's just me coming in to see my mom, rather than anything...else."

"Hate to break it to you, but when a carbon copy of Frisse walks through the door, even the receptionists are gonna pay attention," Gurlien says.

"Then we should go in another way," Maison says, spinning the map around, pointing to an otherwise unremarkable alleyway. "Windows, here, here, and here."

"Or the exhaust vent," Chloe says, twisting the map back

her way. "I checked, they haven't blocked it yet, they don't know it's one of the ways out."

Delina watches her as she swallows. "Would all of us fit through there?"

"No, but one of us can," Chloe replies, grim. "And I can cause some trouble."

41

Another day, where both Gurlien and Chloe gather information and bribe people for copies of access badges; another day, where Delina practices breaking runes and grabbing onto magic with dead bugs and goes almost stir crazy, and another day, where Maison paints the last remaining sheet in his sketchbook and immediately starts on printer paper pilfered from the dusty photocopier that Delina's bio-mother had tucked in one room.

And another day, and then it's Sunday.

There's a pool of dread inside Delina, as she lays in bed, listening to Maison's deep breathing as he sleeps next to her. Their go time is late into the evening, and everyone else elected to sleep as long as they were able to.

Which means a halfway normal time for Delina, based just on the amount of nerves inside of her.

Pushing out a breath, she wiggles out from underneath Maison's arm, creaking the door to the bedroom open and stepping into the cold light of the main room.

In the middle stands the wight, the one with wiry gray hair and a severe expression on her face.

Delina blinks at her, long, before pointing at the coffee machine. "Do you drink caffeine?"

The wight shakes her head, her eyes narrowed.

At least this time, Delina's wearing pants in the main room. "Mind if I do?"

"If you go in there, there's a wight trapped in room eight hundred and nine," the wight says, instead of replying to Delina. "We've been trying to get her out for six years."

The hair raises on Delina's arms.

"If you give me your word you'll get her out, my people will create an escape route, past all the runes and the demon traps and everything," she says, and for the first time, Delina notices that her hand is on the map scroll of the base. "Nobody has been willing to try for six years."

"Uh," Delina says, then rubs her face and grabs a pencil. "Room eight hundred and nine?"

"It's a stasis wing, the entire thing," the wight says, and Delina scribbles that down on another piece of printer paper. "We can't do anything about the stasis spells, only humans can, and not all of them. Take down the entire wing spells, and she'll be able to get out without further help."

"Stasis wing, got it," Delina says, "one of us will be able to?"

"Not the alchemist, not the Half Demon," the wight says. "The spell weaver should know how to direct you, he'll recognize it."

Delina stares down at the map, at the different levels, and desperately wishes at least Chloe was awake, with her encyclopedic knowledge of the base. "That's three floors off where we're trying to get to."

"If you do, you'll be able to escape, even the older woman," she countered. "We will know once you do it."

It is too good of a plan, as the biggest problem with the day ahead of them, is getting back through all the traps. "She'll be able to get past the locking pits?"

The Wight turns her unreal eyes to Delina instead of the map. "Remove the stasis spell and she can get out of anything. Once you drop the stasis, we will provide the way out in one hour."

Delina nods, scribbling it down.

"You will need to get the older woman during that hour, and survive the remaining time," she continues, her eyes eerie. "After an hour, you will be safe."

"Okay, and—" Before Delina can even finish the sentence, the Wight disappears, like she had never even existed. "Of course."

And now she's going to have to explain an additional complexity to the group the day of their mission.

THE GROUP IS SPLIT on whether or not it's a good thing.

"Absolutely not," Gurlien immediately replies, crossing his arms. "The stasis wing is full of monsters."

"It'll eliminate us going past the locking chambers twice and eliminate the fire trap," Chloe points out, and Maison sits at the table, pouring over the map.

"Plus, the monsters might be willing to help," Maison says, lifting his eyes up to Delina's. "We free them, we might be able to get an extra hand."

"When I say monsters, I don't mean the kind that are easy to reason with," Gurlien restates. "I mean they had a cell for Terese there, that's the sort of people they put in there."

"And a wight, apparently," Delina says, though it bothers her in the back of her mind. "Who may or may not have done something."

"They always told me they would keep me in a stasis cell," Maison murmurs, so quiet she almost missed it. "That was the threat."

"Jesus Christ," Chloe remarks, then shakes her head. "Okay, I'm down with breaking the stasis."

"That would be a stupid place to keep you," Gurlien says, crossing his arms again. "You'd be useless."

"Anyone going to explain to me exactly what stasis cells do?" Delina asks, and they all turn to stare at her. "I mean, I can guess, but I'd like solid information."

"The cells don't let you change, at all," Maison says, still squinting at the map. "You can't sleep, you can't eat, you can't heal, you can't age. You're just...aware in a white box that's unchanging. It breaks people, usually within a month."

"And there's a wight who's been there for six years, I have my doubts on her sanity," Gurlien says, before he sighs. "So everyone's on board with freeing a bunch of dubiously sane monsters while we're there?"

"For a guaranteed way out? Yes," Chloe shoots back. "Leave the dubiously sane monsters to tear the rest of the place down."

"We'll hit it first," Maison says, tapping on the map. "Let everyone panic about the chaos, get my mom out with less guards, and have an escape route."

Delina raises her eyebrows at him.

He's hopeful. He's actually hopeful.

CHANCE THE CAT stares at them, wide eyed, as they pack Chloe's backpack, before he lets out a small, pitiful meow.

"Aww," Gurlien says, then crouches next to him to pet his chin, and the cat preens against him. "I'm gonna..."

"What?" Chloe replies absentmindedly.

"I'm gonna leave the entire bag of food where he can reach it," Gurlien says, unsteady. "And I'll text Axel to come rescue him if he doesn't hear back from us."

In case they don't come back.

Delina swallows, then crosses her arms. "We're gonna make it out, Gurlien."

"Obviously, yes," he snips back, but still, a frown tugs on his face. "We might not be able to come back here, we might have to abandon town, I don't want Chance to starve."

Chance perks up his ears at hearing his name, then meows again.

"And now Chance is distressed because you're upset," Chloe chides, her voice fake and cheerful. "Look what you did, you upset the cat."

"Still gonna do it," Gurlien replies, shuffling for the bag of food from the top of the fridge.

42

In the end, the grand Toronto base looks more like a sprawling shipping center than anything sinister. Like the mega Walmart distribution hubs centered in the Midwest, completely unremarkable.

Gurlien's information holds true, and they skirt the alarm runes easily, and Chloe's guidance brings them right to an exhaust vent that's obviously way too small for all of them to fit through.

It's innocent enough for an entrance to a prison.

"And this leads to the cubical level?" Maison asks, skeptical.

The fact that this magical prison, where they kept Chloe locked away, has a cubical level is surreal.

But even magical prisons have bureaucracy.

"Yes," Chloe says, nervy, and there's one of the protection rings on each of her fingers in what's almost certainly overkill. "See you in fifteen minutes at the bricks right there, I'm swooping by the evidence lockers then coming right out."

Delina nods, standing back as Chloe cinches her backpack down tight against her body and fixing the bribed badge over her chest.

"You'll do it in ten," Gurlien replies dismissively. "This is child's play for you, you've been doing things way more difficult since you were thirteen."

"I know that," Chloe shoots back. "I just..."

"Swore you'd never be here again?" Gurlien supplies, and Delina and Maison exchange a glance. "We know, and that's not gonna mean that this bit isn't going to be super easy."

Chloe nods, and Gurlien raises an eyebrow at her.

"This is easy and you're fine," Gurlien says again. "I'm gonna time you."

"Oh fuck off," Chloe says, then adjusts her backpack again and focuses.

The brickwork wavers, unmoving, but the grate covering the vent bends, then goes limp, like it's made out of noodles instead of metal, and Chloe breathes out, shaking the tension out of her hands.

"This is the easy part," she whispers to herself, then, with a boost from Gurlien, pushes aside the vent and climbs in.

The air wavers again, before the metal snaps back into place, and her footsteps fade from hearing.

Gurlien dusts his hands off, then spins to Maison. "If you don't thank her for this, I will punch you."

"Like that would hurt me," Maison says back, but he's nodding. "Obviously. Yes. We get out of this and I'll...I'll be in your debt for a while."

"Of course," Gurlien says, almost neutral. "We'll absolutely call you on that."

Delina raises an eyebrow at the two of them. "That have bigger magical connotations?"

"Not really," Maison reassures her, but he is tense, nervous. "Maybe to full demons, not to me."

"Not that I've encountered, at least," Gurlien says, and he too is bouncing on his toes. "Some spirits, yes. Wights, not really, but they have a big culture of not going back on their words so practically yes."

"So we really get a way out," Delina muses, before scuffing the toe of her boot on the grimy snow of the alleyway.

"Yep," Maison replies, grim, and they all fall silent.

Delina sidles up to Maison, pressing her shoulder against his. They're mostly sheltered from the wind, but it's still...nice.

"She can do this, it's not even a small problem," Gurlien babbles, breaking the tenuous quiet, and this must be his form of nerves. "The bunker we broke into two weeks ago was more difficult, this'll be nothing."

Delina doesn't really have anything to say back.

"Do they burn their dead?" Delina asks, and both Maison and Gurlien flinch. "I get...nothing from out here from in there. Not even a bug or a mouse."

"Dampening spells," Maison replies, and he presses his shoulder back against hers. "Protects the area, doesn't let any magic outside the walls."

"Also doesn't let any in," Gurlien says. "So if we tried to strike the building, we wouldn't be able to. The grate here," he gestures at it, "sticks out just enough that it's outside the spells."

Delina nods, staring at the pockmarked brick. "So I'll get hit by it inside."

"If there's dead, yes." There's a clunk in the wall, and they all freeze, but nothing happens. "That wasn't Chloe, that's the wrong spot," Gurlien says.

"What about a tank?" Delina asks. "Roll up a tank to the front door, would that do it?"

"Oh my god," Gurlien mutters. "You are just like your mom."

"That would explain all the extra guns," Maison deadpans.

Another thunk on the brick, and they all freeze.

"There will be thirty-seven guards on duty," Gurlien repeats in a low voice. "Most on the non-stasis floors. None active on this level. We're okay."

Maison shifts again, and Delina recognizes the motion now to know that he's putting himself in a position he can easily shield her if needed.

He slicked back his hair that morning, just enough to break the silhouette, and combined with the beard he looks just enough like another person that her heart jumps, just a bit.

Delina herself had left her hair down, wispy around her face, softening her features away from what both Gurlien and Chloe called the Frisse facial structure. Away from the appearance that everyone who saw her would immediately recognize her as her mother's daughter.

She doesn't like it too much.

Another scratch at the brick, like a rat trying to eat through the wall itself, and they all watch, still.

Delina touches the pill box with the dead bugs inside, her fingertips soft against the hard plastic.

The very air seems to still around them, the chill far away, before the bricks fall open, revealing a half-sized door, Chloe crouched in the middle.

Gurlien exhales, then checks his watch. "That was only seven minutes."

~

CHLOE LEADS them through a darkened hallway, the only light the glow from runes written into the very walls, illuminating as they walk past.

The cheap carpet deadens all their footsteps.

"There," Gurlien whispers, pointing to yet another security camera, and Chloe silently turns the glass in the lens to opaque plastic.

Delina keeps the pill box of death gripped in her fist.

"There's a demon trap up ahead," Maison whispers, and the sound doesn't carry his words. "After the bend."

Chloe nods, then gestures Delina up.

Because Delina has to do some of the work here, conserving Chloe for the traps that she has no ability to take down.

They turn the bend, and there's...nothing. No paint on the floor, no paint on the ceiling, nothing.

"Under the carpet," Maison murmurs, and she's never taken down something she can't see. "Here."

He taps her hand, and the world bursts into gold.

Gold everywhere. Gold along all the walls, gold in the footsteps on the floor, gold outlining the ancient computers in the cubicles.

And gold, ever so faint, shining in a circle painted under the carpet.

"And another dampening," Chloe whispers, "they must deal with demons up until this point, but no further."

"Interesting," Gurlien responds.

One of the lines of the circle is fainter than the rest, like it's been shifted over and over again, like a gate.

Delina rests her hand against it, and Maison breathes out, before giving her a quick glimpse of his dimple. "This isn't going to be pretty," she warns, before yanking on the line, until the strip of magic shatters.

And, immediately, the entire building slams into focus.

Death, death, and more death floods into her.

Something dead, two floors down, ended by a knife to the heart.

A twisted mound of flesh, so warped that the nerves wrapped itself around the lungs and squeezed until no more air could reach the brain.

A human, completely normal, all but just a skeleton.

A...a demon, foul and bitter against her tongue, dead from a surge of power.

A person, draped over a clinical cot, rotting from the inside, long dead but the skin around them perfectly preserved. They aren't wholly human, not entirely, but her mind skips away from it as soon as it can.

Another person, the body perfectly still, the lungs stopped by a chemical she can't quite taste, long ago...and with a jolt she realizes that she gets the same sensation from him as she does Maison.

A Half Demon. Just like him.

All this information, all this knowledge, and she gets it before her butt even hits the floor, the air knocked out of her.

"Woah, you're okay?" Maison's asking, he's rubbing her back as she blinks through unbidden tears. "What happened, you're okay?"

"We need to keep moving," Chloe says, her voice muted.

Delina swallows down the horror, past the lump in her throat, then clings to Maison's arm, pulling herself up.

"All the...uh...dead in the building, I just got...yeah, just got to where I could sense them," Delina says, rubbing her eyes, trying to see past the stars swimming in her vision. "That broke the dampening."

The other three exchange glances.

"There's a lot," Delina says, getting her feet underneath herself. "They're...some of these died in horrific ways."

Maison huffs out a breath, the lines around his eyes tightening. "I'm not surprised."

"I'm only surprised that they'd keep bodies around," Gurlien says, grim.

"These ones felt..." Delina trails off, unsure of how to describe the careful, deliberate nature of the deaths. "More like experiments."

"Oh my god," Chloe mumbles, then shakes out her hands. "We need to keep moving."

Delina nods, pulling whatever composure she can to her. "I don't think I can raise them all."

Her voice is smaller than she'd like.

"Yeah, definitely don't," Gurlien says, and he ventures forward, a ghost of a frown across his face. "Conserve your energy until we need it."

THEY CREEP through rows upon rows of cubicles, all lit by just the glow of runes as they pass by, and each time the badges they wear briefly warm.

And each step, Delina's able to feel more deaths.

They have to stop, frequently, to undo traps and securities both small and large. A notification spell someone sketched near their desk, so they know if someone's walking up behind them. A trap meant to stop someone unwanted in their tracks, close to the printer. A glowing rune on the bathroom door, keeping track of how many times it's opened and closed, how many rolls of toilet paper inside.

A trap that Chloe says would snap drain the blood of anyone unexpected who steps unknowingly inside of it. It was coded to recognize everyone who should be there, so only intruders would get ensnared.

"We're not pretending this is normal, are we?" Delina mumbles, as Chloe painstakingly clears the way on that one. "Instant death seems a bit rough for an intruder."

"Only if you didn't grow up in it," Maison replies, his eyes glowing red as he watches Chloe. "Everyone here probably did, probably thought it was standard."

"And there," Gurlien points, "is the head of Toronto's office. Anyone doing espionage, anyone trying to steal his secrets, would go through it."

Delina swallows, glancing at the unassuming door. It's just a normal office door with frosted glass and a standard nameplate.

The glowing trap unravels with a snap, and Chloe exhales, standing up and brushing off her hands. There's a spike of pain there, in her fingertips, but Chloe doesn't react to it so Delina's not going to point it out.

"That one was nastier than I thought," Chloe says, and her voice is strained. "Next non-demon one, Maison you need to get."

It's as close to a cry for help as she's ever given.

"Did they use the thorn unravel?" Gurlien asks, and Chloe nods. "You can thank your mom for that, Delina. She designed the traps to hurt when taken down."

"Of course she did," Delina says, and Chloe confidently steps over the barren threads of the trap, so they follow.

They pass another hallway, before both Maison and

Chloe still, sudden enough that Delina almost runs into Chloe's back.

"We tripped something," Maison says, barely moving, like he's afraid extra motion will set something off. "A while back, something just went off."

Chloe breathes out hard from her nose, her eyes narrowing. "I can't tell what it is."

"Me neither," Maison replies, before he reaches a hand out and curves his fingers over Delina's elbow, almost a reassurance.

"We shouldn't stay here," Gurlien says, eyes narrowed. "If it's back there, if it's delayed, we shouldn't be here when it comes to us."

Still, Maison and Chloe don't move, and Maison's hand over her elbow tightens.

Delina watches him, as his eyes move, rapid, across the entire hallway, before all the runes dim, the light fading away.

A chill steals over Delina and she shivers.

"Guys?" Gurlien asks, and there's a hint of fear in his voice, lilting upwards. "What do you see?"

There's nothing, just the light dimming until all she can see is the vague silhouettes of the group around her.

"Don't move," Maison orders, and all she can see is the faintest outline of his jaw. "Just don't move."

Delina forces herself to remain still, to not move, though her heart pounds so loud it must be audible, echoing through her ears.

And nothing happens.

Nothing happens, but for the faintest whoosh of air, tickling over her skin, ruffling her clothes, clattering their badges.

Maison hisses out a breath, his fingers tightening imperceptibly, like he's typing something out against her skin by touch, before the world abruptly brightens, all runes glowing, and he flinches.

"Okay, let's move," he says, dropping Delina's elbow and immediately striding again.

Delina almost has to jog to keep up.

"What was that?" Gurlien demands, though his eyes are wide as well. "What type, what—"

"I don't know, Gurlien," Chloe says, clutching the straps on her backpack tightly. "I don't know, and I don't know if we hid ourselves, or—"

"We hid," Maison replies. "We hid but they know something's up."

"Shit," Delina breathes, and Maison rips up another trap in front of them, barely pausing in his stride. "What do we—"

They turn another corner...to an abrupt dead end, drawing them up.

And Chloe stares at it, her eyes dark, before she lifts her chin.

"You all ready to go into the locking pits?"

43

Before Delina can think, Maison's shifted himself in front of her, and Chloe's hands glow.

Literally glow, not with strips of magic, but like the very air itself is brought to light.

"Delina," Chloe says, her voice remote, "there's going to be dead in here."

There's been dead revealing itself to her in every step, but Delina nods and lets her mind concentrate.

There's the echo of pain, of sudden ends, and a few disjointed bones laying deep beneath the floor.

"No actual bodies, they've cleaned them up," Delina says, and Chloe nods absently, before the air wavers over her hands and the wall in front of them opens.

Splits in two, the stucco and brick peeling away like it's burnt paper.

Revealing a deep chasm, one that can't exist in the building. It's too big, too deep, too spacious.

It's too much.

There's blood slicked along the walls, dried and blackened. A vague hint of machinery whirs, somewhere in the deep, like a maw chewing through something.

Chloe gestures them in, before she seals the wall back up, leaving it without a crease.

"Congrats," Chloe says, and she's not whispering now, her voice echoing down into the depths. "This is the biggest hurdle out of this place."

Even Gurlien looks peaked.

"If we get the wight out, we don't have to do the hard part of this," Chloe says, and her eyes are sharp, surveying the machinery.

"How do the guards get around this?" Delina asks, and her own voice hangs in the air.

"They take shifts," Maison says, and he's tracing his fingertips along the short platform, as if searching for something by touch. "They generally work a week, then have two weeks off, so they only have to cross it then."

"And they know the spells, they know the changes of the runes, and they know who to call when it backfires," Chloe says, then cracks her knuckles.

For once, instead of the remote fear that's been across her for the entire time, an almost content expression filters over her face.

"Maison, you mask any leakage, cover for any traps at our back," she orders. "Delina, you keep your hand on the bugs in case something comes at us, and sense anyone who might be near us. Keep yourself aware." Chloe throws a look to Gurlien, who nods back at her. "Gurlien, stop me from falling over."

There's a breath, where everyone absorbs that information, before Maison turns back towards the door.

A strip of magic twists into his hands and, between one roll of his fingers and the next, he shreds it, and a warping golden wall forms behind them, not unlike the demon bubble.

He keeps his hands against it, his back to the cavernous maw, like his hands hold it up and away from them all.

Delina pops open the bug pill container, and with barely a thought, compels the tiny golden string into the palm of her hand.

After so long in the airless coffin, it's almost joyous against her skin.

Maison inhales, then throws her a grim grin. "Still weird when you do that."

Chloe watches Maison's shield for a split second then slings off her backpack, unzipping it and grabbing a handful of...gravel?

Playing with it in her hands, Chloe crouches at the edge of the platform, peering over. As if ready for it, Gurlien crouches next to her, grabbing her by her shirt collar, bracing himself.

"So the guards get over this by targeted runes and precisely placed keys on four separate points," Gurlien recites, as if it's not something that they all have memorized by that point. "All she's going to do is mimic the keys, and we should get across this."

"Can't do that coming back," Chloe replies, almost mechanically, "not without someone waiting on the other side. So we have to hit the stasis floor."

"Yep," Gurlien says, and it's so practiced that Delina would've believed that they've had the information for far longer than they should've. "Ready on a go."

Delina nods, crouching as well, and Maison braces himself with the golden shield.

"And...go."

Chloe's hands light up again, the gravel floating around them an inch away, and the entire platform lurches.

Biting back a gasp, Delina sits her butt on the floor, and the platform slides along the wall as if on an invisible track in a theme park.

Unable to stop herself, she glances off the edge.

The floor of the cavern, much closer than it looks, whirs into activity. Machinery, grotesque and monstrous, churns on the ground, knives glinting in the light of the runes. Blades, cogs, and teeth all gnash together, in one long continuous machine.

"You broke into the wall here?" Delina breathes, and Chloe doesn't pause to nod.

"There," Gurlien points, keeping one hand wrapped up in Chloe's collar.

Chloe inhales, sharp, then squints, letting one of the pieces of gravel spin off to the floor.

It changes midair, twisting and engorging, before it sockets into place with a clunk.

The platform hitches, then continues to slide along, and for a split second Delina sees the tracks along the wall, before they fade as well.

Maison's back twitches, and he lifts his hands up higher, as if counteracting something that only he can see.

"There," Gurlien whispers, barely audible over the din of machinery.

Another pebble, growing into a metal rod, sliding into place on a lock. It turns, smoothly, and the platform drops a few feet before the track illuminates once more and they slide on.

Delina cranes her neck to look back at the lock. The metal rod fits perfectly, but by the time the next piece of gravel gets socketed in, it disintegrates, the machine crunching to life once more.

So. The locking pits re-lock themselves.

"The thing about the walls," Chloe says, her voice remote, "is that there's scaffolding in them to balance on. Much easier."

She's sweating, in the odd glow from her hands, coming from the pieces of gravel, and her head is starting to pound, so strongly Delina can almost taste the bitterness.

There's a skeleton, somewhere close by, though Delina can't see it, and it might also be in the walls. It's old, aged almost beyond recognition, dry and almost dust.

The lights dim around them, and Maison grunts, lifting the shield higher, and Delina catches a spare glimpse of magic swirling beyond it. Magic, dark and bulbous, striking the shield, as if testing it.

Another piece of gravel, another lock, another chunk of machinery cluttering to a stop and another piece of track illuminated. There's a splash of blood on the lock, the splinters of a bone, as if they didn't fully clean it.

As if they didn't want to take the risk.

Chloe leans forward, almost craning her neck over for the next piece of lock, and Gurlien grabs her tighter. His wrist aches, sharp, at the strain, before she adjusts herself so she's lying flat against the platform.

There's a hint, just something, within the moment, and the only warning Delina gets is the sudden inhale from Maison, before his shield shatters.

Shatters into a million golden pieces, flying around them like shards.

Chloe cries out and the platform drops a few feet, and Delina has no time to think.

No time to think, no time to plan, no time to breathe.

Before the nebulous dark magic swirls towards them, surging, and—

Maison staggers back, falling on the platform, still keeping a hand up on the broken shield. There's a sharp bite of pain in his back, in his knee, sudden.

He's hurt.

The magic forms, hunching over Maison, like it's some sort of creature. Like it's something sentient, like it's something that could hunger, raising itself to strike.

Delina grabs the magic in her fist, spreading it like the paper she was taught, flowing it between her hands.

It glows, bright in the dim light, and the dark magical... thing...turns towards her.

It has no eyes, it has no discernible face, and yet Delina can feel its gaze on her.

"Yeah," she breathes, and her heart pounds. "Look at me, not him."

Maison scrambles back, as much as the platform will allow, and his knee is twisted. Not critically, not irreparable, but hurt all the same.

The creature shifts, as if assessing her, and Delina hitches her breath.

And lets the magic snap out of her hands.

There's a split second where the light reflects shiny over the thing's form, before it splatters out of existence, a high-pitched shriek echoing through the chamber, drowning out the crash of machinery.

Delina's ears ring and her hands smart, before the platform slowly continues on the track, clicking another lock into place.

Maison surges himself up to standing, grabbing Delina and pulling her back down with a quick, practiced motion. His knee buckles, but there's no trace of it in his face.

"What was that?" Delina breathes, as Chloe clicks another lock into place and the track illuminates once more.

Maison shakes his head, like he doesn't fully know. "Some ghoul, something twisted, I don't know."

"You're hurt," she says, turning away from the cavern and to him. "You're hurt, I can tell—"

"I've done a lot harder with a lot worse," he replies grimly, but he clutches her, an arm around her middle, like he could keep her safe with just that.

"Well, that's not coming back," Gurlien says, still keeping a grip on Chloe, but the far wall grows nearer, impossibly so. "Good instinct."

Delina nods, and her breath comes out in huffs, like she just ran a few miles.

"Almost there," Chloe mumbles, and her head blooms with pain with each stone fall. "Almost there, then we can relax."

"We can absolutely not relax," Gurlien corrects. "We can do something marginally less difficult."

Maison adjusts himself so her back is tucked against his chest, and his hands tremble, the fingertips aching. Like the entire weight of the shield had been just on the pads of his fingers.

Delina squeezes her eyes shut, as the platform shudders and drops again, before it clicks into place, socketing against the far wall.

Chloe finally crawls fully back onto the platform, shaking like a leaf, before peeling the wall open to another corridor with white light and polished walls.

"Get in," she croaks, her voice hoarse, and Delina hauls Maison up to standing, stumbling into the hallway.

His knee twists, painful, before the weight on it crumples him, staggering against Delina.

"I got you," Delina murmurs at his hiss of pain, and Chloe and Gurlien follow them behind, before Chloe waves her hand and seals it off.

Closing off the giant maw, all sounds of machinery cutting off, leaving them just in the stillness and bright lights.

44

Almost as soon as the door closes, Chloe lets her legs go out from underneath her and sits down, hard, on the shining white tile.

"Yup, understandable," Gurlien says, grabbing her backpack from her and pulling out one of the 5 Hour Energy shots and a protein bar. "Eat this."

Carefully, Delina nods at Maison, then helps him sit next to her, his knee throbbing.

"It's not broken," Maison says, before she can even say anything. "I'll be okay."

"You'll be slow," Gurlien replies, but he gives Maison one of the protein bars as well, before he eyes Delina. "Do you need something?"

"Give me some of the chocolate," Delina says, then locks eyes with Maison. "I'm gonna touch your knee."

"Is it safe to stop here?" Maison asks, but his voice is raw. "Should we move?"

"Chloe needs to eat first," Gurlien interrupts him, strict. "I don't think you realize how incredible that was."

"Thanks," Chloe mumbles around a mouthful of food.

"No, I think I get it," Maison says, and his face is a bit pale.

Delina takes the distraction to put both her hands on each side of his knee, and he cuts his words off short.

And she lets herself think.

The kneecap isn't quite in place, slipped out of its socket, spearing the nerves on either side of it. It's not broken, there are no tears in the cartilage, just...it's out of place.

"It's dislocated, you need a hospital and a splint," Delina says, and looks to Chloe, who's palely chomping on her food. "Is there anything in the backpack?"

"Ace bandage," Gurlien replies for her, already pulling it out, but his face is grim. "Can you walk?"

"Yes," Maison interrupts, grimacing. "I can walk, I'll be fine."

"I can put it back," Delina says, and he pales further. "I'll put it back and we'll wrap it. This is gonna suck, when will the next rotation of guards be in earshot?"

Gurlien looks up and around, at the blank white walls and hallway that stretches onwards, down and away from them. "It's the stasis ward, they don't need guards, just the occasional patrol."

"Maison," Delina starts, and his eyes snap up to her. "Can I do this?"

It turns her stomach, too, but he nods.

Without waiting, she lets her mind sink into the sensations of his leg, then jerks the kneecap over with her hands.

He chokes, halfway between a yell and a grunt that echoes along the stark white walls, and pain slams into her, sharp before abrupt relief. He sags against the wall, briefly, before blinking, tears in his eyes.

"Oh my god," Gurlien mutters, then Delina quickly tries to wrap the knee, to provide some sort of stabilization. The entire joint feels wobbly, uncertain of itself, but the pressure is another bit of relief.

"I'm so sorry," Delina whispers to Maison, whose head is swimming.

"No, it'll be good," he says, weakly, like he's not even paying too much attention to the words falling out of his mouth. He slumps forward, his head hitting her chest.

"I got you," Delina says, and takes a brief moment to stroke his hair back, before she lets herself look around the hallway.

It's featureless, the fluorescent lights bouncing off the polished tile and walls, stretching on for far too long.

There's a box mounted to the wall, a few meters away from them, and another one at the far edge. No doors to go in and out, no windows, nothing.

And they're going to have to walk down it, with Maison still blinking back tears of pain and Chloe staring numbly in front of her face, mechanically chomping on her food.

She exchanges a quick glance with Gurlien, and his face is grim.

"This isn't good," he says, which echoes what she's feeling, but saying it feels wrong. "Any dead on this floor?"

Strangely, the answer is no, but she squeezes her eyes shut, tries to feel something. Anything.

But there's no other beings but them.

"Absolutely nothing, except for the other bug in my pocket," Delina says, before she lets her hands rest on Maison's knee, stretching his leg out.

He grunts, his jaw clenching, before he raises his chin. "I'll be okay."

"Yeah," Delina says, before handing him another protein bar. "Still eat this."

Gurlien pushes himself up to standing, carefully approaching the box on the wall.

It's roughly the size of a fire extinguisher box, the same featureless bright white of the rest of the hallway.

"It's the first of the control runes," Gurlien says, opening it and peering inside. "Written in India ink."

Maison nods at her. "Can you help me up?"

"Is that wise?" Delina asks, but he braces himself on the wall, then, just like they would do if one of them was sick, helps him to stand, before she tucks her shoulder under his arm, letting him lean his weight on her.

He steps, experimentally, on the bad knee and it wobbles. The bandage helps, the pressure something, but it needs more, much more.

"When we get out, I am finding a safe hospital for you and taking you to it," Delina declares, and he nods, his face pinched. "And then you are gonna stay the fuck off of your leg until I can't tell you're in pain anymore."

Still, she walks him, limping, over to the box.

Sure enough, looping runes, beautiful in indigo brush strokes, incomprehensible.

"Don't ruin these," Maison instructs, leaning heavily against her, and a small, remote part of her, is alarmed at how much. "These aren't to take down, we need both sets intact to deactivate them."

"That's what I thought," Gurlien says, scowling at them. "We need someone to flick this switch, then go to that one," he throws a nod down the hallway, "and flick the same switch."

Delina peers at the beautiful markings. "Then we can destroy it?"

"Should be," Maison says, his voice tight. "Then let's hope the Wight knows what she's talking about."

Gurlien throws a look to Chloe, whose eyes are at least a

bit more aware now, and she swallows down the protein bar.

"I can move," she says, and her voice is raw, like she spent the last hour screaming. "Alarms have got to be ringing, we can't stay here forever."

She takes a deep breath, then hugs her backpack to her chest, standing up, and is far less shaky than Maison is. "I'm okay."

"It'd be more believable if I wasn't aware of your headache," Delina says, and Chloe sighs, pulling out another energy shot.

"I'll be okay, I'll just be hungover once we get out of this," Chloe grumbles, and that, at least, seems reasonably likely. "Let me take a look."

Maison leans his cheek against the top of Delina's head, as Gurlien and Chloe debate the inner workings of the runes, and tremors run up his side.

"If you have to run, it's okay," he whispers to her, "take my mom and run, I'll be okay."

"Oh fuck off," Delina whispers back. "Stop with the self-sacrificial bullshit, we both know I won't do that."

He sighs against her, and she tightens her grip around his middle.

"We'll find something for a splint, and then we'll get out," Delina whispers back.

"I can do this side," Chloe says, with a pale glance to them. "Delina, you'll have to do the matching switch when we get over there."

"Okay," Delina replies, and, despite the exhaustion still on her mind, Chloe deftly draws something in the box, and the entire hallway groans to life.

Maison twitches, like he wants to pull Delina behind him.

Instead, shutters, giant ones, clatter and roll up, on

either side of the hallway, revealing tall windows.

Each into a small, individual room. Hundreds of them, all barely bigger than a closet, stretching down the entire length of the hallway.

Delina's breath hitches.

"Have you ever been down here before?" Chloe asks, voice hushed.

"Not this one, but a different one," Maison whispers, and Gurlien nods as well. "It's only a good threat if you know what you'd be facing."

And with that, they start down the hallway.

In the first room, someone sits in the corner, eyes listless, staring out into nothing. There's blood on the side of their head, fresh, but their clothing is about two decades out of date.

The display plate reads a name, then 'murder.'

They don't react as Delina passes, as if they can't even see out of their little room.

The next room, a young woman stretched out on a cot. Her eyes stare up at the ceiling, and her display plate reads 'insane.'

Another, and a sickly young man, skin clinging to bones, curled up on the floor, with the display plate 'failed Half Demon.'

Next, a twisted mass of flesh, not even identifiable as human, though breath flutters against the skin. Display plate reads 'experiment, won't die.'

Delina swallows, then looks back down the hallway.

There are too many rooms.

"How can a place like this exist?" Delina asks, and her voice echoes hollow through the shining hallway.

"Oh, this isn't even the only one," Gurlien replies, mouth

grim. "There's one in Paris, one in Atlanta, and one in Mexico City."

"And South Korea," Maison says, and his knee sends a pang of pain up at him with each step, despite Delina's support. "The Paris one is the worst."

"Which room is the Wight?" Chloe asks, and somehow she's still eating, though her face twists. "I want to make sure we're releasing someone correctly."

"Eight oh nine," Delina answers, and her own words are remote against her ears.

Another room, and there's someone splayed on the ground, a bloody hole punched through his sternum, but he still breathes.

She stills.

"That one will die if we drop the spell," Delina whispers, certain horror crawling along her spine. "Can he feel that?"

"Can't ignore it," Maison replies. "Can't heal, can't sleep, just sitting with the sensations of when you were locked up." With his free hand, the one not clutching around Delina, he taps the sign.

Which reads Nicholas, Mass Murder.

"So this would be his punishment," Gurlien says. "He can't die, he can't recover, knowing that the moment the spells would drop he'd perish."

Words evaporate from Delina's mind, at the ghastliness of all of it.

They pass another half-demon, body emaciated, curled up on the bed, and she's marked for death, too. The skin is too thin, the arteries too nebulous, the nerves too sharp. She might take a dozen breaths, each one more painful than the next, before her brain would give up, starved.

If Delina clings a bit stronger to Maison, she can't tell.

Another person, bleeding from the eyes and ears, black

and red blood mixing, barely breathing, and the nameplate reads 'Sauv, Terese Project.'

The moment she takes the runes down, he'll die as well.

Goosebumps rise on her arms, despite the relative warmth of the hallway.

"Here," Chloe says, jogging forward a few steps, "eight hundred and nine...oh."

Inside the room, the wight's half transparent, like she had been caught halfway through disappearing, her long curly hair unruly. She's sitting on the floor, staring numbly out the window, her eyes not tracking them.

She's also maybe twelve.

Maybe.

"Oh my god," Delina whispers, covering her mouth.

The wiry hair and coloring echo the Wight from the cabin, almost a younger mirror image.

All four of them stare down at her, and she doesn't react. The display plate reads 'Stella, Ransom Insurance.'

"If she's been here for six years, she hasn't aged in that time," Gurlien says, hushed.

"That's a crime," Delina hears herself say. "It's a crime, she's just a child...you grew up like this?" she asks Maison.

He shakes his head, and there are still lines of pain around his eyes. "Not in here, it was just a threat."

"He was too powerful, too useful," Gurlien replies, constantly looking over his shoulder. "And...alive enough for it."

If that statement wasn't enough to light the fire inside Delina to burn this entire place down, the pre-teen wight comatose in front of them, all gangly elbows, would be.

"Let's do this," Delina says, moving Maison towards the box, and—

The very next room is the demon with the half-shaved head. The one from the bar.

And she's not prone like the rest of the hallway.

Locking eyes with Delina, she paces, right at the glass separating them.

The blackened wound on her cheek, from Delina's strike, still flakes, as if no time at all had passed. Her gut wound still glistens with black blood, and her claw marks from her own fingernails on her neck still bleed.

There's still the leash around her neck.

On the shaved side of her head, three electro patches stick to the skin, wires draping down her back. Medical leads, like ones Delina's seen on EKG machines, all directly into her brain.

"Oh fuck," Chloe says, the moment she sees the demon, and the demon deliberately flickers her eyes over to Chloe, appraising, not stopping in her pace.

Maison straightens, then winces, his knee wobbling, and the demon's gaze immediately snaps to him.

She bares her teeth at Maison, halfway between a smile and aggression, before she mouths something.

Of course, no sound reaches through the glass, and she scowls in frustration at that.

"So this is where they keep her," Gurlien says, stepping close to the glass, and she jerks to look at him instead, an evaluating expression over her face. "Not my first choice, but I guess it's safe."

The Demon paces back over to Delina and Maison, and mouths something again, then tugs a finger underneath the leash.

The nameplate reads 'Ambra, Terese Project.'

"Fuck," Maison says, staring at the words on the name-plate. "They succeeded."

45

They all stare at the nameplate, and the demon—Ambra—paces, her steps short and agitated, before she waves at them for attention.

This time, her gaze locks onto Delina, and slowly, deliberately, mouths, "Free me."

"What are the chances she's going to kill me the moment I bring down the runes?" Delina asks, craning her neck up to Maison.

"She's not going to get to touch you," he growls, staring the demon down, who is currently actively ignoring him to mouth the words to Delina again.

"Can she hear us?" Chloe asks, small. There's more color in her cheeks now, like the walk down the hallway settled more of herself.

The demon—Ambra—nods.

Gurlien straightens, and the demon's eyes snap over to him, mouthing, "Free me," again.

"We are bringing the runes down," Gurlien says, clinical, as if he's remarking on the weather. "You'll be able to go where you want and escape."

The demon shakes her head, then tugs at the leash around her neck again to demonstrate. So she wouldn't, she would still be under whatever control they had of her.

"We have to free the child in the room right next to yours," Gurlien continues, the faux bored tone belaying a tremor underneath it. "Don't hurt one of us, and we will do what we can to free you."

Ambra looks over to Maison, as if gauging his reaction, narrowing her eyes.

"You touch her, you die," Maison says, and the demon nods, something close to relief on her face, like for once she's understanding the context.

"Shit," Chloe breathes, as Ambra resumes her pacing in the tiny space. "Shit, this is going to be bad."

Ambra nods again, at that.

"The moment we bring down the runes, at least eight people are going to die," Delina says, and the demon nods along, as if she knew all of this. "I will use one of the deaths to defend myself."

Ambra mouths, "Good."

"Is there any way to bring down just some of the runes?" Maison asks, and the demon bares her teeth at him.

"Not without the keys," Gurlien responds, and Ambra immediately stops with the outward aggression. "All of them or none."

There are two more cells between them and the rune box. One of them will die instantly, the other is another catatonic person with bones jutting from his face and the nameplate that just reads 'coward.'

And Ambra watches them from behind the glass, until the angle of her cell no longer lets her.

Maison is stiff, his jaw tight, his shoulders aching, and

Delina's known him long enough to know he's doing some mental calculations, some sort of decision making.

"We have to," Delina says.

"I know," Maison mutters, and he leans against the wall next to the box. "I'm trying to gauge how much I'll be able to fight her."

"Hopefully none," Gurlien says, popping open the paneling to the rune box. "Still have a dead bug you can take? Get it ready, so you don't have to panic in the moment to reach one."

Delina does, and pulls out the thin golden string, even though the pull in her gut tells her that the people will be infinitely more powerful, infinitely more useful.

She lets the string slink between her hands, weighing it.

"I think I speak for us all that when we do this, everything's going to be very, very chaotic," Chloe says, slinging her backpack down and handing Maison another chocolate bar. "I'll prep the wall for the staircase."

"Half these people will take hours to fully wake," Gurlien argues, which is a little better. "We make sure the wight is gone, we keep going."

"And there are two failed Terese Projects and one actual, we have no idea how this will go," Maison says grimly.

"Can you make a splint?" Delina asks, at the continued weakness in Maison's knee.

"She should save her power," Gurlien responds, and Maison nods. "We're going to need it for at least two more traps and there's no good material."

"Delina, here," Chloe instructs, gesturing her over to the box. "You disrupt this," Chloe gestures, precise, "and break this, then it'll fall."

Maison straightens, and his knee pangs him, but his face

settles into something detached, before twin strips of magic appear in his hands.

Gurlien tugs Chloe's backpack off of her, his face grim, and pulls out the gun.

The gun from back in the cabin, the one stored in the living room table drawer, the one he pointed at her the very first night.

"That won't do anything against the demon," Maison warns, as Gurlien checks the chamber and magazine.

"Obviously," Gurlien snips back. "I'm worried about what else is coming down the hallway."

Chloe's face is tight, but there's something approaching determination across her features.

"Want me to tie this around you?" Delina asks Maison, and he hesitates.

"Save it for two floors down," Gurlien replies, grim. "We'll need more power there."

"Power down there won't mean anything if we're dead up here," Delina shoots back.

"This is going to ruin them, I think," Chloe says, thoughtful, and they all glance back at her. "All these people, once they wake up, the ones that survive...they're not going to be able to recover from this."

"Good," Delina says, and the two of them share a brief, insane smile. "We ready?"

"Not terribly," Maison grumbles, still leaning against the wall, but he nods anyway.

"If the wight doesn't have a way out, we're gonna be screwed," Chloe warns, but she's already tracing the motions across the runes, fingertips swiping in the dust, where Delina can follow. "Just so everyone knows, this'll be loud."

And so Delina steps up to the box, and with the horror still in her heart, breaks the runes.

The moment her fingertips lift from the last one, death punches into her.

The mass murderer, almost immediately, slamming against her chest and leaving her gasping.

The woman bleeding from her eyes, a spare second later, as unforgiving as a wave in the sea, sending sparks behind her eyes.

And another, and another, until she's choking on it, coughing around it in her throat, clinging onto the rune box, as if it can support her body weight. Her fingertips dig into the metal, nails scratching and breaking, before a scream echoes down the hallway.

A scream and glass shards erupt outwards from the demon's cell, before she crashes through it, shoulder first, panting.

Maison shifts, so he's between Delina and her, though his knee sends a knife of pain up his entire leg.

Ambra stares at them, her chest heaving and eyes glowing, before her face splits into a wide grin and she rips the leads off her head, stomping on them.

"Stop panicking, half-demon," she spits out, and her voice is raw. "And get me out of here."

Fear so strong it's almost pain, Gurlien brushes by her, to the pre-teen wight's room.

"She's still here," Gurlien says, and the demon watches him like a beetle. "Guys, she didn't get out—"

Ambra closes her hand and jerks, and the glass shatters to the Wights cell, showering Gurlien with shards, and he flinches back, but none of them strike him.

It'd be a miracle if Delina didn't catch a split-second shield around him, fast and fluent.

Maison inhales at the casual display of power.

With nary a glance behind her, Ambra pushes past Gurlien, stepping among the glass and emerging with the pre-teen.

Stella's blinking, dazed, but upright. Her head's spinning so hard Delina can taste the dizziness, and her stomach roils.

"Here," Ambra says, then shoves her at Gurlien, who scrambles against the sudden weight to catch her. "Now let's go."

The wight blinks up at Gurlien, then over to the group, to Maison and Delina and Chloe, then opens her mouth and screams.

Screams, screeching, high pitched, before she vanishes, as sudden as anything else.

And all of the sudden, the lights slam off, and an alarm blares through the hallway, before getting flooded with red lights, strobing.

The demon recoils back, clapping her hands over her ears.

"Shit," Maison mumbles, but Chloe's already at the wall, sketching her runes, her hands glowing. "We're going loud."

"Yes, this is the definition of loud, thank you, Maison," Gurlien says. "Okay, she's out, we have an hour to go get your mom." He clicks on his stopwatch, pale.

Another scream ricochets down the hallway, piercing, and Delina grabs the death from the room nearest to her, pulling it to her, and it surges with power in her hands.

Like nothing she's ever felt before.

Ambra flinches back, her eyes wide, at that, before gaping in horror at Maison. Like he's to blame for letting Delina grasp the death, somehow.

"And...here." Remote, Chloe splits open the brick, revealing a staircase down, the red lights strobing.

"That's the wrong way," Ambra says, surging up to Chloe between one blink and the next. "We're underground, you need to go up, that's just to more traps."

"And we're here to rescue my mother," Maison says, staring at the staircase with trepidation. "We'll have a way out in an hour, first we get her."

"You're insane," the demon says, flat. "No human is worth the traps in here."

Maison squares his shoulders down at her, despite the pain in his knee, and Ambra has the temerity to roll her eyes, before they fall on Delina.

For a split second, hunger echoes through her, so sharp it's pain Delina can feel, before she shakes her head, and starts down the staircase.

"Jesus Christ," Chloe mumbles, and Delina tucks her shoulder underneath Maison's arm.

"You ready?" Delina asks, and he nods, and they follow the demon down, Chloe in front of them, Delina and Maison in the middle, and Gurlien in the back, still clutching the gun.

46

The staircase wouldn't be out of place in a public school, with a fire hydrant and medical bag at the landing of the next floor, and Delina rips into it, despite Ambra glowering with impatience.

Inside are several shots of morphine, ready to go, more ace bandages, blood clotting powder, and gauze.

No splints.

"What do you need?" Ambra all but spits out, skirting close to Delina before jerking herself back after Maison straightens. "You're looking for something, what do you need?"

"Something for his knee," Delina responds, though her heart hammers, remembering the threat. Remembering the gold flashes from before, remembering her feet going numb. "We need to go faster."

"Just heal it," Ambra tells Maison, who stares down at her. "That's easy, just heal it."

"I can't," Maison replies, and he's sweating, despite the stoic exterior, and Delina swears she's going to get him out of here and to a hospital. "Half Demon, remember?"

Ambra gapes at him, then closes her fist around the metal handrail, tearing off a chunk like it has no more structural integrity than a pretzel, and tosses it to Chloe.

"Make a splint from this, it'll be faster than him hobbling," she says, scowling down at Chloe. "Shrink it and mold it, it's easy, less effort than with other materials."

"Can you—" Gurlien asks Chloe, but the metal's already warping down, already taking shape of an immobilizing brace, almost immediately.

Ambra paces on the landing, short, agitated steps, her eyes reflecting back the strobing light, until Chloe hands Maison a brace, something they can actually use.

"Here," Delina says, helping Maison down to sit, so he can stretch the leg out in front of him. She loops the string of death over her shoulder, and it tightens, imperceptibly, as if it's holding on as well.

The kneecap gives a pang of pain at that, sharp, and he hisses.

"I know," Delina grumbles at the echo of sensation from him. "This fucking sucks and you're not allowed to get hurt anymore."

She unwinds the ace bandage, as quick as she can, though her hands tremble, then fits the brace over his knee.

And there's another wave of relief from the pain from Maison, at just that, before another death punches through from the level they just left.

Another death, and it's not someone who was in the cells.

"We got to go," Delina says, and Maison pulls himself up with the broken handrail, "that wasn't someone who was there before."

Chloe and Ambra start clambering down the stairs, and

Delina helps Maison swing his leg down the next few steps. It's clumsy, it's slow, but there's less pain echoing from him.

The wall splits open again, and Gurlien fires off two shots, echoing down the staircase, and a death punches through Delina once more.

Gurlien scrambles after them, his eyes wide, like he's choking down vomit.

Delina's not sure he's ever killed someone before.

Chloe stops at the landing, three floors down, and starts to sketch out the runes, before Ambra clenches her fist and the entire wall shatters, brick flying outward, filling the air with dust.

Delina cranes her neck upwards, up the staircase, and more boots thump against the metal stairs.

Unwinding the death from her shoulders, it thrums in her hand, angry hot, as they scramble into the new hallway before Ambra jerks the bricks back into place, melting and warping until they're hotter than slag, glowing with heat.

"Oh wow," Chloe mumbles, at the raw display of power, and Ambra smiles at her, satisfied.

The hallway is more of the cheap carpet, the lights dim and strobing red, but the alarm is more distant. Further away.

And almost immediately there's less pain from Ambra, so much so that Delina hadn't even noticed how much it consumed her entire being, until a little bit of it was gone.

"Now what?" Ambra says, pacing in front of them, her movements jerky. "We're here, now what?"

"This floor, next wing, protected prison," Gurlien recites. "Three demon traps, two displacement wards, and some flamethrowers."

"And then we get out?" Ambra presses. "Then can we try to leave?"

Gurlien checks his stopwatch. "We have forty-two minutes."

Delina twists the magic in her hands, and immediately has both Maison and Ambra's undivided attention. "Can I use this to break the demon traps?"

"Oh yes," Maison replies grimly.

"And you're okay with her having that?" Ambra bursts out, as if that's the pressing issue. "She could end all of us with that, and she's just casually carrying it around."

Maison faces her, squaring his shoulders again, and it's easier for him to do so with less pressure from his knee. "That's the point, self-defense."

"What the fuck," Ambra states, and for a moment Delina almost wants to laugh, at how normal and colloquial it is. "You're insane, all of you are insane."

"That's rich," Gurlien mutters, and his hand is shaking against the gun. "Let's go on, we need to break those traps."

THEY GET MOST of the way down the carpeted hallway, the dust motes hanging in the air, before Chloe and Maison freeze and Ambra backpedals, almost thumping into Gurlien.

Delina stills herself, waiting in the quiet air, before knives slam out of one side of the corridor, imbedding into the wall on the other side, hilt deep into the Sheetrock.

If they hadn't stopped, it would've shredded through all of them.

"I take it you missed that trap," Gurlien asks, and Chloe nods, pale, before she walks up to one of the knives, poking it with her thumb. "Great."

Bracing herself, Chloe yanks one of the knives from the

wall, and grey dust powders through the air, before she flips it in her hands. "They're not spelled, just normal knives. Anyone want one?"

"No," Ambra says flatly, but Gurlien takes one anyways, holding it next to the gun. "They won't do anything against a shield."

"Not everyone here has a shield," Gurlien snips back. "Not everyone here can explode things on command."

She narrows her eyes at him, before resuming down the hall, until she stops at a glowing demon trap, toeing around the edge.

Without even a word, Chloe steps up, and the air above it shimmers.

"There are more demons beneath us," Ambra says. "Not sure your claim on the Necromancer will be enough to stop them."

Delina shivers, and Ambra gives her a wide grin, showing all her teeth.

"You're going to release those ones if you're not careful about which protections you tear down, alchemist," Ambra says, and her voice lilts up, like she can't decide if she's taunting them or if she's warning them. "Some of those down there shouldn't see the light of day."

"Noted," Chloe says, concentrating hard on the circle, and after the locking pits and the splint, Delina can taste her exhaustion, taste her pounding headache. "This is a complicated one, please don't talk to me."

Back down the hall, with the slagged brick blocking the way, the sound of chipping at stone clinks through the air.

They're trying to come behind them.

"How good are you at defense?" Delina asks Ambra, who almost startles at someone else starting the conversation.

"We might need more shields, might need someone else to cover our back."

"They can't attack us if they're dead," she replies simply, which isn't better. "Unless they—" she jerks a finger under the leash, demonstrating it, "—then they can't stop me."

"So we stop them from pulling on your invisible leash, got it," Gurlien says sarcastically. "Good, actionable goal."

Instead of responding to the sarcasm, Ambra just blinks up at him. "You can't see it?"

The air above Chloe's hands shimmer again, the world beyond it warping, and sweat trickles down her face.

"Dud, remember?" Gurlien replies, and a thoughtful look steals over Ambra's face, one that Delina likes not one bit. "No way of me telling that it's there, can't see it, can't sense it, whatever."

"You can, right?" Ambra asks Maison, who nods. "And you?"

"Yeah," Delina replies, and Ambra makes a humming noise in the back of her throat, like she's evaluating them, like she's considering saying something, before the demon trap unravels with a snap.

Chloe staggers back, her fingertips stinging, and there are droplets of blood dotting them, before she throws Delina a nod. "You get next one."

The hallway stretches onwards, impossibly longer than it was beforehand.

"Illusion spell?" Delina asks, and Maison nods, grim. "Sweet."

"You can't see through illusion spells?" Ambra asks, walking backwards, and despite the direness, despite the stress and the injuries and the situation, Delina gets the sudden insight that the demon is having fun, that the demon is actually enjoying having someone to talk to. "Wait, can you?"

"Sometimes," Maison grumbles, and he's sweating again, even with the help of the brace. "Depends on who set it."

"Fascinating," Ambra says, and Delina wishes she could roll her eyes. "There's a door five paces away, it leads to a branching hallway. I've only been down the left."

Gurlien rounds back on her. "Was it a prison there?"

"This whole place is a prison." The demon shoots back. "It's all a prison and you're insane for going further down."

"Great, thanks, but I need to know specifics," Gurlien replies, before he stops Chloe long enough to yank the map out of her backpack. "Does it lead to here?"

"Guys, we should keep moving," Maison murmurs, and the hair on the back of Delina's neck raises. "Something's coming."

The other demon ignores him. "This is a woefully incomplete map."

Delina glances up at Maison, and his mouth is grim.

"Someone's coming, I don't know who, and—"

The wall shatters at the end of the hall, and almost without thinking, Ambra flicks her hand and collapses the roof in front of it, closing off the way.

"You're trying to get here?" Ambra asks, jabbing her finger at Maison's mom's prison cell, as if she hadn't just possibly hurt the structural integrity of the compound. "They're going to protect it, they put the dangerous people there, what did she do?"

"Have me," Maison says, leaning a hand against the wall to brace himself.

"You can't be that special," Ambra replies, disgruntled, before she puts a hand on the wall a few paces away, peeling the illusion up and opening the door. "There's a fire trap and a pressure plate, but this way's easier and there's no demon traps until before the cell."

All at once, Gurlien and Chloe look to Delina, like she's the one to make the decision, so she glances up at Maison.

Who nods, inhaling deep.

"Let's do this."

~

THE HALLWAY IS DEAD SILENT, unlit, and Gurlien pockets the knife so he can pull out his cell phone for the flashlight.

Maison holds back the fire trap, the strips of magic glowing his hands, holding literal flames at bay as they pass through, and Delina gets the overall sensation that it's easier than walking for him at the moment. Chloe whispers Delina through disabling the pressure plate before they walk through it, soft.

Even Ambra is silent, as if worn out by the chattering, her eyes jerky down the darkness of the hall.

"We have eighteen more minutes," Gurlien murmurs, his voice dead in the quiet.

"We're almost to the branch," Ambra whispers back, and her eyes keep on flickering between Maison and Delina, considering.

Maison inhales at the reminder of his mother, but he nods, grim, and he's back to leaning against Delina, so his hand tightens around her waist, still avoiding the coil of magic thrumming angrily.

"We're almost done," Delina whispers to him, and he squeezes her briefly, like he's still not believing it. "We're almost there."

His face is blank, carefully so, his jaw working.

"We'll get her out, we'll get to safety, then we can plan."

Ambra stalks up closer to Chloe, brushing by them, and Maison jerks Delina out of the way, swift, before he tugs her into a hug, burying his face into her hair.

She clings back to him, against his heart beating strongly, before he pulls himself back.

"I'm terrified," he says, his voice low, simultaneously obviously tracking both the death magic in her hands and where Ambra whispers furiously at Gurlien and Chloe. "This could go so wrong, this could—"

Delina stands on her tip toes, and kisses him.

In terms of kisses go, it's far from ideal. There's dust coating her face, his leg is trembling from pain, but he opens his mouth to hers, brutal and brief, before pulling back.

Delina nods at him. "We got this."

He nods, leaning against her, and she ducks her shoulder under his arm, supporting him. He's warm against her, strong despite all the pain, and for a brief, crystalline moment, she wishes that this could stay like this, exactly like this, for forever.

mbra remains true to her word, pulling open another illusioned door, and the pain Delina sensed back at the bar is slowly starting to creep in.

And the door opens to a disaster.

Immediately, Ambra scrambles back, hand flailing behind her, before the leash around her neck abruptly jerks.

She screams, high pitched, and stumbles forward.

"Shit," Chloe breathes, and Gurlien tries to grab for the door, before the wall blasts open.

Delina rocks back, half protecting Maison, half ducking away from the shards of brick.

And in front of them, revealing a hall of prison doors, traditional prison bars, the wall folds open like nothing more than origami.

Delina grips the strip of death tight, pulling it taut, and she can't see a thing in all the dust, can't see a thing in all the smoke, and—

Behind the wall, blocking them from the prison door, is a group of people.

A group of people, all grim, all with weapons, all waiting for them.

With only a beat, Gurlien lifts the pistol and cracks out a shot, but the one in front bats it away like it's nothing.

Maison inhales, deep.

"So, Frederick, this was impressive," the one in front speaks, a man with close cut gray hair and a face that's lined deeper than any that Delina's ever seen. "Got your girlfriend to blast her way down her, free a bunch of criminals, impressive."

Despite the pain, Maison swings Delina behind him, practiced.

The man's hand is clenched around the leash, his knuckles white with the grip, and Ambra struggles against it, clawing at her throat.

There are way more of them than they can go against. Way more, and behind them...

...Sitting in the cell, staring straight ahead, her eyes blank, is the older woman from the pictures. Her hair is whiter, her face thinner, but her jawline echoes Maison's and her brows are the same set as his when he's trying not to think.

The man's eyes fall on Delina, as if evaluating. "So the insane doctor bred a Necromancer, that's typical," he says, and his eyes fall to the ball of death in her hand. "You really don't have any finesse, do you?"

"No," Delina replies, honestly, and the group obviously didn't expect that, their brows furrowing all at once.

Slow, deliberately, the man withdraws a gun. A normal, perfectly non-descript gun, and points it directly at Maison's mother, holding it to her chest.

And he freezes.

"How much do you want to bet you can get your necromancer to her?" the man says, sharp. "Think long and hard about what you're willing to do, Frederick."

Maison stares, panic in his eyes, bleeding through the stance of his shoulders.

Chloe backs up, not fully out of their view, already making herself smaller. Making herself unnoticeable, though one of the groups keep their eyes on her.

And the man smiles, satisfied.

Then pulls the trigger.

The bullet punches through Maison's mother, blood spraying over the small cell.

Too many things happen at the same time.

The demon screams, recoiling away, clapping her hands over her ears.

Gurlien and Chloe jerk back, scrambling away.

Maison's mom slumps over, whatever spell they put on her to keep in silent, to keep in stasis, breaking. She blinks, once, twice, before her heart gives up, blood pouring out of the artery, too deeply.

Death slams into Delina, close, too close, and she gasps, her ears and eyes filling with it. It sparks behind her mind, drowning out her awareness of anything else.

She staggers, her very balance off.

Maison spasms forward, and the man swings the gun over to him.

"Because if you give up the Necromancer, we'll have her raise her, and everyone is happy," the man says, and Maison's shoulders tighten, despite it all. "They can both survive, and it's all up to you."

Maison inhales, terror in every motion, then his eyes flicker back to Delina.

And for a split second, she can tell he considers it. Weighs their chances, weighs what he thinks she can do, before something furious, something subversive, sparks in his eyes.

"What exactly will you do?" Maison asks, turning back to this, and Chloe hisses in anger. "She can raise my mom? You'll let her?"

And, as he speaks, slow and deliberate, he hides his wrist behind his back, presenting it to Delina. His hand shakes, a tremor through it.

To Delina and to the death still in her hand.

She twists it between her hands, clinging closer to him, still gasping. The entire world narrows to just a pinprick, and there's the death in her hands and the death just beyond the cell, just out of her reach.

"Oh, we can guarantee many things," the man says, idly, and Ambra scrambles against the leash to no avail. "Your mom living, the necromancer being out of your hair, and—"

Before she can think twice, Delina loops the rope around Maison's wrist, and everything sparks into motion.

"Hurt only them!" she yells, and Maison jerks forward, between one breath and the next he's in the man's face, ripping the gun from his hand and crushing it in his fist.

The man yells, and everyone bursts into action.

Maison teleports to the bars of the cell, held back by an invisible barrier, then twists back, fear and fury in his eyes. He's panicking, he's not thinking clearly, every line of him is scared. His mother's on the floor, the death so strong Delina can taste it, and he can't get to her.

Gurlien ducks back, as someone sends a spell snapping through the air, jerking Chloe away from the bolt. Chloe scrabbles for the bag, pulling out the knife.

Maison teleports out of the way of another bolt, all pain gone from his knee, then snaps the neck of the magician who sent it his way, and the death punches through Delina's awareness, and he tosses the body to her.

Right. Another death for her to take.

She does, the power twisting in her hands, and she rips it apart and fans it out, just in time to block another bolt of magic that would've hit her face.

"Chloe, get the cell," Delina yells, and Chloe pushes past them, scrabbling with her lock picks, and Delina skids to a halt in front of her, the death blister hot against her palms.

The man holding Ambra's leash yanks back on it, and Amber surges up to Delina, the bobble popping, up, and—

Delina lets the death in her hand snap apart, and Ambra reels away, pain searing through her head, through her neck. Blood wells up in her throat, against her chest cavity.

And it's enough for Maison to grab Ambra by the back of her collar, heaving her away from Delina, teleporting her up and away from her, before he drops her by the side, appearing in front of Delina to block another spike of magic.

His eyes are wild, like a scared little boy, a wrecking ball of emotion and power and fury.

Another dead, and Delina pulls it back to herself, blocking another desperate shot to Chloe, whose hands shake at the lock.

Ambra screams, struggling against the leash, clawing at her neck, and the man tugs it again, spinning her back towards Delina. Tears streak down her face, red and angry, and she screeches in Delina's face, like a monster of old.

She's in so much pain.

"Stop—" she chokes out, and a gunshot rings out, cutting her short.

A gunshot directly into the man holding her leash's head, and he crumples.

A moment of silence, and Gurlien lowers his gun, his eyes wide.

Ambra recoils, then scrabbles away, panting.

The first lock clicks, and Maison breaks the neck of the last person, and then there's nothing else but the sound of their breathing.

"Mom," he says, appearing between one moment and the next in front of the bars. "Mom, can you hear me?"

There's no reaction.

Of course there's no reaction, his mother isn't breathing, there's no spark of electricity in her mind. There's nothing.

"Mom, can you..."

Delina grabs his wrist, untying the death around his hand, and he stumbles forward, his hands coming up to cling onto the bars. The pain blooms back in his knee.

Chloe swears, then moves to the second lock.

Delina sticks her arms through the bars, reaching towards the dead in front of her, but she can't reach. She's out of reach, she can't grab her back, she can't...

"I've almost got it," Chloe mumbles, in the silence. "Give me two more seconds."

His mom's eyes are open, unblinking, and they're the same shade of grey as Maison's.

"Mom," Maison repeats, desperate. "Mom, please—"

Chloe clicks the second lock, and the door swings forward, Maison stumbling inside, until his knees hit the floor next to his mother's form.

He doesn't even react to the pain.

There's blood pooling everywhere, too much blood, and Delina's heart pounds.

Maison cradles his mother's head, pulling it into his lap, and his hands are shaking, before he lifts his eyes back up to Delina.

They're bloodshot, and his face trembles.

"Delly..." he says, his voice rasping, and there's terror there as well. "Delina, please—"

It's enough to spur her into motion, and she scrambles to his side, to his mother's still body.

And despite the exhaustion, despite the headache pounding into Delina's mind, she lets herself sink into the sensation of the death. Into the knowledge she gets by just the touch.

The bullet punctured through the artery, grazing her lung and through her rib cage, chipping one of the bones on its way out of the body. The blood pooled in the chest cavity, in the lungs, all electrical signals stopped.

It's a far worse death than Maison had.

Slow, Delina exhales, letting her eyes flutter shut.

Maison's saying something, but Delina pushes it away from herself. There's too much with the body, too much that needs to be done before she can bring her back.

She seals the puncture first, socketing the chipped rib back into place. It's small, but if she had left it there, his mother would die all over again in moments.

The blood in the lungs take more effort, and Delina pushes it into place, drawing it out drop by drop.

Against her hands, Maison's mother's body spasms. She's not alive, some leftover signal to the brain.

Slowly, too slowly, Delina knits the artery back into place, and sweat drips into the dust on her back. She has to make it perfect, it has to, despite her ears ringing and her hands trembling.

Behind her, remote, she hears the demon Ambra inhale, pained. It's a threat, back there, but she can't think, not when Maison's holding his dead mother, not when she has to do this.

Delina's breath hitches, as the elasticity of the artery isn't perfect, isn't completely smooth, and there's blood still on the skin. There's blood all over Delina's hands, sticky and rapidly cooling, cooling too fast. The rest of her blood will cool, then still, and she won't be able to—

Before she can complete that thought, before she can will herself to even think it, Delina sends a shock of electricity to the brain, sparking it into action.

And then that's all Delina can do, all possibilities vanishing before her.

Delina blinks her eyes open, and Maison's staring at her, stricken. His mother isn't breathing, isn't moving, there's nothing, until—

With a small hitch, her chest moves, a deep, gentle breath, like someone deeply asleep.

Delina sits back, exhaustion prickling her vision with black.

She did it. She did it, his mother's breathing. Alive. The blood sluggishly starting to pump back through the veins, the heart beating.

In front of her, Maison's mother blinks, and the discomfort of it ricochets down Delina's senses. His mother was shot, and she's picking up that her eyes are scratchy.

"Mom?" Maison repeats, and slowly, ever so slowly, the woman lifts her eyes to him. "Mom, can you hear me?"

For too long of a beat there's no reaction, nothing, before her face crumbles and she jolts herself to sit upright, then coughs.

"Maison?" she asks, and her voice is whisper soft. "Maison, is that..."

As if seeing beyond the doors for the first time, she looks past the bars, at the carnage. At Gurlien holding the gun, at

Ambra huddled on the floor. At Chloe ducked behind Gurlien, like she's afraid...Then...

At Delina.

Her eyes are the same grey as Maison's.

Trembling, she reaches a hand down to the ragged hole in her clothing, then over to Delina.

"Mom," Maison says, desperate, and his mother tilts her head up to him. She's also exhausted, she's lost a lot of blood, she's dehydrated, and Delina can feel all of it.

"Maison," his mother repeats, and there's some steel in her voice, something stronger than should come from a woman who was just dead. "I told you not to risk anything."

Still, his mother pulls him into a hug, and Maison all but collapses into it, his face crumbling, before he reaches for Delina and grasps her hand as well.

Slowly, outside the little cell, Ambra climbs to her feet, as if she thinks that any motion will jerk her back down to the ground, and Gurlien twitches the gun back up to her.

Delina just stares over at the room, exhaustion rendering her unable to react.

"Mom, we got you," Maison mumbles. "We got you, we're getting you out, everything's okay."

Ambra eyes them, and Delina tears her glance away from Maison to watch her.

"That was two out of five," Ambra says, her voice wrecked. "Your team killed two out of five."

"So three people out there can still control you?" Gurlien asks, and he's shaking, despite the gun still outstretched.

She nods, her eyes wide.

Delina should get up, should interfere, but the very idea of standing is so beyond her.

They did it. They actually did it.

They actually freed his mom. His mother is alive, despite the blood on her front.

Maison's knee still hurts, but it's almost beyond them now. Delina's hands ache, a headache brews behind her eyes, but they did it.

They actually did it.

"How much time do we have, Gurlien?" Chloe asks, voice hushed. It's so silent there, with just Ambra's ragged breathing and the buzz of the overhead lights.

The remaining death clogs up Delina's nose, like it was waiting for her to notice.

"Four minutes," Gurlien says, tucking the gun back away and staring at his watch, a little dumb founded. "Four minutes, then we get a rescue."

Ambra rockets back up to her feet, and, almost instinctively Delina tries to stand, but the demon stares, a bit too intensely, at Gurlien.

"Rescue by who?" she asks, voice tilting downwards, almost in a warning.

Maison stirs, lifting his head. There are streaks of tears down his face.

The silence is fraught, now, and Gurlien gapes at all of them, like he's asking for help in it.

"The Wights," Chloe answers for him, still sitting on the ground, and Ambra slates her eyes over to her, evaluating. "That was the deal, we rescue the girl—"

"—Stella, yes, her," Ambra interrupts, impatiently. "She cried a lot."

"—and then they'd break us out," Gurlien finishes, rocking back on his heels, away from the conversation, like he's grasping for straws. "You helped, I'm sure they'll help you, we'll tell them."

The demon's glowing eyes narrow again. "There are

three people still out there who can control this," she says, tugging at the leash around her neck again, and even though it's her own hands, Delina gets a hint of pain, sharp among all the death in the room. "Three more. The Wights won't help me, not with three still out there."

Maison pulls away from his mother, his face grim, and even with everything else, even with the pain in his knee, he grasps magic in his hands. Even after all the fighting, he's still ready.

Ambra twitches, then grabs at the leash, and there's some split-second decision in her eyes, a split-second of warning, before she snakes her hand out, grabbing Gurlien by the collar of his jacket, and disappears.

Taking him with her.

Chloe gasps, the air so exhausted it's almost a squeak. "Where..."

And then, the entire building above them opens up, and the Wight strides in, fury along every line of her body.

Maison pulls his mother up to standing, then reaches down and extends a hand to Delina, helping her up.

The rescue is here, and now they can leave.

THE END

EPILOGUE

～

The Wight takes them all to the apartment, just long enough for Chloe to panic call Gurlien—to no result—and grab the cat, before spinning them off to a safe hiding place, deep in the snowy woods of Toronto.

There's a cabin, dizzyingly close to the one on the Washington coast, and the Wights contact a physician to examine them all.

Chloe's panicking, calling Gurlien, pacing in the other room, and all Delina can tell is that Gurlien's not...dead.

She's not sure how she can tell, but she can tell.

Maison alternates between staring dumbly at Delina, hugging his mom, and grabbing Delina's hand. It's like all the words are stolen from him as well.

Before whatever doctor gets there, in the shocked moments of sitting on a couch, Maison's mother turns to Delina, her face intent.

Delina just stares back, beyond exhausted.

"I know enough of this magic to know that should be impossible," she says, and there's the steel in her voice again, familiar.

Delina can't think of a thing to say to that, and just shrugs.

"You're the girl my son's fallen for?" she asks, and it's so incomplete of a question, so beyond anything that she should be asking in this moment, that a smile breaks over Delina's face.

"Yeah," Delina manages out, and Maison makes an embarrassed noise, the only sound he's made since they left.

Maison's mother nods, as if that explains everything, before the Wight swings back into the room.

She's fully visible to everyone, near as Delina can tell.

"We've contacted the West Coast," she says, and Delina can't quite understand it. "The Wights there knew your mother, and know your cousin."

Delina nods, because of course they do.

THEY TRAVEL OUTSIDE of Vancouver in small bursts of tele-portation helped by Wights, until they're greeted outside a sprawling compound. Snow dusts the top of the trees, and dead blackberry canes line the road.

It's a squat set of buildings, ugly and jutting out from the wilderness, and Maison leans heavily against Delina, still wobbling.

His mother is fine, breathing and walking like nothing had happened to her at all that day. Chloe's still dialing Gurlien in panic.

All Delina can tell is he's not dead. She doesn't know

how she can tell it, but she can, her skin crawling with the awareness.

To greet them, six people stand at the base of a sloping driveway, one Delina very much so does not want to pull Maison up unassisted, and Maison straightens, like he's once more preparing for a fight.

Instead, Delina just studies them as they come into view.

The tall woman with the beautiful black hair, from the passport, her golden glasses glinting in the sun, a Wight standing next to her, shoulder to shoulder. A young man, his hair curly and wild, with the now-familiar form of Terese a half step behind him, her eyes colorless and distrustful. Another man, his brown hair pulled back, and he's not quite human, not quite, though Delina's awareness slides off of him if she thinks too hard.

And then...the last person, a young woman, shorter than the rest, her dark brown hair wavy, but when she meets Delina's eyes, she knows...

The other Necromancer.

SNEAK PEEK OF THE GIRL WHO SHOULD BE DEAD

CHAPTER ONE

After everything that had happened that day, Ambra doesn't begrudge herself a little light kidnapping.

Her head still pounds after all the alarms, her eyelids drag with each blink, and both the lingering gut wound and the slash on her face throb. Her mouth still tastes of iron, as it always does when the leash gets tightened, and whatever snap of death magic the necromancer had smashed in her face in the fight still echoes in her lungs.

All that's recoverable, of course, given some time outside the stasis chambers, and they would have to lobotomize her - again - in order for her to go back there willingly.

Straightening the moment her feet hit the floor, she drops her grip on the kidnappee's collar, dusting off her hands.

The kidnappee - a young man with floppy hair and thick rimmed glasses who shot one of the Five in the head - staggers back, gasping. He's still holding the gun in his hand, but thankfully he doesn't aim it towards her

"Where are we?" He chokes out, like the teleportation was less than perfect, which is rude.

She obviously took them to a safe house, so she blinks at him.

Ambra, like most demons she's come into contact with, instinctively crafts safe places to land. A place where she could run to, a place to think, a place to collect whatever catches her fancy, on the rare occasion something does.

She hasn't been to this one since the merge - her mind shies away from thinking about it directly in a way that's distinctively annoying - so a thin layer of dust coats the bench and the bookcase.

"Okay, okay," the kidnappee says, after her silence, as she obsessively lets her mind check her wards, lets it wander to see if anyone else has been in there. "Uh, why am I here?"

That, at least, is a question her mind doesn't have to think about.

"Because of the leash," she answers, and his brows furrow, like the answer isn't intuitive to him.

The leash, the incorporeal, magical leash tied so crudely around her throat by the College. The key to them controlling her. The key to her freedom, and her safety.

He just raises an eyebrow at her, so she turns away.

One of her wards is smudged. Not broken, but someone else had clearly been sniffing around the edges, testing them.

Another demon, if the tang of the power is any indication. Had probably noticed the emptiness and wanted to observe if the person who crafted it was dead or not.

She stalks towards the offending rune, and the kidnappee's eyes widen as she passes him, but despite pulling at the rune, despite squinting at it, she can't tell who it could be.

Another result of the merge. She just...can't do everything anymore.

Careful, his motions so careful it immediately sends up red flags in her awareness, her kidnappee sits on the bench, gripping the aged wood like it could help him.

The gun is still clutched in his hands, as if he forgot it.

He doesn't look too injured, near as she can tell, beyond the scrapes and bruises that come from breaking out of a prison.

He stares at her, his eyes a normal shade of human brown, and in between one moment and the next, she can see his brain kick in and something truly analytical lights up his face.

This, at least, she can talk to.

"You're a dud, you said," Ambra starts, and he nods. "Duds aren't supposed to know about any of human magic, yet you do."

He nods again, his mouth twisting down.

"You've been scarred by some magic, in a huge way," she continues, and it's obvious all over him. Like someone had taken a surge and shocked it directly into his system. "You knew how to read the runes, you knew a lot of the pathways, and you could instruct the necromancer and alchemist."

"Good assessment," he says, cautious, and his knuckles are white against the bench.

He's afraid of her, which is a bit nice.

"The necromancer killed Korhonen, and you killed Rastian," Ambra recites. "There's still Nalissa, Johnsin, and Boltiex out there."

"Boltiex is one of them?" The kidnappee says, immediately identifying the dangerous one out of all of them. It's good he's probably a bit smart, if he's catching on. "Why would they let him get access to a demon, he's almost insane."

"Once they piece through the wreckage your Half Demon left there, they're going to try to get me back," Ambra states, as matter of fact as she can, but a shudder still shakes down her spine at the thought. "Hence, you."

"Still don't follow," the kidnappee murmurs, but his eyebrows are still furrowed. "Can you return me back?"

The unease tightens across her shoulders. "I'm not going back to that prison."

"No, not the base, obviously, but...to my friends. They're heading to...a safe spot with backup. The College can't get to them there, you might be safe."

She squints at him, like that can give her clarity.

"Alright," her kidnappee says, clearly unnerved. "Ambra, that's your name, right?"

It had been a long time since anyone had actually called her that, and a shiver flickers across her body.

He raises an eyebrow, like he caught that. "It was on the nameplate outside your cell."

"I know that," she says, and, in some odd mannerism left over from the body, hugs herself. "Yes, that's my name."

The smudged ward throbs against her awareness, again, the demon testing it. They must've set something, to see if someone would come back, and she likes that not one bit.

She hasn't faced another demon since the merge, and if her less than perfect control is an indication, she's not sure she would win any fight.

"Okay, Ambra," he starts again, the body shivers around her. "I need you to explain to me, in easy, human terms, what's going on."

She doesn't stop staring at the rune, and she doesn't think her protections have weakened enough so that another demon could just teleport in, but the itch to go elsewhere already eats at her gut.

Her gut, with the wound from the first fight at the bar still slowly bleeding. And hurting, far more than such wounds should.

Thankfully, the kidnappee stays silent, as she prods at the physical lines she etched into the wood of the safe room wall.

The safe room is little more than a single structure, deep underground, the air connected through an odd series of tunnels leading up to the surface. A few ages ago, she had teleported in wood plank by wood plank, then wired it when electricity became popular, and had a perfectly good collection of preserved books on the shelves.

It is also blessedly quiet, most of the time, and the presence of a living breathing human in it clashes.

One of the worst things about the merge is the noise.

That's a lie.

But it's an easy lie, kinder than thinking about it more.

READ MORE HERE

ALSO BY ALESSA WINTERS

The Ghost of Riverside County

The Magic of the Living and the Dead

The Paranormal Organization Series

Summer Reads

Follow her on twitter at @writerLyn

Printed in Dunstable, United Kingdom

64652028R00268